By the same author

A Fisher of Slaves
Turbans
New Zealand – A personal discovery

A FAMILY DIVIDED

DICK PARSONS

authorHOUSE®

AuthorHouse™ UK
1663 Liberty Drive
Bloomington, IN 47403 USA
www.authorhouse.co.uk
Phone: 0800.197.4150

Published by AuthorHouse 12/15/2017

ISBN: 978-1-5462-8514-4 (sc)
ISBN: 978-1-5462-8515-1 (hc)
ISBN: 978-1-5462-8533-5 (e)

To Anne and Mary

Acknowledgements

My grateful thanks to Ambrose Barber and George Heller for their comments and advice.

Glossary

*The meaning of words in the text marked so * is given below.*

Achtung, Achtung Öffnen die Tur, Achtung, Achtung. Open the door. This is the
zu offnen. Dies ist der Gestapo — Gestapo

Balfour Declaration — On 2nd November James Balfour sent a letter to Lord Rothschild the leader of the British Jewish Community and a friend of Chaim Weizmann President of the Zionist Organisation in Palestine, stating that "His Majesty's Government view with favour the establishment in Palestine of a national home for the Jewish people, and will use their best endeavours to facilitate the achievement of this object."

Bellbottoms — Sailors' flared uniform trousers

Brownshirts — The colloquial name for the S.A., the Sturmabteilung (Storm troops)

Bund Deutsche Madel — The League of German Girls, the female equivalent of the Hitler Youth. Girls had to take the oath "I promise always to do my duty in the Hitler Youth, in love and loyalty to the Führer"

Clippie	Slang term for female Bus Conductors
Con	The Officer of the Watch normally has the con. That is he controls the navigation of the vessel by ordering changes in the course steered and the speed of the ship. However in certain circumstances such as manoeuvring the ship alongside, or when attacking an enemy, the Captain takes over and indicates his intention to do so by saying "I'll take the con."
Conchies	Men who were pacifists and unwilling to fight had to register and go before a tribunal to be registered as a Conscientious Objector and be excused military service. They were known as Conchies and would be employed in some other wartime employment e.g. the Fire Service. But Conchies were generally ostracised.
Contraband of war	Goods being delivered from a neutral country to a belligerent.
D-Day	Allied invasion of German occupied Europe on 6th June 1944
Dieppe	In August 1942 an allied force mainly consisting of Canadians, but supported by British Commandos, launched a raid on the port of Dieppe. Its aim was to evaluate procedures for an amphibious assault against a defended target and to learn lessons for an eventual assault on mainland Europe. Such lessons were learnt at an exorbitant price in casualties, for almost two thousand troops were

taken prisoner by the German defenders and nearly one thousand were killed.

Eels	German nick-name for torpedoes. The British called them "fish".
Ein Reich, Ein Volk, Ein Führer	One Nation, One People, One Leader
Einsatzkommando	An S.S. force of about one hundred officers and men tasked with ridding the countries occupied by Germany of the Jews. Adolf Eichmann ultimately charged with the Holocaust told the court at his trial that the purpose of the Einsatzkommandos was "to murder the Jews and deprive them of their property"
Escort carrier	Some 40 small aircraft carriers called escort carriers were produced for the Royal Navy by converting a suitable merchant ship hull with a flight deck with a hangar deck below. Swordfish biplanes (often called "Stringbags") flying from escort carriers made a great contribution to the defeat of the U-boat in the Atlantic. In other spheres they carried fighter aircraft such as the Sea Hurricane (a strengthened Hurricane fitted with an arrester hook to pick up one of the arrester wires to bring it to a halt, when landing on the short deck)
G I	The nickname given to U.S. Army soldiers, believed to have originated from the letters G I, meaning Government Issue, stamped on Army equipment
German Volk	German people

Ha'avara Agreement	Transfer Agreement
Haganah	Jewish paramilitary organisation in Palestine
Haggadah	the Jewish text that sets forth the order of the Passover Seder
Heer	German Army
Horst-Wessel song	The Nazi anthem
Hot bed principle	Only the Captain of a U-boat had his own bunk in a curtained off space in the diminutive officers mess. Everyone else shared a bunk. As most worked on alternative watches, the one going on watch would vacate his hot bed to the man coming off watch.
Hydrophone	An instrument for detecting sounds in the sea, especially the sound made by the rotation of a ship's propeller.
I'll take the con	A phrase used by the ship's Captain to tell the Officer of the Watch, that he will take control of the ship's navigation himself.
Kapitanleutnant	Lieutenant Commander
Kippah	Jewish skull cap
Kosher	Food that fulfils the requirements of the Law of Moses
Kriegsmarine	German Navy

Kubelwagen	Light open vehicle capable of carrying four people, similar to the Jeep
Lord Haw Haw	an American born, Irish-German Fascist who presented the English-language propaganda radio programme broadcast by the Nazis, called *Germany Calling*
Lord Woolton	The wartime Minister of Food
Luftstreitkrafte	German Air Combat Force in the 1914-18 War
Meidet alles Judische	Shun everything Jewish
Number One	Naval slang for First Lieutenant, who in destroyers and below is the second-in-command.
Oberfahnrich zur See	A Midshipman in the German Navy
Oberleutnant zur See	A Sub Lieutenant in the German Navy
Oberstleutnant	A Colonel in the Wehrmacht or Waffen SS
Orpo	Originally the Orpo was the regular Police force dealing with domestic matters and crime within Germany and Austria. But in a 1940/41 reorganisation, Police Battalions were established as part of the SS, for use in the occupied territories.
Panzerfauste	A very effective anti-tank single shot, recoilless weapon used by the infantry
Panzerschiff	A Pocket-Battleship (a heavy cruiser) in the German Navy

Peyots	Small twisted side locks worn by devout Jewish men
Pill boxes	Small defensive fortified structures built of brick or concrete with slots through which light machine guns and rifles could be fired by infantrymen at enemy troops.
Rations	One person's weekly allowance at this time in Britain was: one fresh egg; 4oz (110 gm) margarine and four rashers of bacon; 2oz (50gm) butter 2oz(50gm) tea; 1oz (25gm) cheese; and 8oz (225gm) sugar. Meat was allocated by price, so cheaper cuts became popular
RNR	Royal Naval Reserve. RNR Officers all had to have served in the Merchant Navy and with their Nautical knowledge and experience could quickly be integrated into the Royal Navy.
RNVR	Royal Naval Voluntary Reserve. Officers promoted from conscripted men and given quick and limited training for use in specific roles.
Reichswehr	The small German Army allowed by the Treaty of Versailles
Reichswehreid	Oath of Personal Allegiance to Adolf Hitler sworn by all men and officers of the S.S. This oath required them to obey without question the will of Adolf Hitler.
Ruhe Haus	Tranquillity House

Schnellbooten	Motor Torpedo Boat – commonly called E-boats
Scrambling net	A steel wire netting with a large mesh, which can be hung over the ship's side so that men in the water can climb aboard
S.S.	Full name Schutzstaffel. – Protection Squadron, initially formed as the Führer's personal guards but growing into a powerful force including Political Police, the Waffen S.S., an elite military unit, the feared Gestapo and later a force to guard the Concentration and Extermination camps
Sanhedrin	The Jewish supreme judicial and legislative assembly in Jerusalem.
Schnellbomber	Fast bomber the JU88 twin-engined multi-combat aircraft developed for the Luftwaffe
Schutzstaffel	See S.S.
Shtender	Similar to a church pulpit, but with doors behind which religious objects are stowed.
Seder	The Passover meal
Schupo	German Guard Police
Stieglitz	Goldfinch
Stosser	Goshawk.
Sturmbannführer	Major in the SS

Todt Organisation	A civil engineering group named after its founder, Fritz Todt which completed a wide range of military projects in Germany and occupied territories, using forced labour from conquered countries.
Totenkopfverbande	That part of the S.S. which provided the guards for the Concentration Camps, Labour Camps and Extermination camps.
Torah	The Jewish Bible known to Christians as The Old Testament
Untermensch	A term used by the Nazis to describe the Jews, Slavs and Gypsies and those deemed mentally handicapped. The Untermensch were sub-humans
Unterscharführer	Sergeant
Untersturmführer	Under storm leader – an SS rank equivalent to 2nd Lieutenant in the British Army
USSR	Union of Soviet Socialist Republics – the Communist controlled states of the former Imperial Russia
Vielen Dank	Thank you
Volkssturm	A militia of men over sixteen not already in essential wartime employment conscripted by Nazi Germany during the last months of WW 2 to support the Wehrmacht in the battle against the Russians. They had no uniform and wore their civilian clothes with a Volkssturm armband.

VW Limousine	The original VW Beetle
Winter Garden	The railed off platform abaft the U-boat's conning tower on which was mounted the boat's anti-aircraft gun. The British called it the "Bandstand".
Wrens	A division of the Royal Navy formed by Women and called the Woman's Royal Naval Service, a title that quickly became shortened to the Wrens.
Yahweh	The Jewish name for God. When Moses met God on Mount Sinai and asked him "What is thy name?" He was told "I am that I am", rendered in Hebrew as YHWH: but spoken as Yahweh. When the Temple stood in Jerusalem only the High Priest once a year could utter the name Yahweh.
Zig-zag	A zig-zag required a ship to execute a frequent and irregular change of course to make it difficult for a U-boat to calculate the settings needed for a successful torpedo attack

Chapter *1*

"HERR HITLER APPOINTED CHANCELLOR", the headlines screamed!

Golda Boddenburg closed her eyes in horror. Ever since his release from prison that dreadful man Hitler had made no secret of his ambition to become Chancellor, to become what he called the Führer. During the election campaign the Brownshirts the SA, Hitler's brutal private army, had unleashed a reign of terror against the Communists and any who opposed him. Yet many humiliated and enraged by the Versailles Treaty with its demand that Germany should pay astronomical reparation payments, hailed Hitler as the nation's saviour! Like them Golda also wanted the reparation payments ended, for the economic crisis to be resolved and work found for the unemployed millions, but as a Jew she was frightened by his anti-Semitic views. In his book Mein Kampf, hadn't he written how he hated the Jews? He'd called them parasites, spongers and blamed them for Germany's defeat. No wonder the Jews worried he would vent his hatred upon them. Some feared those terrible Russian pogroms might be repeated here in Germany.

Why, why did Hitler hate the Jews? She and her fellow Jews were all loyal Germans. Hadn't she and indeed her father fought for the Kaiser in the war? He a circumcised Jew had served with the 2nd Hanseatiscites, the Hamburg Infantry Regiment and had been badly wounded at Passchendaele. And she'd been proud to serve as a nurse in the Military Hospital right behind the front line. That was where she'd met Klaus her beloved husband, an injured pilot shot down by the English. But now the loyalty of the Jews and their service in the war appeared to count for nothing. Ever since Hitler had formed the Nazi party he seemed to blame the Jews for everything.

1

The doorbell rang. It was Hedwig in her school uniform. Hedwig, clutching her violin, her eyes sparkling.

"Mama," she cried excitedly. "I'll be playing in the school concert!"

"Oh darling, how wonderful! And what will you be playing?"

"Bach's Sonata Number Two".

Golda looked at her daughter, now almost eleven and on the brink of womanhood. With her long black hair framing a face lit up by those excited eyes, she seemed more beautiful than ever. She sighed, lovely Hedwig, she'll break some poor man's heart, one day.

"Mama, I'm really thrilled, and Horst will be playing his flute."

Golda smiled, "Oh Hedwig dear, you're both so talented."

Hedwig's cousin Horst two years older than her, was a handsome young boy with blonde hair, blue eyes and a passion for music. It was no wonder Hedwig admired him so much!

Golda heard the key turn in the front door and went to greet her husband.

"Hitler's the new Chancellor."

He seemed depressed. "Yes, so I've heard."

"I should never have married you, Klaus."

He looked at her troubled face. "Why? Don't you love me any more Golda?"

"Of course I do Klaus, but dearest I'm a Jew."

"So?"

"Hitler hates Jews, he calls us parasites and has made all sorts of threats against us, and he'll hate you too because as a Christian, you married a Jew."

"Golda dear," he studied his wife of thirteen years. How lovely she'd been when they wed and how beautiful she still was!

"Hitler may hate the Jews, but what can he do to vent his hatred? He may be Chancellor, but he hasn't got a majority in the Reichstag, not even if the National People's Party support him. No, Hitler may talk and make threats but we still have von Papen as Vice Chancellor. He and the others will keep Hitler's madness under control."

"Dearest, do you really think so?"

"Yes, I do. He may find some excuse to throw a few Polish or Russian Jews out of the country, but he's got far more pressing problems to deal with. Unless he does something about inflation and unemployment he'll be finished in six months, just like the others. You'll see!"

And as the weeks passed the papers seemed to agree with Klaus, but Golda still worried. The pogroms in Russia and the Ukraine had left thousands of Jews dead. Could Hitler repeat them here in Germany, here in Bremen? The possibility was too awful to contemplate! And though they put on brave faces and said all would be well, she was sure that in their hearts, most Jews were just as frightened as her!

She'd been brought up as a Jew, but she really had no faith. She hadn't been to synagogue for years, not since her wedding, but by the Law of Moses she was still a Jew. Everyone born of a Jewish mother is without question a Jew. Even though their father is a Gentile, her two children Moshe and Hedwig, are Jews simply because she their mother is Jewish! It was a fact of life, just as some were born black, her children were born Jews and nothing anyone could do could change that!

She'd remembered how upset her mother had been, when she'd told her she wanted to marry Klaus. "But Klaus isn't a Jew! How can you marry him?" she'd asked with horror in her voice. "Didn't Yahweh* [the Jewish name for God], tell us we mustn't marry a Gentile, that we must marry a Jew?" And her mother had done all she could to stop the marriage, though her father knowing she loved Klaus had forgiven and supported her!

"It's her decision, Renate. She'll remain a Jew at heart," he'd assured his troubled wife.

But neither synagogue nor church would accept them, so she and Klaus had been married in a civil ceremony. And as her father had prophesied, she'd remained a Jew at heart and eight days after her son Moshe was born, she'd had him circumcised according to Jewish custom and thirty three days later she'd been purified. But having done her duty by her son, she never again went to synagogue, nor indeed did Klaus go to his church. Now she hoped that as a non-practising Jew she and her family might be spared some of Hitler's hatred and for a while it seemed her beloved Klaus could be right about his prediction that von Papen and the others would keep Hitler's madness under control.

But then at the end of February, the nation was shocked by news that the Reichstag building, the seat of the National Government, had been set on fire and totally destroyed. Many like Golda wondered whether, indeed hoped that this could be the end of Hitler.

"Who started the fire?" everyone was asking, wondering who could have had the audacity, courage and daring to commit such an act of rebellion? Their questions were answered by the Press the following day.

*"**Herr Hitler**", the papers announced, "**has unassailable evidence that the fire was the work of the Communists. It was they who had started it! The destruction of the Reichstag building**, Herr Hitler claims, marks the beginning of a widespread Communist uprising. He has therefore authorised restrictions on civil liberties, the freedom of the press and the freedom of association and has given the government wide powers to arrest those deemed dangerous to the state."*

Klaus fearful of a communist coup d'état, supported Hitler's decisive action in arresting large numbers of communists, but the violent nature of the witch-hunt frightened Golda, though she comforted herself it was the communists Hitler blamed, not the Jews. It was they who were being detained in their thousands and incarcerated in the new temporary prison soon to be called a concentration camp, at Sachsenhausen near Berlin. But nevertheless she like the Jewish community as a whole, was alarmed by the violence and kept a low profile.

The next day details of the damage done to the Reichstag building, labelled by the press as the seat of German democracy, filled the newspapers and the following night Hitler addressed the nation on the wireless. He spoke forcefully of his fears that this was the start of a Communist uprising. In a voice full of rage, he declared he was determined to find and punish the perpetrators. Then in a calmer tone he assured his listeners his sole aim was to establish a secure and stable state, where law-abiding Germans could live and prosper. He ended by emphasising his determination to remove the distress caused to hard-working "volk", by the actions of such evil forces as the Communists. In the press the following day, the headlines proclaimed:

'LAW TO REMOVE DISTRESS OF THE PEOPLE AND THE REICH'

*"**Our newly elected Reichstag members will meet in the Kroll Opera House in Berlin now the temporary Reichstag building, to consider a proposed 'Law for Removing the Distress of the People and the Reich'. This law will enable Herr Hitler as Chancellor, to rule by decree***

for the next four years. Herr Hitler has pledged to use restraint and will use such powers only when essential for those measures deemed to be vital. Furthermore he has promised to end unemployment and promote peace with France, England and the Soviet Union. To do these things he needs this law which he refers to as an 'Enabling Act'."

"Have you heard the news?" anxiously she asked Klaus when he came home.

"About the Enabling Act? Yes, everyone's talking about it."

"It frightens me Klaus. The man's power-mad. Look what he's doing to the Communists! If he gets these powers, what will he do next? Vent his fury on us Jews?"

"Golda dearest, he doesn't mention the Jews. He says he wants stability, security and peace for the law-abiding. And he's promised to end unemployment. Perhaps dearest, with all our troubles we need a strong government."

But his repeated assurances did not allay her fears, and as it had been her custom since the death of her mother, she went on Friday to cook a proper kosher lunch for her dear father Chaim. He had always been a great support and she loved him for his wisdom and affection and was eager to hear his views about Hitler and his enabling act.

Letting herself in, she found him sitting in his chair by the window, his kippah* on his head, reading the passage from the Torah destined for the Sabbath. As she leant to kiss him, he rose to greet her, but putting a restraining hand on his shoulder she admonished him.

"Dearest father don't get up for me! Are you well?"

"Yes, Golda dear, I am. Yahweh watches over me!"

"And so he should. You've been a faithful Jew all your life!"

Chaim chuckled. "I hope he thinks so too! And how are Moshe and Hedwig?"

She told him how excited Hedwig was about playing her violin in in the school orchestra and of Moshe's progress with his studies. When he asked about Klaus, "Busy with his plane," was her answer.

Now the formalities were over she asked how he felt about Hitler's enabling act.

"That wretched Corporal's a despot."

"Father, father dear," she interrupted him, "you mustn't call him corporal, if the Brownshirts hear you speaking like that about him, they'll be after you! He's now the Chancellor and even though we may not like him, we have to show him respect!"

"Well whatever you call him, that enabling act of his will give him absolute power."

Golda shuddered, she knew that too. "Klaus says he's promised to use the powers only when essential."

"Well Klaus may be right, but who decides when it is essential, that's what concerns me!"

"It worries me too!"

"He's blamed the communists for the Reichstag fire, but he's yet to prove it. And now he's rounding up everyone he thinks are communists and locking them up in his new concentration camp, without recourse to law!"

"Well of course he hates the communists!"

"Yes, but he hates us Jews as well. He calls us parasites and blames us for losing the war!"

"Yes, but why?"

"He just hates us. I've read his Mein Kamp, where one passage reveals his unforgiving hatred of us. I remember I was so shocked I copied it on a piece of paper." He opened the back cover of his Torah, "Ah!" he said, "Here it is. Let me read it to you." He adjusted his glasses and began.

"If at the beginning of the war and during the war twelve or fifteen thousand of these Hebrew corrupters of the nation had been subjected to poison gas, such as had to be endured in the field by hundreds of thousands of our very best German workers of all classes and professions, then the sacrifice of millions at the front would not have been in vain."

He shook his head in despair and folding the paper carefully put it back where it belonged.

"He blamed us Jews for losing the war, he wanted to kill us then, and Golda dear, he'd like to kill us now!"

Hearing her father predicting with such conviction and clarity the awful fate of the Jews, had dismayed her and nothing she could say could change or moderate his appalling prediction!

They ate their meal in silence, both contemplating the future of the Jews in Nazi-led Germany.

As she bid him goodbye, he kissed her. "Somehow," he said "we need to persuade Hitler that we Jews are Germans too and love our country. He must acknowledge the fact that many, many Jews like you and I fought for the Kaiser in the last war and thousands gave their lives for Germany. We must make him do so, but," his voice tailed off, "how do we do that?"

She kissed him and walking home heard once more her father's voice reading that terrible extract from Mein Kampf.

Chapter *2*

It had been a long day, a very long day, yet his plane had made her maiden flight and Herr Goering had seemed impressed. It had gone without a hitch, but it was only the first of many test flights the Focke-Wulf Stieglitz (Goldfinch) would have to make before they could pronounce her a winner. But already he was sure she'd be a success and it was he, Klaus Boddenburg and his staff who'd turned that initial idea into reality.

He'd arrived early that morning to make sure all was ready for the test flight and Herman Goering's visit. As the Reich Chancellor for Aviation, the future of the Goldfinch rested with him. If he was impressed there could be the government order they all hoped for; sales to the flying clubs would hardly be enough to keep her in production. He'd watched as the Goldfinch was wheeled out of the hangar. She was a handsome little plane, perhaps not a trend setter like the monoplanes that were beginning to fly, but as a biplane with two open cockpits she'd make an excellent trainer or a tug for all the gliders in which so many of the pilots of a future air force might get some flying experience. And of course that was why Herr Goering had come. He wanted to see this Goldfinch and evaluate it as a possible trainer for the air force, his Luftwaffe that he planned to create one day. But would there ever be a Luftwaffe? The right of Germany to have armed aircraft was banned by the Versailles treaty, that dreadful treaty which Hitler condemned as vicious and humiliating. The treaty that had crippled the economy with its demands for excessive reparations. The treaty all right thinking Germans demanded should be re-negotiated. Only then could Germany hold up her head and take her rightful place once again as a great European nation. Surely all Germans hoped Hitler who promised to make Germany great again, would do that. If he did,

Goering might have his Luftwaffe and what a fillip that would be for the nation's fledgling aircraft industry!

He turned and saw Erich Schneyer the Managing Director, approaching. Hermann Goering was with him.

"Mein Herr, this is Herr Boddenburg, our Chief of Design."

The great man hesitated. "Herr Boddenburg I understand you were a member of the Luftstreitkrafte* in the 1914-18 war."

"Jawohl, Mein Herr".

"You were a pilot I believe."

"Ja, Mein Herr, I flew a Fokker D VII."

"Ah!" Goering's face softened. "A wonderful plane. Did you down many of the English?"

"Not as many as your twenty-two Mein Herr. Just six, then I was shot down."

"You did well Herr Boddenburg. We would have won the war if we hadn't been stabbed in the back by the Jews and the Communists!" He'd shaken his head ruefully. "Well, let's see your little Goldfinch fly."

The plane's silver fuselage shone in the sun and the red engine cowling mimicked the red face of the Goldfinch, just as he'd wanted. He felt a great sense of pride. She was the result of his team's efforts, but now she had to prove herself. Would she fly? He was certain she would, but nevertheless he crossed his fingers!

Erich Schneyer, the Managing Director was at Goering's side. "We have a good day for the maiden flight, Mein Herr" he observed as they watched the plane being pushed out of the hangar and the overalled Manfred Hufendiek climb into the rear cockpit and busy himself with his pre-flight checks. They saw him raise his arm, the mechanic swing the propeller and they heard the engine fire with a rhythmic beat.

Klaus studied the sky anxiously. It was clear, the visibility was excellent. He looked at the windsock. It was filling gently, "Good," he muttered, "Pray God nothing goes wrong!"

A throaty roar from the engine broke into his thoughts, he saw the handlers pull the chocks away and the plane slowly begin to move forward. Then with the engine at full throttle she picked up speed, her tail came up and her wheels left the grass. She was flying and as she climbed into the sky the onlookers cheered and clapped. It was a perfect take-off! As he watched the plane turn and climb into the heights, the engine seemed to purr with delight. Manfred he knew would shortly ease the throttle back and fly her on the level, before letting the engine idle and putting her into a gentle dive as had been planned He heard the engine roar as Manfred pulled out of the dive and began to climb once more, then after three tight turns he headed for the airfield for his first landing. With bated breath they watched the plane flying lower and lower, cross the boundary fence and finally touch down for a model landing. When he'd taxied back to the hangar and had emerged from the cockpit Manfred was given a rapturous welcome by those who'd built the plane. As he approached, Erich Schneyer embraced him.

"How was she?" he asked.

"She's very responsive and a delight to fly."

A beaming Erich turned to his guest. "Herr Goering let me introduce Manfred Hufendiek, our Test Pilot."

The great man congratulated Manfred, who answered his questions about the test flight with enthusiasm. Then reserving final judgement he added, "But Mein Herr it is only the first of many test flights I have to make."

But despite that note of caution, Klaus was certain the testing would go well. He laughed inwardly, now he could fulfil that promise he'd made himself and order that crimson Opel P4 saloon to celebrate!

In the coming weeks Manfred would fly the Goldfinch every day completing a full range of tests. Then his reports and recommendations would be carefully studied and, where necessary, modifications to the design would be implemented. But there seemed little doubt that with Herr Goering's interest in the plane, the Managing Director's prophesy of success would be realised. And already the Glider Clubs were enquiring about the Goldfinch for use as a tug.

The test flights were indeed proving successful, with only a few modifications to be incorporated, and so Klaus and his design team began to organise the production line for the plane when the expected orders came in. But despite this heavy workload Klaus began to have an insatiable desire to fly "his Goldfinch." Manfred agreed, "I need a passenger to try the dual controls."

And so on the penultimate test flight, Klaus donned flying overalls and helmet and wearing his parachute had climbed into the cockpit, as he'd done so often in his beloved Fokker D VII.

His musings were interrupted by a voice from the speaking tube. "Klaus are you settled?"

"Yes, Manfred". He saw the control column and the rudder bars moving; Manfred he knew, was doing the pre-flight checks.

Manfred's voice came down the tube, "Well Klaus, here we go." The engine roared and he felt the plane begin to bounce over the grass, then she was turning into the wind. He glanced at the rev counter, the needle was moving to full revs as they picked up speed. Now he could feel the wind on his face and the plane levelling as the tail came up. The bouncing eased and they were flying. Taking off had always excited him, that moment when the plane escapes the clutches of gravity and the land can be seen laid out like a map below. It had seemed effortless with the plane being pulled into the air by that powerful sweet sounding Siemens engine. Memories of his D VII came flooding back. She'd been a joy to fly, light and responsive and fast too, with her BMW engine she could do two hundred kilometres per hour, faster than the Goldfinch, which would only do one hundred and eighty five at best. But then the Goldfinch had a crew of two and was a trainer! He studied the altimeter. They were nearing seven hundred metres.

"What do you think of her?" He heard Manfred's voice over the tube. "How does she compare with your Fokker D VII?"

"She climbs well and seems easy to handle. Maybe she's not as responsive as the D VII, but then she was designed as a fighter!"

"Would you like fly her? I want to check your controls."

"Yes, thank you. I'd like to very much."

"OK then, she's yours. Fly her straight and level."

At first he had to concentrate, watching the instruments and the horizon. Then it all came back to him and with a light hand on the stick the plane seemed to fly herself.

"Make a ninety degree to starboard."

"OK."

With his foot he pushed the starboard rudder pedal forward and pulled the stick gently to the right. She banked nicely and her nose swung round to the new heading. It was like old times! "She does handle well," he shouted.

In the next twenty minutes or so he'd done a few more turns, had put her into a gentle dive and had climbed back up again.

"Take her up to seven hundred metres," Manfred said. "D'you remember how to recover from a stall?"

"OK and yes I know the recovery drill." He watched the altimeter needle moving gently toward the seven hundred metre mark and when it was there, he eased the stick forward to put her on the level."

"What's the stall speed?"

"Eighty. So go ahead."

The airspeed indicator showed one hundred and twenty. He closed the throttle and watched the speed drop. At ninety he eased the stick back, the nose came up, the starboard wings lost lift and the plane began to spin clockwise and lose height rapidly. Instinctively, he applied full left rudder and pushed the stick firmly forward. The spinning stopped, but the plane was diving steeply. Gently he eased the stick back to pull out of the dive and as the Goldfinch's nose came up again, he opened the throttle to regain height.

"You haven't forgotten your flying. That went well."

No, he hadn't! It had all come back so easily! "But then," he muttered. "When you've got a Sopwith Camel on your tail, that's when you learn to fly!"

He'd forgotten how much he'd loved flying. Could he, he wondered, ask Manfred to let him loop the loop? That's what his comrades did on return from a fight after shooting down an English plane. He'd done it five times, but the sixth time he hadn't dared, he'd been very short of fuel!

He asked Manfred.

"Yes, OK. Take her up to seven hundred metres again."

He took her up and heard Manfred again. "Right, off you go."

He put her into a dive with increasing revs and watched the airspeed indicator. The needle passed the 170 mark then 180. As it reached 190 he felt the plane beginning to tremble. He pulled the stick back and saw the land below pass under the propeller until only the open sky appeared. Now she was climbing and her speed was beginning to fall away, but he carried on upward, ever upward! For a moment she was climbing vertically with the airspeed needle hovering over the 100 mark. Then as she passed the vertical, she flew upside down until she began to dive and her speed increased as she dived ever more steeply. Then the land came into view again and he could level out.

"Oh! That was fun!" he shouted.

"Well I'm glad you enjoyed it. You should do more flying! I'll take her now; it's time to head back."

Reluctantly he took his hand off the stick and watched the airfield coming ever closer. He remembered his last landing, that crash landing. He'd not seen that Sopwith Camel diving on his tail. The first he'd known was the pain in his shoulder as bullets tore into the cockpit, one hitting him. Automatically he'd kicked the rudder bar and had banked sharply to starboard. As he did so he'd seen the Camel dive past him. Struggling to gain control he'd seen smoke coming from the engine, which was now misfiring. He'd pushed the throttle hard forward but the engine hadn't responded and slowly the propeller came to a halt. Putting her into a shallow dive he'd searched the sky, but thankfully the Camel had disappeared. Perhaps his enemy thought he was a gonner! Well he was almost! Losing height over No-Man's Land he'd searched desperately for a safe place to make some sort of landing. All he'd been able to do was to glide behind the German lines. At three hundred metres he'd seen the German trenches with what looked like flat land behind. Gently he'd coaxed her down. His chosen landing place was fast approaching, but now he could see there were shell craters. He glanced at the altimeter. With the needle moving ever lower he'd seen a crater right ahead! He'd kicked the rudder bar and her nose swung to starboard and she landed heavily, spinning as she did. His straps had saved him and as he scrambled free, he'd seen that the port wings had been torn off and she was lying on the edge of a crater. It was then that he'd become aware of the blood and had felt the pain of his wound. He'd been lucky and doubly so for in the hospital he'd met his beloved Golda!

A change in the engine note interrupted his musing. He looked around. Manfred was on his approach course. He watched the land coming ever closer and then felt a gentle bump as the plane touched down.

Chapter 3

As she'd foreseen her husband's optimism about the future, that nothing would change, that Hitler's enabling act wouldn't threaten the Jews, now seemed mere wishful thinking. The State sponsored boycott of Jewish businesses set for the first of April, left little doubt that Hitler's avowed hatred of the Jewish race would be translated into action!

In his latest aggressive speech, Hitler had declared Germany wouldn't tolerate the provocative action of the Jewish Congress of America, which had planned to boycott the sale of German goods in the United States. In retaliation, he ordered a one-day pre-emptive boycott of Jewish businesses in Germany.

Early the next morning men from the S.A. the Brownshirts, could be seen stationed outside all Jewish shops where placards reading "Meidet alles Judische"* ("Shun everything Jewish") had been pasted on the windows. Golda had seen several herself, one outside Gustav Dudevich's tailor shop and another by the bakery. Like most Jews she'd been worried indeed frightened, but had expected the S.A. to turn shoppers away peacefully, but not the Brownshirts! They'd been their usual aggressive, violent selves, pushing and insulting the Jews and shouting falsehoods about them. It had been quite terrifying and she'd hurried home, concerned about the safety of Hedwig and Moshe.

In the safety of her apartment, she'd turned the wireless on and heard Goebbels exhorting all German people to take action, defensive action he called it, against the Jews, *the guilty ones in our midst who misuse the hospitality granted to them by the German Volk.* *"The Jews,"* he'd screamed, *"are a race apart and the Jews in Germany must take responsibility for the actions of their fellow Jews in America."*

Such anti-Jewish vitriol scared her, the hatred it espoused was unbelievable! Yet she'd seen it with her own eyes, that unmistakeable hostility of Hitler's Brownshirts. But surely not all Germans were like them! Weren't they mostly good hard-working people, people like her who longed for peace and stability, who wanted to forget the hatred and suffering of the war?

Frightened by this manifest hatred, she waited eagerly for her children to come home. They arrived early, Hedwig with tears in her eyes and Moshe with anger in his. "They ignored us," he fumed. "None of our classmates would speak to us. Not even our cousins Horst and Heinrich!"

"No, not even Horst!" Hedwig sobbed, "Though Heinrich did whisper sorry."

"It all started before classes began," Moshe went on. "There was a lot of whispering going on and when we started kicking the ball around as we usually do, they never kicked it back to, us. We couldn't understand it, and when we asked what was up, they wouldn't reply!"

"But Ante, the bossy one made it clear!" Hedwig interrupted, "She'd shouted Meidet alles Judische*".

"Well I hope you didn't start a fight, Moshe." Golda looked at him anxiously.

"No, Mama, I didn't, though I wanted to."

"Well Moshe dear, you did the right thing. If we retaliate it will only make things worse."

Moshe scowled, "Why should they treat us like that? What makes them think they're more German than we are?"

"They've been listening to that dreadful man Hitler, that's why! But tell me." Golda asked, "Why are you home so early? Were you sent home?"

"Well at lunch-time, we Jews thought it best to go home. The boycott is only meant to last one day, so we hope things will be back to normal tomorrow."

Klaus had come home late as usual, pleading problems with the production line for the Goldfinch. He arrived as they were about to have supper.

"That aeroplane seems to dominate your entire life these days." Golda muttered angrily. Klaus seemed not to hear, for he made no reply, but asked

Hedwig and Moshe about their day at school. They told him how they'd been ignored, how none of the non-Jews had spoken to them.

"Not even Horst and Heinrich," Hedwig added petulantly.

Klaus gave his daughter a hug. "I saw Brownshirts outside the Jewish shops with their placards but," he added, "I never thought Jewish children would be boycotted in school. It must have been very distressing for you darling."

"Yes Daddy," a tearful Hedwig replied. "It was horrible."

Moshe frowned. "When they started shouting Meidet alles Judische, I got so angry I wanted to fight them, but the others stopped me!"

"Moshe, they did the right thing. You mustn't react. Just try and ignore them!"

"Yes, do as your father says," Golda urged him. "We don't want to provoke them, but Klaus dear what will they do next?"

Klaus shook his head ruefully.

"Goebbels said it was to be a one day protest against the American boycott. So hopefully there'll be no boycott tomorrow."

And Klaus was right, for on the following morning the S.A. and their placards had disappeared and the boycott seemed to be over, leaving the Jewish shopkeepers to clear up the broken glass, repair the damage and re-open for business. Nevertheless the boycott had triggered many worrying articles in the press whether the Jews had the right to be part of German society. It seemed the one-day boycott could be just the start of Hitler's persecution of the Jews. And not long afterwards the newspapers and the wireless began announcing new anti-Jewish laws. Laws which made it clear that Hitler was determined to exclude the Jews from the German community.

The first of the new laws decreed the immediate dismissal of all civil servants of "non-Aryan origin". This as Golda knew would affect thousands of Jews since all teachers, professors, doctors and nurses in addition to national and local government employees, were listed as 'civil servants'.

"Does that mean," she asked herself "that Benjamin my brother, will lose his professorship at Bremen University? If so how will he and Ruth survive?"

A second law was published a day later. All non-Aryans were to be removed from the judiciary. And a third set a maximum quota of Jewish students in any one school. The quota was set at five percent and within days both Moshe and Hedwig came home with letters declaring that in order to meet the quota, neither would be allowed back in school!

"Dearest," she looked accusingly at Klaus as he came home. "You said the persecution of the Jews would die down. Read these!"

He studied the letters anxiously.

"What will Hitler do next?" She asked fearfully.

Klaus reached for her hand. "How can anyone tell? He seems to have a resolute hatred of the Jews. But how can he govern the country without all the civil servants he's going to dismiss?" He shook his head. "Two of my best engineers are Jewish and for all I know there may be more!"

"But Klaus dear, what are we going to do about Hedwig and Moshe? They're both very upset".

"Yes, dearest, I'm sure they are, but where are they?"

"They're in their rooms. I'll fetch them."

A worried Hedwig came in. "Daddy we've been expelled from school. Why do they hate us?"

"Because they're ignorant pagans," an angry Moshe declared. "They can't accept that we're God's chosen people and they're jealous of what we Jews have achieved!"

Klaus smiled involuntary. Moshe is a fighter, he knew he'd never give in.

"Well Moshe," he said, "The Jews have a long history of persecution, yet somehow they've survived and your God will be with you. But now you'll have to stay home for a while."

He turned to Golda, "There's a Jewish school in town, isn't there? Surely they'll take Hedwig and Moshe. Perhaps you should talk to your Rabbi, maybe he can help."

The following morning Golda had gone to the Synagogue to see the Rabbi. As she'd expected other parents were there too, many perhaps forty or maybe fifty! They all looked distressed, all talking about Hitler's hatred of them. Only two seemed to recognise her, but she hardly knew either of them, they were mere shopping acquaintances. It made her feel an outcast, and perhaps she should be, she hadn't been to Synagogue for years. She didn't even know the Rabbi. In fact she didn't know many Jews at all. With a Gentile husband and in-laws, most of their friends and acquaintances tended to be non-Jewish. But Hitler by his invective had made her recognise that she and her children were Jews, and now she must seek Yahweh's forgiveness and plead that in His mercy, He would make the Rabbi look kindly on her a lapsed Jew, and he would help. At long last it was her turn.

Your name?" the Rabbi asked politely.

"Frau Boddenburg, Frau Golda Boddenburg."

"And your children?"

"I am blessed with two. Hedwig my daughter who is eleven and Moshe my twelve year old son."

She watched him taking notes in a painstakingly clear hand. Then he hesitated. "Boddenburg" he repeated the name. "It's not a Jewish name."

"No, Rabbi. I married a Gentile. Before that my name was Leobowitz."

"Ah, a good Jewish name. Are you the daughter of Chaim Leobowitz?" She nodded. "Yes, I'm proud to say he is my father."

"He is a good man and a faithful Jew, but I don't recall seeing you in synagogue"

"No, I'm ashamed to say I haven't attended synagogue for many a year."

He reached out and took her hand. "Well our God is merciful and compassionate, and if you ask him he will forgive you."

A few more questions followed with her answers neatly recorded in his book. Then promising to do what he could, he asked her to come back on Thursday, when he'd tell her what if anything he'd managed to achieve.

Heading home she thanked Yahweh for his forgiveness and prayed the Rabbi would be successful. If he wasn't, she dared not think what she could do with Hedwig and Moshe. But if he was successful, she was sure they'd be happier in a Jewish school where there'd be no boycott. What a frightening country Germany was becoming, a country divided by race and ruled by a Dictator, whose word was law. The future worried her, what, she wondered would be the end of it all? But despite her worries she had to admit she was luckier than most Jews; she had a loving husband with an assured job. Not like her dear brother Benjamin, sacked simply because he was a Jew! Passing his apartment, on impulse she'd knocked on his door. Benjamin was there, looking stunned and bewildered!

"I've been sacked like all the other Jews. We were told the university had no option; the law had to be obeyed! I've been given a month's salary and told not to come back!"

Ruth looked at Golda in dismay. "He's been Professor of Mathematics at the university for over three years and now without warning he's been dismissed! Yet only last year he was told how well he was doing!"

"Oh! Benjamin dear, what'll you do?"

"Well, no university will employ me now, but I suppose I might find a job teaching in a Jewish school."

"Maybe." Golda replied telling him Hedwig and Moshe had been expelled from their school as Jews, and how she hoped Mount Carmel school would take them.

"Perhaps," she added to comfort him, "Schools like Mount Carmel with more pupils will need more teachers."

"Yes, that's possible, but they can't take us all!" Benjamin glanced at Ruth, "We might have to emigrate; that is if we can find a country to take us." Suddenly he looked angry. "Would you believe it, Golda? When I said good bye to my students and wished them good luck in their exams, one didn't seem to hear me properly. He turned and looked me up and down as if I was some diseased animal. "Sir," he said "isn't it time you emigrated?" He paused and looked at Ruth. "Well Ruth dear, isn't that what we must do?"

Walking home Golda felt her world was being savagely destroyed. What future was there for the Jews? Why were they so wrongly denied the right to live like other Germans, in their own land, the land of their fathers?

Over supper that night, she told Klaus and the children how she hoped to find a place for them at the Jewish school, but it was not until they were in bed that she told Klaus about Benjamin and Ruth.

"Dear Benjamin felt humiliated by that student. He'd wished him luck and for his kindness he was treated as if he was some contagious animal! It was so offensive, downright insulting! What right do these so-called Aryans have, to treat us so?"

She paused to let her anger subside. "And now the poor dears," she continued, "have no income, only the little Ruth can make with her knitting and crochet. We may have to help them Klaus dear."

"Yes of course Golda, but let's hope he gets a job in a Jewish school."

Reading the papers the next day Golda could find no outcry about the new anti-Jewish laws. It seemed clear that Josef Goebbels, the Minister of Propaganda, would not allow Nazi policy to be criticised. However two days later she read his more conciliatory statement:

"Jewry can rest assured that we will leave them alone as long as they retire quietly and modestly behind their four walls, as long as they are not provocative, and do not affront the German people with the claim to be treated as equals".

At first the statement seemed to offer some hope for the Jews. If they made themselves "invisible" it seemed they would be tolerated. But the message to vanish soon became clear. On walls and windows all over the country signs were being posted. **"Jews not welcome", "No Jews served here", "Jews and dogs not admitted", "The Jews are our misfortune".** And many shopkeepers were refusing to sell to Jews. Libraries and museums were closed to them too and they were refused entry to theatres and cinemas.

Then there was the book burning. The ***Volkischer Beobachter*** the Nazi newspaper, gleefully reported that in Berlin the Brownshirts aided by university students, had thrown twenty-five thousand books onto a pyre, where they had been engulfed in flames. It continued:

"The Horst-Wessel song rings out like thunder and the flames still crackle while heaps of Jewish subversive writings are thrown into them. With this demonstration, the continuing fight against the non-German mind has been started."

Goebbels' response was more concise, praising the action of the Brownshirts as an appropriate response to the *"trash and filth of Jewish gutter literati."*

As the burning of books spread to the university towns of Heidelberg, Gottingen, Munich and Munster, the Jews began to feel themselves locked into a kind of ghetto, not one with walls, but one of isolation and separation from the social life of the nation.

With such discrimination, the Jewish community had begun to draw together, to meet their needs from their own resources. But many like Benjamin and Ruth, could see no future for themselves in Germany and had begun to think of freedom, freedom in foreign lands where so many of the more eminent Jews, actors, artists, musicians, academics and scientists had already fled. They were the lucky ones! One needed an entry visa from the chosen country in order to emigrate. For the famous getting one was not difficult, but for the ordinary Jew getting a visa was the first and most difficult hurdle, for even in 1934 many countries still struggled with high unemployment resulting from the 1926 depression, and so would only give visas to those with their own financial support, or who had a sponsor guaranteeing them work. So every Jew wishing to escape began searching desperately for a guarantor, a relative now settled in some foreign country, or perhaps a foreigner who had become a friend during a visit to Germany. Old family records were desperately searched and foreign telephone directories eagerly scanned for names and addresses to which letters could be sent pleading sponsorship. The great majority were to be disappointed, but now and then the miracle happened and with sponsorship a visa could be obtained. Then the punitive Reich Flight Tax had to be paid, which meant they would arrive in their new country with little money and few possessions. But only a few were lucky and for most emigration was an unfulfilled dream; they remained trapped in a hostile Germany.

A few days after the book burning she heard the dreadful news about her father. There'd been a loud banging on the apartment door and opening it she'd found Levi her father's old friend with a bandage wrapped around his head. His appearance shocked her. "Whatever's happened? Have you fallen?" she asked him.

"No, no I haven't fallen. It's the work of the Brownshirts. But my injury is nothing, they've killed your father."

"My father's been killed?"

"Yes."

"Oh!" She closed her eyes in distress. Her dear father killed? How could it be? "Levi please tell me what happened."

"Chaim your father," he told her, "had wanted to demonstrate the loyalty of the Jews to their native land Germany, and he persuaded me to help him. We found our old Army caps bearing the badge of the Hamburg Infantry Regiment and wearing them we stood outside the synagogue holding a placard adorned with the Star of David and the Swastika. On the placard we'd written 'We Jews fought for the Kaiser and we love our country Germany.' As we stood there, several other Jews joined us and though some passers-by shook their fists and a few even spat at us, many people seemed to tolerate our presence, indeed we felt some support."

"Oh!" Golda interrupted him. "He told me only last Friday, that we Jews must show we are Germans too and that we too love our country, but Levi, I never imagined he would organise a demonstration!"

"Well your Father was a man of principle and it was a peaceful demonstration. We never criticised Hitler or the Nazis!"

"But surely he must have known it's dangerous to protest against the regime."

"Well he reckoned our regimental cap badges would protect us, would show our loyalty to Germany and I did too. But the Brownshirts ignored our Army cap badges and calling us filthy Jewish traitors, began beating us with their rifle-butts. The others fled leaving us at their mercy. They hit your father first and when he fell they turned on me. I don't recall much more, they left us both unconscious! Then our Jewish friends returned and carried us into the synagogue. I came round and while they dressed our wounds, I was able to tell them what had happened. But your father," he shook his head sadly, "well no-one could make you father come to. When a doctor arrived he declared him dead!" He held her hands, "Your father was a brave man."

"Yes, he was. I think he preferred to die rather than succumb to Hitler's hatred. But you dear Levi are brave too, as brave as him. But where is my father now?"

"The Rabbi has him."

She ran to get her coat, "I must go to him."

"Golda dear, it's dark now. See him and the Rabbi in the morning."

He was right she knew, and when she had asked who would care for him, he assured her his dear wife Chema would and left.

Though in a state of shock, she had to make sure her brother knew, so having broken the sad news to the children she went to tell Benjamin and Ruth.

Custom demanded that his funeral be held within twenty-four hours of his death, so there was much to do, but with the Rabbi and Benjamin's help all was ready and the family set off for the funeral. Entering the synagogue, the low murmuring of psalms proclaimed the sadness and grief of the occasion. Her father's earthly body lying in a plain casket in front of the shtender*, emphasised the finality of it all. Never would she see his loving face again. Holding back her tears, she led Hedwig and Moshe to join Ruth in the women's gallery. Looking for her beloved Klaus, she saw him in the men's stalls, sitting alongside Benjamin, looking uneasy in his kippah*.

The children had never been to synagogue before, and almost at once Moshe began asking questions.

"Is that the Ark?"

"Yes," she whispered. "It contains the Scrolls. The Scrolls of the Law."

"What are they?" Moshe asked. She promised to tell him later, but then he began asking about the Seven Armed candle stick.

"It's called the Menorah, but we must be quiet," she berated him.

"The Rock, his work is perfect," the Rabbi was intoning, "For all his ways are judgement; a God of faithfulness and without iniquity, just and right is he......."

She closed her eyes and saw again her dear father, his dark eyes shining as he told her how he believed the Jews should demonstrate their loyalty to the nation. She shook her head. "How could he have been so reckless?" she asked herself. But he'd been a man of principle, who wouldn't accept Hitler's vilification of the Jews. He'd been a kind and loving man, a man who always saw the best in people. Fighting back her tears, she looked around. The synagogue was full "and so it should be," she muttered. He was a well-respected and loving member of the Jewish community. She saw Eli her father's closest friend mount the shtender. He spoke of her father's patience, wisdom and learning and the great shock felt by everyone when they heard he'd been killed by the Brownshirts. He paid tribute to his courage and that of his friend Levi, for trying to demonstrate the loyalty of German Jews to the state. Such loyalty, he reminded them, had been amply shown when Chaim and so many other Jews had fought for the Kaiser in the war. Chaim he told them, had fought at Passchendaele, where he was badly wounded. Then in despair he shook his head and declared, "But such Jewish loyalty seems to count for nothing in Nazi Germany now!" Then reminding them of her father's kindness and generosity he ended by saying, "Chaim Leobowitz was a Jew of the old order, one who lived by the Law of Moses and strove to be obedient to Yahweh. We shall miss his dedication and fine example."

"Yes, we most certainly will," Golda muttered. She knew her father's faith had been his lynchpin and how in his later years he'd found great comfort communing with Yahweh in the synagogue.

After a moment of silence the Rabbi began leading the congregation in a psalm and as they sang: "for thou O God will not abandon my soul to the grave: thou wilt make known to me the path of life", the pall bearers shouldered the casket and led the procession to the graveyard.

There the close relatives would rend their garments. When she'd told Moshe and Hedwig how they, their father and their grandfather's friends would tear their garments with their bare hands and wail with grief for the loss of their beloved Chaim, they'd looked mystified.

"Your shirt or blouse must be torn," she told them. "I will make a small cutting close to your heart, to help you tear it. We tear our clothes near the heart to show we're heart-broken and as the casket is lowered into the grave we must all murmur 'May he come to his place in peace'".

When the burial was over, everyone spoke to her and Benjamin, offering their condolences and admiration of her father. Having her own high regard for her father bolstered in such a way made Golda proud to be a Jew.

Chapter 4

Klaus sipped his coffee, all was well this morning, there seemed to be no problems. The production line workers had now finished their training and hopefully knew their jobs; now it was up to the Supervisors to ensure they did!

As he savoured the strong sweet coffee, he mused about Golda's oft repeated remark "That aeroplane seems to dominate your life!" It always worried him when she said that, but though he kept telling her how much he loved her, that she was a wonderful wife and mother and how proud he was of his talented daughter Hedwig and of his determined and principled son Moshe, she still seemed to resent the Goldfinch. Yet it was the Goldfinch which gave him the salary that enabled him to feed and house his family!

The Goldfinch had indeed become an important, a challenging part of his life. To have translated that original idea into a machine that defied gravity with such ease, had fulfilled all his hopes and expectations. It had been a truly gratifying experience! He sighed, the thrill of conception and delivery was now behind him. Now he had to be satisfied with a production line! He lit a cigarette and leant back in his chair. He was certain the Goldfinch would do well; potential buyers were already showing a great interest in her and the first plane now being built was as good as sold to a flying club, and three others were considering a purchase. "Yes," he mused, "Goering's subsidy to the flying clubs will be a great help, but will he order her as a trainer for his Luftwaffe? Only then could he say the plane was a success!

But now he felt empty, as if he had no real purpose; nothing of his was on the drawing board, though the idea of a fighter aircraft had begun to exercise him. It would be a monoplane, just the one wing, without the need for the struts and bracing wires of a bi-plane. Getting rid of them would reduce drag and powered by his choice of engine the new Daimler-Benz DB 601, it would have a speed to match or better that of the Hurricane the English were building. But he sighed, for the moment he had to concentrate on building and selling the Goldfinch and be satisfied with an occasional flight when a Goldfinch was being test flown.

But despite his dissatisfaction, he had to admit that unlike some men, he often felt happier at work than at home. At work he could forget the problems of the Jews, for these days the moment he got home Golda would invariably tell him of yet more problems her people were facing. Problems he couldn't begin to solve! And now that her father had been so brutally killed by the Brownshirts, his beloved Golda was becoming more and more anxious and withdrawn.

Involuntarily he shook his head. He'd hoped his new car might have lifted her spirits. He'd bought it only a few weeks ago. He'd not told the family about his plans to buy a car! He laughed as he remembered driving home that first day. He'd parked it on the other side of the road and had summoned the family to the window to announce, "There she is," pointing to the crimson Opel with its shiny black mudguards. "That's ours. Now the Goldfinch is flying, I thought I'd buy us a car, to celebrate!" He'd squeezed Golda's hand and laughed, "Dearest, we can have some picnics in the country now."

"Wow!" Moshe exclaimed. "She's a beauty. How fast will she go, Daddy?"

"Fast enough Moshe, but I must nurse the engine for the first 500 kilometres."

"Oh Daddy, let's have a picnic on Sunday," Hedwig demanded.

He'd taken them out to inspect the car. Moshe wanted to see the engine, while Hedwig explored the interior. Even Golda looked happier!

Since then most Sundays, they'd driven in the country and had found some special picnic spots. Now it seemed that only in the car, was Golda able to forget her Jewishness.

"Is it any wonder," Klaus asked himself, "that I'm happier at work?"

His dearest Golda looking ever more care worn, had acquired a few Jewish friends. That pleased him, they gave her support and advice. Like them Golda waited anxiously for Thursday to come to learn what the

Rabbi had to say about their children's schooling. Arriving, Golda found the synagogue crowded with worried parents. When at last the Rabbi arrived, they were delighted to see he was smiling. Did he have good news they wondered? And he had; he told them everything they'd hoped to hear. Mount Carmel School would take all the children, though not for a week or two, as the school had to be reorganised. Golda could scarcely wait to get home to tell Moshe and Hedwig about Mount Carmel and its offer to take them, but Hedwig didn't seem so pleased.

"Will there be any violin lessons?" she asked plaintively. "And is there a school orchestra? It was such fun playing in the orchestra with Horst and his flute, and my other friends."

"Well Hedwig dear, it'll be good to get you back to school and I expect we can find a violin teacher for you."

Moshe took the news philosophically. "But," he scowled, "I'm still angry that we were expelled because we're Jews."

"Moshe dear," she tried to calm him, "It's no good getting angry or fighting the Nazis, it'll only make things worse. Remember how they killed Grandpa! We have no choice but to accept Hitler's orders. All we can do is to try to live with them as best we can."

That evening when she told Klaus the news, he was pleased. "Persecuting children like this is unforgivable, it's completely unjust. How thankful we must be to your fellow Jews for what they've done! Let's hope Hitler will be more reasonable in future."

"Yes dearest, we must pray that he will."

For a while their hopes for the children seemed to have been fulfilled. They had started at Mount Carmel now divided into two, with one half being taught in the morning and the other in the afternoon. It seemed to work well and with the children being taught in a Jewish school, Golda told Klaus she ought to take them to synagogue on the Sabbath.

"Dearest, we are Jews," she reminded him, "and we must get closer to the Jewish community. We need to learn from them how best to deal with our problems. We Jews must support each other."

She was pleased that Klaus had agreed.

When she told the children of her plans, Moshe was delighted. Since being at Mount Carmel he'd embraced his Jewishness and had begun to study the Torah every day. He'd also drawn a Star of David, which now hung proudly above his bed.

But Hedwig displayed no such interest. She was just happy that a violin teacher had been found, and as before was always busy practising!

But while the problem of her children's education seemed to have been solved, Golda couldn't help worrying about her brother Benjamin. She knew he was having great difficulty finding a job and was grateful to Klaus for giving them a weekly allowance. Delighted with his generosity she had taken the money to Benjamin and Ruth the following Thursday, promising to bring the same amount each week. Though reluctant at first, they had accepted the money gratefully.

"It's very kind of you and Klaus, very kind indeed," Golda saw Ruth's tear-stained eyes. "I'm afraid my knitting earns so little and we're falling behind with the rent."

"Dearest Golda," Benjamin reached for his sister's hand, "We are truly grateful". Embarrassed by their effusive thanks Golda changed the subject.

"Benjamin dear, have you managed to find a sponsor?"

"No, no, we've had no luck." He looked depressed. "I had a letter only yesterday to say my English friend has died and as yet I've had no reply from America."

"We can only hope our American acquaintance will help us." Ruth put on a forced smile. "We'll find a sponsor somehow." Then she added more hopefully "We've got our passports, here look."

Golda smiled. She opened the passport Ruth had given her. She read the name

Ruth Heidi Sarah LEIBOWITZ.

"But Ruth dear, you're not called Sarah, there must be a mistake!"

"No Golda dear. Here look at Benjamin's."

Golda opened his. It read Benjamin Ezra Israel LEIBOWITZ.

"What's happened? Benjamin was never called Israel."

"No, and I was never called Sarah, that is until now. The Nazis have decreed that on their passports all male Jews should have the name Israel added and female Jews the name Sarah. Then there can be no doubt whether or not we are Jews!"

"Oh dear, Hitler really does hate us doesn't he?"

Ruth nodded unhappily. "Yes, I'm afraid so. But tell me about Hedwig and Moshe, how's their schooling?"

Golda told her about Mount Carmel School and how she'd even found a violin teacher for Hedwig. Ruth was delighted, but added "You must be worried about their future."

"Yes like all Jews, we worry about our children. We see only unhappiness, persecution, the possibility of imprisonment, even death for them in Hitler's Germany and we desperately want them to go to another country, where they'll be safe."

Golda hesitated, the problem facing her and her children seemed overwhelming. "We've talked to them both about the possibility of leaving Germany, and that Klaus and I may not be able to go with them; that they may have to go on their own." She paused to control the anguish growing inside her. Then with a deep breath, she continued, "Breaking up the family is wicked, cruel and unforgivable, but surely it's our duty as parents to save our beloved children from the fate Hitler seems to have in store for us Jews". She shook her head, "We have to be realists".

Ruth reached out for her hand. "Oh! Golda."

Golda sighed, "Ruth dear, our children like those of other Jewish families will have to go on their own. Klaus and I believe Moshe given the chance would go, but dear Hedwig bursts into tears whenever we tell her that Daddy may not be able to go too and that I won't leave without him, so," she shrugged her shoulders, "we have no plans, only worries!"

"Oh! Golda dear, we've always envied you and Klaus for having two such lovely children. Benjamin and I have always longed for children of our own, but our hopes have been denied. But now," Ruth glanced at Benjamin, "we're glad we've none."

"Yes," Benjamin nodded. "Thankfully we've no children to worry about. But perhaps when we've managed to emigrate, Yahweh will look on us more kindly!"

But a new decree published a few days later, ***"forbidding anyone to leave the country without permission",*** raised yet another hurdle for Jews hoping to emigrate.

When on the following week Golda took their money to them, she asked Benjamin, "What'll you do now?"

"We'll have to escape somehow," he looked defiant. "We must. There's no hope for us here in Germany!"

That evening she told Klaus. "Benjamin says there's no hope for Ruth and him in Germany and they want to leave." She saw him nod.

"Yes," he said, "but how?"

"They won't tell me and I do worry about them. And Dearest I worry about Moshe and Hedwig too. What future do they have in Hitler's Germany?"

It was a question she knew Klaus couldn't answer. But then that other question, the one that had plagued her ever since her last visit to Benjamin and Ruth, demanded an answer.

"Dearest, Benjamin and Ruth are planning to escape. Can't we do so as well? Can't we try? Can't we? Can't we all go as a family? I'm sure Benjamin would tell us how he and Ruth plan to go."

"Dearest, I daren't even try! As an aircraft designer with the reputation I seem to have acquired and my knowledge of our aircraft industry, I've become too important to Herr Goering and his plan to build a strong Luftwaffe. I'd never be allowed to leave Germany. And if I was to plan an escape and was caught, well the consequences for all of us would be terrible. I'd be charged with treason and you for helping me, and for that there would only be one punishment, death!"

He shook his head ruefully. "No, Golda dear, I can't even try to emigrate, let alone escape. You and the children can go, but I cannot!"

Golda looked dismayed, yet she had known his answer, even before she'd asked the question. The man she loved was trapped inside Hitler's Germany as much as any Jew. She reached for his hand. "Dearest, I can't go without you!"

And so while they wondered how Benjamin and Ruth would escape, the possibility of them following was never mentioned again. But Golda, like all Jewish parents, agonised about the future of her children.

Then an article published in many of the papers gave a spark of hope. It read:

The fundamental idea of the Zionists to organise the Jews as a nation among nations, in their own land is sound and justified, as long as it is not connected with any plan for world domination.

That became the prelude to negotiations between the Jews and the Nazis, who both saw Palestine as the solution to their differing problems. The resultant Ha'avara (Transfer) Agreement established the way Jews could raise the money required by Britain (the Mandatory Power) for unrestricted entry into Palestine. The Jews would sell their possessions for marks to be deposited in a German bank. This would then be used to buy German goods to be shipped to Palestine. There they would be sold for Palestinian pounds and the money would be used to pay the entry fee for German Jews wishing to enter the new Zion. But the Zionists seeking to build a new nation, wondered how many people Palestine could absorb. Unrestricted immigration was out of the question. Intellectuals and professionals were deemed not to be necessary, but if they came, they would finance their own entry through the scheme. What was needed was a young labour force to build roads, bridges, and accommodation or to till the land. But such youngsters would not be able to pay their entry fee, so they would be financed by the Palestinian Jews.

The opportunity to give their children a new life in Zion, was welcomed by many Jewish parents; it would give their children a future, even if they themselves had none. So the Youth Aliyah Movement was formed to organise the necessary training in an establishment at Eberswalde near Berlin, where young Jews would be taught the practical skills needed for work and life in the Jewish community in Palestine. Their training would also include the study of the Hebrew language, the history of Zionism and the geography of Palestine.

Golda read these developments eagerly and was convinced this would be best for her beloved Moshe, now becoming ever more Jewish, wanting only to eat Kosher and studying his Torah daily. She discussed it with Klaus. "Even if we can't escape, we must get Moshe out of Germany somehow!"

"Yes Golda dear, but he's only thirteen. He won't be accepted until he's fourteen".

"Yes dearest, but I pray Hitler won't have ended this scheme by then".

Klaus nodded. "And Golda what about our dearest Hedwig?"

"She's too young at the moment, but everyone is saying girls should learn domestic skills and a foreign language too. The English are said to want domestic servants and England would be a good country for her!"

"But surely Golda dearest, our clever Hedwig is destined for better things than domestic service!"

"Yes, Klaus we both know she dreams of being a violinist, but will a foreign family want to employ one? Surely they only want domestic servants!"

So it was agreed that Golda would explain the Ha'avara Agreement to Moshe and see how he reacted. He was excited, his eyes shone.

"What an adventure it would be! I'd be a pioneer helping to build the new Zion!"

Then his excitement faded. "But what about you and Daddy?"

Somehow she assured him they'd be alright; that Daddy's job would keep them safe, though in her heart she knew it was probably wishful thinking.

"And what about Hedwig?"

She was afraid he might ask about her.

"Well," she said lamely, "at the moment she's too young and we don't think a pioneering life would suit her."

She saw a grin spread over his face as he nodded. "So what'll she do? Will she stay here?"

"Well, Moshe dear, we haven't talked to her yet, but if you're happy about going to Palestine, we'll do what we can to get you there."

"Yes, I'm happy, but when will I be going?"

She found the newspaper article and read it to him.

"We'll apply for a place for you then and hopefully when you're fourteen, you'll go off to Eberswalde and join the Youth Aliyah Movement and then after a month or so you'll be on your way!"

Moshe was very excited and asked endless questions about the training at Eberswalde and Palestine. She answered them as best she could, and giving him an atlas, left him studying the map intently.

She felt relieved, for the first time in months she felt assured that providing he was accepted, her beloved Moshe might have a future. But what about Hedwig?

As she had hoped, a few days later Hedwig put her precious violin aside and came and sat with her.

"Mummy," she had a puzzled look on her face, "Is Moshe really going to Palestine? He keeps telling me he's going to be a pioneer! He's not teasing me is he?"

"No, Hedwig dear. He teases you a lot I know, but he's not teasing you this time."

A look of horror spread across her face. "You mean he really is going?"

"Yes, darling. Let me explain."

She told her daughter about the Youth Aliyah Movement and how excited Moshe was. Then she said "And we must do something about you too, Hedwig dear"

"What do you mean, Mummy?"

Carefully she explained that there was little hope or future for the Jews in Hitler's Germany and that everyone was wanting to emigrate. The Youth Aliyah Movement gave youngsters a way of escaping to Palestine but that was the only scheme sponsored by the Nazis. But there could be other opportunities for Jews to leave Germany. "It may be possible for young Jews to leave for employment as domestic servants in private households."

"But Mummy," there were tears in her eyes, "I don't want to go without you and Daddy. Why can't we all go?"

Golda had foreseen her question and having told her that she and Daddy would stay, had voiced her well-practised answer, "Daddy's job making aeroplanes for Hitler means he cannot go and I won't go without him. His job will keep us out of danger so we'll be alright, but for you and Moshe it isn't safe, not with that dreadful man Hitler in charge. You must go!"

"But Mummy, I don't want to leave you and Daddy. And I don't want to be a chamber maid or a kitchen maid, I want to be a violinist in an orchestra," her eyes became dreamy, "one day I might be another Alice Pashkus!"

Golda put a protective arm around her troubled daughter. "Hedwig dearest, Daddy and I love you and we want you to have a happy life in a country where you'll be safe. Dearest we don't want to lose you, but you must go sooner or later."

It was all too much for Hedwig. She burst into tears and fled.

Chapter 5

Was it good news or not? Golda and her fellow Jews couldn't believe what they were reading. The vicious bullying S.A. had been disbanded by the Reichswehr* and Ernst Rohm its leader and other high ranking officers having been accused of organising a coup d'état, had been executed in what the papers called "The Night of the Long Knives". Now there were no S.A. men on the streets and surely that could only be a good thing. On the wireless later that evening, Hitler had addressed the nation, ranting in his usual violent aggressive manner about the deception of the S.A. Though they had sworn loyalty to him, he claimed they had planned to assassinate him and seize power.

If the S.A. had been successful in their coup, Golda wondered whether they would have made life even more difficult for the Jews. Some thought they would have and saw the disbanding of the S.A. as a small mercy. When she'd discussed this with Klaus he'd said briefly

"There'd have been no difference."

But he was distant, seemed distracted by other things and talked of an early night. She knew he had a heavy workload coming home late most nights and even working on Saturdays! She changed the subject.

"It's your nephew Horst's birthday on Sunday week, and we've been asked to his party."

"Yes Golda dear, I haven't forgotten. I've bought his present."

"Oh! Have you! I thought you'd be too busy. So what have you got him?"

"A piccolo. Now he's fourteen he'll be joining the Hitler Youth and the piccolo is smaller and handier than his flute. It'll fit into his kit bag more easily."

"Oh! That dreadful Hitler Youth, its only purpose is to train young boys to be ardent Nazis!"

"Golda you're exaggerating. It gets the boys camping, playing sport and gives them a healthy life, rather like the Boy Scouts of old. It's a pity Moshe can't join, but now he wants to be a pioneer in Palestine, he'd probably refuse anyway."

It was a lovely summer's day for Horst's birthday party and he was the centre of attention, proudly wearing his new Hitler Youth uniform. How could he be so insensitive, Golda wondered in despair? Didn't he know his Aunt and cousins were Jews that her father had been killed by the Nazis and that Jewish boys like Moshe, were excluded from the Hitler Youth? She glanced at her dear loving, naïve Hedwig. She seemed totally unaware of the uniform's significance with its Hitler Youth badge boldly showing the Nazi swastika! Her gaze was focussed on Horst, not his uniform! Golda sighed, she could understand why, for with his blue eyes, fine complexion and straw blonde hair, he was indeed a very handsome young boy. When Horst came to unwrap the present Klaus had given him, he was ecstatic, as if it was the only thing he wanted! "Now," he joyfully exclaimed, "I can pack this in my rucksack when I go to camp. My flute's too long." He fingered it and putting it to his lips began playing. Then suddenly he stopped and looked at his brother, "Come on Heinrich sing; sing the Horst-Wessel song."

Golda grimaced, it was that awful Nazi song. Hedwig didn't seem to like it either and when they stopped had begged Horst to play "Lorelei". It was his favourite she knew; it had almost become his signature tune! When he'd finished, she gave him her present. It was a framed postcard of Lorelei, the big rock on a bend in the Rhine, named after the mythical siren who distracted the helmsmen of the barges in the river below, by combing her golden tresses and making them steer onto the rocks! Poor Hedwig, he quickly unwrapped it, gave it a quick glance and had hardly thanked her, before turning to receive another present. Her poor darling Hedwig had looked disappointed and hurt!

"The uniform fits well!" Moshe slapped his cousin on the shoulder as he handed over his gift. "When I'm fourteen I hope to be a pioneer in Palestine." Horst had looked surprised but other than saying "Really?" had made no comment.

When it was Golda's turn, Horst had taken her present and avoiding her eyes had given her a grudging thank you. She'd felt offended, surely he could show his aunt some affection and thank her properly! Horst had always been more reticent unlike his brother Heinrich who always welcomed her with a hug and a kiss. But why was he now being so impolite to Hedwig and her? Was it because they were Jews? Had the Hitler Youth infected him already?   Afterwards when they were having tea, Liesel had told her she and Wolfgang her husband had tried to persuade Horst not to wear his uniform, but it was his birthday, he'd been excited and had insisted he must; he told them he was proud to serve Hitler. At that point Liesel had given Golda's hand a friendly squeeze and said she hoped she and Klaus had not been offended.

"No, no we quite understand," Golda assured her, "It is his birthday after all."

Liesel had clearly been relieved by her assurance and they'd talked about the children, how Heinrich was doing well at school and how he was becoming a fine swimmer.

"He swam a kilometre only last week, that's twenty-five lengths of the pool." Liesel saw her blue eyes twinkle. "I asked him how he managed not to lose count!"

Hedwig came to join them and Liesel gave her a big hug.

"Oh! I wish I had a lovely daughter like you. You know Hedwig you're getting prettier every day!" Then she'd asked about her violin playing.

"They do miss you in the school orchestra, Hedwig dear. They've not yet found anyone to play solo as well as you!"

Later that night Golda learnt that Klaus too, had been concerned by Horst's rudeness and his insensitivity in wearing his Hitler Youth uniform. Looking angry, Golda told him, "He ignored Hedwig, Moshe and me and hardly thanked us for his presents. Yet he was exuberant in his thanks to you! What's got into him? Has the Hitler Youth taught him to hate us for being Jews?"

Klaus shook his head in despair. "I really don't know Golda dear, but the boys have to swear loyalty to Hitler. Perhaps he's taking his loyalty too seriously. I'm sure Liesel and Wolfgang will have a word with him."

"Well, Liesel did apologise to me about him, so perhaps they will." Golda sighed, "Poor dear Hedwig is terribly upset and Moshe, well as you'd expect, he's angry."

Klaus shook his head ruefully. "I'm afraid Hitler's driving a wedge between our two families. Germany's fine for Horst and Heinrich, but it's no place for our two. We must do all we can Golda dear, to get them out of Germany, while it's still possible."

"Yes dearest, though I dread the time when we must say goodbye! Life without them will seem awful, empty, pointless! I don't know what I'll do, though I keep praying that Moshe will be accepted for the Youth Aliyah scheme, and that we can do something for Hedwig."

"Yes, Golda dear, I keep praying for Moshe and for Hedwig too, but how do we persuade our dearest Hedwig to go without us?"

"Well, somehow we must." Persuading her would be difficult, she knew. It might even be impossible! She changed the subject.

"You and Wolfgang were having a lengthy discussion. What was that about?"

"Really nothing much."

"Well it took you a long time to talk about nothing much. Klaus, are you hiding something from me?"

"No, dearest," He hesitated. "Well, Wolfgang's Law firm has been involved with a mixed marriage couple who claim they were victimised and harassed by the S.A. He told me it had been almost impossible to do anything for them now that Hitler makes the laws! He just wanted to warn me, and tell us to be on our guard."

"So, what can we do?"

"Well, at least we don't have a Jewish name. That must help, but otherwise we just have to keep a low profile and do nothing to upset our non-Jewish neighbours. That's what happened to Wolfgang's couple. They'd upset theirs and in revenge their neighbours told the S.A. that the husband was Jewish. And you know how the S.A. hate anything Jewish." He saw her nod despondently.

"Dearest, I'd better have a word with Moshe, he must learn to accept unpleasantries from the Aryans without reacting, or he'll have us all in trouble!"

"Yes, that's all we can do I suppose, but Moshe's still very young and sadly has a quick temper. We can only hope he'll learn!" She hesitated, "And Klaus dearest, I do worry about you. You seem to be working such long hours, and even on Saturdays!"

"It's just a temporary problem Golda dear. I'll have it fixed soon."

He sighed inwardly. He couldn't tell her about the Stosser (Goshawk), the prototype of an advanced trainer Focke-Wulf were making. Everyone had been sworn to secrecy and it was the Goshawk that Goering had wanted to learn about, when he'd visited for the Goldfinch test flight. And now he knew why, for recently Hitler had openly defied the hated Versailles Treaty. In a message to the nation broadcast over the wireless, he'd announced in his usual forthright, decisive and unyielding manner, that:

No more would he abide by the terms of the Treaty that restricted the Army and Navy to mere defence forces! No longer would Germany remain defenceless against the growing might of France and England. He had therefore enacted a "Law for the Reconstruction of the National Defence Force". Thus the Reichswehr and Reichsmarine would become the Heer* and Kriegsmarine*, and a new air force the Luftwaffe would be created. These three military forces would be enlarged and equipped with modern armaments to make them effective instruments of a strong Germany.

It had been a bombshell, but a welcome one, one which promised more employment, one that was received with adulation by the nation, now becoming bewitched by Hitler. But despite their joy, many were fearful that violating the Peace Treaty would bring retaliation from the "Versailles Powers". But as the weeks went by it seemed the "Versailles Powers" were rent with indecision and were impotent!

Erich Schneyer the Managing Director was excited. "It's good news, very good news," he said with delight. "Now, we have the Luftwaffe there'll be a huge demand for aircraft. No doubt trainers will be needed first, so we must get the Goshawk right. We must persuade Herr Goering she's the best advanced trainer for him."

But the Goshawk had trouble. During its initial test flight it had suffered marked vibrations in the fuselage and now that the Goldfinch was in production, the Goshawk's problems had been given to Klaus to sort out. Taking over someone else's project at this late stage and correcting the design faults had been difficult and though the modifications made for the second test flight had given a better flight, some problems still remained! And the pressure was building, for both Heinkel and Arado were developing advanced trainers. Comparison flights would clearly be made before the Luftwaffe decided which to order, but Klaus was hopeful, even confident that the vibrations would be eliminated totally in the third test flight. Then he believed the modified Goshawk would out-perform the Arado Ar 76 and the Heinkel He 74 too!

So despite Golda's concern, Klaus continued to come home late. It was an anxious time for him, for though he was certain he had diagnosed the faults correctly, his intended modifications were proving difficult to implement. And still waiting for a third successful test flight, Erich Schneyer was constantly sending for him to ask what progress was being made. For him and his staff, overtime had become the norm and one night after a difficult day as usual, he'd come home late to find Golda in tears.

"Dearest what's happened?"

"Oh Klaus dear," she sobbed. "Is there no end to Hitler's hatred of us?"

He put his arms around hers. "What's he done now?"

"He's taken away our citizenship. We Jews are no longer Germans!" she gave him the newspaper. "Read this. Oh! Klaus, you should never have married me!"

REICH CITIZENSHIP LAW

The new Law for the Protection of German Blood and German honour prohibits marriage and sexual relations between Jews and citizens of the Reich. The new Reich Citizenship Law identifies citizens of the Reich as subjects of German or kindred blood. Jews therefore are no longer German citizens.

He laid the paper aside. This was unbelievable! It was appalling, terrible! It seemed the Jews no longer had any rights. He embraced her, trying to console her.

"Dearest it prohibits marriage between Jew and non-Jew, but that surely must be for future weddings. He can't separate those already married!"

"Do you think so? I'm not so sure. Hitler will do anything to hurt us. And if we're no longer citizens, will our passports be valid?"

"I don't know, but Golda dear that won't affect us, we don't have any."

"No, but Benjamin and Ruth do. They've only just managed to get theirs and now they may be worthless! If they succeed in getting sponsorship somewhere, how are they going to get out of Germany without passports?"

There seemed to be no answer to the questions raised by these new laws. The only hope was to flee, and the Jewish community began redoubling its efforts to escape if not as a family, then to send their children to a place of safety, in any way possible.

That the new law affected him and his family Klaus knew only too well, but he hoped, even had some confidence that his skills in the aircraft industry might really be of value to the regime. Goering had been impressed with him and his Goldfinch and now he'd been given the job of rescuing the Goshawk. If that went well, he could become valued as a successful aircraft designer and then maybe his marriage to a Jew might be overlooked. It might be a forlorn hope, but it was all he could hope for. But the children must go. He must find a way to send them to a country where they would be safe. And Golda too, though she always said she would never go without him. But for him escape was impossible. His only hope was to make himself valuable to Goering and the Nazis. The Goshawk must succeed! If it did, his skill in making it fly, might help save him and Golda.

Chapter 6

After the frosts and snow of winter, spring was at last near. The crocus and daffodils were in bloom and the sticky buds on the chestnut trees were fast expanding. Hedwig and Moshe were excited, Passover was near and with it the traditional eight day holiday from school.

The thought of Passover had stirred old memories in Golda; how her parents always celebrated Passover without fail, how important the Seder, the Passover meal, had been to them and how before the first day of the feast, her dear mother Renate would clean the kitchen thoroughly, searching every nook and cranny to find and remove all traces of chimetz, the Hebrew name for yeast, for during Passover only unleavened bread would be eaten.

As children she and her brother Benjamin had learnt the Jewish Festival of Passover told how Yahweh had brought the Hebrews up from slavery in Egypt into the Promised Land, a land flowing with milk and honey, and how with his help they had driven out the Canaanites. In thanks to Yahweh and to glorify him, the Jews had built a temple on Mount Zion, the highest point in the city of Jerusalem, as a sacred home for his name, and they called their new land Judah. But since the diaspora Judah no longer existed, now it was part of Palestine where the Zionists were trying to re-establish a home for Jews, and where Moshe her beloved son, now fired with an unquenchable desire to be a pioneer in the New Jerusalem, hoped to go.

Golda sighed, she couldn't bear the thought of losing him, but he would be safe there. And Hedwig? She must find sanctuary for her too. In her misery she asked herself what she'd done to deserve this. Was it because she'd been unfaithful as a Jew? Well, to atone for her sin she was now going to Synagogue, but to her shame she hadn't celebrated Passover since she was wed. She'd always made the excuse that her Roman Catholic husband might not wish to support her, though she'd never asked him! Nor had he asked her to go to his church. They'd led a secular life, both ignoring their God. Yet she could have gone to her parents for Passover and taken the children with her, but despite her father's urgent entreaties she hadn't. Now too late, she knew she should have done and her children should have been brought up in the Jewish faith.

Her parents had been pious Jews, always celebrating the Feast of Unleavened Bread as her father insisted on calling Passover. Their Seder always included Benjamin and Ruth and Aunt Annie and Uncle Liam and their children. It had made a wonderful family gathering and it was that which she really missed, rather than the significance of the meal. That had never made much impression on her! She shook her head, no she'd never been a real Jew. She and many others seemed to have forgotten the covenant that Yahweh had made with Moses and the Israelites. Surely now was the time to change her ways and honour that covenant once again. Then perhaps Yahweh might have compassion on them and save her and her family from Hitler's wrath! Yes, she must celebrate Passover, but if she did organise a Passover Seder, she should celebrate it like her parents did, with the whole family sitting around the table. But there wasn't much of a family left now! Her mother and father were dead, her brother Benjamin and his wife Ruth hoping to go to America and dear Moshe wanting to go to Palestine. Well they must go and Hedwig too! So, she shook her head bitterly, this could be the last time she could celebrate Passover with the family! This time she must! She glanced at the clock. She must stop thinking about Passover, it was time to go to Benjamin and Ruth's and give them their money.

She found her hat and coat and after locking the door walked quickly along Breslauer Strasse and turning into Wagenfeld Strasse noticed people outside Herr Dizengoff's tailor shop. As she neared she could hear voices.

"Some Nazi youth painted Juden on the shop window," a lady was saying. "Saw it myself, but I kept on the other side of the street, to be safe."

Herr Dizengoff' had appeared. "I was coming out to clean off the words, when a young boy, he couldn't have been more than fourteen, threw a brick at the glass. He shouted 'Filthy Jew', and ran off."

As the crowd made sympathetic noises, a policeman appeared. She stayed to watch and heard him telling the people they were causing an obstruction and they were to move on. He urged them to move on with his arms, but showed no interest in the broken glass or Herr Dizengoff. He with Frau Dizengoff had begun moving suits and garments from the window to a place of safety. Poor people Golda thought, they'd done nothing to deserve that! They'd been attacked merely because they were Jews. And what of their assailant? Would he be punished? No, of course not! The Police would take no action and when he got home, the boy would probably be welcomed as a hero!

Suddenly feeling frightened, she walked quickly away and turned into Galen Strasse. Finding their apartment block, she climbed the stairs to the third floor and thankfully rang Benjamin's bell. Ruth opened the door, her knitting in hand.

"Come in Golda dear. Are you well? You're looking very pale, has anything upset you?"

Golda frowned. "I've just seen some of Hitler's handiwork. It frightened me."

Ruth guided her to a chair. "What did you see?"

Golda told her all that had happened to Herr Dizengoff and his shop. "What have we Jews done to deserve this? Oh! Ruth dear, I'm frightened, one day it'll happen to all of us."

"Maybe, Golda dear, but let me get you a cup of coffee."

Though still scared Golda pretended the coffee had restored her courage and putting on a brave face asked, "How are you both?"

"We're well enough," Ruth's face brightened. "Benjamin's found some work."

"Oh! What good news! Has he finally found a teaching job?"

"No, no. He helps the kosher butcher."

"Oh! Is my dear brother learning the butcher's skill?"

"No." Ruth shook her head sadly. "He helps clean the shop before it opens. He starts at five in the morning and is finished by eight. He's having a nap right now."

"Well Ruth dear, at least it gives you a little more money." She opened her purse and counted out the marks Klaus gave them each week.

"Oh, Golda you are both so kind. I just don't know what we'd do without your generosity!"

Golda smiled, it was good to help them. "Have you managed to find a sponsor?"

"No, I'm afraid we've given up hope."

"Oh my dear. But you must keep trying."

"How can we? We have no other friends or even acquaintances to approach!"

"But you can't stay in Germany!"

"Hello Golda dear." Benjamin appeared. "I gather Ruth has told you we've had no luck finding a sponsor."

Golda nodded. "Yes, but you must leave Germany somehow!"

"Yes, Golda we know that. We have plans."

"Oh! How wonderful. What are they?"

"Well Golda, I will tell you because you are my sister, but you must promise not to tell anyone else. Not Moshe, nor Hedwig, not even your dear husband Klaus."

"Dear brother Benjamin, of course I promise not to tell anyone, not even Klaus."

Benjamin took a deep breath. "We want to go to Switzerland, where we've heard the local Jews are helpful. But to enter Switzerland we need visas, which of course we can't get and Switzerland has strong border checks."

"So, how do you plan to enter?"

"Well, apparently there's an area where a sympathetic Police Chief issues false entry papers to us Jews".

"Oh! Do you know where that is?"

"No, but we've heard of a man who for a price, will take us there."

"Benjamin dear, are you sure this man can be trusted?"

"That's a risk we must take Golda."

"But what if he's a swindler, what if he takes your money and lets you get caught?"

"Well," Benjamin he gave a dry laugh, "I suppose we'll be handed over to the Gestapo, but it's a risk we must take. We can't stay in Germany."

"Tell her about Jacob." Ruth gave him a postcard.

"Thank you Ruth. Golda, we're fairly confident about this man. Jacob told us about him and how he was planning to escape with his help. If he arrived safely he promised to write us a postcard signed Fritz and send it in an envelope. And," he held up the card, "here is his postcard. It says 'enjoying a few days here in this pleasant town of Frauenfeld', and look its signed Fritz!" He grinned. "So it does look hopeful!"

"Will you have enough money?"

"Yes dear sister, we've not paid the rent this month."

"When will you go?"

"We really don't know, but soon we hope. It depends on our contact. We'll just disappear one day. We won't be able to say good bye, but we'll send you a card from," he smiled, "from Ernst and Ingrid."

"Well I'll be praying for you with all my heart, but before you go we must celebrate Passover together. I haven't celebrated it since I was wed and I want to do so now for Moshe and Hedwig's sake. Will you come too?"

"We'd love too, if we're still here, wouldn't we Ruth?"

"Yes, yes, it would be wonderful."

They spent time reminiscing about their father and how he used to lead the feast. A thoughtful Benjamin declared, "He made it all so real!"

Golda smiled and nodded, "Benjamin dear you'll have to lead us and maybe lend Klaus a kippah. He must cover his head too!" She saw him laugh. "It'll be a great honour," he said.

As she hurried home, past Herr Dizengoff"s tailor shop, now with its windows boarded up, a feeling of emptiness began to engulf her. To celebrate Passover would be good, but it would be so final, like a prisoner's last meal! Soon they'd be gone, but gone safely she prayed. And then? Would she ever see them again? She walked home in deep thought; scarcely noticing she'd turned into Schwerbrock Strasse, with her own apartment block ahead. Relieved to be home, she comforted herself with the prospect of a Passover Seder with all the family present. It would be good, but what if Klaus objected? Would he? The thought worried her, it would be the last opportunity she'd have for a family Seder. But she couldn't tell him that! No, in doing so she might reveal their plans to escape! Keeping their plans secret, was a burden she must carry alone,

Chapter 7

The day of the test flight had arrived. Klaus watched the Goshawk being pushed out of the hanger. She was the first monoplane they'd built and after the second test flight when she had suffered those marked vibrations, she'd become his problem. For the first test flight she'd had wooden wings, but for the second these had been replaced by metal ones. Vibrations on the second test flight had been even worse and so he'd decided to revert to the original wooden wings. Wood he felt was more flexible than metal and might be less likely to be the cause, though he had to admit even on the first test flight with wooden wings there'd been vibrations, but not so severe. What else might be the cause? Could the problem lie in the tail section? He'd studied the position of the elevators and horizontal stabiliser. Unusually they were set before the fin and in line with the base of the rudder. The more he thought about this, the more he became convinced its positioning was wrong. It should be set higher. So he'd designed a small mounting to be fitted ten centimetres above the fuselage, on which the horizontal stabiliser and its elevators would be set. He'd have liked to test his solution in the new wind tunnel, but it was not yet complete.

When Erich Schneyer, the Managing Director, saw his modified tail assembly he said it spoilt her looks and it did, but hopefully it would stop the vibrations. Now it was time for the next test flight and they would find out. This was the moment of truth!

Erich Schneyer was talking with Manfred Hufendiek the test pilot, "I'm afraid Klaus has spoiled her looks, but he tells me it'll cure the problem. I hope he's right! We have to get her operational. I hear Heinkel's trainer has done well! We've got to do better than Heinkel, haven't we Klaus!"

"Jawohl Mein Herr."

"Well Klaus," Erich Schneyer gave him a critical look, "Let's hope our problems are finally cured. The Goshawk has great potential, so let's pray she'll do well." He turned to Manfred. "Good luck. Third time lucky eh?"

As he saw Manfred manoeuvring the plane ready for take-off, Klaus crossed his fingers. Test flights always made him nervous, but at least this time he knew she'd fly, but had he cured those vibrations? Together they watched the Goshawk take off and go through the programme of climbing, circling and diving again and again until at last the plane came in to land. Having taxied towards the hangar, Manfred climbed down and walked towards them, his face lit up by a huge grin.

"She may not look as good as she did Herr Schneyer, but she flies beautifully. We touched 275 kilometres per hour in level flight, and there's not a trace of vibration, not even in a dive!"

Erich Schneyer smiled broadly, all his hopes for the test flight seemed to have been fulfilled. "Good," he said turning to Klaus. "We must hope the remaining test flights go as well, then we can offer her to the new Luftwaffe."

Klaus had taken Manfred to his office for him to complete his flight report. It was excellent! Relieved and delighted, he shook Manfred's hand, "If all your other reports are as good as this, we'll get the contract!"

Manfred nodded, "She really does fly well. She'll make an excellent advanced trainer!"

Buoyed with the day's success, Klaus had gone home early. Golda was surprised and pleased. "I wasn't expecting you home so soon. Did your Goshawk fly well?"

"Yes, Golda dear. Everyone is delighted. Now if the remaining test flights go as well, we hope she'll sell well."

To celebrate he'd taken the family out for supper, to a little Kosher restaurant nearby. The Goshawk had indeed dominated his life recently, but now he was determined to have more time with Golda and the children. Hedwig was excited about eating out. In her new summer dress she no longer looked the gangly child, now a budding young woman. How beautiful she was, Klaus mused as he looked at her with fatherly admiration. Some lucky man will want her for a wife, he was sure, but please God he begged, not here in Germany!" He eyed his son Moshe, now almost fourteen. Moshe fancied himself as a sprinter and was absorbed in the forthcoming Olympic Games. He spoke knowledgeably and with surprising authority about the competitors and their abilities. "We must do better this time," he'd said. "Last time Germany was ninth, one place behind England!"

For weeks now the newspapers led by the Volkisher Beobachter the Nazis' own paper, had contained articles and photographs about the immense Olympic Stadium being built in Berlin for the Games. There would be seating for one hundred and ten thousand spectators, and a special stand was to be built solely for the Führer. Forty-nine nations, the largest number ever, would participate in the games, with almost four thousand athletes competing. Whilst everyone wanted Germany to do well and win lots of medals, the Volkisher Beobachter saw the Olympiad as an opportunity to promote the Führer and his ideals of racial supremacy. He promised it would show a new and strong Germany rising from the ashes of the Versailles Treaty.

With the Games imminent the Volkisher Beobachter had published an article proclaiming that Jews should not be allowed to participate. This had caused uproar in many of the competing nations, who threatened to boycott the games if Jews were banned. Faced with this international pressure Hitler and the Nazis unwillingly withdrew their proposal, so in the true Olympic spirit, people regardless of race, religion or colour were welcomed and allowed to compete. But nevertheless many German Jewish athletes found themselves excluded.

"Moshe dear," Golda spoke with pride in her voice, "the papers say that Helene Mayer will be fencing again for Germany. She won a gold medal in the 1928 Olympics, and came fifth last time. Whatever's happened? Everyone knows she's Jewish. Is Hitler being more reasonable?" Her short-lived joy however was soon dashed, for the following day she read that the Jewish shot-putter and discus thrower Lilli Henoch a four-time world record holder, had been excluded from the German team. Then another Jew, Gretel Bergmann was removed a few days earlier despite having set a world record of 1.6 metres in the high Jump! Golda was mystified and angry.

"Why," she asked her beloved husband Klaus, "Why have Lilli Henoch and Gretel Bergmann been excluded, but Helene Mayer hasn't?"

She handed him the newspaper and watched him as he read. His craggy face was still handsome, though marred by the lines of age, or was it worry and overwork? His hair was thinner too and now liberally flecked with grey. Age had given him an air of authority, purpose and confidence, yet when he laughed, that youthful charm returned. She remembered how the handsome, laughing young air ace had captivated her and how all the other nurses had been green with envy! But she sighed, he didn't laugh much these days, and it had been ages since he'd told her he loved her! It troubled her. And worse still, though they shared a bed, she no longer seemed able to rouse him. Involuntarily she shook her head, a barrier seemed to have grown between them. Was it those wretched planes? Or? That fear which had inexorably grown returned, had the Nazi poison infected him too? Had the venom that Hitler unleashed, that postulated the Jews as sub-human parasites, who threatened the purity of German blood, tainted him as well? Had her Jewishness begun to repel him?

She saw Klaus put the paper aside. He appeared to be talking, but in her distress she heard nothing.

He reached for her hand. "Are you alright, Golda dear? You look worried. Did you hear me?"

"No, dearest I'm sorry I didn't. Suddenly I felt faint, but I'm alright now."

He put a supportive arm around her.

"Dearest you do look pale. Let me get you a glass of water."

A feeling of relief spread over her as she watched him go. It's those wretched planes! It's them that keep him from me. She drank the water thankfully, yes, yes; it was those planes!

"So dearest," he reached for her hand, "Why have Lilli and Gretel been excluded? Well, Henoch and Bergmann are good Jewish names aren't they?"

Golda nodded "Yes, yes they are."

"But", Klaus continued, "Mayer isn't. That's a good, solid German name. Helene's father's unlikely to be a Jew. It must be her mother who's the Jew!"

Golda nodded. "Theirs is a mixed marriage, like ours, dearest."

"Yes." A smile lit up his face, "that's right. So that makes Helene only partially Jewish, at least in Hitler's eyes. Perhaps that's why, she's been allowed to compete, and of course she's likely to win a gold medal too! But the other two, well their parents are both Jews, so they're fully Jewish; that's why they've been excluded!"

"Well," Golda saw a ray of hope. "By that reckoning, Klaus dear, our two are only partially Jewish!"

Klaus nodded. "Yes. Maybe that's good news!"

The Führer opened the Games on 1st August and following the protocol introduced at the 1928 Games, the Olympic Flame was to burn throughout the games in a special stand by the Marathon Gate. But the Nazis also introduced a new ritual. This time the flame was to be lit in Greece in the original stadium at Olympia, and brought to Berlin by a series of runners in a grand Torch Relay. On the opening day, when the runner carrying the flame entered the stadium and ran up the steps to light the flame in its stand, the crowd thundered its approval.

During the Games newsreels in the cinemas were avidly watched, as the nation kept a tally of the medals awarded. But Jews, many of whom were still loyal Germans, were banned from cinemas and had to rely on the wireless or the papers for news of the games. As German athletes began to win medal after medal, the nation became ecstatic with joy and pride, many believing that such success affirmed the Führer's ideals of racial supremacy. For the Jews ecstasy came when Helen Mayer won silver!

In the closing ceremony, the athletes' lap of honour of the stadium bedecked with Nazi Swastikas was led by the German team. The honour had been rightly earned for the Fatherland, as Hitler now called the nation, had become Champion of the 1936 Olympiad, having won more medals than any other nation, beating the United States of America into second place! It was a glorious triumph and the Germans delighted in seeing the "old enemies" France and England languishing in seventh and tenth places respectively! When the final lap of honour came to an end, a jubilant Adolf Hitler surrounded now as always by black uniformed S.S. men, declared the Games closed. And as the Olympic Flame was extinguished and the Nazi Ensign lowered, the euphoric Germans revelling in their great victory, hailed their adored Führer with the Nazi salute and a rumbling chorus of "Heil Hitler". One English reporter commentating on the ceremony wrote, "It was like a great religious festival. When at last the Nazi Flag was lowered and the band played the Horst Wessel, the massed ranks of spectators burst into song, singing the new national anthem and swaying in unison as if entranced by Hitler!"

The Nazi newspaper the Volkisher Beobachter, reflecting on Germany's great victory, ended its article by saying:

"Thanks be to our beloved Führer, for by his inspired leadership he has given the Nation new confidence and a determination to restore the Fatherland to its rightful place in Europe."

Yet, pleased as he was with these splendid results Klaus was even more excited by the testing of the Goshawk, for each test flight proved to be successful, with Manfred reporting only minor items for improvement! With such good results, she had been offered to the Luftwaffe as an advanced military trainer. During the Olympiad all had worried whether their bid would be successful, but finally an ecstatic Erich Schneyer announced to all concerned that four Goshawks had been ordered by the Luftwaffe for further tests. Now there were high hopes for the plane.

So Klaus found himself busy organising all the design drawings and instructions to be carefully followed by the Work's Manager's team on the production line, a job which had to be done, but one which never really motivated him. No, his metier was design, and the concept of that single seater monoplane fighter began to occupy his mind again. Once the Goshawk production line had been organised, he hoped he could happily return to the drawing board! But in the meantime the production line demanded all his energy, though now he was working normal hours and able to get home early and see more of Hedwig, Moshe and Golda.

One morning as he reflected on the production line and its progress, the phone rang. It was Erich Schneyer's secretary, "Herr Schneyer would like to have a word with you, mein Herr." He went to the Managing Director's office.

"Guten Tag, Herr Schneyer."

"Guten Tag, Klaus. Sit down, I have some exciting news for you!" He was smiling. "You've found favour with Herr Goering, the Reich Minister of Aviation!"

"Have I?" Klaus looked puzzled.

"He was impressed with our Goldfinch and has heard about the good work you did to overcome our problems with the Goshawk. And he remembers you flew as a pilot in the war. As I've said you seem to have found favour with him and now he wants you to help with the completion of our secret dive-bomber."

"Well, I should be honoured to help, but I know nothing about this plane."

"Of course, I know only a little myself, but I must swear you to secrecy before I tell you anymore."

"Yes, I understand, Herr Schneyer. You can trust me, I'm a loyal German."

"Well Klaus, let me tell you the little I know. The plane is to be built by Junkers at Dessau and is to be called the Stuka, the Ju87. It was designed by Ulrich Hofmann as a dive bomber, a plane that has the ability to deliver bombs accurately, a most useful weapon in anyone's armoury! Unfortunately on its test flight it crashed killing the pilot, and now Ulrich Hofmann's design is suspect! I must remind you that the Stuka, its development and its crash is a closely guarded secret and like me, you must maintain its secrecy."

Schneyer Erich stopped to adjust his spectacles. "Herr Goering," he continued, "as I'm sure you can imagine, is extremely disappointed. He'd hoped the Stuka would be a successful and effective bomber for the Luftwaffe he is developing. And having heard about the good work you did to cure the problems with the Goshawk, he wants you to take over as Chief Designer of the Stuka and put things right."

Astonished, yet delighted by Goering's high opinion of him, Klaus was lost for words. Could he believe what he was hearing? Was he up to the challenge? Could he fix the Stuka? If he did it would be a great feather in his cap. But what if he failed? It was a worrying two-edged sword! However, it seemed he had little choice in the matter!

"Herr Hofmann," he said, "is a greatly respected Aeronautical Engineer. Succeeding him will be a challenge, but if Herr Goering wants me to do so, I have little choice but to accept."

"Good, good. Of course I shall be very sorry to lose you, but as you say we have little choice, we must bow to Herr Goering's wishes. So Klaus, I will inform him of your decision immediately."

For the rest of the day the problems of the Stuka never left him. Erich had told him there were doubts about the strength of the airframe and in pulling out from a dive the aircraft had mysteriously spun out of control and crashed. That was indeed a serious problem. Everyone in the industry knows there are considerable forces on the airframe when a plane reaches its top speed in a dive, so the problem was serious. Yet altering the airframe would affect the plane's overall performance, its speed, ability to climb and manoeuvre, all the essential qualities a plane needed to fend off attacks by enemy fighters. Would he, could he, solve the problem, without damaging her performance? Of course he was honoured to be selected by Goering himself, but he didn't enjoy sorting out other people's problems! Why couldn't he just be allowed to develop his own designs, like he had with the Goldfinch? His concept for a monoplane fighter was good and almost ready for presentation to the board. He was certain it had great potential, but now he must abandon it to sort out this dive-bomber, and with a strange staff probably still loyal to Ulrich Hofmann. "Mmm," he muttered, "It could be difficult dealing with them!" And then the thought struck him, he'd have to move the family to Dessau, nearly two hundred and fifty kilometres away. None of them would like that! Moving to a new city would make it difficult for them to make new friends! And the children had barely settled into Mount Carmel! Involuntarily he shook his head, there would be problems, great problems! And he'd been sworn to secrecy too, so until he received confirmation of this new assignment, he couldn't say a word about it to Golda!

That evening he'd hardly known what to say to her; the news of the Stuka and the need to keep it secret dominated his thoughts. She'd seemed strangely quiet too! A worrying silence prevailed until Moshe appeared. "It'll soon be Passover time," he announced with apparent new found authority, "It's our most important feast." "We've been reading about it in the Torah, in the Book of Exodus. Everyone's been talking about their family Seder. Why've we never had one?" He looked at his father. "Is it because of Dad, because he's Roman Catholic?"

"Moshe dear," Golda spoke quickly before Klaus could intervene. "Our marriage is a mixed one, your father a Christian and I a Jew. He could have worshipped in his church and I in the synagogue, but we both felt that would or could divide us, so he ceased going to his church and I stopped going to synagogue and we've led a secular life."

"But you go to Synagogue now, don't you? You take Hedwig and me!"

53

"Yes, indeed I do. With Hitler's anti-Semitism your father and I felt that we should get closer to our Jewish brothers and sisters. We felt we needed their communal support! And surely it was because the three of us attended Synagogue that places were found for you both at Mount Carmel. But perhaps now Moshe," she gave Klaus a hopeful glance, "you should learn more of your Jewish heritage."

"Yes, Mother dear, we should." Moshe was grinning, "So, shouldn't we have a Passover Seder? It's an important part of our heritage isn't it?"

"Yes Moshe, it certainly is".

She was smiling too, she hadn't known how to broach the idea of a Passover Seder to Klaus, but now thanks to Moshe it was easy.

"Well Moshe, if your father agrees, perhaps we might this year. We could ask Uncle Benjamin and Auntie Ruth to join us and it would be a lovely family affair. Klaus dear may we, and would you join us?"

"Of course Golda dear, but you'll have to explain its ritual to me, otherwise…"

"Otherwise what dear?

"Otherwise as a Gentile," he chuckled, "I may make some awful gaffe and upset you all!"

Chapter 8

Delighted with Klaus's agreement, Golda had invited her brother Benjamin and his wife Ruth to celebrate Passover with them. They'd happily agreed and now she was busy preparing for the festival. It was women's work and she'd coaxed a reluctant Hedwig to help her.

"I don't want to be a Jew," Hedwig had said. "I just want to be an ordinary person. I don't want to be hated by Hitler or anyone. Why, why does he hate us?"

It was a question Hedwig had asked before and one which she couldn't answer. Yet Hitler did, and for the Nazis hatred of the Jews seemed to have become a founding creed! She put her arm around her troubled daughter, "Dearest we just don't know why he hates us. All we know is that he does and uses us Jews as scapegoats for all his problems."

Hedwig's questions worried her. Unlike Moshe, she'd never shown any enthusiasm for being a Jew and had always wanted to be as she put it, "just ordinary".

"Hedwig darling, when I was your age, I didn't want to be a Jew either, but I am and so are you and Moshe. We have to put our hopes in Yahweh, our God who made us his chosen people. Surely he will keep us safe." Involuntarily she shook her head, she was no Rabbi. How could she make Hedwig understand?

She gave her distressed daughter a smile, "Come Hedwig dear, help me get ready for the feast. Even if you don't want to be a Jew, you can enjoy the meal. Uncle Benjamin and Auntie Ruth will be with us and it'll be a lovely family celebration."

She saw Hedwig smile and look a little happier. "Now," she said "we must search for every bit of chimetz".

During the festival she explained, there mustn't be a scrap of it in the house and only unleavened bread can be eaten.

"Do we have to smear blood over our doorway?" Hedwig suddenly asked.

"No dear, we don't do that anymore."

"But they used to. Why?"

"Well, when Yahweh wanted to bring the Hebrew slaves out of Egypt, he sent Moses to ask Pharaoh to set them free, but he wouldn't. So Yahweh sent nine plagues on the Egyptians, but still Pharaoh refused. Once more Yahweh sent Moses to tell him to let the Hebrew slaves go. If he didn't agree, Moses was to tell him that Egypt would suffer one more plague when every firstborn son of the Pharaoh and his people would die. But to spare the Hebrews, Moses was to tell them to smear blood over their doorways, so that Yahweh could see their houses and pass over them, without killing their first born sons."

"Oh! But whose blood was it?"

"Yahweh made Moses tell the Hebrews they must find a year old lamb, a perfect lamb, a lamb without any defects and kill it as a sacrifice to Yahweh. It was the sacrificial blood of the lamb that they were to use."

"Oh! Did Yahweh really kill all the first born sons of Pharaoh and the Egyptians?"

"Yes, he struck them down at midnight and there was much grief and anguish in the land. And so at last Pharaoh relented and allowed the Hebrew slaves to go."

"But didn't he change his mind and send his chariots and army after them?"

"Yes, he did."

"And that was when Yahweh parted the Red Sea to allow the Hebrews to escape?"

"You're right Hedwig, but when the Egyptians followed the Hebrews, Yahweh made the water flow back and Pharaoh's army was drowned. That's how he rescued the Hebrew slaves and led them into the Promised Land. And that's why we celebrate Passover, our most important feast. But Hedwig dear, we've spent too long talking, we've a lot of work to do."

Passover evening came, the lamb had been roasted, the unleavened bread made and all was ready. Klaus was wearing a smart suit and Moshe was helping him to adjust his kippah, when Benjamin and Ruth arrived and the Seder could begin. Benjamin as the oldest male Jew, spoke about the significance of the food laid out before them. The lamb he told them symbolised the sacrifice made to Yahweh, and the roasted egg with its hard yoke represented the Hebrews' determination not to renounce their faith during their slavery in Egypt.

Then he asked everyone to take a lettuce leaf, dip it in the salt water and eat it; this he said, was to remind them of the tears shed by the slaves. Then they sampled the paste Golda and Hedwig had made from apples, walnuts and wine. This represented the clay from which the slaves made bricks for Pharaoh. Moshe wondered why he made no mention of the dish of herbs, which they then all shared.

"Now we begin to eat," Benjamin declared, "So lean back on your cushion and drink your wine while I read from the Haggadah* and remind you how the Hebrews slaves escaped."

While they ate and each drank their four small glasses of wine, all in turn read a further passage from the Haggadah. When they'd finished reading, Hedwig and Moshe were invited to ask the two questions they had been given.

Hedwig's first was to ask why they ate unleavened bread.

Moshe keen to air his Jewishness immediately said "because the Hebrew slaves left in such a hurry their bread didn't have time to rise." Golda saw Benjamin smile and nod his approval.

Hedwig's second wondered why they'd eaten the bitter herbs. Benjamin looked at Moshe for an answer, but seeing him hesitate, said it was to remind them of the bitter suffering of the Hebrew slaves.

Moshe then asked, "Why do we have cushions to lean on?"

Benjamin waited for Hedwig to answer, but seeing her shake her head he said, "We have the luxury of cushions to remind us Jews that we're no longer slaves, but free."

Hedwig had been eyeing the untouched glass of wine that had been placed at the head of the table throughout the Seder. Mystified she had one further question.

"Whose wine is that?"

Uncle Benjamin smiled. "That glass is for the Prophet Elijah. You may have noticed that we have left the door ajar." He saw her nod. "Well

Hedwig, we believe that one day Elijah will come to our Passover Feast to announce the coming of the Messiah, but for the moment we must give thanks to Yahweh for leading our ancestors to freedom and making us his chosen people."

For Golda the meal had been very emotional. How she missed her beloved mother and her courageous father, so recently murdered by the SA. Their unswerving faith in Yahweh had always illuminated the meal! Now it was their son, her brother Benjamin, who presided over the feast and he had done so with the wisdom and authority he'd learnt from their beloved father. As the tale unfolded memories of previous Passover Seders, when the table had been crowded with uncles and aunts and cousins had returned to fill her with joy, but then she'd heard that inner voice proclaim, "Never again will all of us celebrate Passover together." As that certainty and finality struck home, she'd had to fight back the tears. How could she live without her children and Benjamin and Ruth? Why, why was life so cruel? She found herself praying involuntarily, "If we are to be separated, please Yahweh I beg you, forgive us our sins and keep us safe."

With an effort she managed to compose herself. She looked at Klaus. Had the finality of the occasion struck him too? She couldn't tell, his face showed no emotion. She wondered what he thought of their Passover celebrations. Did he believe Yahweh had rescued the Hebrews, that he'd parted the sea so they could cross over? Or did he think was it some ancient myth? Rarely had they discussed their faiths. She didn't know if he had a faith even though he'd been brought up as a Roman Catholic. Many years ago when they were newlyweds, he'd told her he had none; that for him there was no God! But now, now when he was more mature she wondered, indeed hoped, that perhaps he'd changed. Her own faith had been dormant she admitted, but faced with Hitler's hatred it had grown. Now all she could do was put her trust in Yahweh. Hadn't he rescued the Jews before, from slavery in Egypt and from exile in Babylon? Surely he'll rescue his Chosen People once more!

Feeling a little happier, she became aware of the others. Moshe was talking earnestly with Benjamin. "In David's time," she heard him say, "The Jews were strong and able to defeat those who were against them. Why can't we do the same now?"

Benjamin had smiled ruefully. "If only we could, Moshe! But in King David's time the Jews had a homeland, where they were a nation, a nation that could unite and defend itself. But since Titus the Roman General destroyed the Temple in Jerusalem and drove the Israelites out, we Jews have been spread all over the world and no longer are we a nation. We've had to adopt the nationality of the country in which we live, so some are Germans like us, others Russians, Poles or nationals of almost every country in the world. So it's difficult for us to unite against the Nazis in any effective way."

"Well Uncle Benjamin, I shall soon be going to Palestine where we hope to build a Jewish nation. Perhaps one day we might all live together there!"

Moshe's enthusiasm for Palestine and for its possible future as a Jewish nation was a small comfort to Golda. If only she could give Hedwig some similar cause to believe in, to make her happy to leave Germany!

Hedwig had been talking almost non-stop with Auntie Ruth, but theirs had been a conversation unconcerned with the plight of the Jews. Theirs had been about clothes, music, cooking and other everyday topics. Hedwig seemed determined to put everything Jewish aside, to be "just ordinary". Perhaps she was right! Was there any point in worrying? Maybe it was best to live each day as it came and be as happy as possible!

As the minute hand neared the midnight hour, Ruth and Benjamin made moves to go with Benjamin thanking Klaus for his generous financial support. Then it was her turn to say goodbye. As she hugged and kissed them both she managed to stop her tears, for unlike the others she knew this could be the last time she would see them. How could she bear their going? Yet she knew they must escape. Like them Moshe her dearest son would soon go too, and then her precious daughter Hedwig. Yes, they must go! Germany was becoming a dangerous place for Jews.

Clearing the table and washing the dishes had helped ease her misery, but in their room as she prepared for bed, she could hold back her tears no longer. She threw herself into her husband's arms. "Passover will never be the same. Benjamin and Ruth are determined to escape somehow, Moshe will be gone soon and so will Hedwig. How can we live without them?"

So many Jewish parents were asking that same question! But what answer could any loving parent be given? That their children would be free from Nazi persecution, that they would be safe? Yes, she and Klaus both knew that, that was the object, the prize to be won, but that prize had to be paid for. And the price? Separation from one's loved ones, separation with little or no hope of reunion, never again to hold one's beloved child in one's arms. That was the price that had to be paid! But that didn't answer her question, how can we live without them?

Klaus tried to comfort her. "Dearest, it's best for them. It's the only way they'll find happiness and security and fulfilment. The knowledge that they are safe must be our consolation. We must let them go, we must learn to live without them. Our love for each other must comfort us."

His answer did little to cheer her.

"Dearest," her troubled eyes sought his, "Could we not go too and take the children with us. There are means and ways to slip out of the country".

"Yes, there may still be and we might find a safe country, but how would we earn a living?"

"Don't France and England build aeroplanes too?"

"Yes they do, but that's why I can never leave Germany lawfully or unlawfully. I know too much about the German aircraft industry and now I've been asked to help with the design of a secret warplane and dearest," he shook his head in despair, "it's not possible for me to refuse. So Golda, I daren't try to slip out of the country. If we were caught Hitler would accuse me of treason and you too!"

She didn't reply. It seemed she was beaten.

"But Golda dearest, you could go with Hedwig."

"Klaus, I couldn't do that. Without me she'll have a job, but who would employ the two of us. It wouldn't work and dearest I happen to love you too." She kissed him and moved his hand towards her breast. At first he seemed unsure of himself. It had been some time since they'd been intimate, but then the consoling joys of love overtook them.

Chapter 9

The day after Passover was Sunday, a lazy day, a day for a lie in. Golda woke, the rays of the sun lighting the room, but Klaus still slumbered. Strangely she felt happy and fulfilled, the concerns and worries of the night before forgotten. They'd been lovers again. She revelled in the warm glow that spread over her. She saw him stir and felt his hand reach for her waist. She turned and kissed him.

He gave her a comforting hug, "Dearest I'm glad you won't go without me. Y'see I love you dearly".

"And I love you Klaus. We need each other."

He kissed her, his hand caressing her back.

"Dearest there's something I have to tell you. I should have told you last night but you were so engrossed with Passover."

"What is it Klaus? Tell me."

"I'm afraid I have to move to Dessau."

"Dessau? Why? Why do you have to go there?"

"Dearest, Junkers have their factory there and their latest aircraft has crashed on its test flight."

"So?"

"Well having sorted out the problems with the Goshawk, I seem to have found favour with Hermann Goering, the Reich Minister of Aviation. He wants me to help Junkers find out what made the aeroplane crash and cure the problem," he hesitated. "I hope I'm up to it!"

"But we're settled here and the children are happy at their schools, and we have Benjamin and Ruth and your brother and Liesel nearby. Can't you refuse and stay with Focke-Wulf?"

"Dearest, I have no choice. These days if Hermann Goering wants something, he has to be obeyed!"

Her warm glow vanished, the worries and wretchedness of the night before now compounded. Klaus saw the look of anguish on her face.

"Dearest I'll find us a home and schools for the children just as soon as I can."

His promise did nothing to comfort her.

"When will you go?"

"In a week's time."

It seemed fate had no mercy. Destiny was determined to break up the family. All she could do was pray that they would survive Hitler's hatred; that one day they would be re-united somewhere safe.

They told the children at breakfast. Moshe appeared unmoved. Nowadays all he seemed to think about was his future in Palestine, his promised land for the Jews. Bur poor dear Hedwig took the news badly.

"Not another new school! I'm just beginning to make friends at Mount Carmel. Must we go?"

All that day their conversation seemed to focus on the move, with Klaus trying to portray the few good points he could muster. "It's a fine city and perhaps we can find a house instead of an apartment." But his efforts to cheer them were of little avail, Golda complaining that they'd be complete strangers in Dessau; that they'd have no friends there. It was only later that night that he was able to expound the opportunity the move offered.

"Golda dear it could be a blessing."

"A blessing? How can it be?"

"Well dearest, our surname is a good solid German one. Why can't we forget you're Jewish? No one need know! You and the children don't wear traditional Jewish clothes like the orthodox Jews from Russia and Poland do. Why can't you be just "ordinary"? Hedwig would like that."

"Moshe wouldn't."

"No, but he doesn't wear traditional Jewish clothes and maybe we could persuade him to forget his Jewishness for all our sakes. After all he's hoping to go to Palestine soon."

"But dearest my first name is Jewish and so is Moshe's! Surely we'd soon be found out." Then she laughed. "But Hedwig would be alright, she'd be pleased to know her name is just "ordinary!"

She saw Klaus grin. "Well Golda dear, you and Moshe would have to adopt new German first names. Perhaps you could become Gerda, that's not so different from Golda, is it? And Moshe? Could he be called Max? I don't know, we'll have to think about him. But what do you think about it? Surely it's worth a try!"

"If we know no one in Dessau, I suppose it might work, but it'll be hard for all of us to remember the new names you want to give Moshe and me!"

"Gerda," he couldn't help smiling, "We'll have to practise using the new names here, before we go."

The following Sunday Klaus packed his gear in the car and left. "I'll find a house for us and then you can join me. So till then it's goodbye Gerda dear and to you Max and Hedwig," he grinned. "Keep practising. I'll be home again on Friday evening."

Practising! How difficult it was. The children always called her Mummy or Mum and though she asked them to call her Gerda they always forgot, so she had adopted the practice of saying "Max (or Hedwig) my name is Gerda." Yet she too often called her son Moshe not Max, yet they had to get the names right if Klaus' plan was going to work.

He'd talked about the family going to the Roman Catholic church instead of the synagogue! She knew Hedwig would come, she would be pleased to be "ordinary"! But Moshe uh, uh Max? Since they'd gone to synagogue each Sabbath he'd adopted Judaism with growing enthusiasm and conviction. She was certain he wouldn't accept the Christian faith; if anyone gave the game away it would be him.

Poor Moshe, "Oh," she mumbled to herself. "I must remember to call him Max!" She couldn't help admiring his determination to remain a Jew. She called him, "Max dear." She saw him grin. "You remembered!" he said.

"Yes, for once! I must try harder. But Max dear, if Daddy's plan is to work, if we are to succeed in pretending we're Christians, we shall have to go to church and you mustn't let your new-born Jewish faith betray us. You must keep your Jewishness secret for all our sakes, and not just in church but in school too. You must dearest."

Moshe looked troubled. "Well, I'll try, but I shan't enjoy being disloyal to Yahweh!"

"But Moshe dear, I mean Max dear you can be loyal to Yahweh at home."

He nodded. "Yes Mum, I'll do as you want."

She thanked him, she knew it would be difficult for him and she too had reservations about becoming a pseudo Christian! What she wondered would her father think? He could never accept Christ as the Messiah, he always said he was a false prophet, a blasphemer. But nevertheless Klaus' plan seemed a good one, if only they could make it work.

It was Wednesday. She eagerly awaited Klaus's return on Friday, waiting to hear what he had discovered about schools for the children and housing for the family. And more importantly did he really think his plan would work? Without him she'd felt lonely and vulnerable and prayed they'd soon be reunited.

But moving to Dessau was not her only worry, she was very concerned about Benjamin and Ruth and their plan to escape. Tomorrow would be Thursday, when their money was due. She found the cash and tucked it into her purse wondering when the family were settled in Dessau, how she would be able to give them their money? Perhaps she could persuade Klaus to give them some in advance, some to carry them over until they left. She shook her head in desperation, Benjamin and Ruth had to go, but their escape plan seemed so dangerous! Were they doing the right thing? Could they trust this man who promised to guide them? What if he betrayed them? What if they were caught? The possibility terrified her, yet she could understand how they felt. They had little option, somehow they must escape! They had no future in Germany. As a Jew it was becoming almost impossible to find work; only last week another Jewish firm had closed down. It had been a large ironmongers with branches throughout the region, but the Nazis had boycotted it and with falling sales it had gone into liquidation. A German Aryan had quickly snapped it up and it had re-opened with non-Jewish staff. The Nazis were determined to aryanise all Jewish enterprises, their plan was simple, boycott them, make their sales fall and close them down. Then an Aryan could buy the business for a few marks!

Thursday came. On the way to Benjamin's she met Sheyna Yanait, a new friend made when the children changed school. She was looking distressed.

"Have you heard about the synagogue?"

"No! What's happened?"

"Some Nazi youths have stoned the windows and daubed paint over the walls."

"When, when did it happen?"

"The Rabbi says it was late last night. He heard the noise and when he approached, some youths ran off shouting obscenities at him."

"Oh! Sheyna, will this hatred never end?" This constant harassment frightened her.

"The broken windows are being boarded up," Sheyna told her, "and the Rabbi wants everyone to be at synagogue on Sabbath. You and your children will come, won't you?"

Golda assured her they would be there and giving each other a reassuring hug they parted. But the hug did nothing to disperse the fear that was ever present. Nowadays every strange man or youth seemed a threat. Would he be an arrogant Nazi, with a hammer in hand, ready to smash Jewish windows or Jewish heads? With head downcast, looking neither to the left or right she hurried on. Only when she reached Benjamin's block did she begin to feel safe. Hurrying up the stairs, she reached their door and rang the bell. There was no answer! She rang again. Still no answer, could that mean.........? She rang the bell a third time listening for any sign of life inside, but there was none. Concerned now that her continued presence might draw attention to their absence, she turned and left quickly. Had they gone? If they hadn't, surely they'd have opened the door. Surely they'd be expecting her, she came at this time, every Thursday! But there was no sign of them! They must have gone! If they had, she must tell no-one, not even Klaus. She hurried home rehearsing what she would say when the children asked how they were. She must say the same thing to each, and must remember what she had said. She must give them no reason to think she was lying!

That night as she lay alone in bed, she was certain the children suspected nothing, but nevertheless she couldn't sleep. Terrifying images of Benjamin and Ruth being caught and turned over to the Gestapo filled her every thought. In the morning after the children had left for school, she set out again for their apartment, praying that her distress wouldn't show and walked unhurriedly as if she hadn't a care in the world. It was a hard act to follow with so many worries and by good fortune she met no-one she knew. Arriving at their apartment she rang the bell. There was no answer. She tried again, this time giving it a much longer ring. But still no one came. Had they really gone? She rang once more. Again the door remained firmly shut. They must have gone! She must tell no one, she must keep their absence secret. Praying for their safety and success she walked home hearing her brother's voice again, "there's an area where a sympathetic Police Chief gives Jews false entry papers". She prayed it was true. But could this man who said he'd take them there be trusted? She remembered her brother's dry chuckle as he told her it was a risk they had to take!

Again that night she slept badly, tossing and turning in an empty bed, and missing the warmth and assurance of Klaus. Yet perhaps it was a good thing he was away, for had he been with her she might in a moment of anguish have unburdened herself and so betrayed the secrecy of their escape. Earlier when Hedwig had asked about her beloved Aunt, she hoped she'd lied convincingly.

Now she was certain they'd gone and that they were now in the hands of that stranger who promised to lead them to safety in Switzerland. And she was the only one to know! The burden of keeping their secret bore heavily down on her and she prayed to Yahweh for his help and support. How would she know if they'd been successful? How would she? It all seemed so impossible. Then she remembered that postcard! The card they'd promised to send if they reached Switzerland safely. He'd told her they couldn't sign it themselves, but that it would be signed by....... who? What were the names? How could she have forgotten? Then with relief the names came, ah! That's right. Ernst and Ingrid, they were the names! She sighed, now all she could do was wait, wait desperately for that card! If it never came she'd know that fate had overtaken them, that they'd been caught. She shuddered, they would be in the hands of the Gestapo!

Chapter *10*

As Klaus drove through the impressive gates, that self-doubt hit him again. Could he do it? Could he resolve that problem with the Stuka? If somehow he could, if he could get her flying again, if he could make himself valuable to Herr Goering perhaps the authorities might accept his Jewish wife. But if he failed? That didn't bear thinking about!

He saw the main building ahead and parked his car alongside the others. Looking at himself in the overtaking mirror he straitened his tie, grabbed his brief case, got out and walked through the big glass entry doors. A uniformed door-keeper enquired who he was, asked his business and then summoned a messenger.

"Take Herr Boddenburg to the Managing Director's office."

He was led up a flight of stairs into a small office and introduced to a smartly dressed woman. She offered him a seat before disappearing through a door marked "Herr Otto Tauber, Managing Director".

He studied his surroundings; they were modern and smart and the framed photograph of the highly acclaimed three engined commercial transport the Ju52, which hung on the wall, emphasised the company's success; a success now tarnished by the crash of its Stuka dive-bomber.

She'd returned. "Herr Tauber will see you now, Herr Boddenburg."

Otto Tauber rose from behind his desk with outstretched hand to greet him. He was a tall powerfully built man, a confident man, a man whose authority was evident.

"Welcome to Junkers, Herr Boddenburg. I hope your hotel accommodation is suitable." Klaus assured him it was.

"I understand you know Herr Goering."

"I've met him and we both flew Fokker DVIIs in the war. He was the last commander of the famous von Richthofen Squadron and victor of twenty-two dogfights, but I can't say I know him."

"Well, whether you know him or not, he thinks highly of you. He was dismayed when the Stuka crashed. He's always believed in the accuracy of dive bombing and the Stuka concept appeals to him, so much so that he's placed provisional orders for one hundred planes. Now he wants the Stuka put right and he believes you're the man to do it!"

"Well, I'm very honoured to be chosen and I hope I'll not disappoint him." He saw Tauber nod his head quietly in agreement. "But as yet, I know very little about this plane. Please tell me what happened."

"The Stuka was designed here by Ulrich Hofmann and two prototypes were secretly built by AB Flygindustri in Sweden."

"In Sweden?"

"Yes. As I'm sure you know, the Versailles Treaty forbids Germany to build warplanes."

"Yes, of course."

"As I said, AB Flygindustri built two prototypes and delivered them to us for re-assembly. One was carefully rebuilt and everything checked against the original plans, and in September it took off for its maiden flight. As usual the first flight was very gentle and all seemed well, except that the Rolls-Royce Kestrel liquid cooled engine began overheating due to its small-sized radiator."

"It had a Rolls-Royce engine?"

"Yes. As the Stuka was built for us in Sweden, it was decided it would be inappropriate for Germany to send the Jumo 210 the preferred engine, to Sweden, though the plan is to fit the Jumo to all production aircraft. Well, we designed and fitted a larger radiator and the next test flight, a more exhaustive one, was planned for January."

"That's when it crashed?"

"Yes. Having completed two relatively gentle dives, Willy Neuenhofen the test pilot put the aircraft into a steep dive emulating its flight when delivering a bomb. As it pulled out of the dive the aircraft entered an inverted spin, the twin fins and rudders broke free and the plane crashed, killing Willy and Heinrich Kreft his crewman.

"So we have no Pilot's report?"

"No".

"Has the wreckage been recovered?"

"What was left of the tail section was found almost a kilometre from the rest and we've also recovered bits of the wings, fuselage and almost all of the engine."

"I'd like to see what we have. And of course I shall need a complete set of the aircraft's plans and its specification."

"Of course."

"I'd also like to meet Herr Hofmann."

"That will not be possible. He has resigned."

"Oh! Well then, I'd better get down to work."

"Yes. Let me get your assistant Helmut Schmidt to show you to your office." He rang the bell and Schmidt was summoned.

"Have you any other questions?"

"Not at the moment, but on a personal level I shall need some time off to arrange accommodation for my family."

"That will be fine. Take a whole day or two half days."

So started his first day at Junkers. He'd been installed in his office, introduced to the members of his design team, given plans of the Stuka and shown the recovered wreckage that was being pieced together. It had been a true baptism of fire! But he decided the problem of the Stuka would have to wait, leaving Golda and the children alone in Bremen worried him. He must bring them to Dessau. He would take a day off on Friday and search for a suitable home. He telephoned an agent and discussed his requirements.

Friday came and the agent arrived. As they sat in the hotel foyer he perused the accommodation details given him. He discarded the more expensive properties leaving three apartments and two houses to view. Of the three apartments one appealed greatly, it was on the first floor, was light an airy and he was sure Golda (Oh! He must remember to call her Gerda) would like the spacious modern kitchen.

Then they'd gone to look at the houses. He hadn't liked the first. It was too far from town, but the second set in its own little garden, seemed to have everything they'd want. It had a telephone and was close to a bus route into town. Gerda would like it he was sure, so he'd agreed to rent it. The agent had taken him to his office to complete the deal and had then driven him back to the hotel where his own car waited for the journey home to Bremen. That little house, number 3 Kirchestrasse excited him. He liked the name too, Ruhe Haus (Tranquillity House). He decided he must look at it again, so he could answer all the family's questions.

With some difficulty he found it. He knew she'd like living in a house rather than an apartment and she'd enjoy the garden too! He stood examining the house, trying to etch its details onto his memory; the symmetrical set of the windows, the pretty porch bedecked with climbing roses, and the panelled front door. Opposite on the north side of the road stood the church, built in the Gothic style. He wandered in. Its stillness and peace engulfed him. Without thinking he crossed himself and sat in one of the pews. He'd not been to church for ages, not since the war! Then with the perils of aerial combat he'd come to pray for his fallen comrades, or he asked himself cynically, was it to seek his own survival? Well, whatever the reason after the war like so many, he'd given up the church. And when he'd married Golda they'd both felt their different religions could become divisive, so they'd decided she would give up synagogue and he the church. Now with Hitler's persecution of the Jews, Golda had returned to synagogue, from which she seemed to draw strength. But with the family moving to Dessau she had agreed somewhat reluctantly perhaps, that she, Moshe and Hedwig would forget their Jewishness and attend church as Christians. Making the promise was easy, but they knew nothing about the ritual of Roman Catholic worship and their ignorance would easily be noticed. He would have to prepare them and they would have to learn well and quickly, otherwise their hopes of masquerading as Aryan Christians would be dashed. He shook his head. It all seemed so difficult!

He felt a hand on his shoulder. Turning he saw a priest. "Welcome my son", he heard a voice saying. "You seem a little troubled."

He didn't know what to say. How could he tell him of his plan to present his Jewish family as loyal Christian Germans?

"Would it help if you confessed?"

He hesitated, if his plan were to succeed he'd have to win this priest over. "Yes Father, I think so."

He followed the Priest to the confessional and entering settled himself on the kneeler and heard the lattice screen being pulled back ready for him to begin. For a moment he wasn't sure what to say, but then the ritual began to come back.

"Forgive me Father", he heard himself saying. "I have sinned."

He heard the Priest ask, "When did you last confess your sins?"

"Sadly many years ago. It was during the war."

"Tell me, my son, what stopped you confessing your sins?"

How could he tell this priest it was because he'd married a Jew? What could he say? The Priest waited patiently, then spoke.

"My son, tell me what is troubling you. Only God, you and I shall ever know what you tell me."

That was the crux of the matter. Could he trust this Priest to keep what he wanted to say, secret? "Father," he said, "I trust God implicitly. Can I trust you?"

"My son, by my ordination I have authority from God to forgive sinners. What I hear in a confessional I hear on behalf of the Father and nothing you say during your confession will be repeated to any mortal."

There was a long silence, then he heard the Priest say "Do you wish to continue?"

"Yes Father, though I hardly know where to begin."

"Open your heart to the Holy Spirit, my son. He will guide you."

He prayed for the Almighty to help him and then in a low voice said he'd met and married a Jewess. How their children were therefore Jewish and how he feared for their future in Adolf Hitler's Germany. He reminded the Priest that many Jews had suffered death, persecution and violence from the Nazis and that many were seeking sanctuary abroad. But for him and his family that option was not possible. "I am an aeronautical engineer," he continued, "building aircraft and I am therefore well informed of the capabilities of the aircraft being produced for the emerging Luftwaffe. So I would never be given permission to emigrate. If I did so illegally, I'd be accused of selling state secrets to an enemy country." He stopped, wondering whether this priest understood what he was telling him. And then as if to assure him, he heard the Priest saying, "May God bless and protect you my son, and your family."

"I have more to tell you Father."

"I am listening, my son."

"Well Father, at some time in the future our two children may seek sanctuary elsewhere, but my wife tells me she will never be parted from me and will stay with me come what may. Being married to me Father, she has a non-Jewish surname and so have our children. Now my family will shortly be moving to join me here, to Dessau where we know no one. So Father we hope that with non-Jewish surnames we might be able to forget the Jewishness of my wife and children and the four of us be welcomed as loyal Germans into this Roman Catholic Church."

Suddenly he felt naked. He'd revealed all to this unknown Priest. Could he trust him? Would he allow these Jews to masquerade as Christians in his church?

"Would our Heavenly Father", he heard himself asking, "Look with favour on me and welcome my Jewish family into the church of the Gentiles?"

The voice replied," Our Heavenly Father is full of compassion and love and welcomes all who turn to him, but to show their commitment they would have to be baptised."

That was better than he'd dared hope, but would Golda and the children agree to be baptised and forsake their Jewishness and become Christians? He'd thanked the Priest telling him how grateful he was and heard the Priest saying "Now my son do you wish to confess?"

"Yes, Father, but I have so many sins to confess."

"The Lord is patient."

"All my many sins have stemmed from one great one, Father."

"What is that my son?"

"Until today, I have forgotten God. I have forgotten and ignored the God who has given me life and created heaven and earth. I have been proud and felt I could live without Him, but now I wish to live a new life, a life that pleases Him."

The Priest gave him Absolution; he crossed himself but remained in the confessional. He could feel a presence, a presence which enveloped him with peace and hope.

A few minutes later he left, found his car and set off with joy in his heart for home, for his beloved Golda and the family.

Chapter *11*

Excited by the news he had for Golda, Klaus was eager to get home, but with the road blocked by a broken down lorry, it was almost ten o'clock before he arrived to be met by a tearful Golda. He'd hugged her and told her how much he'd missed her and asked her what was upsetting her. "They want Moshe," she said as she gave him a letter.

He knew its contents before he read it. It was from the Youth Aliyah Training Institute at Eberswalde. Its message was short and to the point:

A place has been found for your son Moshe Boddenburg on the preparatory course for migration to Palestine, which starts on Monday 17th October. On completion of the course it is planned that he will leave for Palestine on Friday 19th December.

He should join by five pm on Sunday 16th and should bring with him the items listed overleaf.

He put the letter aside and held out his arms to comfort her. "Dearest it's for the best. It's what he wants. He'll be safe there."

"Yes", she sobbed. "But will we ever see him again?"

He looked at Moshe. "This is what you want, isn't it?"

"Yes, Daddy," his eyes expressed his anguish. "I don't want to leave you and Mummy, but I hate the Nazis and I want to fight for a Jewish homeland, for a new Zion, where we Jews can be free. Now I've been given this opportunity to do so I can't refuse." He put his arms around Golda. "Please forgive me Mummy."

As Golda hugged Moshe, Klaus reached for Hedwig, silent with tears in her eyes. He pulled her to him and whispered, "We'll have to support Mummy; losing Moshe will break her heart."

"Yes, Daddy. I'll do all I can and I'll never leave her."

It had been a traumatic home-coming, with Moshe due to go in a fortnight's time and nothing he could say or do could lift the despair. At last they retired to bed and they were alone, he waiting for the right moment to tell her his news. Without a word she climbed in beside him. He felt for her hand.

"Dearest we must be thankful. Moshe will have a future now. Letting him go is the best gift we can give our beloved son."

"Yes, I know that, but my heart asks will we ever see him again?"

"Dearest, Hitler's madness can't last forever. Surely we'll be reunited somehow, sometime, but if not," he paused, "we shall at least know he'll have escaped Hitler's vengeance."

In the dimness he saw her nod. "That's all we can pray for I suppose, that he'll escape this madness." Her voice was empty as if there was no hope.

He drew her to him and kissed her tenderly. Somehow he must tell her about the house and his talk with the Priest. He held her tight and gently wiped the tears from her eyes. It seemed to comfort her.

"I've found us a house," he whispered.

"Have you dearest? I hate living here without you."

"And I miss you."

"A house you say, not an apartment?"

"Yes, a little house standing in its own garden."

"It has a garden?" Her voice was more cheerful.

"Yes, and a telephone. I'll be able to ring you from the office!"

"When can we move in?"

"In a week or two." He told her how pretty it was with its rose bedecked porch and all he could remember about the kitchen and the other rooms. It seem to hearten her.

"What about a school for Hedwig?"

"Dearest, let's leave that till we've moved."

That seemed to settle her and soon she was asleep in his arms. In the morning at breakfast, he told Hedwig and Moshe about the house he'd found, and how he hoped they'd move to Dessau the following weekend.

"So, we've got a busy week ahead, preparing for our move and today Moshe and I must go shopping," he turned to his son.

"Where's that joining letter of yours? We need that list of things you need."

And so the two of them went into town to buy his "stout boots, drill trousers, sun hat" a large rucksack and the other items on the list. As they shopped he'd seen Moshe in a new light; still the son they'd always cherished, but now a young man of determination, with a clear purpose in life, to help build a state where Jews would be free to govern themselves. But while Moshe was clearly excited about his great adventure, Golda was inconsolable, his imminent departure heralded the break-up of the family, for surely one day her beloved Hedwig must go too!

When they got home Golda met them. Klaus could see she was making every effort to be cheerful and while Moshe unpacked the shopping, she checked that everything Moshe needed, had been purchased. Then she produced the pullover and socks she'd been knitting for him. As Moshe tried on the pullover, the imminence of his going brought tears to his eyes, but he managed to hold them back. Now the possibility indeed the probability of never seeing his parents and Hedwig again struck home. No longer could he hide his anguish behind the thrill of starting a new life in Palestine. He struggled bravely to hide his tears. For everyone's sake his own included, he had to put on a brave face. "Mum, it fits me well," he hugged her, "And I love the colour."

Moshe's impending departure dominated all their thoughts and conversation that day, yet despite the distress and finality of his going, Klaus desperately wanted to tell Golda about his talk with the Priest, but not until they were in bed, was he able to broach the subject.

"Dearest," he whispered, "Do you remember me saying that since we know no one in Dessau and as the family has a real German surname, we might be able to forget that you and the children are Jews?"

"Yes," she sighed. "If only we could!"

"Well, the church stands directly opposite our little house."

"So?"

"So dearest, I wandered in. I hadn't been in church for years and I was quite overcome by its peace. I sensed God's presence and I felt the need to pray. I prayed for you, Moshe and Hedwig that you might all be kept safe from Hitler."

"That's very loving of you darling, but all Jews must surely be saying the same prayer. But," she hesitated, "It doesn't seem to work does it?"

"Well, dearest it could. You see as I was sitting in the church, the Priest said how troubled I seemed and asked if he could help me. I thanked him and before I knew it, he was leading me to the confessional. Well, I hadn't made a confession for years and I hardly knew how to start. But then all my worries about you and the family seemed to pour out in an unending flow."

"So, he knows the children and I are Jews."

"Yes".

"So how can we pretend to be otherwise?"

"Dearest, what is said in a confessional is secret and only known to God and the Priest who takes the confession. He will not betray me."

"How can you be certain?"

"He is an ordained minister of the church and he assured me that whatever is said in the confessional is for the ears of God and the priest alone. Nothing a priest hears in a confession will ever be repeated to any mortal."

"You believe him?"

"Yes, absolutely."

"But why did you tell him?"

"Because I wanted to ask him if God would look with favour on me and welcome my Jewish family into the church of the Gentiles."

"Oh! So, how did he reply?"

"He said Our Heavenly Father is full of love and compassion and welcomes all who turn to him."

"He said that?"

"Yes, dearest, but then he added that to show their commitment your wife and children would have to be baptised."

"Baptised? Renounce our Jewish faith?"

"Yes, dearest. If you and the children were baptised and attended church regularly, surely you'll be safe, especially with your non-Jewish surname."

"But we'd have to become Christians, we'd have to abandon our Jewish faith. Moshe would never do that!"

"No, he wouldn't, I know that, but he won't be with us. He'll be off to Palestine. But surely Hedwig won't object. She's always wanted to be "just ordinary", hasn't she? Well, now's her chance."

Golda didn't answer. He knew it would be a big step for her to take; he could understand how she felt. He broke the silence.

"And what about you, dearest?"

"Klaus dear, what would my father say? It may be a good idea, but how can I do such a thing?" She sighed. "I don't know!" Then in a weary voice she said, "Dearest you must be patient, I really can't give you an answer now."

He gave her a hug and said he understood, but she made no reply. He knew giving up her Jewish faith would be a huge and painful step for her; one which would appal her beloved father, if ever he knew.

In the silence that followed he tried to think of something to ease her worrying, something to change the subject. Then he remembered her brother.

"How are Benjamin and Ruth? I must give you some money for them. Remind me in the morning, in case I forget!"

She thanked him and said she would. But how could she say how they were? She didn't know herself! How could she tell him they'd disappeared, that twice now she'd gone to see them, but no one answered the door? That she hadn't seen them for the past two weeks. She remembered their plans to escape. Had they gone? Had they made it or had they been stopped at the Swiss border? She desperately waited for that post card. The card that would tell her they were safe. Would, it ever come? She was sick with worry, yet she couldn't share her worries with anyone, not even Klaus! For their safety their absence had to be kept secret. Trying to hide her fears, she spoke. "The last time I saw them they were alright. Benjamin's working for Yigal Maimon, the butcher. He's cleaning the shop for him, but he's only paid a trifle."

"Oh, when did you see them last?"

"Yesterday," she lied. "I usually go round on Thursdays."

Now it was she who wanted to change the subject, to stop his questions about Benjamin and Ruth but she could think of none, so squeezing his hand, she said they must sleep, they had a busy day tomorrow.

But she knew she wouldn't sleep. She'd not had a proper sleep for days now tormented by the prospect of losing Moshe and worrying about Benjamin and Ruth. And then there was her father! She was haunted by her father's face and could hear him reciting his daily acclamation,

"Hear O Israel: The Lord our God is one Lord". Would he, could he ever forgive her if she became a Christian? Never would he accept the idea of the Trinity; that the Father, Jesus and the Holy Ghost formed one being, one God. To him that was blasphemy. To him there was only one God, Yahweh, who had led his people to freedom from slavery in Egypt. While he could acknowledge Jesus as a prophet, like the Sanhedrin he could never accept Jesus as the Son of God, for then he was claiming equality with God, equality with Yahweh! To him and to all right-thinking Jews, that was utter blasphemy and for that Jesus was justly crucified. No, her father would never become a Christian and he would find it hard to forgive her, if she did.

Yet many Jews had become Christians, even Saul the Pharisee! Even he! He who had hunted down the Jews who followed Christ, and brought them before the Sanhedrin for judgement. Even he had turned to Christ! Long after Jesus had died on the Cross, he Saul claimed to have met Christ on the road to Damascus. He was convinced it was the Risen Christ, but her father like all faithful Jews could never believe that. Yet Saul was adamant and thereafter claimed to be a follower of Christ himself and set about recruiting others. He even changed his name to Paul!

Such thoughts kept sleep at bay, but as the morning sun eventually lit the curtains, cold logic seeped into her exhausted mind. It was her father not she who was the ardent Jew. It was he who put his faith in Yahweh, the God who in his lifetime had given him a good life. But where is Yahweh now? Where is he? Why isn't he defending his faithful Jews? Why isn't he saving them from Hitler's wrath? Why does he allow Jewish families to be torn apart as their children seek safety in other lands? His faithful people, the Jews, have been oppressed throughout the centuries, persecuted by the Egyptians, the Babylonians, the Romans, the Russians and now Hitler. Their persecution is never ending! Why, why does Yahweh allow it? Why does he never punish those evil people, who hate and oppress the Jews?

In despair she sighed. If Yahweh can't help, could it be that the God, this Trinity that Klaus and his fellow Christians worship, might keep her and her children safe? Could it be that destiny was sending them to Dessau? To a place where they knew no-one and no-one knew them? Is this an opportunity for her to forget her Jewishness? Should she? Should she worship the God that Jesus claimed as Father, this God bound up in this incomprehensible Trinity? Should she be baptised and become a Christian? If she did, would their God keep his side of the bargain? She shook her head. How could she bargain with Him?

She felt Klaus stir. She put her arm around him and kissed him. "If it'll keep us safe dearest, I'll be baptised."

Chapter 12

It had been a hectic week with the Stuka, but he'd found time to sign the contract to rent the house, their house. He was sure Golda would like it, he certainly did, and in a house called Tranquillity House he hoped they could live in peace! He'd driven home for their last weekend in Bremen with fresh hope; it could be a new start for the family. They might be able to forget their Jewishness!

Golda had had a busy week too, packing their possessions and arranging for the removal of their furniture to Dessau. When Klaus arrived, her hard work was plainly evident, for no longer were there any pictures on the walls, the mantelpiece and shelves were clear of trinkets and the bookcase empty. The home they'd had since their wedding day no longer seemed theirs!

She met him with a hug and seemed more cheerful than last week. Even Hedwig looked happier, it seemed she'd accepted the move. Almost at once he was told Liesel and Wolfgang had asked them to tea on the Saturday. It turned out to be a sad party, everyone knowing it could be a long time before they met again. Klaus had told his brother about Moshe's future, how he'd soon be off, how final his going seemed to be, yet one day they hoped to be re-united with him, if ever Hitler's madness could be cured. Wolfgang had sympathised and in an effort to comfort his brother, had assured him they'd made the right decision. When he asked Klaus where they would be living in Dessau, Klaus told him about the house.

"It's called Tranquillity House," he said with a smile. "Maybe we'll have some peace there!"

Then telling him what he was about to say was secret and for his ears only, he spoke of his conversation with the Priest, how the Priest had agreed to baptise Golda and Hedwig, and how he hoped that with their good German surname, they could forget they were Jewish. "And Golda", he added "has agreed to lose her Jewish name and be called Gerda. And Moshe will be known as Max." He gave a dry laugh, "Now we're trying hard to remember and use their new names!" Wolfgang shook his head more in despair than hope, "Well my dear brother, we shall be praying for you. You must let me have your new address in Dessau."

"We shall value your prayers Wolfgang, but I don't want to give you our address. I want to keep it secret from everyone here in Bremen. We don't want to be traced by anyone here who knows Golda is Jewish. "We want to disappear. And please keep what I've told you secret, please don't even tell Liesel or your two sons."

Wolfgang nodded wisely. "Of course. But perhaps you could phone me. We must keep in touch dear brother, phone me just occasionally from your office!"

He'd agreed and in the silence that followed he'd heard the youngsters chatting. Moshe was telling Heinrich about Palestine and how he hoped to go there. "I want to help build a new Jewish state," he said with evident pride. Heinrich had seemed impressed and wishing him well had told him how excited he was about the new Kriegsmarine. The *U-1*, the first U-boat to be built by Germany since the war, had just been launched and the first heavy cruiser, the *Deutschland* had now been joined by two others of her class, the *Admiral Scheer* and the *Admiral Graf Spee*. And recently the battleship *Scharnhorst* had been launched. He was impressed by the modern fleet Germany was building and said when he was eighteen he wanted to join the Navy.

"What do you want to do, man the big battleships or join the U-boats?" Moshe asked. Heinrich had given him a wry grin.

"Battleships, I like the fresh air, but who knows!"

Klaus looked around the room. Hedwig was gazing at her cousin Horst with adoring eyes. That worried him, Horst was an ardent supporter of Hitler and couldn't be a friend or be trusted by a Jewish girl. Yet he had to admit he was an uncommonly handsome young man with blue eyes, blonde hair, a real Adonis, no wonder Hedwig was besotted with him. "How is your piccolo?" he heard her ask

"It's fine." Horst replied. "I play it a lot at my Hitler Youth Meetings, and you know I'm really proud to be a Hitler Youth. One day I hope to join the Schutzstaffel*

Hearing Horst say that had shaken him. He knew Horst admired Hitler, but he'd never thought he had aspirations to join the S.S., the instrument Hitler used to ensure his anti-Semitic policies were implemented. How could his lovely gentle daughter admire such a man? Yet there she was wishing him well and telling him sweetly of her ambition to play her violin in some great orchestra. What contrasting aspirations these four cousins had! And how divided their two families were becoming!

Suddenly a vision of the handsome Horst in S.S. uniform, dutifully obeying Hitler by leading his aunt and doting Hedwig off to a concentration camp, crossed his troubled mind. Involuntarily he shook his head, Horst couldn't be trusted. It was indeed a good thing they were leaving Bremen. Never must Horst know their address in Dessau!

It was time to go, they made their sad emotional farewells and left, strangely silent as they drove home. There a postcard awaited them. Klaus picked it up and saw it was from Ernst and Ingrid. The names meant nothing to him. He gave it to Golda.

"Who are Ernst and Ingrid?" he asked.

For a moment she seemed mystified, then a blissful smile spread over her face.

"I'll tell you later," she said.

The card intrigued him, she'd been so melancholic before, but after reading its contents, her mood had suddenly changed to one of joy and unmistakable relief! But she'd made no comment and it wasn't until they were in bed, that she enlightened him.

"The card was from Benjamin and Ruth," she said. Klaus didn't understand.

"I thought it was from Ernst & Ingrid, whoever they are. Didn't they sign the card?"

Golda chuckled. Klaus couldn't believe it! She hadn't laughed or chuckled for ages!

"Dearest," she continued, "Benjamin promised to send me a card when they were safe in Switzerland, but to keep their identity secret and to save us being involved in their escape plan, they wouldn't use their own names on the card. He told me they would sign it Ernst and Ingrid. So now dearest we know they're in Switzerland and safe. Isn't that wonderful?"

The next morning after the first good night's sleep she'd had for a while, Golda felt and indeed looked much happier. And swearing the family to secrecy, she told them that Uncle Benjamin and Auntie Ruth had gone to Switzerland, where they'd be safe from Hitler and the Nazis. "And now," she told them, "We must keep our new address in Dessau secret, since we are to be baptised and become Christians. It is important, indeed vital that we are not traced! We must tell no-one here including Uncle Wolfgang, Auntie Liesel, Heinrich, and, "she gave Hedwig a stern look, "not even Horst, our new address in Dessau. She looked at Moshe and Hedwig, "Is that understood?" She saw them nod their agreement. "Dearest," she sought to comfort her daughter. "It's not that we don't trust them to keep our address secret, but in talking to their friends they might accidentally reveal it. So it's better if they don't know!"

Klaus had taken a few days off for the move and by Friday evening the family were in Dessau with their possessions finally unloaded and the removal men gone. Tranquillity House, their new home in Dessau, had begun to regain a little of its tranquillity, and happy to have the family with him, Klaus left for the office the next morning.

However the family's joy at being re-united was dampened by Moshe's imminent departure for Eberswalde and in due course Palestine on the Monday. On Sunday evening Klaus took the family to a well recommended restaurant for a farewell meal. He tried desperately to make it a celebration for Moshe's new life, but his efforts met with little success. It had been a sad occasion and on the following day they drove their beloved son to Berlin and on to Eberswalde. When they arrived at the main entrance Golda hugged her son for an age. It seemed she would never let him go, but with tears in her eyes, she gave him a last kiss and released him. Hedwig was crying too, even Klaus was struggling to hold back his tears as he helped Moshe to shoulder his rucksack, before hugging him too and giving him a hundred marks. "Keep them safe Moshe," he said. "You'll be a great pioneer." Then Moshe pushed open the door and vanished.

With Moshe gone life for Golda seemed empty and nothing Klaus could do or say would comfort her. The following morning he left for the office worrying about her, but at work he was quickly buried in the problems of the Stuka. At a Board meeting on the coming Friday he had to present his solution. His were radical proposals which he feared the

Board might find difficult to accept, yet he was sure they would enable the Stuka to survive the stresses imposes upon it when pulling out of the steep dive needed to deliver its bomb accurately. He was convinced the original assembly with its twin fins and rudders had not broken off as a result of the crash, for their debris had been found well away from the main wreckage. He therefore concluded that the tail assembly had broken off before the Stuka struck the ground and that was why the Stuka had failed to pull out of its dive. He was convinced it was the strange tail-plane assembly that had caused the crash and he proposed replacing the twin fins with a single fin version. But he feared opposition from the Board for he'd heard that the original design with its twin tail plane assembly had received great support for it was argued that it would give the rear facing gunner a clear field of fire at an enemy fighter approaching from right astern. That had been the raison d'etre for the twin rudder design, but he would suggest that the number of enemy fighters attacking from absolutely right astern would be minimal. They could come from many differing bearings astern. And with two tail-planes two preventers would have to be incorporated in the controls to stop the gun firing at either fin. He would therefore argue that in fact, a single fin gives less obstruction to the gunner firing at a fighter plane coming from astern, than a double fin.

On the day however to his surprise and delight, the board had approved his re-design, but pleased as he was, he knew he couldn't tell Golda. All he could do was hope the garden might help ease her distress and on the way home he'd bought her some daffodil and tulip bulbs. She took them without a smile and had clung to him like a drowning child. He'd kissed her. "Dearest, he'll be safe," he said, but as he tried to console her, the doorbell rang. It was a lady with a smile on her face and flowers in her arms. "Welcome to Kirchestrasse," she said. "I am Christel Hoffmann and live next door. I hope we'll be friendly neighbours."

Klaus thanked her for her kind welcome and as he introduced Gerda, she gave her some flowers. Hedwig appeared and was introduced. Christel smiled again, "I have a granddaughter about your age," she told her and turning to Golda continued, "But sadly I have no grandsons. You're lucky to have a son, my dear. Boys are a rarity in my family."

A son! The word raced through Klaus's head. How can we explain our son's imminent departure for Palestine? Then Golda spoke. "You mean

Max? He's not our son, he's our nephew. He came along to help us with the move and we took him home on Monday."

Klaus sighed inwardly. Golda's tale seemed to satisfy Christel and talking of the garden, Golda said how much she enjoyed its peace. Christel laughed. "Yes, the house is aptly named! Being opposite our beautiful church helps. And will you and your family be attending mass on Sunday? It begins at half-past nine."

Klaus smiled. "Yes, I shall be there with Gerda and Hedwig."

"Good, I shall look forward to seeing you. Till then," she smiled and left.

Sunday came. Going to a Christian church with its strange ways would be a challenge for Golda, he knew. Hedwig would be nervous too. But when he told them that in Christian churches, women sit with their menfolk Golda had looked happier.

"So," he assured them, "I'll tell you what to do and don't worry, all will be well."

They'd arrived deliberately just as the service was due to begin, so they could sit in the pews at the back, where they would be least noticed. And with guidance from Klaus they'd managed to follow the strange service that emphasised the divinity of Jesus.

As they were about to leave Christel found them, "Oh? There you are, it's good to see you in our church."

"It's good to be here, isn't it Hedwig?

Hedwig nodded shyly as Golda said how much she'd enjoyed the service.

They chatted for a while and then managing to catch the Priest's eye, Klaus led them over to his presence.

"Father," he said. "May I introduce my wife Gerda and my daughter Hedwig?"

Golda found the Priest friendly and felt a little more relaxed.

"Welcome to St Hildegard's. I understand you're new to Dessau and live opposite the church?"

"Yes," Golda replied. "We are indeed fortunate."

"Your husband," the Priest looked at Klaus, "tells me you and your daughter Hedwig wish to be baptised. Is that so?"

"Yes, we do," Golda replied as Hedwig nodded.

"Good, as you are both adults I feel I should prepare you for this rite. Baptism is often called 'the door to the church" as it's the first of three sacraments leading to a true Christian life. The other two are confirmation and the Eucharist. So", he smiled, "we shall need to set aside some time for me to prepare you both."

Chapter 13

Baptism? Golda remembered Father Ulrich had said it was the first of three sacraments leading to a true Christian life. A Christian life! What had she done? She'd agreed to be baptised! It troubled her. What would her father think? Once again she heard his voice "How can you worship that impostor, didn't he claim to be the son of God, the son of The Most High? Didn't his disciples believe his mother Mary was a virgin? That Jesus had no earthly father? That he was conceived by the Spirit, whoever that is? Well," she could see her beloved Father shaking his head in despair, "Who can believe that? The Sanhedrin* didn't, they saw Jesus as a fake, as a blasphemer and so do I. He was rightly crucified."

Her father had been a faithful, practising Jew. He'd shaped her life, given her the faith and culture that had made her the person she was. How could she abandon him and her Jewishness? How could she? Yet it was no longer safe to be a Jew in Hitler's Germany. Why, why did Hitler want to persecute us so? Why does he hate us? Aren't we loyal Germans too? As always, there seemed to be no answer to her questions! Then that terrible question came again. The one she always tried to ignore! But it persisted. It wouldn't go away! "Was Yahweh using Hitler to punish his wayward Chosen People? Was it Yahweh's work?"

Yahweh had been angry with the Jews in Nebuchadnezzar's time. They'd been worshipping Baal and in their desire for riches, success and power, it seemed they'd forgotten Yahweh and he was angry with them. They'd broken the covenant, they were worshipping idols; they were being disobedient. Was Nebuchadnezzar doing Yahweh's work when he captured Jerusalem and sent the Jews into exile in Babylon? Surely he was! "And could it be", her inner voice asked once again, "Could it be that like Nebuchadnezzar, Hitler is doing Yahweh's bidding? Is Yahweh still angry with the Jews? Had he never forgiven his Chosen People for crucifying Jesus? Jesus, his only begotten son? If he hadn't, was that why he was using Hitler to punish the Jews? Golda shook her head, it was all too frightening; she really didn't know what to believe!

As their first meeting with Father Ulrich approached, Golda became ever more concerned about rejecting her Jewish faith. When she'd disclosed her fears to Klaus he'd tried to comfort her by reminding her that Jesus was himself a Jew, who preached a new way of worshiping God his father, one based on faith rather than obedience of the Law, that Judaism demanded.

The evening arrived and Golda and Hedwig crossed the road and entered the church, where Father Ulrich was waiting. Though he was clearly aware of their Jewishness, he made no reference to it, and without hesitation began. He spoke about the meaning of Christmas and the birth of Jesus. How Mary the mother of Jesus was a virgin and how he was conceived by the Holy Spirit. It was everything her father had told her was false, yet Father Ulrich recited it with undeniable conviction. It was an enigma! When their meeting was over, Father Ulrich gave them each a bible and asked them to read Saint Luke's Gospel before their next visit.

Hedwig had seemed to accept Father Ulrich's teaching without question, as she was to do at their next meeting, when Father Ulrich spoke about the Crucifixion of Jesus, the empty tomb and his rising on the third day. But as Golda listened to the Priest, once more she could hear her father denying all that Father Ulrich was saying. Yet her reading of Saint Luke had made her more receptive to this new yet strange belief that Jesus was human and at the same time divine, and as she left she began to feel it could be right that she and Hedwig were to be baptised.

Father Ulrich baptised them privately three weeks later on a Saturday and afterwards Klaus had congratulated them and had given them each a golden crucifix to wear as a necklace.

But that was not the end of it. To be a practising Christian, Father Ulrich told her it was necessary for her and Hedwig to be confirmed, then they could join the others in receiving the sacrament of communion at the altar. But to be confirmed needed further preparation culminating in the laying on of hands by the local Bishop. This time fortunately, they were not alone and were pleased to find they were joined by two other adults and five youngsters, one of whom was Christel's granddaughter Brigitte.

So they began to be accepted into the local community, and with Hedwig attending the nearby school with Brigitte, it seemed their worries as Jews could be behind them. Yet there remained an aching void in Golda's heart as she mourned her lost son Moshe, from whom she could expect no letters, for it had been agreed there should be no correspondence between them so that the family's Jewishness would not be revealed. But the reward was his safety and the promise of a new life for him, free from Nazi persecution. For that she had to be thankful and now as a confirmed Christian named Gerda, she had to admit to a measure of relief and contentment as the peace and serenity of the house and garden encompassed her. Hedwig too seemed more at ease, happy with her new violin teacher and filling the house with her music.

Klaus too was less concerned for Golda and Hedwig now that their Jewishness seemed to be behind them, and was becoming increasingly absorbed with the challenge presented by the Stuka. His remedial proposals for the plane had been accepted and were now being implemented, with the board waiting impatiently for the first test flight. A successful flight could lead to a bright future for Junkers with confirmed sales to the new Luftwaffe. Success was equally important for Klaus, not only for his own sense of achievement, but making the Stuka airworthy would enhance his reputation as a warplane designer and in Hitler's new Germany that would surely be no bad thing!

But their relief was short lived. A tearful Hedwig came home from school. "The Headmistress sent for me," she said her voice quivering with fright. "She asked me why I'm not a member of the Bund Deutsche Madel*. It's compulsory for all girls over the age of 16," she said. "All but Jews," she added. Then with a nasty look she'd said "You're not a Jew are you?"

"I was frightened but I denied being a Jew." Then she told me I must join, gave me this form and said that you and Daddy should complete it to confirm that I am of pure Aryan stock."

Hedwig gave her mother the form. It required the names, and nationality of Hedwig's forbears and whether or not they were Jewish. A quote from the Nuremburg Laws at the bottom of the form, stated that "anyone with three Jewish grandparents is a Jew, those with two Jewish grandparents are "half-Jews" and those with one Jewish grandparent "quarter-Jews".

Golda shut her eyes in horror. That form when completed would reveal Hedwig's Jewish ancestry and their attempt to pose as Christians would be uncovered. And furthermore if Hedwig was banned from the League of German Girls, everyone at school would know she must be Jewish and they would surely bully her and make her life intolerable!

A tearful Hedwig shook her head, "What can we do Mummy?"

"Dearest your father and I will think of something." She gave her daughter a kiss. "We must!"

But what could they do? While she waited for Klaus to come home she could think of nothing else, and after giving him his usual cup of tea, she told him about Hedwig and showed him the form.

"We're done for," he exclaimed. "When that form is completed they'll never let her join the League and if she doesn't join, everyone will know she's a Jew!"

"Yes, but at least with your parents as grandparents, she's only a half-Jew!"

"Yes, but she has to be a non-Jew to be eligible and our hopes of hiding your Jewishness and Hedwig's too will be dashed!"

They fell silent. Neither could think what they could do.

Golda picked up the form and sighed. Whatever they did would lead to trouble, unthinkable trouble at the hands of the Nazis! She shut her eyes in dismay, the sword of Damocles hung over them. If they completed the form truthfully, Hedwig's Jewishness and hers would be confirmed. If they lied they would surely be found out, then they would be at the mercy of the Gestapo. But the Gestapo was never merciful! Lying was not an option. How she wished they could ignore the form, but she shook her head in despair, that was impossible. Taking a deep breath she took up her pen and wrote:

Name of child <u>Hedwig Boddenburg</u>

"Golda, what are you doing?" Klaus held her arm.

"Dearest we have no option, we must tell the truth and pray that our Christian God will protect us."

Chapter 14

Hitler's strong and unopposed leadership had resulted in the stabilisation of the mark and a huge fall in the number of unemployed by the building of the new autobahns and other military and infrastructure projects. The ending of the Weimar hyperinflation and the marked fall in unemployment was welcomed joyfully by the German people and admired by other countries. But his enlargement of the German army, the modernisation the Navy and the creation of a German air force in complete defiance of the Versailles Treaty, caused great concern in Europe. Though Hitler's defiance was discussed endlessly in the newly formed League of Nations, nothing the League did was able to bring Hitler to task. His unresolved hatred of the Versailles Treaty was always at the centre of his strategy for his new Third Reich. Not only did he object to the cruel and unreasonable reparation payments, but he was equally outraged by the Treaty's demilitarisation of the Rhineland, a sovereign and integral part of Imperial, Weimar and Nazi Germany. That meant no fortifications could be built and no military forces could be stationed in the Rhineland on Germany's border with France. This he claimed, rendered Germany defenceless in the West and he determined to rectify this humiliating imposition. In March 1936 without warning and despite the fears of the German General Staff that the French would react strongly, German troops marched into the Rhineland. Not a shot was fired and despite earnest discussion in the League of Nations, no action was taken to enforce the terms of the Versailles Treaty. Hitler was cock-a-hoop and the nation glorified in this show of German strength and confidence.

There was good news at Junkers too when, to the firm's delight, the redesigned tail plane on the Stuka proved itself in the initial test flight. The remaining test flights were equally successful and all the firm now had to do was to persuade the Reich Chancellor for Aviation that the Stuka was a worthy addition to his embryonic Luftwaffe.

Having prepared plans for the Stuka production line, ready for the hoped-for order, Klaus had become involved with the Ju88 a twin-engined aircraft known at Junkers as the Schnellbomber*. Its first test flight had revealed a number of technical problems which he was helping to resolve. Then the good news came. The Luftwaffe had placed an initial order for thirty Stukas. Now his planned production line had to be brought into operation and for the next two months he was frantically busy and again Golda began complaining that she hardly saw him. But eventually the first Stuka came off the production line ready for its test flights, and the Luftwaffe order began being fulfilled.

But now Nazi Germany was no longer the principal interest of the International Press Corps, for in Spain a coup d'état had been launched by the Republicans seeking to depose the King and wrest power from his right-wing government. Colonial troops from the Spanish protectorate of Morocco rebelled, took control of the colony and sent troops to Spain to support the Republicans, now occupying Seville and Cadiz. But the initial success of the Republicans was halted when their troops in Madrid were overcome by Government forces, now known as the Nationalists. So began almost three years of civil war.

The Union of Soviet Socialist Republics (USSR) and Mexico quickly announced their support for the Republicans, and provided weapons and munitions. Other nations became involved too, aiding one side or the other. Hitler was opposed to the Republicans, whom he considered little more than Communists and wished to support the Nationalists not just with munitions, but with military force. So German air and army units forming the Condor Legion were sent to Spain to assist the Nationalists, now under the control of General Francisco Franco. The actions of the Legion were reported with enthusiasm and pride by the Nazi media and its participation in the war gave Germany the opportunity to test its new weapons and tactics and gave important training opportunities to the military. And soon the Junkers management were to learn that a squadron of Stuka dive-bombers had taken part in the bombing of Guernica. Later they were to receive exemplary reports of the plane's performance.

But for Golda and Hedwig the civil war in Spain had been of little interest. Both had been confirmed in the Christian faith and were now attending communion regularly. Hedwig's acceptance into her new school had eased their worries and Golda tried hard to feel Golda the Jew no longer, but Gerda the Christian, and thankfully Klaus and Hedwig rarely called her by her Jewish name. But despite her conversion, at heart she remained a Jew and hoped thereby to have made her peace with her father Chaim.

Christel had become a good friend and with her help she had got to know many people from the church. Hedwig and Brigitte had become friends too and Golda in her prayers thanked God for the sanctuary and the relief that Dessau had brought. But she missed Moshe greatly and mindful of Hitler's never ending hatred of the Jews was sure that, one day, she and Klaus would have to seek asylum for Hedwig too. It was for that reason that she now insisted Hedwig learned to speak English and become proficient in the domestic skills required of a maid. Such skills could, if need be, facilitate her resettlement in England, a country she admired for its tolerance. Yet England like so many countries was struggling to recover from the Great Depression of 1929 and, with millions unemployed, showed scant interest in helping Germany's Jews. So all Golda could do was pray.

In the winter of 1937 and the spring of 1938 the media endlessly reported rioting in Austria and the repeated call of the Austrian Nazis for unity with Germany, the Anschluss forbidden by the Versailles Treaty. Now in his ever-more bellicose speeches the Führer, himself an Austrian, unequivocally demanded Anschluss. "Ein Reich, Ein Volk, Ein Führer". One Nation, One People, One Leader, he kept proclaiming. His call for unity excited and motivated the German people not just in Austria and the Fatherland, but also those living in the new nations bordering Germany that had been created as a result of the Versailles Treaty. These German-speaking minorities claimed they were being victimised because of their German roots and sought support from the Fatherland.

In Austria a coup d'etat had been launched by the Nazis without success, though Chancellor Dollfuss had been assassinated. Despite their failure, however, the agitations, demonstrations and rioting organised by the Nazis continued unabated. Later in February, the world learnt that

Schuschnigg, the new Austrian Chancellor, had been summoned to a conference with the Führer in his alpine eyrie at Berchtesgaden. But it was no conference! Hitler gave Schuschnigg an ultimatum! Comply with his demands for the appointment of named ardent Austrian Nazis to lead the Foreign and Interior Ministries, and release all imprisoned Nazis within three days, or the German Army stationed and ready on the border, would invade. Schuschnigg had little option. He had to obey!

On 20th February Hitler addressed the Reichstag in the Kroll Opera House in Berlin, the replacement for the burnt out Reichstag building. With Nazi influence in Austria now assured, Hitler spoke of his triumph and insisted not only on Anschluss, but also demanded that the three and a half million German-speaking people in the Sudetenland a province of Czechoslovakia, be given the "right of self-determination". His rousing speech was wildly applauded with the unified, rhythmic howling, with which the German people showed their adulation and support for the Führer.   "Sieg Heil! *Sieg Heil!* SIEG HEIL! Heil Hitler! *Heil Hitler!* HEIL HITLER!

In public this was how Klaus voiced his sympathy with Hitler's ambitions too and though Golda in her role as Gerda the Christian outwardly supported him, inwardly Hitler's new-found aggression struck a fresh note of terror in her Jewish heart.

As the Nazi-organised demonstrations in Vienna grew and became more violent, Chancellor Schuschnigg called a plebiscite to decide whether the Austrian people wished to remain independent or seek unification with Germany. But Hitler concerned that the plebiscite might support continued independence, and having little fear of intervention from the League of Nations or the old enemies, France and England, issued a second ultimatum to Chancellor Schuschnigg on March 11th. Not only must the plebiscite be cancelled, Schuschnigg must resign and the pro-Nazi Seyss-Inquart be appointed Chancellor in his stead. A time limit of four hours was given in which to comply, or German troops would march into Austria.

In an emotional statement broadcast to Austria and the world, Chancellor Schuschnigg told of his resignation and his succession by the pro-Nazi Seyss-Inquart. When the Austrian National Anthem was played to conclude his announcement, Schuschnigg finished with an emotional salutation to Austria. Then a few seconds later another anthem struck up. This time it was "Deutschland, Deutschland Uber Alles" the new German anthem and this was followed by the Horst Wessel song, the anthem of the Nazi Party.

The following day the German Army crossed into Austria. There was no resistance, the troops being welcomed with Nazi Swastika flags and flowers. The next day the Austrian Nazis began taking a swift and terrible vengeance against those who had led the struggle to remain independent. Many Austrian army officers were interned and thousands of civilians arrested and sent to concentration camps in Germany. A few days later black-shirted men of the S.S. became masters of the streets and every aspect of German Nazism was introduced. Most important were the anti-Jewish laws that had been introduced in the Fatherland. Jewish shops and homes were looted and thousands of Jews attacked and beaten. Given buckets of water some Jews were forced on their knees, to clean the pavements with toothbrushes, whilst fellow Austrians, standing nearby, laughed and derided them.

In the weeks that followed German laws depriving Jews of the right to own property, to be employed or to participate in their professions, were rigorously enforced. A small minority managed to escape and find refuge in other countries, but countless Jews unwilling to face a bleak, hopeless and dangerous future, killed their families and themselves, while thirty thousand of Austria's two hundred thousand Jews, were arrested and sent to concentration camps.

The news that in Austria the hated Jews were getting their just deserts was received in Germany with satisfaction and quickly spawned a revival of Jewish persecution in the Fatherland.

In her new guise as Gerda the Christian, Golda dared not show sympathy for the Jews in Austria and insisted that Hedwig should follow her lead. Now her agony at losing Moshe was replaced by thanks. Thanks that her beloved son was safe from the vicious Nazis. But Hedwig's future and safety dominated her every thought. As she worried about her precious daughter, sleep became a rare luxury and what little she had was often disturbed by nightmares.

"We must do something for Hedwig." Once again she made her plea to Klaus.

"Yes, dearest but what can we do?"

"Well she's not safe here. I have nightmares now about that form we completed. It shows two of her grandparents were Jews and whether or not she's a converted Christian, to the Nazis she's a half-Jew and the best we can hope for is that she's expelled from school. But like all Jews, she can expect nothing but persecution in Hitler's Germany."

"Dearest, like you I constantly worry about Hedwig and you too for you are a full Jew. Would you go with Hedwig? If you did we might be able to smuggle you both into France or Holland. I'm sure Hedwig would refuse to go on her own."

Golda gave a great sigh of despair. "If only we could all go dearest! But with your knowledge of the aircraft industry I realise you can't and dearest I won't leave you, you're my husband, so somehow," she shook her head in misery, "Hedwig must go on her own, if we can only find a way."

Chapter **15**

At the Junkers factory morale was high, for not only was the Stuka now in full production, but the Ju88 the Schnellbomber, had successfully completed all its test flights and the Reich Air Ministry was showing great interest in the plane.

But though the Stuka had performed well in the Condor Legion's Spanish campaign and had been the subject of many excellent reports by its aircrew, it had faced no real opposition from fighter aircraft and its vulnerability to such attacks was being questioned. An exercise to test the Stuka's ability to defend itself against enemy fighter aircraft had therefore been designed and carried out. Its findings had been documented in a Top Secret report, a copy of which had been sent to Junkers where Otto Tauber the Managing Director, studied it carefully before sending for Klaus.

"Read this", he handed the report to him, "but remember it's Top Secret! Then come and tell me what can be done."

The report summarised the results of a series of mock air battles between a Messerschmitt BF109 Germany's latest fighter aircraft, and a Stuka, both aircraft being flown by highly regarded pilots. The pilot of the BF109 which had a maximum speed of 640 kilometres an hour, had little difficulty in overtaking the Stuka with its maximum speed of 410. And with its higher speed the BF109's pilot found it easy to place his aircraft in the best attacking position right astern of the Stuka, from which a "kill" would be almost certain.

The Stuka's pilot reported that in none of the exercise flights was he able to manoeuvre his aircraft so that his two wing mounted guns could be aimed at the BF109. The fighter with its superior speed had always been able to approach from astern and though his rear gunner always had a good view of the BF109, the mechanism designed to prevent him shooting at the Stuka's single tail fin had frequently triggered the interlock which had prevented him from firing his blank ammunition! So he'd only been able to place a few 'shots' on target and thus claim only two possible 'kills'.

The report ended "The exercise clearly demonstrates the vulnerability of the Stuka from attack by enemy fighter aircraft."

Kraus laid the report aside. It was not good reading! His redesigned tail fin had clearly hampered the rear gunner, yet the original twin fin design had been the cause of that test flight crash. Clearly a new tail fin which did not impede the gunner was required, but what could that be? The Stuka was too slow as well, he'd have to reduce drag. Making the landing gear retract as it did on the BF109 would help. Such thoughts ran through his mind as he returned the Top Secret report to the Managing Director.

"It's not good news about our Stuka, Klaus."

"No, Herr Tauber."

"Klaus, I need to assure the Reich Air Ministry that we are well aware of the problems with the Stuka and that we are working on modifications to lessen the plane's vulnerability." His eyes pierced Klaus. "Otherwise we may well lose orders for the plane."

"Yes, Herr Tauber."

"So Klaus, please let me have your proposals by this time next week."

A very worried Klaus returned to his office. The Stuka had shown itself to be a very successful dive bomber able to attack its target with considerable accuracy. Indeed there was no other aircraft built or being designed in Germany that could compete with it! Yet because of its low speed and inability to shoot without impediment at aircraft coming from astern, it was clearly vulnerable to enemy fighters. But how could he increase its speed and solve the tail fin problem without designing a new aircraft? Over the next few days he could think of nothing else. Reducing drag, especially that caused by the fixed undercarriage, was essential, but modifying those gull-like wings to accept retracted wheels and struts was impossible. Entirely new wings would be needed. And for greater speed a more powerful engine too, and that would require a re-design of the aircraft's nose!

So far so good! But what could he do about the tail fin? It seemed whatever he did would impede the rear gunner's twin guns.

"It's a pity the damned thing can't be mounted on the underside of the fuselage," he muttered. But that was a ludicrous idea! How could the plane land with a tail fin protruding from the underside of the fuselage?

He went home that night mentally exhausted. It was a problem which seemed to have no solution!

Golda was worried about him. "Dearest you're home late again. You're working too hard."

He tried to reassure her all was well, but of course he couldn't say what was worrying him, it was Top Secret as Otto Tauber reminded him only too often!

Changing the subject Golda told him of the two Jewish owned shops in town that had been attacked by Nazi ruffians. One of the owners had been badly beaten. It seemed part of an organised upsurge in anti-Jewish behaviour throughout Germany. Though that damned Stuka ruled all his thoughts, he tried to comfort her.

"Well Gerda dear, with your Aryan names and your attendance at church, no one knows you and Hedwig are Jewish, so we'll be safe."

"Yes, until they examine that form we signed, the one we had to complete for Hedwig to join the League of German Girls."

That form he feared could be their downfall. He'd correctly given his occupation as "Chief of Aircraft Design, Junkers" hoping that would impress Hedwig's Headmistress and perhaps make her forget, overlook, Hedwig's half Jewishness! But he was sure that wouldn't wash! Yet all they could do was hope!

"Gerda dear," he took her in his arms and gave her a reassuring hug, "all we can do is hope and pray they don't."

That's all he and Gerda could do, he told himself; though he knew their hopes and prayers would go unanswered.

And he had his worries at Junkers. His expertise in aircraft design could yet save him and Gerda and Hedwig too and in five days he had to give Otto his proposals to rectify the Stuka. With a major design he could reduce drag and so increase speed, possibly enough to match that of the BF109. But the tail? All he could think of was that crazy idea of mounting the tail fin under the fuselage. But that was a ridiculous, idiotic idea, yet it dominated all his thinking. And he was finding it difficult to sleep, and last night after what seemed hours, he'd eventually dropped off. But his sleep had been short-lived and disturbed by a dream. In it he'd seen a plane with those familiar gull-like wings in a dive with its engine racing and its siren screaming. Then the plane had pulled out of its dive and he'd seen it! Seen its tail fin. It was protruding from the underside of the fuselage! In his dream it had seemed not at all unusual, but as he awoke he remembered thinking "he'll have to do something about that tail before he lands". But what could he do? That question had dominated all his thoughts. Could it be rotated? Rotating it would cause problems of stability. And beside that surely there'd be steering problems, for if the rudder was in the left rudder position when then tail fin was up, the plane would turn to port, but when the tail was down the plane would turn to starboard! How could the plane be flown with a steering problem like that?

In the morning with his dream fresh in mind, he'd left for the office, still no nearer to finding a way of clearing the line of fire for the stern gunner. As usual he'd been welcomed by his secretary with his customary coffee and with a reminder that he had an appointment with the Managing Director at 10 a.m. the next day. He didn't need any reminder, that meeting would be his downfall, for he still had no idea what to do about that cursed tail fin. However, he'd thanked her and drew some small comfort from the hot sweet coffee. Then he remembered that dream. In his mind's eye he saw it, that fin pointing downward. Idly he sketched what he had seen on the pad in front of him. It looked very odd with the tail protruding from the underside of the fuselage! Then the thought struck him, the instability caused by rotating the tail fin could be cured by the judicious use of the ailerons, but what about the steering problem? Could he arrange a mechanism to change the direction of the rudder when the tail was in the down position? Suddenly he could see a possible solution!

Yes that was it! Now he had to do some serious work to get the details right. He'd sent for his assistant, he'd need all the help he could get to prepare his proposed modifications.

The day came for Klaus to give his proposals to the Managing Director. He dealt with the need to increase speed by reducing drag. This he would achieve by fitting a retractable undercarriage which would require a redesigned wing and other minor modifications. He also spoke of the need for a more powerful engine, which would necessitate the redesign of the nose section. Otto accepted these ideas without question. Then he asked what could be done about the rear facing guns?

"My proposals to clear the gunner's line of fire are more radical," Klaus paused. Suddenly his confidence went! How could Otto or indeed any sane person, accept his revolutionary idea?

"I'm proposing to rotate the tail fin once the plane is airborne so that the tail fin points downwards from the fuselage. The rear-gunner will then have a clear line of fire at any plane approaching from the rear."

Otto looked surprised, "Surely the act of rotating the tail fin will affect the plane's stability and control."

"Yes, mein Herr, but I will include instructions for the pilot to use the ailerons to counteract the effect of rotating the tail fin."

"Oh! And how do you propose to stop a forgetful pilot landing with his tail fin in the down position?"

"I will design an interlock to prevent the undercarriage being lowered when the tail fin is in the down position."

"Well, it's certainly a revolutionary proposal, Klaus. Let's make it work, eh? But," Otto paused, "We need to build a new plane, we can't incorporate all these proposals in the Stuka. Draft me a letter to the Reich Air Ministry outlining these modifications and I will propose we incorporate them in a new design, which I suggest we call the Ju187."

Chapter *16*

As the nation glorified in the success of the Anschluss, the Führer began to voice his concern for the Germans left behind in Czechoslovakia when under the terms of the Versailles Treaty it had been carved out of the old Austro-Hungarian Empire. The issue dominated his ever more bellicose speeches and on 6th September 1938 Nazi Party Day, Adolf Hitler speaking at the annual Nuremberg Rally, presented himself as the champion of the German people living in the Sudeten Province of Czechoslovakia. "Three and a quarter million Germans living in Sudetenland are being victimised by the Czech government. Germany cannot tolerate this unwarranted persecution of its German folk," he raged.

Six days later in a speech broadcast throughout Europe, he declared that "the oppression of the Sudeten Germans must end. Czechoslovakia," he ranted, "is a monstrous formation created without thought by those who wrote the treaty."

Edvard Benes the President of Czechoslovakia, offered to seek a fair solution to the Sudetenland problem, but Hitler doubted his integrity and accused him of mendacity! The Sudeten Germans," he demanded, "must be given self-determination. The whole power of the German Reich is behind them in this."

Hitler's aspirations were welcomed in the Fatherland as one more step in promoting the new Germany as a powerful European state. But the manner in which Hitler tackled the so-called Sudetenland problem was much disliked in Europe. Czechoslovakia sensing a degree of moral support, refused to be bullied. Indeed France's Prime Minister Edouard Daladier, sided openly with Edvard Benes, but tension grew in May when the Sudeten German Party began organising demonstrations and disturbances. When rumours spread that a German invasion was imminent, the Czech government took immediate action, sending troops to garrison the province. But this did nothing to ease the tension and Herr Ribbentrop, the German Foreign Minister, sent for the Czech diplomatic representative in Berlin, and warned him that unless Czechoslovakia changed its policy towards the Sudeten Germans, Germany would be forced to march to their rescue.

Neville Chamberlain, the British Prime Minister, now became involved. Daladier had suggested that Britain should join France in guaranteeing Czechoslovakia against German aggression, but Chamberlain refused, maintaining that mediation between the Czechs and the Sudetenland Germans was no longer possible. Therefore he told Daladier, there would have to be a plebiscite.

Chamberlain and Daladier had three meetings with Hitler in Germany. On the first, Hitler reluctantly agreed to the proposed plebiscite, but on the second he insisted a plebiscite was not needed in areas where more than fifty per cent were German speakers. Chamberlain agreed with Hitler.

A final meeting was held at Munich on 29th September 1938, when during twelve hours of talks, Chamberlain, Daladier, Mussolini and Hitler drew up a detailed plan for the transfer of the Sudetenland to Germany. The Czech representatives kept in a room nearby were not invited to attend the meeting. Only at midnight, when the meeting had ended, were the Czechs told what had been decided, and invited to accept the plan and given no chance to amend the decisions.

Without further ado, on the first day of October, German troops began their occupation of the Sudetenland and like the Anschluss, German troops met no resistance, only cheering crowds. Hitler had gained yet another territory for the Reich and the nation applauded him as a hero; he was making Germany great again.

Like many Klaus had been concerned lest Hitler's determination and aggressive speeches might lead to conflict, a conflict that might escalate into another war. But Hitler's nerve had won the day. Klaus was relieved that peace had prevailed and happy that the Sudetenland and its German folk were now part of Greater Germany. "After all," he told Golda, "they are Germans and they found the land they thought was theirs incorporated in this strange new country called Czechoslovakia."

"Yes dearest." Golda wasn't as happy as Klaus. "But surely not everyone living in Sudetenland is of German origin and no doubt there are a great number of Sudetenland Jews who will now be persecuted like the Jews here and in Austria!"

Hedwig, however sided with the German minority. "Everyone at school", she told them, "thinks the Führer is wonderful. He's making everyone respect Germany. We were made to sing the Horst-Wesel (the Nazi anthem), for today our Head Mistress told us the whole world hears us."

Hedwig's viewpoint horrified Golda but she saw the irony of it all. Her Jewish daughter was doing what she wanted her to do; to behave as an Aryan, and she seemed to be doing it well!

Now everyone hoped that the Führer's demands had finally been settled, and in a message broadcast over the wireless for all the world to hear, he delighted them by saying "I have no more territorial claims in Europe." The whole world sighed with relief, though wiser heads urged re-armament, for by now Germany had a large and well equipped army, navy and air force, tried in battle in the Spanish Civil War.

In the German armed forces morale was at an all-time high. Adolf Hitler had made a defeated, disunited nation wracked by high inflation and massive unemployment, feel great again. Through his masterly leadership Germany had regained the Rhineland, achieved the forbidden union with Austria and had occupied the Sudetenland, liberating the oppressed Germans from Czech persecution. And all this had been done without a shot being fired! The military adored him. Even the General Staff, earlier concerned about international reaction to German occupancy of the Rhineland and his march into Austria, were impressed by his undoubted success.

Klaus's nephew Horst was excited too. He had done well in the Hitler Youth, his great admiration for the Führer and outspoken support for Hitler's desire to rid the country of the Jews, had been noticed and on his eighteenth birthday, he had been singled out as a suitable S.S. candidate. He was vetted for political reliability, racial purity and, found medically fit, had begun training as an officer cadet in the Gestapo, eager to serve his great hero Adolf Hitler.

His brother Heinrich Boddenburg, now wearing naval uniform had completed his initial training at Wilhelmshaven and was serving as an

Oberfahnrich zur See, a Midshipman in the *Deutschland*, one of three new Panzerschiffs known to the English as Pocket Battleships! These were formidable vessels carrying two catapult-launched seaplanes and armed with six eleven inch guns, eight six inch guns and eight torpedo tubes. With her two sister-ships the *Admiral Scheer* and *Admiral Graf Spee* and the battleships *Bismarck, Gneisenau* and *Scharnhorst,* she formed part of a formidable surface fleet. To have joined such a mighty symbol of Germany's growing strength filled Heinrich with pride, a pride shared by many eager to avenge the so-called defeat at the hands of the British at Jutland. And his ship the *Deutschland* was no stranger to battle, for she had served as part of a four-nation Naval Non-Intervention Patrol during the Spanish Civil War. Now she was at home, based at Wilhelmshaven and flying the Flag of the Fleet Commander.

Only a few weeks after the incorporation of the Sudetenland into the German Reich, the Führer announced another goal. It was a purely anti-Semitic one; to expel all Polish Jews. On October 28th, twelve thousand were ordered out of their homes and taken by train or lorry to the border with Poland. The deportees were only allowed to take with them whatever they could carry. All other possessions, including their homes and things needed for their livelihood, had to be left behind and were acquired by the state.

Some days later seventeen-year-old Herschel a Polish student in Paris, angered by the humiliation of his Jewish parents and their sudden and unjustifiable expulsion, entered the German Embassy in Paris and in an act of vengeance, shot and seriously injured the German Third Secretary, Ernst von Rath, who later died. Hitler was outraged. In retaliation he ordered a physical attack on the homes and synagogues of Jews in Germany, Austria and the Sudetenland. Starting in the early hours of November 10th, the Gestapo accompanied by members of the German Labour Front, swept through the towns in an orgy of violence, damaging and setting fire to Jewish shops, houses and synagogues.

Kristallnacht, the Night of the Broken Glass as it came to be called, lasted for fifteen hours, but in that relatively short time some two hundred synagogues were set on fire, seven-and-a-half thousand Jewish shops looted and countless Jewish homes ransacked, and any furniture not looted was piled up in the streets and burnt. Almost one hundred Jews were murdered that night and over the next few days twenty thousand were arrested and interned in the Concentration Camps at Sachsenhausen, Buchenwald and Dachau.

The following day German newspapers portrayed the orgy of violence and destruction as a righteous retribution enacted upon an evil section of the community and wrote of the need to purge the nation of the canker of Jewry. Herman Goering, the second most powerful man in the Nazi hierarchy, added to the misery of the surviving Jews by issuing a decree ordering Jews to make good at their own expense the damage done to their synagogues and property and ruled that all money received as a result of insurance claims and the like was to be handed over to the German Government.

The events of Kristallnacht were welcomed by the Nazis, who praised the Führer for his decisive action, but a minority were disturbed by the seemingly unwarranted killing, brutality and destruction meted out to the Jews. However, in the atmosphere of fear now gripping the nation, they kept silent. No-one dared criticise the Führer. The international press however could not be restrained, and over the following days proclaimed its outrage, horror and disgust at the events of Kristallnacht. On the morning after, the leading article in *The Times* declared:

'No foreign propagandist bent on blackening Germany before the world, could outdo the tale of burning and beatings, of blackguardly assaults upon defenceless and innocent people, which disgraced that country yesterday.'

Such comments by the international press were not welcomed by the Nazis and those newspapers that criticised Kristallnacht were removed from circulation. But Kristallnacht became a turning point in how Hitler and his Nazi Party were perceived abroad, and many could no longer condone his unwarranted persecution of the Jews, though such feelings did not result in any worthwhile support or relief.

Chapter 17

Golda had been traumatised by Kristallnacht. Was there to be no end to the persecution of the Jews? Was it to be like the Russian pogrom, when half a million Jews were murdered? She wept in despair. Why, why are the Jews persecuted so? Why are they murdered just because they're Jewish? Why does Yahweh allow Hitler to persecute and murder us so? We Jews constantly plead for his protection from Hitler's wrath. Does he not hear us? Why does he ignore us so? Whatever have we done to make him so angry? Maybe some have worshipped money and success and have forgotten Him and His Covenant, but many like my dear father Chaim have remained faithful. And if Yahweh were to look, surely he would see how on the Sabbath our synagogues are full to bursting. At least they were before they were burnt down on Kristallnacht. So why, why has Yahweh forsaken his chosen people?

Has he never forgiven us Jews for our refusal to recognise Jesus as the Messiah? For crucifying him? Is that why we Jews have been persecuted throughout the ages? God has used mortals before to do his will, to punish the Jews. Is he using Hitler like he did Nebuchadnezzar, to punish us now? Such terrible thoughts had bedevilled her before, but now she was beginning to think they might be true. Her prayers, it seemed, would go unanswered and all she could do was to be thankful that her beloved son Moshe was safe in Palestine and her dear brother Benjamin and Ruth safe in Switzerland. But what about her daughter? She'd delivered that form they'd signed to her Headmistress a week ago. They'd delayed returning it as long as possible, but after Hedwig had been reminded twice they'd had to give it in. Now in perpetual fear, they awaited its consequences. What would happen to them when they discovered she and Hedwig were Jews? She dared not think! And now more than ever before, she was certain that

Hedwig must go; only in another country would she be safe. Now at last, she might be able to persuade Hedwig she must go? And she herself? She would never go without Klaus.

When she voiced such fears to Klaus, he kept saying Hedwig might be expelled from her school, but that was all. However, nothing would allow him to condone the brutal carnage of Kristallnacht.

"Surely," he said, "no decent person could. We can only hope that now Hitler has created his Greater Germany and wreaked his vengeance for the murder of that diplomat in Paris, he'll be satisfied, but" he continued, "neither she, nor Hedwig nor he himself, must voice any criticism of Hitler or the Nazis. The Gestapo have eyes and ears everywhere!" That was all he would say. He was becoming ever more detached and difficult to talk to! She was sure something else must be worrying him but when she plucked up courage to ask, all he said was "I've got problems at work." And he had! His innovative idea of rotating the tail fin needed careful design work, and progress was slow.

The next day when he was asked into Otto's office, he found him smiling.

"I've had a letter from the Reich Ministry of Aviation. It says the Ministry is very interested in the new design and is intrigued by the proposal to rotate the tail fin. 'This innovative design,' the Reich Marshal declares 'shows the genius of the German Aryan race'. He wishes to visit Junkers on November 18th, to be briefed on the design and its progress."

Klaus was gratified by Goering's interest and though preparing for his visit would add to his heavy workload, he knew the presentation had to be clear and convincing. Herr Goering had to be impressed by his efforts!

After Kristallnacht, Golda's days were full of fear and uncertainty. She dreaded to think what the Nazis would do next. Hedwig was frightened too and wanted to miss school, but Golda had insisted she went. Coming home that night, she told her many girls at school supported Kristallnacht and seemed unaware of the human suffering. She said they viewed the Jews as little more than animals! And that night Klaus came home late as usual looking even more tired and worn.

The design of the Ju187 was Top Secret, so he was unable to tell Golda about it and its problems, nor could he mention Hermann Goering's visit tomorrow. He pleaded for an early night and almost immediately had fallen into a deep sleep. But sleep avoided Golda, the terrible events of Kristallnacht still plagued her, but at last she drifted off, only to be woken by loud and repeated knocking on the front door.

"Achtung, achtung. Öffnen die Tur, zu offnen. Dies ist der Gestapo"*

Klaus was up in an instant and grabbing his dressing gown headed quickly for the stairs. Terrified, Golda followed him. She saw Klaus opening the front door and S.S. men bursting in. They seized Klaus.

"You are Herr Klaus Boddenburg?" the Gestapo officer demanded, pointing his Mauser pistol at him.

"Yes, but why are you invading my house?"

"Because Herr Boddenburg I am arresting you for breaching the Reich Citizenship Law. Your wife here is a Jew and so is your daughter Hedwig. Get some clothes." With that he bundled Klaus up the stairs and stood over him while he dressed.

A terrified Hedwig appeared and flung herself into her mother's arms, "What are they doing?"

"They're arresting Daddy."

Klaus re-appeared, prodded by the Mauser. He stopped and kissed them both. "Don't worry," he said. "If I'm not home in a few days talk to my brother Wolfgang." Then he was pushed away.

"Where are you taking my husband?" she screamed.

"To Buchenwald."

At Junkers, Otto Tauber had arrived early. The great Herr Goering, was coming at 10 o'clock and he wanted to make sure all was ready. He'd been to the conference room where the projector and screen had been rigged and the chairs laid out. The steward was already there with coffee, biscuits and wine, but there was no sign of Klaus. Surely he should be here checking all was ready! Worried he made his way to Klaus's office, but still there was no sign of him. He found one of his assistants and asked where Klaus might be.

The assistant shook his head. "We don't know where he is. We thought he'd be in early. We've looked in the hangar, but he's not there. Perhaps he's not come in yet".

"Really?" Otto looked at his watch. It was five minutes to nine and Herr Goering would be arriving in an hour's time. "Could he be ill?" he asked. The other shook his head.

"Wouldn't have thought so, he seemed well enough yesterday."

Now very concerned, Otto headed for his own office. He rang for his Secretary.

"Guten Tag, Herr Tauber."

"Guten Tag, Frau Lutter. There's no sign of Herr Boddenburg this morning and he's due to make a presentation to Herr Goering in an hour's time. Do you have his telephone number?

"Ja, mein Herr."

"Good, well ring him, tell him to hurry and find out why he's late."

She sped off. Otto waited impatiently; it seemed an age before she returned.

"I had trouble getting through, mein Herr. There was no answer at first, but I kept on trying and at last the phone was answered. It was Frau Boddenburg. She sounded distressed, very distressed. I managed to calm her a little and enquired about Herr Boddenburg, but I couldn't understand what she was saying. She was sobbing, she was hysterical! She kept saying they've taken him. Somehow I assured her we were very worried about her husband and asked her who had taken him. The Gestapo, she replied, the Gestapo. Now I began to understand why she was in such a state!"

"The Gestapo? Oh my God. Did she tell you why?"

"She mumbled something about the Reich Citizenship Law. Do you know what that is?"

"No, not really, it concerns the Jews, I believe. Did she tell you where they'd taken him?"

"Yes, Buchenwald."

"My God! That's one of the new Concentration Camps. This is serious." He glanced at his watch. Goering would be here in twenty-five minutes. Hastily he called an urgent meeting with his fellow directors. They'd better know! Perhaps they might suggest what they could do about Goering!

None could suggest who could make the presentation, other than Klaus. The whole project was Top Secret and only those who had a need to know, knew anything about it and even then, they were only conversant with their own particular part. Only Klaus knew the whole picture! All agreed honesty was the best plan, in fact it seemed the only one! Otto should be truthful with Herr Goering and explain what had happened. But Otto was terrified of the great man's reaction and with only ten minutes before Herr Goering's arrival, he ended the meeting and with fear and trepidation went to the main entrance to greet him. He saw the Mercedes coming through the entrance gates. There were three of them. As they drew to a halt, armed S.S. men leaped from the first and last vehicles as Goering stepped leisurely out of the middle one.

Otto raised his right hand in the traditional Nazi salute. "Heil Hitler," he shouted. Goering raised his right arm in return. "Heil Hitler," he said.

"Welcome mein Herr to Junkers. Your visit is a great honour for us."

The great man nodded, "Vielen Dank*, I am interested in this novel project of yours."

Otto lead him to his office where his secretary was ready to offer him refreshments. Goering settled himself in an armchair and began to sip his coffee, while Otto took a deep breath to steady his nerve.

"We have a problem, mein Herr."

Goering gave him a quizzical look. "Problem?" There was air of aggression in his voice. "I hope it's not with the Ju187".

"No, no, mein Herr, it's to do with Herr Boddenburg. He is the chief designer of the Ju187."

"Well, where is he? I'm waiting for him to tell me all about his new design."

"I'm sorry to tell you mein Herr, he was arrested last night by the Gestapo."

"Arrested! Why? Why has he been arrested?"

"His wife says it's to do with the Reich Citizenship Law."

"The Reich Citizenship Law? He's not a Jew is he?"

"No, most certainly not, mein Herr."

"What about his wife?"

"She's no Jew either. Both Herr Boddenburg and his wife worship in the same Roman Catholic Church as I and my family do."

The great man didn't respond. He seemed lost in thought. "Mm," eventually he spoke. "Boddenburg, yes I remember him. He was a pilot in the war, though not in my squadron. He had a few kills before he himself was shot down, I believe. I came across him a few years ago during the test flight of the Focke-Wulf Goldfinch, one of the first aeroplanes we built in Germany after the war. He was the chief designer and his Goldfinch has proved itself to be a good plane and is an excellent trainer for the Luftwaffe." He paused as he marshalled his memories. "Yes, and it was he who sorted out the problems with the Goshawk. That was why we sent him to you to correct the design faults in the Stuka, and it was he who made it the outstanding dive-bomber it is."

He gave Otto Tauber a piercing look. "Boddenburg's an outstanding engineer and now he's come up with this novel design. We can't have him rotting in some concentration camp. Germany needs his talents to build a modern Luftwaffe", he paused. "Where did the Gestapo take him?"

"To Buchenwald."

"Right, get the Commandant of Buchenwald on the phone. I want to speak to him."

A few minutes later Otto's phone rang. It was his secretary. "I have the Commandant of Buchenwald on the phone." Otto thanked her and passed the phone to Goering, who drew himself up in his seat.

"Who am I talking to?" he demanded.

"Standartenführer Gustav Wirth, Commandant Buchenwald, mein Herr."

"I am told that Herr Klaus Boddenburg was arrested last night and brought to Buchenwald. Is that so?"

"Mein Herr, over the last twenty-four hours we have had many brought in. I must check my records. Will you kindly wait a moment?"

The great man gave a grudging response and held the instrument to his ear, but as the minutes ticked by he became ever more impatient. Finally Gustav Wirth spoke.

"Yes mein Herr, Klaus Boddenburg is being held here."

"Well, he is to be released. He is an irreplaceable aircraft designer, who has a vital role in the production of aircraft for the Luftwaffe. Release him at once."

"But, but, but mein Herr I cannot release him on the authority of a telephone call. You must understand that. This could be an elaborate plan to free the prisoner from his just detention. I ask your forbearance mein Herr. How do I know you really are Herr Goering?"

The great man was becoming visibly infuriated. "But I am. Here ask the Managing Director of Junkers to confirm it."

But Gustav Wirth could not, dare not accept such dubious confirmation. If he was talking to an imposter and on his orders released the prisoner, he would surely be thrown into a Concentration Camp himself!

"Mein Herr, you must understand I cannot accept your order over the phone. If you are Herr Goering I will do as you say, but only if I receive a letter delivered to me by your S.S. guards instructing me to release Klaus Boddenburg into their custody. I shall need a receipt for him, then he can be delivered to you."

"Standartenführer, you are a wise man to be so careful. I will do as you ask. My guards will be with you tomorrow." He put the phone down.

"Herr Tauber, you will have your chief designer with you in a few days. I will have him released into my hands at the Reich Ministry of Aviation, where he can brief me on his revolutionary design. Then I will send him here to you."

Chapter *18*

Buchenwald! That's where they said they were taking him. Buchenwald, one of the new concentration camps, where they took the Jews. "Oh! My God," Golda shuddered. "What will they do to him? Will I ever see him again?"

Hedwig clung to her as if she was drowning, "Why, why have they taken Daddy?"

"Because of that form we signed for you to join the League. It showed both you and I are Jews."

"Oh!" Hedwig wiped the tears from her frightened eyes. "What will they do to Daddy?"

"Hedwig, I don't know. I daren't think! In Hitler's eyes being married to a Jew is a crime."

"What will happen to us, Mummy?"

Questions, questions, how could she answer them? Her world had become full of fear, turmoil and uncertainty. Desperately she tried to comfort her daughter, but her own fear hindered her. To console her all she could do was to share her bed with her, but those questions continued to torment them as they struggled to sleep.

Golda awoke from a fitful doze and the terrifying events of the night returned to haunt her. Would she ever see her beloved Klaus again? How could she live without him? Without ever seeing him again, holding him, talking to him, being with him? The future terrified her. The questions overwhelmed her. Were there any answers? Perhaps death was the only answer. No more fear, no more anxiety, no more suffering, surely nothing but peace! No, no, death wasn't the answer, no not yet. There was Hedwig. Hedwig with her whole life before her, yet saddled with Jewish ancestors and a target of Nazi hate. Somehow she must save her. But how? The questions multiplied! Then suddenly another came. Money! How would she be able to pay the rent? Call my brother, if I'm not back in a few days, she remembered Klaus saying. In a few days? How could she wait that long? She must call him today.

The clock was surely slow! She checked her watch, no it was only half past eight. She waited impatiently rehearsing what she would say to Wolfgang, while watching the minute hand make its slow progress. Nine o'clock came, he must be in his office now! She picked up the phone, but almost immediately replaced it. She couldn't ring now, she must let him settle at his desk. The waiting seemed never-ending. The minute hand reached the figure five. She braced herself, another five minutes! Then the phone rang!

Who could it be? It continued to ring without ceasing. Frightened, she picked it up. A voice said "Hello, Hello. Is that Frau Boddenburg?" In a moment of panic she couldn't answer. The voice came again. It was a woman's voice. "Hello, Hello. Am I speaking to Frau Boddenburg?" It was a woman's voice. It gave her courage.

"Yes, yes. I'm Frau Boddenburg."

"Thank you", the urgency of the voice became apparent. "It's the Secretary of the Managing Director of Junkers speaking. We are concerned about Herr Boddenburg. He hasn't come into his office today and we are very worried. Is he ill?

"My husband?" Golda could hear voice tremble. "My husband Klaus," she began to sob uncontrollably. "They've taken him, they've taken him," she howled.

"Taken him? Who's taken him? Is he in hospital?"

"No, no! The Gestapo came early this morning and arrested him."

"The Gestapo? Oh! My dear. Do you know where they have taken him?

"To Buchenwald," she sobbed, "I don't know if I'll ever see him again."

"Oh! My dear how terrible. I am so sorry for you, but I must tell Herr Tauber the awful news. Good bye."

Golda put the phone down. What would Herr Tauber do? Could he do anything to help? She shook her head miserably. She looked at the clock. Five minutes to ten. Picking up the phone she dialled the number.

"Guten tag. Herr Boddenburg's Secretary speaking."

Golda took an anxious breath. "May I speak to Herr Wolfgang Boddenburg please?"

"I am sorry but Herr Boddenburg is not in the office today and won't be until Tuesday. May I take a message for him?"

"No, no thank you, I'll ring again on Tuesday."

She put the phone down and closed her eyes in despair. "Yahweh if you are the God of Jacob and our father Abraham, please help me. Please, please bring Klaus back to me." She sat in silence repeating her prayer over and over again. Then a feeling of utter exhaustion came over her, nothing she could do would bring him back.

Hedwig appeared half-dressed with tangled hair. "What can we do, Mummy?" Golda put a protective arm around her and began telling her about the morning's telephone calls.

"Well," she said wiping her eyes, "Junkers know about Klaus and at least the woman who rang seemed sympathetic."

"Do you think they can do anything to help?"

That question had already joined the hoard of others which plagued her. As she struggled to find an answer, the telephone rang again. Warily she picked it up.

"Hello"

"Hello, the voice said, "Is that Frau Boddenburg?"

A ray of hope surged through her. It was the same voice. Did it have any news of Klaus?

"Yes, I'm Frau Boddenburg."

"Good. This is the Secretary of the Managing Director of Junkers again. I have some news about Herr Boddenburg."

News? Was it good news or bad? "Is he safe, they haven't harmed him?"

"No, no my dear. He is to be released tomorrow and will be brought to our offices, when we will return him to you."

"He will be released? You say he'll be released tomorrow? But how can you be sure?"

"My dear, his release has been ordered by the Reich Minister of Aviation Herr Hermann Goering. He says his work is very important, but I cannot tell you more as it's secret. You must trust me, my dear. I promise I will ring you tomorrow afternoon when we expect your husband here at Junkers, then I'll tell you what time he'll be home with you."

"Oh! It's a miracle. I can hardly believe what you're saying. Tell me it's really true?"

"Yes, my dear it's true, really true. Trust me."

Chapter *19*

That woman said she'd ring. But she hadn't and now it was nearly six o'clock!

"That phone call yesterday, it was real wasn't it Mummy? They really did say Daddy would be released?"

"Yes, yes, Hedwig. That's what she said." At the time she'd found it hard to believe, but now? Was that woman really the Managing Director's Secretary? She said she was, but how could she be sure? That worrying thought troubled her again. What if she was some imposter? Some cruel Nazi intent on hurting her for the fun of it? Was it something they might do for a laugh?

They waited impatiently with growing despair. Then they heard the sound of an engine. Rushing to the window they saw a big black car drawing to a halt. A door opened and she saw him, her beloved Klaus. She ran out and threw her arms around him. "Klaus darling," she sobbed, "I thought I'd never see you again!"

"Dearest and I you. It's a miracle." He stretched out his arm to hug his daughter too. "And it's wonderful to see you too, dearest Hedwig."

Golda drew herself back to look at the husband she thought she'd lost. "But what have they done to you?" Tenderly she touched his bruised face.

"Oh! They hit me during my interrogation, but it's only a bruise."

"Let me bathe it for you." She pulled him in and rushed off to get water and a dressing.

"Daddy it must have been horrid."

"Yes Hedwig, it was, but luckily it didn't last long!"

As Golda dressed his battered face, he told them that Herr Goering, the Reich Chancellor for Aviation, had ordered him to be released.

"It was unbelievable!" he said. "Yesterday he came to Junkers for me to brief him on the new plane I've been designing for the Luftwaffe. But I wasn't there! Otto the Managing Director told him I'd been arrested by the Gestapo and Goering was astonished and enraged. Somehow I seem to have found favour with him, for he told Otto he couldn't have an outstanding engineer like me rotting in some concentration camp. He said Germany needed talents such as mine, to build his modern Luftwaffe. Then I'm told he rang Buchenwald and ordered my release and this morning I was collected by his men and taken to his office in Berlin. There he wanted me to tell him about the new plane. Well, without the drawings and papers I'd prepared, I couldn't do a good job, but it seemed to satisfy him and he wants to see the plane later. I just can't believe my luck, dearest wife and daughter," he shook his head in amazement, "That plane seems to have saved us!"

It was indeed incredible! Her loving husband Klaus had been rescued by none other than Goering, one of the highest ranking Nazis! Were his talents so valuable? The thought that Klaus seemed to be so important gave her hope for the future. Might it be possible that now they could live without fear? She hugged him, it was the most wonderful turn of events! But in bed that night Klaus was less optimistic. While his engineering talents might possibly keep him and her safe he told her, he was not so sure about Hedwig. "It mightn't work for her, dearest. Our cover as a Christian family has been blown and sooner or later Hedwig will want to live a life of her own, to find work, to marry but," he hesitated, "you know as well as I do, for a Jew in Hitler's Germany that's only a dream. She must go, or sooner or later she'll be in Buchenwald too!" Sadly Golda knew he was right! "But how do we persuade her, dearest?"

It was a problem she'd struggled with before, but she tried afresh over the next few days. Now however, she began to feel more hopeful, for Hedwig had been petrified, indeed traumatised by the Gestapo's arrest of her father and his incarceration in Buchenwald. And unlike the murder of her grandfather by the S.A., or the escape of Uncle Benjamin and Auntie Ruth, it seemed that at last Hitler's irrevocable hatred of the Jews had been brought home to her clearly and unmistakably! Now Golda hoped Hedwig could no longer ignore her Jewishness and feel herself to be just "ordinary", that at last she would acknowledge that she too was a target for Hitler's hatred? That his hatred was real and frightening! But nevertheless she still refused to be parted from them. "I don't want to leave you and Daddy. Won't his favour with Herr Goering protect us too?" she asked plaintively.

"Your father," Golda told her, "may well be protected, but as for you and me? I don't know. Maybe I'll be lucky, but dearest we fear for you. Hedwig darling, for your own safety and future you must go. Daddy and I beg you to go. You must! Already you're too frightened to go to school. What future do you have in Germany as a Jew? Only misery, fear and brutality! Dearest Hedwig, please say you will go." But Hedwig said nothing.

However Golda comforted herself, Hedwig hadn't said she wouldn't! But then she began to worry that if she did agree, how would they find a country to give her refuge? Never would she let her go like Benjamin and Ruth. There must be better way, a safer way.

A week or so later to her joy, it seemed a way might be found, for she spotted an article almost hidden away on the inside of the newspaper.

Kindertransport

It has been announced that the British Government will fund the transport of Jewish children under the age of seventeen, to Britain and arrange volunteer host families for them. Parents wishing to avail themselves of this offer should apply in person to the British Embassy in Berlin or to one of the British Consular Offices in Dusseldorf, Munich, Hamburg, Hanover, Bremen, Frankfurt, Kiel, Nuremburg and Stuttgart. Passports and entry permits will not be required, but valid birth certificates are.

What a wonderful and God-sent opportunity this seemed to be! And thank God, Hedwig was only sixteen! She discussed it eagerly with Klaus and together they prevailed upon Hedwig, telling her what a wonderful chance it was for her to escape from Hitler's hatred, how Britain was noted for its tolerance and how she must not refuse. Finally to their joy she had reluctantly and tearfully agreed. Concerned that many other parents would want their children to be included and certain that numbers would be limited, Golda and Hedwig set off for Berlin the very next day. Finding the

Embassy had been difficult but when finally they arrived, to her horror she saw it was besieged by a long queue of parents and children. Hastily they joined the queue, Golda praying for Yahweh to help them and after what seemed an age it was their turn to be directed into an office and questioned by a middle-aged, bespectacled Englishman. Initially he seemed concerned with Hedwig's non-Jewish surname, but after Golda had given him her Jewish maiden name Leibowitz, and having told him she had married a Gentile, he seemed content that Hedwig was Jewish. She saw him entering her answers on a form, then he laid his pen down. "Tell me please, what anti-Jewish persecution have you and your family suffered?"

She told him how her father had been killed by the S.A., how her brother had been dismissed from his position as a professor in Bremen university, about the expulsion of her son and daughter from school and of the arrest and imprisonment of her husband. Finally she said, "Our only crime is that we are Jews."

He seemed concerned. "The British Government is aware of the plight of Jews in Hitler's Germany. We offer you our sympathy and are pleased to help with the Kindertransport scheme, though many of us know we should be doing more, a great deal more."

He made another note on his form, then he spoke again, "You have a son I understand, what about him?"

She told him Moshe was safe from the Nazis; that he had gone to Palestine under the Ha'avara Scheme.

She saw him writing again, then he smiled, "I'm pleased to tell you, your daughter Hedwig is now included in the Kindertransport scheme." And giving her a certificate, he directed her to another room where a smiling lady told them about her daughter's travel arrangements.

"Hedwig must be at Dessau railway station on Friday June 12th", she told them. "Her train will leave promptly at half past nine for IJmuden and the ferry to England. Please remember that Hedwig may only take one suitcase with her."

As they were ushered to the door, Golda thanked her and the British people for their kindness and generosity. "We are very grateful, very grateful indeed but before we go, I have one last question. Please tell me who will be Hedwig's host family and where do they live."

"I am very sorry," she replied, "I am unable to tell you. Your daughter will not be allocated to one of the many families who wish to host the Kindertransport evacuees, until she arrives in Harwich. Only then will Hedwig know."

On the train home they hardly spoke, both had much to ponder. Hedwig sat in the corner, her face reflecting her misery and anxiety as question after question begged an answer, 'Where will she be going? What will England be like? Will her host family be nice? "Will she ever see Mummy and Daddy again? But as yet there were no answers!

But Golda felt strangely at peace. It was what she'd wanted for a long time, for her daughter to be offered safe refuge from Hitler's murderous persecution. At last a place had been found for her and in England too, a country believed to be tolerant to Jews. Well, she should be pleased and of course she was, but the price? A price too much? After Friday she may never see her again! Never see her blossom into womanhood. Never see her married and a mother. Never knowingly be blessed with grandchildren. It was a heavy price, an exorbitant one, but one she must pay! She had paid a similar price for her son Moshe, now she must do the same to ensure Hedwig's survival. Her family was being torn apart by that fiend Hitler, she prayed one day his soul would rot in everlasting hell.

Chapter 20

After three years of bitter fighting, the Spanish civil war had at last come to an end and General Franco had been declared Head of State with full dictatorial powers. A few weeks later in June 1939, the German volunteers of the Condor Legion, some fifteen hundred in all, returned from Spain and paraded through the streets of Berlin. Hitler took the salute and in his speech of welcome told them that their success in Spain was 'a lesson for his enemies'. Not only was it a lesson for his enemies, but it was also a lesson in modern warfare to be learnt by the German armed forces, now rapidly being expanded.

For Junkers and Otto Tauber the build-up of the Luftwaffe was excellent for business, with production lines working at full capacity. The Ju88 the Schnellbomber, had a full order book and despite its vulnerability to enemy fighters, so had the Ju87, the Stuka. And within its own secret hangar the revolutionary Ju187 was being assembled under the direction of Klaus. Her rotating tail plane had been tested in the wind tunnel, her retracting undercarriage had been fitted and a more powerful engine the Jumo 213A developing 1,776 horsepower, had been installed. This together with the reduced drag gained by retracting the landing gear, would give a better speed, possibly as much as five hundred kilometres an hour, an increase of about twenty per cent on the Stuka. But would that be enough to lessen its vulnerability to enemy fighters? Klaus had his doubts! If only he'd been able to start afresh with that earlier idea he'd had at Focke-Wulf, of a monoplane fighter. He'd have done away with the rear guns, relying on speed and manoeuvrability for the plane's defence. Such a plane would be better in all ways than the Ju187, but he'd been overruled, the Stuka had had to be modified.

Well, now everything rested on the outcome of tomorrow's test flight. He was as certain as anyone could be at this stage that the Ju187 would fly, though handling the plane during tail fin rotation could test the pilot. He waited eagerly for Manfred's comment on that in his test flight report. And what speed would the Ju187 achieve? He expected five hundred kilometres an hour, which was only an increase of a fifth! Would that be enough to make the Ju187 markedly less vulnerable? The Ju187's vulnerability from attack by enemy fighters was critical and his favour with Hermann Goering depended on its reduction!

But tonight there was nothing more to be done, so he cleared his desk, locked his office, found his car and drove home. There was the usual traffic jam at the junction of Bodelschwingh Strasse and Franziska-Gratz Strasse, and there as usual was the paper boy, with his placard reading:

FÜHRER DEMANDS
DANZIG AND CORRIDOR BE RETURNED
TO GERMANY

He called the boy over and bought a copy. Arriving home he searched for Golda wondering indeed hoping, that she might be a little more cheerful tonight. Hedwig had been gone for nearly three weeks now and still she grieved. She'd come to terms with the loss of Moshe or so he thought, but with Hedwig it seemed her grief would never end. She seemed to mope all day and hardly ever went out. He prayed things would get better. Last Sunday he'd succeeded in persuading her to come to church. She must do, he'd told her if she is to maintain her claim to be Christian! Of course questions had been asked about her absence, some enquiring about her health, and Hedwig's continued absence had been noticed too. They'd both agreed to say she'd gone to Munich to stay with her aunt for some tuition on her violin. Whether or not it had satisfied their curiosity, he couldn't say. However he'd had to tell Father Ulrich the truth, though he took care to do so in the privacy of the confessional.

Golda was in the garden. Did he detect a slight improvement in her malaise? He kissed her. "How are you darling?" She ignored his question. "There'll be war this time for sure," she said. "Have you heard the news?"

"About Poland? Yes. The papers say he wants Danzig and the Polish Corridor returned."

"Yes, yet only the other day, he told the world he had no further territorial demands in Europe! Do you think England and France will let him hoodwink them again?"

"I don't know. But they don't want a war, that's for sure!"

"Well Klaus dear, I'm sure war is now nearer than it's ever been."

He nodded, "You're probably right, darling."

"If I am right, I'm truly thankful that our two beloved children are gone. Like you I miss them terribly, but I thank God they won't be caught up in a war and are no longer a target for Hitler's hatred."

He gave her a hug. "Yes beloved, we have much to be thankful for."

Strangely that evening they were happier. Could it be that Golda's grief was at last beginning to ebb? That it was moderated by her thanks that Hedwig and Moshe were safe?

As they retired to bed, she surprised him by asking "How's your special plane?" Since Hedwig had gone, she'd not shown the slightest interest in his work!

"Well it's hush hush dearest. We're working on a revolutionary design and we're all praying it'll fly."

"Oh! Dearest I hope it does. When will it have its first flight?"

"Tomorrow."

"Is Herr Goering still interested in it?"

"Yes. In fact he's coming to see the test flight."

And he did, and as before the red carpet had been laid out to welcome him and he'd been shown the Ju187 while last minute preparations for its first flight were being made.

"She looks vicious enough! That's what we want, eh?" Goering laughed and so dutifully did Otto and he. The great man turned to Klaus.

"What's her top speed?"

"We think she'll do at least 500 kilometres an hour in level flight, mein Herr, possibly more."

"Oh! I'd hoped she'd do better than that. The English Hurricane is reputed to do five hundred and fifty."

They heard the engine start. It was the Jumo 211A he'd fitted. It would give 40% more power than the Jumo 210 in the Stuka, but would that be enough to power the heavier Ju187 to 500 kilometres an hour? Its rhythmic purr comforted Klaus, it was a fine engine. He prayed it would. With the hatch cover open, he could see Manfred Hufendiek in the cockpit, saw him wave the chocks away and taxi to the take-off position. As the plane turned into the wind and stopped, he knew Manfred was carrying out his pre-flight checks and as he expected, he saw the elevators and the tail rudder moving. Then the engine roared, the plane sped down the runway and was airborne. All eyes were glued to it as it climbed, levelled out and turned towards them. The distant speck grew as it drew closer and then this weird-looking aeroplane he'd designed flew past and he could see its tail fin protruding from the underside of the fuselage. It had worked and the plane was flying straight and level!

"That's the strangest looking plane I've ever seen!" Goering muttered before turning to Klaus. "But your strange plane seems to fly well enough!"

"Thank you, mein Herr. So it seems. Let's hope Manfred has found it easy to handle!"

By now the plane was high in the sky and as planned Manfred put her into a steep bombing dive. As the plane dived, everyone could hear the screech of its sirens that had become part of a dive-bomber's psychological armoury. Then Manfred pulled out of the dive and to everyone's relief all seemed well! Only the landing remained. For that Manfred would have to check that the interlock prevented him from lowering the undercarriage until the tail fin had been rotated to the "up" position. This was perhaps the biggest test yet. Through his binoculars he watched the plane turn onto the down-wind leg, the tail fin being rotated to the up position and saw to his relief the undercarriage being lowered. Reassured he saw the plane turn onto his final approach leg, begin to lose height and make a perfect landing.

Everyone was talking about the success of test flight, including the great man himself. He seemed impressed.

"Your revolutionary design seems to work well, Herr Boddenburg, but is she fast enough?"

His qualified praise worried Klaus but then he was delighted when Manfred, having been introduced to Goering, told him the plane had achieved five hundred and ten kilometres an hour in level flight.

But the great man didn't seem so pleased. "Mn," Goering had muttered. "the English Hurricane," he said, "is reputed to do five hundred and fifty and the Spitfire is thought to be faster."

Chapter 21

What a moon it was! Moshe remembered that great harvest moon that lit up the night as he'd followed Boas and his friend Tzadok up the tower and onto the lookout platform.

"It's beautiful, isn't it?" Boaz said. "We can see for miles, so they won't attack tonight! But keep your eyes skinned, you never know what the Arabs will do!"

"Shall I test the lamp?" Tzadok asked. As Boaz nodded he switched on the search light. In the moonlight it wasn't very effective nor was it needed, but when a cloud hid the moon, it shone out bright and clear. It had been three weeks since the tower had been erected and with rifle in hand he'd begun another night's duty as lookout.

Now a year or so later, he recalled with pride how he'd helped build the kibbutz with its tower and stockade. It had been one of the first things he and Tzadok had had to do when they'd arrived after that long train journey from Berlin to Baghdad and that final leg on the Haifa line. He and Tzadok had been excited; at last they were in Palestine, eagerly scanning the land as it slid by. As they'd learnt at Eberswalde, much of it was dry and arid, unlike the green and fertile land they knew at home. They'd seen little sign of habitation, though now and then little groups of buildings set around a tower would come into view, and occasionally they saw the black tented camps of the Bedouin. And now and then a shepherd and his flock could be seen searching the dry hills for pasture. That last leg of their long journey had seemed never-ending with the train stopping constantly at every station, stations hardly more than huts! But at last it was theirs. Just another tiny hut but it bore the name Yagur. As Moshe read it again to make sure, Tzadok had pointed to a man waiting for them.

"Moshe Boddenburg, Tzadok Karlstadt.," the man kept calling.

"Shalom, welcome to Yagur," he'd shaken their hands, "My name is Boas Schonfeld, our kibbutz is not far". As they'd walked he told them it had been built only five years ago, that it was a couple of miles away and was named Kfar Ha Horesh. In the heat of the sun when the track led them through a plantation of young trees, they were thankful for the shade. Boas had pointed to them proudly. "They're ours, they're orange trees and on this side the ones with silvery grey leaves are olive trees. We've had no olives yet, we have to be patient, but they'll give us plenty in time. And over there behind the oranges we're growing wheat."

With their heavy rucksacks it seemed they'd been walking forever, but then Boas had pointed to a tower and a number of white buildings set among trees. "There it is. That's our kibbutz, Kfar Ha Horesh." And finally they'd arrived to be welcomed by the Chairman.

"We need strong young men like you, to help us build our new kibbutz, so we're very pleased to have you with us," he'd told them. "And Boas here will be your mentor and introduce you to life in a Kibbutz."

And Boas had taught them all about their new life as kibbutzniks and in doing so had become a great friend. And it was he who'd told them a month or so later they'd be moving to a new kibbutz at Alonim a few miles away.

"When will we be going?" he'd asked.

"Well, Moshe," Boas had chuckled. "It has to be built first and you two are going to help build it!"

"Good," Tzadok had grinned, "when do we start?"

"When we're ready! You see when we start building, we can't expect any help or support or even protection from our British masters. The bastards have reneged on the promise Balfour made to establish a national home for us Jews here in Palestine. They're frightened of the Arabs, who want Palestine for themselves. So when we build our new kibbutz, the British will do nothing to support us and the Arabs know that! So once the Arabs see us building, they'll want to attack us."

"Well if they attack us, can't we fight back?" he'd asked.

"Yes, we'll have to, won't we?" Tzadok like him, seemed ready for a fight.

Boas had grinned at these two pugnacious youngsters.

"We must defend ourselves of course, and we may have to, but we don't want to shed blood if we can help it. And once we've built a tower like this one, and a stockade too, we can finish the rest of the building in comparative safety." He'd paused, "Now, we're sure the Arabs know we plan to build a kibbutz at Alonim, after all we've bought the land! But they don't know when we'll start building. So", he'd tapped the side of his nose with his forefinger, "we intend to surprise them, by building our tower and stockade in one day."

"Yes," he'd seen the look of surprise on their faces, "in one day! The tower will be built here in Kfar Ha Horesh, ready to be erected at Alonim on the day. And the stockade wall?" he anticipated their question. "Well, we shall build it in sections here too, ready to be transported to the new site for erection there. The tower and stockade must be completed in one day! That's how this kibbutz was built and that's how we'll build at Alonim."

Soon almost everybody had been busy building the wall sections and the tower; only those preparing and cooking the meals had been exempt. For Moshe it had been an exciting time; everyone was in high spirits, singing and joking as they worked.

"First we have to make the walls for the stockade," Boas explained. "They'll be 6 feet tall and made of two wooden walls with an eight inch gap between them. When the wall has been erected we'll fill the gap with gravel to make the walls bullet-proof."

Moshe remembered grinning, "What a good idea! How big will the stockade be?"

"Forty yards square and the tower will be forty feet tall."

Tzadok had looked surprised, "And you plan to build this in one day?"

"Yes. We'll assemble the pre-fabricated parts in one day!"

And they had! He remembered it well. The night before, everyone had gathered in the hall for the Rabbi to lead them in prayers for safety and success. The following morning they'd been called hours before dawn and after a hearty breakfast they'd set off in the darkness on the two mile march to Alonim laden with their tools. The kibbutz trucks had followed, bringing the prefabricated parts of the stockade wall.

He smiled as he remembered that when they were nearly there, the fiery red rays of the rising sun had lit up the site where the kibbutz was to be built.

"Yahweh is blessing our work," someone had shouted gleefully. Everyone was delighted, all agreed it was a good omen and soon they'd been digging holes with a will, inserting poles, attaching the prefabricated wall sections to them and clamping everything together, to make a strong stockade wall. Then the trucks had come this time laden with gravel, and all had been busy shovelling the gravel into the gap between the outer and inner walls to make the stockade wall bullet-proof. It had all gone as planned and still there'd been an hour or two of daylight left! Now they'd had to erect the tower which lay horizontally on a trailer brought by the tractor. The drill for erecting it had been practised at Kfar Ha Horesh and everyone knew his or her part, and with much pushing, shoving and heaving the tower had been raised to the vertical and secured in position. Then the dynamo and searchlight had had to be fitted and the searchlight switched on to light up the surrounding countryside. Then everyone had cheered and hugged each other. The kibbutz had been created!

The pre-fabricated accommodation huts, the dining room and kitchen, the ablution block and shelter for the animals had been assembled within the protection of the stockade wall, during the days that followed. The speed with which the kibbutz had been erected had indeed taken the Arabs by surprise and though one or two came riding by on their donkeys to inspect the new buildings, they made no attempt to attack.

Now a year or so later he felt proud to have taken part in building the Alonim kibbutz which everyone hoped would be worthy of the great new Zion, the national home for the persecuted Jews.

But while he'd been busy building his new Zion, he'd never forgotten his family and that tearful parting in Berlin. They'd agreed not to write for fear their letters might be intercepted and so confirm his mother and Hedwig were Jews. But without any news, all he could do was worry about them. Were they still safe? On the wireless he'd heard about Hitler's occupation of the Sudetenland, the brutal savagery of Kristallnacht and of his demands for the return of Danzig and the "Polish Corridor". He feared for their safety and like everyone at Alonim, wondered how Hitler's apparent determination to exterminate the Jews and dominate his neighbouring countries could be stopped. Everyone in the Kibbutz thought only a war could do so.

But it was not only in Europe where the Jews were being attacked. Their safety in Palestine was threatened by Arab raids on the more isolated kibbutzim. Such attacks had recently become more frequent. So all Arabs, especially those who showed any interest in the kibbutz and its activities, were watched with suspicion and at night the searchlight was kept busy probing the approaches. Then in August the attack came. He'd been on watch on the tower that night and as usual they'd swept the approaches with the searchlight. There was nothing to see, but shortly afterwards they'd heard the sound of rifle fire and bullets crashing into the kibbutz. They'd not been able to see their attackers, but they'd fired in the direction from which the Arab rifle fire had come. When the firing stopped they'd searched the area with the searchlight, but to no avail. Then an accommodation hut had burst into flames and they'd seen people tumbling out. Again they'd searched the surrounding area with the searchlight, but saw nothing. When more gunfire was heard, they'd seen them, three Arabs caught in the light's beam. They'd opened fire and the men fled. When the attack was over, they'd heard Tzadok groaning. Blood was pouring from his arm. He'd seen Boas tear off his shirt and had helped him apply it as a tourniquet. With the flow of blood easing, they'd lowered him to willing hands below. Happily Tzadok had survived and since then had had the doubtful honour of being the first kibbutznik at Alonim to be wounded by the Arabs!

Despite the efforts of those fighting the flames, the fire in the accommodation hut had taken some time to extinguish. Come the dawn, all that had remained was a smouldering heap of cinders, but luckily all had managed to escape unhurt.

The next morning an army patrol arrived. The British had heard of the attack and the young Subaltern in charge wanted details. He was concerned about Tzadok and his wound, but was assured he was being well nursed. Then to their surprise, he promised them some rifles and ammunition.

"We'll arrange for a member of the Haganah* to visit you and if you agree to work with them, we'll let you have some rifles and ammunition."

To Moshe it seemed a strange world! In Palestine, despite the British reneging on their promise of a land in Palestine for the Jews, the Jewish para-militaries of the Haganah were co-operating with them! That for him was a difficult pill to swallow. How he asked himself could anyone forgive them! Yet now the Jews were hoping that Britain would join France and together put an end to Hitler's evil plans. It was indeed a strange world!

Chapter 22

Like almost everyone else onboard the *Deutschland*, Midshipman Heinrich Boddenburg had no idea where the ship was going. The previous day she'd fuelled and had embarked stores and ammunition, then early in the morning of 29th August she'd sailed for exercises. But there'd been no exercises and later that day they'd left the northern-most exercise area astern and the ship's powerful diesel engines were driving her on a northerly course at twenty knots. Only the Captain and the Navigating officer seemed to know where they were bound. But with tension at breaking point with the Poles over Danzig and the corridor, Heinrich and his mates had begun to think the ship was heading for her war station. Later they were proved to be right, for at suppertime the Captain spoke to the ship's company over the broadcast system, telling them the ship was bound for the North Atlantic, so that *"should France and Britain declare war on Germany, the Deutschland will be on station ready for hostilities."*

Now in November, the *Deutschland* was once again in Wilhelmshaven secured in her familiar berth, ready for docking. Since the outbreak of war in September, she'd been on patrol in the Atlantic intercepting trade bound for enemy ports. Ordered to obey international prize rules, she had stopped and searched all the merchant ships she'd found, looking for contraband of war*. Those found to be carrying contraband were sunk, even if the vessel was from a neutral country, though the crews of such neutral ships were given time to abandon ship. But they'd had only limited success for despite stopping many ships only two had been carrying contraband. He'd been on watch on the bridge, when the first was sighted in early October. As they got closer, all could see she flew the red ensign identifying her as British. As an enemy ship there was no need to stop and search her, so with her six inch guns ready to fire, the Captain had ordered the British to abandon ship. Through his binoculars Heinrich had seen men running towards the lifeboats and the boats being lowered. Then when the lifeboats were clear and with the target barely half a mile away, the Captain gave the order to open fire. Within seconds the British ship had been hit, and only two salvos were needed before the ship was in flames and beginning to settle by the stern. For many like Heinrich, it was the first time they'd seen a seaworthy ship, which without doubt had weathered many a storm, slide stern first into the depths. It was a blow for the Fatherland, he'd felt thrilled, as if he'd scored the winning goal!

He was thankful the British had been allowed to abandon ship safely, though surprised that no effort had been made to rescue them! Instead the Captain had ordered full speed and steered westwards. Later he was to learn that the British ship had been heard giving her position and reporting the presence of a German battleship. That was clearly why the Captain wanted to clear the area as quickly as possible!

Two days later they'd found a Norwegian ship, the *Lorentz Hansen* bound for Liverpool with a cargo of wheat and sugar. Her crew was ordered to abandon ship and the *Lorentz Hansen* was quickly sent to the bottom. As her crew were neutrals, they were rescued and transferred to the next ship they'd stopped, a Danish freighter carrying no contraband and making for Copenhagen.

The *Deutschland's* two seaplanes had proved their worth in searching their area, but as November approached the weather had begun to deteriorate making the landing and recovering of the seaplanes in the rough seas difficult and without air reconnaissance it was hard to find their quarry. By then fuel was beginning to run low so it was time to make for home, but the short cut through the English Channel was not for them. That would be dangerous for it would expose them to the full strength of the British Navy and Air Force. So they'd had to take the long route through the Iceland Faeroes gap into the North Sea, and giving the British naval base at Scapa Flow in the Orkneys a wide berth. Finally they'd arrived at Wilhelmshaven to be welcomed by the Port Commander. Though some might be disappointed by their limited success, Heinrich felt he and the ship's company could be justifiably proud of what they'd achieved on their first war patrol.

Given two weeks leave, he headed home to Bremen to be welcomed with pride and joy by his mother and father pleased to have him home safely and delighted to hear that he would soon be promoted Oberleutnant zur See (Sub Lieutenant).

Wanting to hear about his brother Horst, they told him they'd only received a few letters from him, and it was clear he could not divulge much, but as far as they knew he was well and in Poland as part of the occupying force. When he asked about Auntie Golda, Uncle Klaus, Moshe and Hedwig all they could tell him was that they'd moved to Dessau, but they didn't have their new address. Despite his further questions, they could tell him no more. That worried him, for Auntie Golda and his two cousins were Jews.

Bremen seemed largely unaffected by the war, though there were fewer young men around and those that were wore some uniform or other. His mother told him there'd been the occasional air raid warning and they'd seen bombers flying overhead, but they hadn't dropped any bombs! Instead they'd unleashed a veritable shower of leaflets, propaganda leaflets. The authorities had demanded that all the leaflets be handed in to be destroyed, but his parents had kept one. They gave it him to read, but warned him it was very long winded. It most certainly was and all he managed to read was the last paragraph:

"You cannot win this war. Against you are arrayed resources and materials far greater than your own. For years you have been subjected to the most stringent censorship, and by means of an incredible system of secret police and informers the truth has been withheld from you.

Against you stands the united strength of the free peoples, who with open eyes will fight for freedom to the last. This war is as repulsive to us as it is to you, but do not forget that England, once forced into war, will wage it unwaveringly to the end. England's nerves are strong, her resources inexhaustible. We will not relent."

He laughed as he gave it back to his mother. "Who will believe that? Our Führer will have them begging for peace before long!"

Yes, he was sure Germany would win the war. But a few days later he read disturbing news in the paper:

KMS ADMIRAL GRAF SPEE

The pocket battleship Admiral Graff Spee damaged in a battle with three British cruisers, has sought temporary sanctuary in the neutral port of Montevideo to effect urgent repairs.

The *Graf Spee*, a sister ship of the *Deutschland* damaged in battle? She'd been on a similar mission as the *Deutschland*. He wondered what damage she'd suffered. It must be serious, for it had driven her into a neutral port for repairs, and the papers were saying she'd have to effect the repairs herself, for if Uruguay was to assist a belligerent, she would cease to be neutral! Involuntarily he shook his head. With the *Graf Spee* trapped in the South Atlantic far from home, the outlook seemed pretty grim.

The following day the news was even worse:

KMS ADMIRAL GRAF SPEE

With the ending of twenty-four hours sanctuary in the neutral port of Montevideo, Captain Hans Langsdorf has had no option but to take his ship to sea to face the British cruisers waiting for him. With intelligence that a British Fleet including an aircraft carrier was bearing down on him, Captain Langsdorf decided rather than fight a battle against overwhelming odds, he must scuttle his ship and save his crew from pointless death. Accordingly after clearing the harbour, and minutes after the crew was seen taking to the boats, a series of explosions erupted through the Graf Spee and its burning hull settled on the sea bed. Captain Langsdorf is reported to have shot himself in a hotel bedroom in Montevideo.

The news had shocked and dismayed him. He found it difficult to believe that Captain Langsdorf had refused to fight, that he had scuttled his ship, and that he did so before the eyes of the international press! Surely that was the act of a coward, not that of an honourable officer of the Kriegsmarine! Was that why he had committed suicide? When he returned to the *Deutschland*, he found he was not the only one who felt like that!

But for him, there was good news. His promotion had been confirmed and now on his sleeve he was able to wear that coveted single ring of gold lace surmounted by a golden star. A second less welcome letter informed him that he had been selected for U-boat training and was to report to the U-boat School at Holstein. That was not what he'd wanted. When the Kapitanleutnant (Lieutenant Commander) had spoken to him about his future career, he had told him he wanted to serve in one of the Schnellbooten, in the fast E-Boats. He was very disappointed, being cooped up in a U-boat did not appeal to him!

But there was still other news. Naval High Command had issued instructions that the *Deutschland* was to be re-named *Lutzow*! Everyone was dismayed, indeed angry that the ship should be deprived of its great name, the name of the country they loved and were proud to serve! No reason was given, but wise heads suggested that the Führer was concerned about the propaganda value to the English, should a ship named after the Fatherland be sunk in battle.

Chapter 23

Everyone was dismayed and glued to the wireless waiting for the next BBC news and the papers were full of it. Hedwig saw the headline:

BRITISH ARMY DRIVEN BACK TO THE CHANNEL

Calais is still in British hands but the bulk of the British Expeditionary Force is surrounded at the port of Dunkirk. Urgent plans are now being made to evacuate the BEF, though it seems nothing but a miracle can save our soldiers.

Hedwig shuddered and put the paper aside. Everyone was alarmed by this sudden and worrying turn of events, wondering whether the Royal Navy could possibly rescue the British Army. To many it seemed a forlorn hope. A few soldiers might be brought back though their tanks, vehicles and artillery would surely have to be left behind. The country would then be left virtually defenceless. And to make things worse, rumours were spreading that the French were seeking a separate peace with Hitler! Britain would then be alone, left to fight the Nazis single-handed! But without an army how could she? Surely Hitler could be invading England any day soon!

Her Kindertransport host Mrs Bamber reached for her hand. "We must pray for God's guidance and help my dear. Somehow he'll deliver us, I'm sure. And even if the Royal Navy doesn't rescue all our soldiers, they'll stop the Germans crossing the channel."

Her kind encouragement had fortified her for a moment, but the fear of the Nazis, which had lain dormant since her arrival in England, returned to haunt her. It was almost a year since she'd escaped from Hitler's

Germany, but since then his rule and hatred of the Jews had spread over most of Europe. Would his hatred be brought to Britain too? To Britain, her safe haven? If Britain was to surrender too, as France seemed about to do, her escape and separation from her beloved parents would have been futile, a tragic, heart-breaking mistake! Woefully she shook her head, never would she forget that awful day when she'd seen them for the last time, on that platform surrounded by hundreds of tearful children. How she'd clung to her parents praying for time to stand still, praying that the moment of separation would never come. But it had, and they'd gently guided her towards the queue of children boarding that train, the train that would separate them for ever. As she'd looked back for one last glimpse of them, a voice yelled "Only one suitcase" and a hand had grabbed her violin. Her violin! She could do nothing, but the loss of her violin was nothing compared with the loss of her beloved parents. Unable to stop her tears she'd yielded to the crowd as it forced her relentlessly into the packed carriage. Then she'd heard the whistle and the train began to move. She'd pushed her way to the window for one final glimpse and saw them waving and waving until they were lost in the distance. It had been so final, there was no turning back. Life, she'd felt, no longer had any purpose, she remembered wishing to die.

With so many tearful and despondent children it was a dismal journey, but as one of the older girls, she'd done what she could to comfort the younger ones, but it was an impossible task. Eventually they arrived at IJmuden where they'd boarded the ship bound for England. It was then as she searched for her suitcase that the loss of her violin really hit her. Her violin was the only thing she could treasure now, but that awful man, that evil brute had taken it! Her violin had become part of her, a constant companion that shared her world, a world of beautiful consoling music, into which she could happily escape. With her violin she could remember who she was, that girl who wanted to be a violinist in a great orchestra, maybe even a soloist! Now that dream was lost. Never would it come true! Was there to be no end to her wretchedness? In her misery she followed the others and found somewhere to sit, a place by herself where she could be on her own. But kind words from a lady crew member comforted her and reluctantly she joined the others and with them watched the land glide by as the ship headed down the estuary. Then they met the sea, an unkind sea which gave the ship a horrible motion adding the misery of sea sickness to their wretchedness. It was not until many hours later when the welcome coast of England was in sight that the waves had begun to subside and soon they were entering the port of Harwich. There all one hundred and fifty-three of them were taken in buses to a huge hall, to be welcomed by friendly ladies, who called out their names and told them who was to be their English guardians.

"Hedwig Boddenburg?" Hesitantly she answered "Yes?"

"The Reverend Ronald Bamber and Mrs Dorothy Bamber have offered to give you a home. They live near Liverpool. Here let me pin this label on the collar of your coat." She smiled, "We mustn't lose you!"

"Liverpool, where is that? She asked.

"It's a port on the West coast of England, my dear."

"And the Reverend Bamber is a Priest?"

"Yes, yes. He's the Vicar of St Luke's, Crosby." Then she moved on calling out another name.

A Priest, she remembered thinking. What would he and his wife be like? The thought of living with complete strangers and foreigners at that, troubled her. But later she found she couldn't have been luckier. The lady holding a placard with Hedwig Boddenburg written on it when she arrived at Liverpool station had been so kind and welcoming. Having introduced herself, she'd led her to a bus that drove through strange streets and alongside a river. Then as they passed a line of huge warehouses, with cranes towering above them, Mrs Bamber had told her, "That's Bootle my dear, Crosby's not far now, only about a mile." Then the bus drew to a halt opposite a church.

"Is that St Luke's church?" She'd asked.

"Yes my dear and the Vicarage, where you'll be living with us, is next door."

It was a big house, much bigger than Tranquillity House and it too had a garden. She remembered how pleased she'd been when she was shown her bedroom, her own bedroom in the attic, with an uninterrupted view of the river.

"And here my dear," she was led down to the floor below, "Is the bathroom. Now you must come and have some tea. I hope you like crumpets. They'll warm us up on this chilly day. And perhaps you'd like some scones with Devonshire cream and strawberry jam. I'm afraid I have a weakness for them." And so she chatted, with Hedwig doing her best to understand.

"Oh my dear. I mustn't prattle on so." She smiled. "You must be finding it hard to understand!"

"No, no Mrs Bamber," she assured her, "I can understand most of what you say. My mother made me learn to speak English."

She saw the door opening.

"Ah!" Mrs Bamber exclaimed, "This must be my husband." In came a tall balding man, a little older that her father. His friendly blue eyes surveyed her.

"Welcome to England my dear. We're delighted to have you with us, aren't we Dorothy?" And so they introduced themselves, he telling her that he was the Vicar of St Luke's and had met and married Dorothy just after the war, when he'd finished his wartime service with the Navy.

"That was nineteen years ago," Dorothy interrupted. "And we have a son, Alan who is eighteen."

"Moshe's nineteen," Hedwig heard herself saying. Whatever had made her say that? She'd broken the rule she'd made, that she must try not to mention the family she would never see again! That seemed the only way to contain her grief!

"Moshe?" Dorothy asked. "Who is Moshe? Is he your brother?"

Hedwig nodded, "Yes."

"Would you like to tell us about him?"

"Yes, but I can't tell you much. You see he escaped to Palestine five years ago and we've never heard from him since."

"Oh my dear, did you not write letters to each other?"

"No. No. We were sure that letters to and from Palestine would be intercepted by the Nazis and that would give our address and reveal us as Jews. And I won't be writing to my parents either, for the same reason."

Dorothy reached for her hand. "Well my dear, you must treat us as your family now." Then she poured the tea and introduced her to scones with Devonshire cream and strawberry jam!

As they ate, Mrs Bamber told her how good her English was. "You'll be chatting as one of us in no time my dear."

Hedwig felt a little happier. She'd been concerned about her English guardians, whether they would think her a nuisance, as an intruder, as someone they would regret having, but the Vicar and his wife were kind and welcoming.

In her room as she unpacked her case, she looked through the window at the river, it was a lovely view and there was a ship moving on the water, a big ship. She'd not seen ships before coming to England only photographs, and fascinated she watched it as it went past churning up the water and leaving a trail of smoke from its funnel. It looked huge and she'd wondered where it was going and what it carried. Then when it had gone she started to put away her few items of clothes, and reaching the bottom of her case she saw her music folder. As she picked it up her eyes had filled with tears. "What good is music without a violin", she screamed? In her anger and despair she threw it down. The folder broke and her precious sheets of music were strewn all over the floor. Controlling her anger and chastened by her stupidity, she picked them up and returned them to their proper places in the folder. Then putting it neatly in the drawer she tried to be positive telling herself that if she couldn't play her violin, at least she could read the music!

She felt a little happier then and remembered the crucifix Daddy had given her and Mummy, when they'd been baptised. Mummy had sewn it into the lining of her coat along with five marks. Hastily she cut the stitches and hung the crucifix round her neck. Though born a Jew, she was a Christian now. Could it be, she wondered, that her Christian God had given her a Christian priest and wife to be her hosts in England?

As the days of her new life in England passed, Hedwig realised how blessed she was to be living with the Bambers, who did all they could to make her feel at home. Mrs Bamber even suggested she should call her Aunt Dorothy and her husband Uncle Ron.

"We can't have you calling us Mrs Bamber and Mr Bamber!" she said. But though Hedwig tried, she found it very difficult! Mrs Bamber had also suggested she should call herself Hettie.

"Hedwig is such a German name my dear, and we English will never pronounce the w in your name properly. To us it's as a W, but to you Germans it's a V, and anyway," she'd laughed, "for the moment Germans are not very popular here in England!" So Hettie she'd become!

They'd talked about her going to school, but as she was almost seventeen they'd decided she shouldn't. Then Mrs Bamber had asked if she wanted to attend synagogue.

"It'll be very difficult for you I'm afraid as the nearest one is in the centre of Liverpool. There are buses you could catch, but dear Hettie we wouldn't like you to go on your own. So we don't know what to suggest."

But then Mrs Bamber had seen her deliberately handling the crucifix that hung round her neck. Her eyes had lit up, "Is that a crucifix my dear?" she'd asked.

"Yes, Mrs Bamber, I mean Aunt Dorothy." She showed her the golden crucifix! "Though I'm a Jew by birth, my mother and I were baptised and confirmed in St Hildegard's in Dessau. We'd hoped that as Christians we'd be safe from Hitler's hatred, but it wasn't to be!"

"Oh my dear, your family must have suffered a great deal!"

"Yes, but not as much as many. But my Grandfather was beaten and killed by the Nazis, my uncle and his wife have escaped to Switzerland and my father was arrested by the Gestapo and thrown into Buchenwald concentration camp. But thankfully he's since been released.

"Oh Hettie dear how your family has suffered. And you told me before your brother has escaped to Palestine! We must pray for your parents and for Nazi Germany to be defeated. And Hettie dear, you're safe with us."

The following day was Friday and Mrs Bamber seemed very excited. "We're expecting Alan," she explained, as she took clean sheets from the airing cupboard. "He has some leave from the Navy, and I've saved our weekly meat ration for a welcome supper tonight."

"Oh you must be pleased. Can I help you?"

"Yes, Hettie dear. Perhaps you can help me get his bedroom ready."

His room was on the floor below hers, and it too looked out over the river. In a strange way it reminded her of Moshe's, for its walls hung with pictures too and over the bed where Moshe had placed his Star of David, there was a map of the world in which many countries including Canada, Australia, New Zealand, South Africa and India like Britain herself, were coloured red.

Mrs Bamber had seen her studying it.

"Our dear Alan has had that map on the wall since he was eleven. He's always been proud of the British Empire and rightly so too, for in two wars now the Empire has come to our aid. Adolf Hitler should remember that!"

But it wasn't the only thing in that bedroom that had caught her eye. She saw a violin case! Her heart beat with excitement. Did it contain a violin? Was it Alan's?

"Does Alan play the violin?" she asked as nonchalantly as she could.

Mrs Bamber switched off her vacuum cleaner. "What did you say, Hettie?"

"I just noticed the violin and wondered whether it was Allan's and whether he played it."

"Well, he did for a while. We gave it him for his twelfth birthday, but he never mastered it. He was always playing rugby, or cricket, or rowing. So I'm afraid it's just been collecting dust for many years now. He ought to give it away, he never plays it."

Hedwig's heart beat even faster. Could she ask him to lend it to her, perhaps even give it to her? Mechanically she helped make his bed, but she could think of nothing else, her fingers moving as if they caressed the strings.

"Hettie, dear," she heard Mrs Bamber say, "We put the top sheet on before the blankets!"

Hedwig shook her head, she must stop thinking of that violin. "Oh dear. How silly of me, I wasn't thinking."

Dorothy Bamber saw her Jewish refugee glancing again at the violin. "Hettie dear, did you ever learn to play the violin?"

"Yes, yes but I had my violin taken from me as I was about to board the train for England."

"Oh! My dear."

"The man told me I was only allowed one suitcase and tore my violin from my hand."

"Oh! Hettie dear, how cruel the Nazis are," she hesitated, "Well I don't know if Allan's is playable, but as he doesn't use it, I'm sure he'll let you have it."

"Oh! Mrs Bamber, sorry I mean Aunt Dorothy that would be wonderful!"

What would this son of hers be like? Hedwig wondered. Would he give her that violin? Suddenly she found she too, was eager for Alan to arrive.

He came in time for tea, a tall dark haired man with an eager smile, dressed smartly in the blue naval uniform of a Sub Lieutenant in the Navy, and welcomed with hugs and kisses by his mother and father.

"My word, you do look smart, Alan. Last time we saw you were wearing sailors' bellbottoms*," his mother said.

"So," his father interrupted. "You've been promoted, well done Alan. Now tell us what's in store for you."

"Well Dad, I managed to pass all my exams and now I'm to join a corvette. She's called *Foxglove* and is one of the first Flower class corvettes being built as Convoy escorts. They're great little ships fitted with Asdic and depth charges."

"Oh! A newly built ship eh? And fitted with Asdic you say? What's that?"

"It's the Navy's submarine detection equipment. Once it finds a submarine we drop our depth charges on it."

"That sounds good. We need to sink those U-boats!"

"Yes Dad, but we don't always hit the U-boat, somehow they wriggle away. But we get them sometimes!"

"So you'll be escorting convoys?"

"Yes, I expect so."

"Well, your mother and I will be thinking of you and praying for your safety, Alan."

"Thanks Dad."

"Now Alan dear," Dorothy Bamber broke in, "you must meet Hettie. She's one of the Jewish youngsters rescued from Hitler's tyranny."

He shook Hettie's hand politely. "Welcome to England. I hope you'll be happy here. But where are your parents?"

"In Germany, with no means of escape. I pray for them every day."

Dorothy put a protective arm around her. "Poor dear, we must all pray for them."

The plight of the Jews in Hitler's Germany brought conversation to an awkward end and Mrs Bamber summoning up a cheerful and business-like tone, announced it was time for Alan to change into something more comfortable and led him up to his room.

"And how much leave do you have Alan dear?"

"Ten days, Mum. Then I join the *Foxglove* in Middlesbrough, where she's being built. Oh! Here's my ration card."

"Oh. Bless you. I was wondering how we'd manage with one more mouth to feed. Lord Woolton* has just reduced our ration of butter to two ounces and margarine to four!

Chapter 24

"Well," Untersturmführer (Second Lieutenant) Horst Boddenburg reflected during a temporary halt in the advance into Poland, "but for their intransigence we'd still be at peace. Danzig and the so-called Polish Corridor have been part of Germany since Bismarck's time!"

They'd been fighting for a week now, a hard fight against frequent counter-attacks by the Poles, who'd fought bravely, storming over the fallen bodies of their comrades in their repeated counter-attacks. But they'd been greatly outnumbered and faced with superior artillery and armour they'd been unable to stop the Germans. And the Stukas that Uncle Klaus had helped design, had given great support. Lodz, the third largest town in Poland, was now their target and was barely five miles away. Everyone was certain it would be theirs within a day.

And they'd been right. Lodz had been taken on Friday 8th and within a week all resistance had ended and the Swastika was flying proudly over the city that was now part of the Greater Reich.

He'd joined the Waffen-S.S. as an enlisted man and had served in the ranks before being selected for officer training at the S.S. Officer Cadet School at Braunschweig. There having successfully graduated, he'd sworn his Reichswehreid*, his personal oath of obedience to Adolf Hitler. He'd never forget those words!

"I swear to you, Adolf Hitler, as Führer and Chancellor of the Reich, loyalty and bravery. I promise you, and those you have appointed to have authority over me, obedience unto death."

Swearing that oath had been the final testimony of his desire to serve the Führer, a desire fostered by his admiration yes, his adoration of the Führer that had grown since that day he'd first worn his Hitler

Youth uniform! And now he was part of an Einsatzkommando* ready to implement the Führer's plan for the Jews in Lodz.

Hardly a week had passed before the Nazi Governor of Lodz called a meeting to promulgate his plan to make the city Judenrein, cleansed of Jews. Though only an Untersturmführer, a junior officer, as an S.S. officer he'd attended the meeting held in the Governor's headquarters in the Hotel Savoy, the biggest and most luxurious hotel in the city.

"The Jews, and there are about two hundred and thirty thousand Jews in Lodz", the Governor paused as if to emphasise the size of the problem, "are to be rounded up and moved into a ghetto until their future can be decided. The slum district known as the Baluty quarter will become the ghetto." A staff officer indicated the area of the proposed ghetto on a map hanging on the wall.

"Its non-Jewish residents," he continued, "are to be ejected to make room for the Jews. They are to be given temporary shelter wherever it can be found, until they can be rehoused in the homes vacated by the Jews. When the Poles and Jews vacate their homes, they're to leave everything behind, except for whatever they can each carry in one suitcase. One suitcase only. But before the relocation begins, a wall to enclose the ghetto is to be built with only one entry gate. When the wall is completed the gate is to be guarded at all times."

The building of the wall had taken longer than expected, but finally it was completed and the ejection of the non-Jews from the projected ghetto began. That had proved to be relatively easy, but finding where all the two hundred and thirty thousand Jews lived proved to be more difficult. But to their delight the many ethnic Germans resident in Lodz were only too keen to show where many of the Jews lived. Many, however, tried to deny they were Jewish, but whether the menfolk were circumcised or not, settled the matter.

The slow progress displeased the Nazi Governor and a plan to reduce the number of Jews in the city was prepared. On the Sabbath Horst and men from the Einsatzkommando were deployed to surround the Great Synagogue as the Jews came to worship. When the last Jew was seen to enter, Horst and his men had smashed the windows of the synagogue and had pushed burning torches into the interior. And as planned, when the flames spread and the Jews rushed out, he and his men had met them with withering rifle fire. As the flames consumed the synagogue there'd been no need to search for more Jews; those who might be hiding in the synagogue were left to die in the flames. But some who had escaped had only been wounded by the rifle fire and he and another officer had had to despatch them with their pistols.

When the last Jew had been killed they loaded the bodies onto the waiting trucks and counted them. Four hundred and seventy-three Jewish men, women and children had been exterminated.

Though disappointed with the numbers, the Governor had been satisfied with the outcome, but the killing had shaken Horst badly. It had been the first time he'd obeyed the Führer's command to kill Jews. Seeing women and young children cut down by that hail of bullets had been horrendous! The memory of that day haunted him and he saw again those contorted bodies lying before him prostrate in death and worse, those eyes, those accusing eyes, staring at him as he'd pulled the trigger to finish off that Jewish woman. It made him tremble and sweat, but then he would tell himself it had been his duty! Hadn't he sworn loyalty to Adolf Hitler, to be obedient unto death? And he would console himself; they were money grubbing Jews, the parasites who exploited the hard-working, decent Aryan folk. He would feel better then, could feel his shoulders straighten and the pride of serving the Führer as an officer of the Gestapo, return.

News of the burning of the Great Synagogue and the killing of the Jewish worshippers had spread like wild fire. Now the Jews were frightened. Now they were submissive. Now they were obeying the order to sew that six-pointed yellow star on their clothes.

Notices telling the Jews they were to be moved into the ghetto with whatever possessions they could carry in only one suitcase per person, had been posted throughout the city and a few days later the evacuation began. With loudspeakers blaring the Jews were ordered to leave their homes. Men of the Einsatzkommando made sure they did so by banging on doors and breaking them open, if no answer came. And the frightened occupants would emerge struggling with heavy bags, supporting the sick and elderly and trying to comfort their frightened children. The long march to the ghetto followed. There they would be crammed into the empty blocks, eight or ten to a room.

The men had been told that resistance was to be met with gunfire, but after the massacre at the synagogue, the Jews offered none, though their transfer to the ghetto was a slow business. When after five days the transfer was complete the former homes of the Jews were searched for things of value to be taken, before the Poles of the Baluty quarter arrived and found to their delight that they were re-housed in the homes of the Jews.

Now with the Jews settled in the overcrowded, dilapidated slums that formed the ghetto, a Council of Elders, all Jews, was appointed by the Nazi Governor to organise and manage the ghetto in accordance with his instructions. The Jews would be required to pay for their rations but since they no longer had a source of livelihood, the two abandoned textile factories adjacent to the ghetto were to be re-commissioned. They were to be enclosed within yet another wall, and a bridge over the road between the factories and the ghetto was to be built to give the Jews guarded access to them. Then during a twelve-hour day, the Jews would earn their keep making uniforms and other garments for the Reich. Inspectors to be appointed by the Council of Elders were to visit all apartments to keep a record, to be updated weekly, of the occupants, showing the name, gender, age and health of all living there. The elderly, infirm or sick unable to work could at the discretion of the Inspector be given relief in the form of a meagre allowance of rations.

As a Gestapo officer, Horst's primary duty was to prevent any revolt or sabotage within the ghetto. Fear of the Gestapo and the fate which befell those interrogated was a useful weapon for Horst and his colleagues. And to make their presence known in the ghetto, Gestapo officers were ordered to change from their field grey uniforms into their distinctive black Gestapo uniforms with jackboots, and caps adorned with the S.S. death's head emblem. Now the hated Gestapo officers were readily seen and everyone was on their guard when they were near. And to maintain Jewish fear of the German authorities, frequent arrests were followed by long, tortuous interrogations.

By the middle of November one of the factories had been re-commissioned and Jews were at work stoking the boilers and tending the machines. Though they were working for their German masters, many found some satisfaction in their labours. The factory was warmer than the freezing hovels in the ghetto. In the icy winter coal had become a distant luxury. Only when some at great danger was smuggled home from the factory boiler-room, or when children rummaging through the former rubbish dumps found a few spent nuggets of coal, did they have the luxury of a coal fire. Without coal the stoves were fed with anything that would burn and slowly but surely furniture was being burnt to give a little warmth.

Horst would often wander through the factory on the lookout for any signs of sabotage, theft or possible uprising and it was good to see those wretched Jews working for the Reich. Often he would also accompany the Inspector when he visited the apartments to update the Record of Occupants. His first visit with Inspector Tabacznik took him to Gnieznienska Street, to a large run-down apartment block. The entrance hallway was unlit, but in the gloom they found the stairs and climbed to the fifth floor, the top floor. On the landing to his surprise, he saw that none of the doorways had doors. Had they too been burnt for warmth? Now only ragged curtains guarded the doorways. With his torch, Tabacznik had been searching for the Apartment number.

"Number 51. Ah! Freund family." He pulled the curtain aside and they entered. The smell hit Hurst at once, that repulsive smell of a filthy public latrine, but Tabacznik seemed not to notice as he strode into the second room.

Horst lingered surveying the first room. Apart from a couple of mattresses and blankets on the floor, and a pile of rags or clothing, the room was empty.

He could hear Tabacznik talking.

"Name, Pessia Freund?" a tired voice answered "Yes."

"Female?" "Yes"

"Age?" He heard a sigh, then "Forty-two, though I feel like sixty-two!"

"Health?" Having joined Tabacznik he could see her lying on the bed, a gaunt, hollow-cheeked old hag with matted grey hair and a blanket drawn tightly around her. But it wasn't her condition that had struck him, it was the fact that she had a bed to lie on. He wondered when it too would be burned, then close examination revealed it to be a cast-iron bed"! That indeed was a treasure to be guarded!

"Health?" Tabacznik repeated his question.

She sighed again, "It's my bowels. They won't rest!" she paused, "I'm dying, at least I hope so. What is there to live for?"

Tabacznik ignored her question. "Where is Lemel your husband?"

"In the factory."

Tabacznik nodded as he marked his record. "And your children Riva and Yaakov?"

"Searching for anything to eat or burn."

Tabacznik leant over and gave her shoulder a gentle pat. "I will organise some relief for you."

With that he withdrew and went to the next apartment. Horst stayed with him to visit the remaining five apartments on the fifth floor, then he'd had enough. He felt contaminated by their squalor and sought the clean fresh air in the street outside.

Visits to the factory and to the apartments became his regular routine, a routine which made him dissatisfied and disillusioned. What was the point of it all? He often remembered that synagogue fire, the guilt that had pestered him then was now fading. It had killed four hundred and seventy-three Jews, a mere fraction of the Jews in Lodz, but surely that was the sort of action the Führer required! Keeping Jews locked up in a ghetto hardly fulfilled the Führer's vision of a land free of Jews! And like the Führer, he too had grown to hate these filthy Jews; they were evil, they must be exterminated.

But then what had he done? That very afternoon! He'd betrayed the Führer and himself! He scrubbed himself harshly in the warm water of his bath. He glanced at his vest and pants thrown hurriedly on the floor. Like his body, they were contaminated too, contaminated by that girl and that filthy mattress in the ghetto. How could he have let it happen? How could he let himself be seduced by a Jew? Hadn't he always despised, hated that evil, despicable money-grubbing race? He'd seen that girl before and whenever he did that tantalising, seductive body of hers had caught his eye. How he'd lusted over that body of hers, that slender figure that graced the ragged dress she always wore as if it were some ball gown! But it had always been just a passing dream, a dream that helped him escape from the Jews and this filthy ghetto to a happier world. But it hadn't been a dream that very afternoon, when having found her name and where she lived, he'd gone to her apartment block on his own on the pretext of finding weapons. He'd entered her apartment and there she was. She accepted his presence without surprise and began pleading for some relief for her sick mother wheezing on a mattress in the corner. He looked around counting the occupants; five children ranging in ages from five to nine, and a grey-bearded old man with twisted peyots*, a kippah* on his head and a prayer shawl wrapped around his shoulders.

"I'm the only one here who works," she'd said. "I work in the factory, but the wages are small." She'd begged him for an increase, but he said nothing. Then she changed tack.

"Come see, the eight of us all live in these two rooms." She led him into the other room and pulling the ragged curtain over the door, lifted her skirt.

"Have me for five zlotych," she said.

That supple body of hers flexed seductively as she pulled off her dress revealing those tawny breasts and coffee coloured nipples. As a Gestapo officer, who'd sworn loyalty to the Führer, he should have hit her across the face and walked away, but he didn't. That long-felt, recurring need for a woman drove him implacably on, nothing could stop him. And as he lay on her, her body was soft and compliant. Then for a moment or two the tensions of war and the ghetto vanished. Those seconds of peace were blissful. But as he left, a feeling of contamination overwhelmed him, tormented him until at last he'd sought relief in the bath.

The guilt of associating with a Jewish prostitute engulfed him. He'd always been proud of his Aryan ancestry and his membership of that superior, honourable, clean race led by their irreplaceable Führer, Adolf Hitler. But now he, Untersturmführer Horst Boddenburg, had betrayed the Führer! Had contaminated himself with the body of a Jew! How could he have done such a thing?

Chapter 25

Britain rejoiced in the miracle of Dunkirk, for in the space of eight days under constant attack by the Luftwaffe, the bulk of the BEF had been rescued from the beaches. Some seven hundred vessels of all sorts and sizes ranging from destroyers and lesser warships of the Royal Navy, to civilian vessels ranging from tugs to pleasure boats, braved the worst the Germans could do and brought more than three hundred and thirty-nine thousand troops back to England. But all their equipment, tanks, artillery, machine guns, and motor vehicles had had to be abandoned, and almost a third of the rescue fleet had been sunk. The air warfare above the beaches had taken a heavy toll too and in the fighting the Royal Air Force had lost one hundred and six of its Hurricanes and Spitfires, though they had "downed" one hundred and seventy German planes. Though it was a victory for the RAF, their losses were worrying for they had been greater than the number of replacement aircraft coming off the production lines!

With the surrender of France on June 22nd, the Germans were ecstatic in their praise and adoration of the Führer. He had achieved so much, union with Austria, freedom for the Sudeten Germans, restoration of Danzig and the Polish Corridor to the Fatherland, the defeat and occupation of Norway and had brought the old enemy France to her knees and the surrender table. Now Britain was left to fight alone. Surely the British would soon be suing for peace. But they were showing no signs of surrendering and reconnaissance flights revealed anti-invasion defences were being prepared. Pill boxes* were being hurriedly built to guard possible landing beaches, where anti-landing craft obstacles were being installed and barbed wire laid. Similar obstacles to deny gliders a safe landing for airborne troops, were appearing in many fields and open spaces. It seemed there would be no easy surrender and the Führer instructed his Generals to prepare a plan for a sea-borne invasion. The plan was given the name Operation Sea Lion.

With invasion imminent, Winston Churchill the new British Prime Minister, rallied the nation with his never-to-be forgotten speech, "We shall fight on the beaches, we shall fight on the landing grounds, we shall fight in the fields and in the streets; we shall never surrender." His leadership inspired the nation; the sole aim was to be victory. Now as the nation determined "never to surrender", women in ever growing numbers manned the machines in the factories producing the weapons of war, ploughed the fields and worked the farms, manned the buses and essential services and freed the men for service in the Armed Forces.

The nation struggled to supply the remnants of its army with munitions brought from America by the Merchant Navy under constant attack by U-boats. As merchant ships were sunk in ever increasing numbers, more and more shipping space had to be reserved for the weapons of war, leaving less for the import of food and essentials. Early in the war all those who had cars were entitled to a small monthly ration of petrol, but now only those who could show they used their car or motor cycle for essential war time purposes were allowed a small ration of petrol. Delivery firms with vans and lorries, doctors, vets and farmers were the main recipients. And again the food ration was reduced and a "Dig for Victory" campaign was launched. This encouraged householders to grow their own vegetables and lawns in parks and gardens, even the "rough" in golf courses were brought into cultivation too. And the Government needing ever more steel ordered wrought iron railings around homes, buildings and parks be cut down and recycled to provide steel for ships and tanks. And housewives were invited to hand in their aluminium saucepans to be melted down for use as metal for Spitfires and bombers. And household rubbish had to be sorted into separate piles. Paper and cardboard in one, empty food cans in another and left overs (if there was any) in another to be collected separately for pig swill. Beer bottles and the like had always been reused, for when a bottle of beer or lemonade was bought its price included a deposit for the bottle, to be refunded when the bottle was returned.

As the German General Staff drew up the plans for Operation Sea Lion, it became clear that launching an invasion fleet against the strength of the Royal Navy could only succeed if the Luftwaffe could guarantee air superiority over the Channel. But the Luftwaffe never achieved air superiority, and in the four month Battle of Britain which followed, the Hurricanes and Spitfires flown not only by British, but also by Polish, New Zealand, Canadian and Czech pilots destroyed 1,733 German aircraft for the loss of only 915 of their own. Every evening the British listened eagerly to the wireless for the daily score, almost always in favour of the British. The daily score reached its peak on 15th August when 75 German aircraft were shot down for only 34 British.

At the end of October with winter approaching and without the much needed air superiority, Hitler had little option but to postpone his invasion. Now the Luftwaffe was instructed to bomb the cities and to do so under cover of darkness so as to reduce losses. The brunt was borne by London where much of the population took shelter night after night in the Underground system, sleeping on the platforms and emerging in the morning to go to work among the rubble. But ports and other cities were bombed too. First would come the warbling sound of the air raid siren, warning people to take shelter. Many like the Bamber family and Hedwig in Crosby some six miles from the Liverpool docks, would sometimes ignore it and with lights switched off, draw the blackout curtains back and watch the searchlights probing the dark sky for the bombers, listen to the sound of distant explosions and see the clouds over Liverpool turn red as they reflected the fires below. Rarely did Crosby receive a bomb; it was only, some said, when Jerry had been hit and had to drop his bombs to lighten his load.

With the war so close and so many women serving in the armed forces or doing men's jobs in the factories and farms, Hedwig felt an insistent but unsatisfied desire to do something to help defeat that monster Hitler. With her mother and father still in Germany, Moshe somewhere in Palestine and Uncle Benjamin and Auntie Ruth in Switzerland, she worried constantly about them. The family had suffered so much at the hands of Hitler and the Nazis, and only when he was defeated could there be any hope that they might be reunited. But what could she do in this war against Hitler? She was German by birth, would the English trust her? Many mightn't! "After all", she fancied them saying, "She's German; she could be a spy!" Even in church, where she helped with the Sunday school, some made little effort to acknowledge her, while one or two were downright unfriendly! Yet she desperately wanted to do something in this war against Hitler. Was helping Mrs Bamber with the housework and tending the vegetable garden they'd dug in the lawn, all she could do? But that did hardly anything to help the war effort! In her frustration she muttered it was not enough. There must be something worthwhile she could do! But what?

Whether Mrs Bamber was aware of her despondency she didn't know, but one evening when reading the local newspaper, Mrs Bamber looked up.

"Hettie dear, would you like to do some translating? Your English is so good."

"Of course. What would you like me to translate?"

"It's not for me," Mrs Bamber chuckled, "It's for the Navy."

"For the Navy? Surely they wouldn't want a German. They wouldn't trust a German!"

"Well, perhaps not, but who knows? They may look upon a young Jewish girl like you, in a different light!"

"What do they want translating?"

"It doesn't say. The advertisement merely asks for people who have a good mastery of German to do some translating."

"Oh! Well if you think they'd take me, maybe I should apply, but how do I?"

"It says apply in writing. Here look it's in the paper. Yes, you should definitely apply! I'll get you some writing paper. You must do it now. There's no time like the present and remember," she smiled, "the early bird gets the worm!"

And so Hedwig wrote:

Dear Sir,

I have read your advertisement in the Liverpool Evening News calling for people who speak German to do some translation for you and I would like to offer you my services.

I am an 18 year-old German Jewish girl who came to England in 1938 by means of the Kindertransport scheme, for which I am truly grateful. As a Jew I want to do all I can to help defeat Hitler and the Nazis.

I learnt English while I was in Germany and since I have lived in England for over two years, I am now quite fluent in English and feel able to translate well.

My kind English hosts, the Reverend and Mrs Bamber have offered to give me a reference if that should be required and I hope you will call me for interview.

She'd posted it the following day and had waited impatiently for a reply which never seemed to come. But then some ten days later the postlady delivered a letter addressed to Miss H Boddenburg. It looked very important with the words ON HIS MAJESTY'S SERVICE printed on the envelope! Hastily she tore it open. It must be about the translation job! The letter was short and to the point:

Dear Miss Boddenburg

"Your application has been noted and you are asked to report for an interview at Derby House, Water Street, Liverpool on Tuesday 19th November at 10 a.m. A reference will be required."

Excitedly she'd shown the letter to Mrs Bamber.

"Oh! They want to see you, that's good. At Derby House? Mmm, we'll have to find out where that is!"

And so the following day they'd caught the bus into Liverpool and after being told Water Street was close to the Liver Building and behind St Nicholas Church, they'd found a white stone office block, with a policeman standing guard outside.

"Yes," he assured them, "This is Derby House. Have you a pass?"

They'd told him they were merely finding the place as Hedwig had an interview there on the Tuesday.

"Then bring the letter calling you for interview and you'll be allowed in," he told them.

Their reconnaissance had been worthwhile for on the day she'd found Derby House easily and having produced her letter had been allowed entry. She was ushered in and led to a young woman in a blue uniform who she was to learn later was a Wren* Officer. She was asked questions about how she came to be in England and about her family. Finally when at last it had been accepted that she was a Jew, and a refugee from Hitler's persecution, she was passed on for yet more questioning. This time her interrogator was a Naval Officer.

"Now what I am about to tell you," he said, "is secret, and you must sign this paper to confirm you understand and that you will not reveal anything I tell you about what we do here, to any other person. Is that clear?"

She nodded emphatically, "Yes, quite clear, sir"

He waited while she signed, then he continued, "This is the Naval Headquarters of Western Approaches, from which we direct the war against the U-boats attacking our convoys in the Atlantic. And to gain intelligence of the capability and tactics of the U-boats we interrogate naval prisoners of war, survivors from German warships and submarines. They'll have been rescued by our ships." He waited a moment to see how she reacted, but her face revealed nothing. "As prisoners of war they rarely divulge any useful information when interrogated, other than their name and rank. But by other means we sometimes overhear their conversations with each other and this can reveal good intelligence. So," he paused, "we need people who understand German to translate what they say." Again he paused, "Do you understand what we want?"

She nodded. "Yes."

He gave her some earphones. "This is a tape I want you to translate for me. You can stop the tape at any time, if you want to have more time to think. And you can rewind it to hear a phrase again. The voice on the tape is that of an officer from a U-boat"

Gingerly she switched it on and began translating;

"During the night," she began, *"we reloaded our torpedo tubes"* she didn't hear the word properly so she stopped the tape and re-wound it. Then she continued, *"our torpedo tubes and charged the batteries and at first light on Sunday April the fifth we spotted smoke on the horizon"* again she hadn't heard the word properly so again she stopped the tape and re-wound it. She continued *"spotted smoke on the horizon and steered towards it. Later we saw a destroyer approaching and had to submerge at once."*

Having checked her translation against his pre-translated script, her interrogator leant over and stopped the tape.

"I'll move it on to something more interesting," he said. "There, start again when you're ready."

She flicked the switch and began again. *"We heard the destroyer's propellers racing as she drew near and passed right overhead. Then"* – again she stopped the tape, rewound it and started again, *"Then depth charges started exploding. One was very close, the boat shook, the lights went out and water began coming in. The Captain ordered us to surface and thank God we were able to do so, though water was flooding in."*

He smiled and switched off the machine. "You've done very well. I shall recommend we employ you. You'll get a letter in about a week's time to tell you whether or not we want you."

Would they want her, she wondered. She hoped they would. She hadn't heard German being spoken now for more than two years! Hearing her native tongue had affected her. It had brought back memories, memories of the family, memories of life under the Nazis and worries about her dear parents. Memories that made her want do whatever she could to help defeat Hitler.

Chapter 26

Acting Sub Lieutenant Alan Bamber Royal Naval Volunteer Reserve, ducked as the bows dipped into the breaking sea sending seawater cascading over the fo'c'sle and a torrent over the open bridge, where he was standing the middle watch. His sou'wester and oilskins kept out most of the water, but some found a way in, as it did into the messdecks below. It had been blowing a gale for the past twenty four hours or so, making it difficult to maintain station on the port bow of the twenty-four ship convoy, while down below it was impossible to sleep or cook anything. All one could hope for was a bully beef sandwich and a hot cup of tea.

When he'd been told to join *HMS Foxglove*, a corvette being built by Smiths at Middlesbrough, he'd never expected life at sea to be so hard. The "Flower" class, he'd learnt, was a new design based on a deep-sea trawler hull, fitted with Asdic, and depth charges. She was to be a convoy escort. He remembered when he first saw her, how smart she looked with her hull and upper-works freshly painted grey and her Pendant Number K125 in black on her ship's side. But now after nearly a year on the Atlantic convoys, her hull was streaked with rust and her upperworks discoloured by soot from the funnel.

He was one of five officers in a crew of eighty. The Captain a Lieutenant, Royal Naval Reserve, had previously served in the Merchant Navy as a First Officer in the Shaw Savill Line. Then there was the Engineer and three watch-keeping officers of whom he was the youngest. He was also the ship's gunnery officer, not that the *Foxglove* had a huge armament, just one 4-inch gun for use against a surfaced U-boat, and two twin .50 inch and two .303 inch Lewis anti-aircraft machine guns.

Two days after he'd joined they'd sailed for Tobermory, where with other Flower class corvettes they'd been given a rudimentary training in anti-submarine warfare. They'd fired the four-inch too, and had hit a target moored in the bay representing a surfaced submarine! But that seemed an age away now, with the *Foxglove* escorting her sixth convoy across the Atlantic. In the first she'd not even had a sniff of a U-boat, though five of the merchant ships had been sunk. She'd spent most of the time rounding up stragglers, those ships with engine trouble that in the gale, had been unable to keep up with the convoy.

In a later convoy homeward bound from America with forty-six ships, the first few days had been plain sailing with calm seas and no sign of the enemy. Though the Asdic kept searching the seas ahead, nothing was found and everyone was relaxed enjoying the balmy weather. But they didn't know what was to hit them that night. There'd been a full moon and the sea calm, making it easy for the escorts to maintain their station on the screen. It was a glorious night with the stars sparkling like diamonds and vying with the moon to light up the convoy.

Then the *Foxglove* gained an Asdic contact.

"Possible submarine zero six zero, fifteen hundred yards" came the operator's voice.

Alan called the Captain and altered course to put the contact dead ahead. Within seconds the Captain appeared, just as the Operator shouted:

"Confirmed Submarine."

And as the Captain said "I'll take the con*", the voice of the Asdic operator came again,

"Lost contact."

Desperately they tried to regain contact but to no avail.

The Escort leader *Wolverine* was informed they'd lost contact by signal lantern, who replied telling them that *Cyclamen* on the other side of the convoy, had also found and lost a submarine. The escorts were ordered to reverse course, close the convoy and hunt for any U-boat that may have penetrated the screen. But still there was no contact. Then in the moonlight, a U-boat could be seen moving at speed like a Motor Torpedo Boat, towards the merchant ships. And there was another on the other side of the convoy too and yet another. As the 4-inch gun's crew readied their gun, explosions were heard and ships could be seen bursting into flames. In the chaos that followed, no-one could be sure whether there were three or four U-boats running amok within the convoy, torpedoing ships at will. They caught occasional glimpses of them, but there was little they could do for the U-boats were now close to the merchant ships and it was dangerous to engage them with gunfire! Then as quickly as the battle had begun the U-boats submerged and vanished, leaving the Escort Commander to count the cost. Three ships were still burning and three others were missing, presumably sunk. Lifeboats could be seen in the water, but whether they should stop to rescue the occupants was as always, a difficult decision for any Escort Commander; ships stopping to rescue survivors made easy targets for a U-boat. But nevertheless *Primula* was sent to do what she could, while *Wolverine* circled around her hunting for any U-boat that might attack her. Meanwhile *Foxglove* and the remaining ships closed ranks and sailed on.

It had been a frightening battle with the final score, U-boats six Merchant ships sunk, Escorts no U-boats sunk or even damaged! Penetrating the screen and surfacing within the convoy to attack the merchant ships was a U-boat tactic they'd not encountered before. And once the U-boats had surfaced within the convoy they could move at speed and attack at will, while seeking shelter from gunfire by dodging among the merchant ships. This new tactic foretold great trouble ahead!

Once order had been restored in the convoy, the Escort Commander signalled his escorts "Every effort must be made to stop U-boats penetrating the screen." But it was exceedingly difficult to do so and though a few days later *Cyclamen* and *Wolverine* did detect and prevent another U-boat penetrating the screen and eventually sank it, three others U-boats managed to do so and surfaced to attack once again like Motor Torpedo Boats, sending four more ships to the bottom. The convoy was now reduced to thirty-six vessels and the score U-boats ten merchant ships sunk, Escorts one U-boat sunk.

"Signal from Escort Commander, sir. Convoy is to alter course to 040°. Escorts adjust position on screen."

The Captain gave Alan a nod "Maybe the Admiralty has some intelligence about a pack of U-boats up ahead and is steering us clear. Let's hope so."

And indeed it seemed so, for the passage was completed without further loss and with the convoy safe in Liverpool, the escorts retired to Bootle to refuel and replenish ammunition, stores and victuals. Half the crews were given a week's leave, while the other half remained onboard to prepare the ships for the next convoy.

Though he hadn't been in the lucky half, every other day when he wasn't duty officer, Alan had been able to take night leave and visit his parents in nearby Crosby. It was good to see them and be cossetted in the luxury of the Vicarage. And there was Hettie too! He'd forgotten how pretty she was. He found it difficult to keep his eyes off her! And when he'd given her that old violin of his, which he hadn't played for years, she'd hugged him with delight. It was then that he'd kissed her.

Their ten days in Bootle had been all too short, but it had been long enough for the ship to be fitted with HUFFDUFF the newly invented High Frequency Direction Finder, capable of detecting wireless signals on the frequencies used by U-boats, and for the Leading Telegraphist to be shown how it worked. Hopes were then high that HUFFDUFF would help them find a U-boat.

The lucky ones who'd been on leave came back refreshed, to a ship once more ready for battle with both the U-boats and the elements. As they sailed down the Mersey he'd hoped he might get a farewell wave from Hettie and his Mum. He'd told Hettie when they'd be sailing and had asked her to keep an eye open for the good ship *Foxglove*. He'd told her she had the number K125 painted in large black letters on her ship's side. Would she be there to give him a wave, he wondered? When he'd spotted St Luke's Church spire and the Vicarage nearby, he'd looked for her anxiously and there to his delight he saw her and his mother waving. He took off his cap and gave them a good wave in return. Next time hopefully it would be his turn for leave!

The thirty-eight ship outward bound convoy to America had an easier passage. With summer approaching the weather had been kind and it seemed the U-boats were more interested in the heavily laden ships bound for Britain than those in ballast heading westwards. Nevertheless as they neared Halifax one ship was torpedoed and sunk.

It was the homeward bound convoy which took the beating. On the third day out they'd sighted the Kondor that four engined long range reconnaissance aircraft the Germans had. Without air cover nothing could be done to shoot it down and stop it radioing the convoy's course, speed and position to U-boat headquarters. Now they knew all U-boats in their vicinity would be ordered to converge on them. It was a bad omen.

The first sign of the battle ahead came when the Telegraphist's voice was heard through the voice-pipe.

"Enemy signal contact ahead, bearing zero-eight-zero."

The Captain woke from his slumber on his bridge seat.

"That's our HUFFDUFF. Could be a U-Boat signalling headquarters, so Full Ahead then Alan, and steer for her."

As the *Foxglove* accelerated to her top speed of sixteen knots, the signalman was busy on the signal lantern reporting the contact to the Escort Commander in the *Wolverine*. Meanwhile all eyes strained to catch sight of the U-boat. How far away it was no-one could tell, but everyone was hoping it would remain on the surface charging her batteries and filling the boat with fresh air, until it could at least be sighted. The rough sea hindered the *Foxglove,* but the *Wolverine* was making easier progress with her slender hull and the more powerful engines of a destroyer and was well ahead.

He remembered that day as if it were yesterday. Soon the *Wolverine* had signalled she'd gained Asdic contact with the U-boat and then they'd seen depth charges exploding. To watch the *Wolverine* dropping her charges and not be in the hunt themselves, was frustrating for those on the *Foxglove,* but slowly they came nearer and then the long-hoped for "Contact bearing one zero five degrees, two thousand yards", came loud and clear through the voice-pipe, followed shortly afterwards by "Confirmed submarine." As the *Wolverine* drew away the *Foxglove* began her attack, but before she was able to launch her depth charges the cry "Lost contact" came through the voice-pipe.

Where was this damned U-boat? Had it gone deep? The two ships continued the hunt, if they couldn't sink the submarine they must at least keep it submerged. Keeping the U-boat down was important, for this would allow the convoy to draw away from it.

So the two ships continued the hunt until the convoy had drawn well ahead when it was time to abandon the hunt and re-join the convoy. But by good fortune the *Foxglove* gained good contact with the U-boat and held it long enough to make an attack. He remembered seeing the depth charge throwers hurl the depth charges into the sea and waiting for the great plumes of water as they exploded. Then they'd seen what they'd all been hoping for, the bows of a U-boat breaking surface. She'd been hit! As the rest of the submarine appeared, first the gun, then the conning tower with her number U 92 painted on its side, he'd seen men scrambling onto the deck and as the boat began to sink, he'd watched them jumping into the sea.

"Signal from Escort Commander Sir." It was the Leading Signalman. "Well done *Foxglove*. Am returning to convoy. Re-join when you have rescued survivors."

The Captain pointed the ship at the men in the water, ordered slow ahead and shouted, "Lower the scrambling nets" The wire netting to help men in the water to climb aboard was hung over the ship's side and everyone who could be spared went to be ready to help the Germans climb aboard. As the ship neared the men in the water, Alan tried to count them but it was difficult in the rough sea. He counted twenty-nine. Surely there could be no more for he saw the U-boats bows rising higher and higher and then when the hull was almost vertical, the boat slid gracefully into the depths as oil and great bubbles of air rose to the surface.

He looked down at the scrambling nets. The Germans were struggling to get a footing and were being hauled onboard by the crew and taken below. They were breathless, wet and cold, but they were the lucky ones. They were safe, there'd be no more war for them, unlike the poor devils who'd gone down with the boat. He saw again that crippled U-boat surfacing. It had a certain beauty, slim and purposeful, designed to lie hidden until it could strike with such deadly consequences. He'd heard the Germans called them "grey wolves". It was an apt name for the predators which hunted the convoys in those fearsome wolf packs. He wondered how many merchant ships U-92 had sunk, leaving their crews to perish in the cold, cruel, hungry sea. For a moment he felt the U-boat survivors should have been left to drown too, like the men of the ships they'd sunk. But then he caught the look of anguish and fear on the face of the last German struggling in the water; like him he was some mother's beloved son bravely doing his duty for his country! Yes, he was glad to see him reach the net and grasp it firmly.

"Have you put something in the log?" the Captain asked.

"No sir, not yet, I was waiting to see how many we've saved." He found the ship's log and wrote:

'U 92 sunk by *Foxglove* in company with *Wolverine* at 1652, in position N 47°20′, W 38°42′. Twenty-nine crew members rescued.'

Chapter 27

Oberleutnant zur See Heinrich Boddenburg climbed the ladder to the conning tower of U-15, and stood for the last time watching the Skipper shaping course for Wilhelmshaven. He like the seven others of his training batch, had now completed their training and tomorrow would be awarded the revered U-boat badge, a replica U-boat surrounded by oak leaves and surmounted by the German Eagle and Swastika. Then they would be appointed to an operational U-boat sailing for the Atlantic, where the U-boats were achieving such great success against the British convoys. Like him all his class mates were in high spirits, eager to see action and follow in the footsteps of their hero Korvettenkapitan Gunther Prien, who only six weeks after the outbreak of war and having already sunk three British merchant ships, had navigated the submerged U-47 through the narrow entrance of the British Fleet Base at Scapa Flow to torpedo and sink the British battleship *Royal Oak*. Gunther Prien had become a national hero and had been decorated with the Knight's Cross of the Iron Cross by Adolf Hitler himself in Berlin. In the Kriegsmarine he'd been given the nickname "The Bull of Scapa Flow" and thereafter the emblem of a snorting bull embellished the conning tower of his boat.

As the U-15 neared the submarine pens she passed the *Deutschland* his old ship. Her old name he saw, had been erased from the stern and replaced by *Lutzow*. It made him feel angry, the *Deutschland* had been a great ship, had done well and in no way did she deserve such humiliation! He'd been happy onboard her, had expected a career in the surface fleet hoping to join the fast E-boats, but it was to be the U-boats for him. It was a challenge he must accept and humbly too, for it was the U-boats that were taking the war to the British, as day by day they sank the ships bringing the vital supplies needed to feed and arm the country. And now that the French Biscay ports gave the U-Boats immediate access to the Atlantic, the battle against the convoys would surely soon be won. Already in Britain food, fuel and even clothing were strictly rationed; the starving British would have to sue for peace!

The following day he and his fellow trainees had paraded before the Commandant to be awarded their U-boat badge. Now they were members of the elite U-boat force! Then they'd received their appointments, he to join U-71 in Bremen, where she had been built. He was to be the Third Watch-keeper, the most junior of the five officers. U-71 he knew was a brand new Type VII boat, much larger than U-15, with an 88mm gun on the foredeck and a twin 20mm anti-aircraft gun mounted on the platform abaft the bridge, which he was to learn, was called the "Winter Garden!" She would carry nine torpedoes, four loaded in the bow tubes and one in the stern tube. The remaining four would be stowed in the bow compartment as re-loads, and among them some twenty men would share bunks on the hot bed principle*. On the surface using her two diesel engines she could make 18 knots and had a range of 9,000 nautical miles. As they needed air for combustion, her diesel engines could not be used when submerged, so U-71 like all U-boats was fitted with two electric motors powered by the boat's array of batteries. Using the electric motors U-71 had a maximum underwater speed of 8 knots, but at this speed the batteries would quickly be exhausted, so high speeds were reserved for emergencies. Normally underwater speed was restricted to 4 knots, when the batteries would last for about 20 hours.

Like all her sisters, the U-71 would normally proceed on the surface using her diesels both for propulsion and for the charging of her batteries, only submerging when danger threatened. Being able to submerge quickly, especially when an enemy aircraft armed with depth charges appeared out of nowhere, was a vital drill which had to be mastered.

When he'd arrived at the pontoon where U-71 was berthed, he'd stopped for a moment to admire her clean streamlined shape and watch the busy crew loading stores and victuals. Then he'd stepped onto the gangplank and went on board to be met by Walther Schweiger the 1st Watch-keeper. He took him to the Officer's Mess to meet the Captain, Kapitanleutnant Manfred Karf, who welcomed him and told him the boat would sail for Wilhelmshaven the next day for work up. On completion she would sail for her first patrol.

Most of the crew he discovered were new like him; only the Skipper, the four other officers and the senior Petty Officers had served in a U-boat before. He however was a novice and though he'd won his cherished U-boat Badge, he knew he had a lot to learn, had to prove his worth and like the rest of them must become well-practised in his duties and drills and form a crew that worked and thought as a team.

In the work up every possible drill was exercised. They'd fired the guns, launched two practice torpedoes and had practised crash diving time and time again until they'd achieved a full dive in just twenty seconds. Finally they'd been declared fit for operations and then they'd sailed to war.

That first patrol had been a real challenge! He'd thought his training in U-15 had prepared him for life in the cramped conditions in a submarine, but U-15 had never spent more than a few days away from base and the accommodation ship, where one could luxuriate with a shower and sleep in one's own bunk. But the U-71 had spent seven weeks on that first patrol, during which time the crew of forty-four had had to share just one lavatory! Nor had there been anywhere to have a shower and there'd been only sufficient fresh water to clean one's teeth! Like everyone else during those seven weeks, he hadn't shaved or washed his face, let alone his body and had never changed his clothes. After a week or so he'd got used to the stench of body odours and diesel oil, only noticing it when he came down from watch on the conning tower! Then there'd been that claustrophobia that would grip him now and then when they were dived. Then he felt trapped in this steel tube. Then he'd wonder if he'd ever survive, ever walk on dry ground again! Not for nothing were the boats called Iron Coffins! Others must have felt like him too, but one was too ashamed to admit it and anyway nothing could be done! All one could do was live for the moment, join the banter, mostly crude with fanciful tales of sexual exploits, and laugh.

Their first success had come when they found an east-bound convoy and had torpedoed and sunk an oil tanker. He remembered how the cheering erupted when they heard the dull thud of the torpedo exploding, and more had followed as the Skipper peering through the periscope said, "Navigator make a note in the log "Tanker estimated 8,000 tons sinking and enter time and position."

Now that U-71 had made her first kill, everyone was in high spirits, but then they began to hear the enemy's Asdic transmissions. As they came ever closer it was clear it was their turn to be the hunted. Then all were quiet as they listened to the pinging of the enemy Asdic. In an effort to escape, the Skipper took her deeper and changed course, but it was to be of no avail. Still the enemy's Asdic pinged away!

"Don't worry", the Navigator gave him a reassuring wink. "He'll lose us when he's overhead. When he drops his charges he won't know where we've got to. That's when the skipper will order full speed and put the helm hard over and the charges will miss us!"

He'd prayed the Navigator was right. As predicted, he heard the Skipper ordering full speed and changing course, and seconds later the boat shook violently as the charges exploded. He was sent sprawling and the lights went out.

In the darkness he could see the light of torches as a search was made for leaks and damage. Then the emergency lights came on and thankfully the enemy's Asdic transmissions began to fade. As U-71 crept silently away, his terror of being trapped in a sinking boat began to ease and the look of fear and anxiety on the faces of those around him began to disappear. Then there were laughs and smiles as someone shouted, "Well done Skipper that fooled 'em!"

For the next few days they enjoyed the welcome sun and fresh air as surfaced, they'd searched in vain for their next target. It seemed fate had decided to give them time to recover from their baptism of fire. They'd sunk a ship for the Führer, helping to avenge the Fatherland's defeat in the last war, and they'd withstood that depth charge attack. Now he and the other novices could feel they were real U-boat men! Never would he forget that feeling of triumph and joy that had swept through the boat as they heard their torpedoes exploding. That was why they were here in the middle of this unforgiving sea, why they endured the filth, the stench and the incarceration in this steel tube! Now their appetite had been whetted! They wanted more! But here the sea was empty yet they still had six eels,* as everyone called the torpedoes, yet to use.

A day later spirits rose as the look-out reported smoke on the horizon; was this the first sign of the hoped-for convoy? But where was the forest of masts? The two specks of masts grew taller, then they could make out the funnels, but there were no other ships. They counted three funnels rising out of a huge hull. She was going fast, about 25 knots. All eyes were studying the ship as it altered course away.

"She's a lone ship and zig-zagging*" the Skipper said. "Looks like the British liner the Queen Mary. She's too fast, damn it. We'll never catch up with her!"

What a prize they'd missed! For the next two days the sea remained stubbornly empty, but then their patience was rewarded. Another convoy was sighted and they dived deep hoping the escorts would pass over them undetected. They were indeed lucky and once clear of the escorts, U-71 fired a fan of three torpedoes, sinking a freighter. A second fan of three hit a tanker, which exploded in a huge fireball, but then they were caught by a tenacious escort that rained depth charge after depth charge on them. Again they suffered the terror of several near misses until the escort gave up, possibly fooled into thinking they'd sunk the boat, by the diesel oil and the bubble of air the Engineer had released. Then with fuel running low and only one torpedo left in the stern tube, the Skipper headed for Lorient, their new base on the French Biscay coast.

Three days later escorted through the swept channel by a minesweeper, they motored into their new base at Lorient. New base? They saw an ancient liner with a U-boat alongside. A boat came to meet them, "Berth alongside U-58, mein Herr" a Petty Officer shouted.

And as the crew of U-71 revelled in the luxury of hot showers, clean clothes, plentiful lavatories and food that didn't taste of diesel oil, they spun their yarns of sinking two tankers and a freighter and of the depth charge attacks they'd survived.

And then there was the pay they'd earned, seven weeks' worth! Money to spend on their two weeks leave and in the bars and brothels of Lorient.

Like most Heinrich had gone home to Bremen where he was overwhelmed by the love and affection of his parents. It was as if he'd come back from the dead! Clearly they were worried about him and wanted to know what he was doing in his U-boat. He told them the minimum he could, enough he hoped to satisfy their concerns, how his boat had sunk two freighters and an oil tanker, but he didn't mention the depth charge attacks, nor the squalor and stench!

"The U-boats are mauling the convoys," he said. "The British will soon be starving, then they'll have to sue for peace."

His mother listened, her face etched with concern. "We pray for you Heinrich dear every night. When will this war be finished?"

"Well," his father spoke more cheerfully, "Our U-boats nearly brought the British to starvation in the last war. Perhaps you'll finish the job this time eh?"

He'd nodded. That's what they all hoped for! But he wouldn't tell them how many U-boats had been lost! He changed the subject.

"Have the British dropped any more of their leaflets?"

"No. They're dropping bombs now," his father replied. "Your uncle's Focke Wulf factory has been damaged and the Atlas Werke shipyard too, and the town's suffered, but we're alright at the moment, living as we do on the outskirts."

He'd asked about Uncle Klaus, Auntie Golda and Hedwig, but was told they'd heard no more of them since they'd moved to Dessau. They'd wanted to keep their address secret for fear that Golda and Hedwig would be exposed as Jews, so they'd not given them their address.

Once more he changed the subject. "And what news of Horst?" They told him he wrote occasionally, was well and was at Lodz in Poland, serving with an Einsatzkommando*. Einsatzkommando? He and his parents had some idea of what an Einsatzkommando did and the conversation suddenly ended.

His days of love and affection sped quickly by and though he was loath to go early, he left for Lorient on the twelfth day. These days the railways were often disrupted and he daren't return from leave late. But of course for him, the trains ran perfectly and he was the first to return! He found U-71, but there wasn't much he could do, the dockyard workers were crawling all over her, checking everything.

Lorient itself looked like one huge building site. Cranes, drills and steam engines were everywhere, building they were told concrete covered pens and workshops for the new base. Now and then the RAF came at night and dropped their bombs causing some damage, but it was said that when the concrete pens were completed they would be impervious to bombs. Then boats could be refitted and repaired in safety.

Work on the U-71 was soon complete and the crew were busy packing and labelling the possessions they would leave behind, and many like Heinrich enclosed a last letter to their loved ones in case they failed to return. Then it was time for a quick trial in the Bay, before U-71 left for her next patrol. But now from the moment they left the safety of Lorient, U-boats were at danger of attack from British bombers that now flew regular patrols over the Bay. Already several surfaced U-boats had been caught unawares, and had been attacked with depth charges. Yet boats had to stay on the surface when sailing for or returning from their patrol stations in order to make good speed. Only when danger threatened did they submerge.

A good lookout was therefore vital, as was proved on their second day, when an RAF Sunderland was sighted. U-71 crash dived but the Sunderland's aim was good for the depth charges were worryingly close! That concentrated their minds. They were the hunted too! U-71 remained submerged for a while before coming to periscope depth for a thorough search of sea and sky. When nothing was sighted she surfaced, switching to her diesels to drive them on at fifteen knots. Two days later as they neared their patrol station, an arm appeared from the Radio room with a piece of paper. "Message from U-boat HQ," the Radio Operator said. Heinrich took it to the Skipper. It read "Form Wolfpack "Reaper" with U-69 and U-71 under the command of U-65 to attack convoy with 3 escorts in position N 48° 55′, W 35°10′, course 080°, speed 8 knots. Acknowledge."

Then a signal from U-65 ordered them to their designated starting positions. U-71 was to attack from the Convoy's port bow.

The next morning as the sun began to climb over the horizon, they caught the first glimpse of the convoy and waited for U-65 to give the order to attack. It came and like the others, U-71 dived and conserving battery power, steered slowly for the gap between two escorts. The Radio Operator had already begun hearing the convoy on the hydrophone, but then he reported the sound of propellers, possibly those of an escort. They listened for any asdic transmissions, but could hear none.

"We must be nearly through the screen," he heard the Skipper say. Then a few minutes later he ordered. "Come to periscope depth."

He watched the Skipper move the periscope round as he surveyed the scene above. Then he said "Surface, surface, surface."

Almost immediately he could feel the deck tilt as the boat began to rise and he, the guns' and conning tower crew all moved towards the ladder. The Skipper climbed it first and they followed, going with familiar practice to their surface stations.

Once surfaced he could see the convoy clearly. There were about forty ships in four columns, with the three escorts ahead. The Skipper was busy selecting his target, he chose a large freighter in the nearest column, "Standby to fire tubes one and two" he shouted, followed later by "Fire." He watched the target through his binoculars and saw the torpedo explode. The freighter had been hit. He stole a quick glance at the Skipper and saw a flicker of satisfaction cross his face, but it vanished as he ordered "Standby to fire tubes three and four". Having selected another freighter, he steered for her. Again the Skipper shouted "Fire". As he watched the new target, waiting for the torpedoes to hit, he saw an explosion on the other side of the convoy. That meant the other boats were at work too! Then their target exploded.

He saw a delighted Skipper raise his fist in a victory salute and shout. "Report when tubes 1 and 2 have been reloaded."

Clearly the Skipper hadn't had enough yet! He watched him as he turned the boat about to keep up with the convoy and saw him selecting his next target. But time was running short, for a destroyer could be seen heading towards them.

"Tubes 1 and 2 reloaded and ready", came the report.

"Standby to fire tubes one and two," the Skipper replied as he pointed at yet another vessel.

After the next two torpedoes had been launched, he counted the number of ships now on fire or stopped in the convoy. There were seven. Then as their torpedoes claimed another victim, he caught sight of a destroyer. It was heading for them. He shouted, "Destroyer Green 140" as plumes of water rose some 400 yards ahead. The destroyer was firing at them!

The Skipper yelled "Dive, dive, dive". And as the bows began to dip, there was a scramble for the ladder. It was a good dive, one of their "20 seconds" dives and as the last man closed the upper hatch, water was splashing around the sill.

Now the boat slowed to a quiet two knots and altered course towards the convoy. "They can't attack us in the middle of the convoy," the Skipper muttered.

But then they heard the pinging again, the destroyer had found them. Speed was increased and the noise of the convoy became louder. Then the steady beat of propellers was heard and the boat turned to steer the convoy's course. It was a good move and for a while they enjoyed the safety the enemy convoy gave them. But it wouldn't last for long, for dived they couldn't maintain the convoy's speed. So eventually the convoy would draw ahead of them and as the last ship overtook them, they began to hear those worrying Asdic transmissions again. For the next hour or so they suffered attack after attack, each countered by the Skipper's successful evasions. But with depth charges exploding close to them, they suffered more damage and worrying leaks. But then miraculously the hunt ended. Perhaps the escort had been ordered to re-join since they all knew U-71 was no longer a threat, for without surfacing she couldn't catch up with the convoy.

The next few days and nights were spent on the surface with every eye straining to find the next convoy. But it was no hardship, for they welcomed the fresh air which the diesels sucked into the boat, and enjoyed the sun as it warmed and dried their damp smelly clothes. And they felt safe for no aeroplane with its prying eyes could reach them here in mid Atlantic. At last their patience was rewarded. A blur of smoke was sighted on the horizon. Slowly it grew into a forest of masts and then the hulls of ships. U-71 made a sighting report to U-boat HQ, dived and waited. Later the hydrophone heard the rapid beat of propellers and a quick search through the periscope revealed an escort a mile and a half distant. U-71 descended to two hundred feet hoping to remain undetected. The noise of the convoy could now be heard and a quick search through the periscope revealed a line of ships. The Skipper chose a freighter.

"Stand by to attack ship bearing Green two zero" he shouted and began passing estimates of the targets course, speed and range to be fed into the Torpedo Fire Control box. Then came the order "Fire tubes one, two and three". Again everyone listened for the explosion. When finally it came the whole crew cheered, but a hurried search through the periscope to check on the target, revealed an escort heading their way. Soon those worrying Asdic transmissions were heard. The pinging was regular and becoming more frequent, the escort was getting close. A radical change of course was ordered and the boat taken deep. For a moment it seemed to work, for the pinging stopped. They began to relax. But then the pinging began again. The escort was getting nearer. When it was overhead the Skipper once again took decisive evading action. Depth charges exploded. They were close, again the boat shook violently, but seemed undamaged. Would he attack again? They all knew he would and he did. He made two more attacks but each time U-71 managed to evade the charges. Then it seemed the attacks really had ended, for though the enemy's Asdic could be heard, it came no nearer as it would do for an attack. Quietly confident, U-71 stole slowly away.

Then there was an explosion, a huge explosion. They'd been hit and water began coming in.

"Surface, surface, surface," the Skipper shouted, the bows began to tilt upwards and as the survival instinct struck home, everyone rushed to escape. He was lucky; being near the ladder he'd been one of the first to reach it and the welcome fresh air. He saw a corvette nearby, her gun aimed at them though she didn't fire. It must be obvious to her that the boat was mortally wounded, there was no need to fire. But would the corvette rescue them? With four others he struggled to get the big life raft loose.

Chapter 28

"Hettie dear, here's a letter for you." Mrs Bamber gave her the manila envelope. "It must be about that translating job of yours, dear."

"Oh! But they won't want me, I'm German. They won't trust me!" It was only the second letter she'd received since she'd come to England. Like the first it had the words ON HIS MAJESTY'S SERVICE printed in bold above her name and address.

Cautiously she slit the envelope open. "They want me!" she exclaimed. "They want me to report on Monday!"

"Oh! Hettie dear that is good news. I'm sure they'll trust you."

Hedwig was elated, how she wished she could tell her mother she'd be helping Britain to fight Hitler, to help overturn the evil, murderous regime he was imposing on their country and those he now occupied. But how could she? And would anything she did make any real difference? Hitler and his armies seemed to be unstoppable, he seemed to win every battle in France, in Greece, even in North Africa! And as if to emphasise his invincibility the sirens sounded that night and the war came again to Liverpool. At Crosby she'd felt safe enough to pull the blackout curtains back and in the darkness watch the city burn as the Luftwaffe dropped its bombs.

It was a cold mid-November day, when Hedwig caught the bus for Liverpool to start her new job. From the top deck she studied the remains of houses and shops flattened by the bombs in the recent air raids, and as they neared the city the bus had had to slow down as it wound its way through streets being cleared of yet more rubble. A lady visibly shocked called her attention to the shell of a building.

"That was the Custom House," she said in dismay. "But," she pointed to a statue, "They haven't hit Queen Victoria. She's still standing there defiantly!"

And the good lady continued "I've heard that flames from some of the warehouses set on fire by the incendiary bombs, spread to a ship which caught fire too. The port's been badly damaged." She shook her head in desperation.

The bus stopped at Water Street and getting off Hedwig made her way to Derby House where on production of her letter she was allowed to enter. Further interrogation by a receptionist followed and a man in naval uniform came to collect her. He was the one who'd interviewed her.

"Good morning Miss Boddenburg. My name is Mathews," he said, smiling. "It's good to have you joining us. Let me take you to the office where you'll be working."

Hedwig followed him down the stairs to the basement, where she could see men and women in uniform moving symbols around on a huge table in the centre, while the walls were covered with maps and information boards.

"This is the Ops room," he whispered. "We reckon it's safe from the bombs!"

Leaving the Ops room, they walked past a few doors until they stopped and he opened one. They were met by a girl in uniform.

"Good Morning Sue, meet our new recruit, Miss Boddenburg," he looked at Hedwig. "Can we be less formal? Do you have a Christian name?"

"Yes, please call me Hettie."

"Well then Hettie, you'll be working with Sue, Leading Wren Sue Perkins. She'll have the tapes for you to translate, and she'll show you how to start and stop the machine. And, he grinned, "Sue is one of those clever people who understand short hand and she'll take down what you translate and type it for you to check. Do you have any questions?"

Hedwig shook her head. "No, not at the moment."

He gave her some headphones, showed her the stop/start switch and told her the tape he was loading was a record of prisoners chatting at a nearby Prisoner of War camp. "They're all German, all officers and mostly U-boat men. Some of what they say is mere chatter, but now and then there's some useful intelligence, so please translate everything no matter how irrelevant it may seem."

He saw her nod. "So," he concluded, "I'll leave you two to make a start."

Sue gave her a smile and started the tape recorder for her and Hedwig began translating. As the Lieutenant had said, it was mostly chatter which was easy to translate. But then it changed:

A voice said *"Good morning sir, we have three new arrivals today. Let me introduce Korvettenkapitan Erich Hauser,* she stopped, rewound the tape and played it again to check the name. Satisfied she began again. *Korvettenkapitan Erich Hauser who commanded U–52.* Now it was a different voice.

> *Good morning Korvettenkapitan. You commanded U-52?*
> *Yes, sir.*
> *So how many patrols did U-52 complete?*
> *Three, all in the Atlantic, sir.*
> *And how many ships did you sink?*
> *In total 6 merchant ships and an escort, sir.*
> *That's a good score Korvettenkapitan, thanks to you and your brave U boat men we'll soon have the English starving and on their knees begging for peace. Where was U-52 based?*
> *In the French port of Lorient, sir. That gave us easy access to the Atlantic Convoys. Before that we were based in Kiel and our route to the Atlantic took us through the North Sea and the Iceland/Faroes Gap. A long and dangerous passage, sir*
> *You were based in Lorient? I hear the bases on the French Atlantic coast are being fortified with bunkers. Is that so?*
> *Yes, sir. The Todt Organisation* is building huge concrete bunkers over the U-boat pens. They're incredible, they give the boats complete protection! The English keep bombing them, but their bombs can't penetrate the concrete, they just bounce off! But they've done a lot of damage to the town and killed many of the French. I tell you, sir, the English aren't popular in Lorient!"*
> *"That is good news. So these bases give you quicker access to the Atlantic and the convoys."*

"Yes. At first we could proceed safely on the surface day and night to our patrol areas, but now the English Air Force patrols the Bay, and by day when we are making good speed on the surface they attack us, so we often have to stay dived. But at least until recently, we could stay surfaced at night and make good speed then, without fear of being detected.

………and so it went on until Sue lent forward and switched the recorder off. "It's time for lunch," she said.

In the dining room on the second floor, Sue had introduced her to her fellow Wrens.

"Hettie's joined us to help translate some German documents we have. She's signed the Official Secrets Act, so," she grinned, "she's one of us now!" They'd all welcomed her but when one of them asked how she came to be in England, and she'd told her a little shyly that she was a Jew given refuge through the Kindertransport scheme, the conversation had suddenly stopped. Whether it was because she was a Jew, or because they knew little if anything about the Kindertransport scheme, she couldn't tell. But after an awkward moment or two, Sue broke the silence and turning to another girl, asked, "How's your latest boy-friend? He's a soldier isn't he?" Giggles followed and the tension was broken.

After lunch, with Sue, she'd continued translating and the following afternoon Sue had given her a typescript.

"Please check it Hettie and make any corrections."

Hettie read it carefully. Most of it was just chat, but to her the last few paragraphs of it seemed useful intelligence:

But now the English seem able to detect a U-boat on the surface even at night! Then they attack us without warning".

"You have no means of detecting them?

"Well we have the Biscay Cross but it just doesn't work."

"Biscay Cross?"

"Mein Herr, it's a radar detection device given to U-Boats to pick up an aircraft's radar and give them time to dive. But it's useless. It just doesn't work. By day with a good lookout we might see an aircraft and crash dive, but at night we have no warning. The first we know of an attack is when the aircraft is almost overhead and then suddenly we are illuminated by his searchlight. Then he can drop his depth charges accurately. When U-52 was attacked like

this, we were very lucky for the bombs fell astern of us and we were able to dive and escape. But many boats have not been so lucky..............."

Hedwig put the typescript down. "That's fine Sue."

"Well then Hettie, please sign it."

In the bus home that evening, Hettie realized she'd enjoyed listening to her native language. But hearing men recount the dangers they faced in the U-boats had disturbed her. So many of their shipmates had not survived, dying a most terrible death by drowning, often trapped inside their sinking U-boat. She found herself worrying about Alan and whether he was safe and had he and the *Foxglove* sunk any U-Boats? Then there was Heinrich, he'd always wanted to join the Navy. She remembered him telling her he wanted to serve in the fast E-boats. She hoped his wish had come true, that he was serving in anything other than those awful U-boats. And what about his brother Horst? She closed her eyes as a vision of him appeared. He'd been so good looking! Involuntarily she sighed. With that tall, slim figure of his, that unruly blond hair and those blue eyes, he was the very archetypal Aryan that Hitler admired and wanted for his Volk! She remembered when music was the most important thing in his life, how they'd both played together in the school orchestra, he on his flute and she on her violin. She wondered whether he still had his flute and that piccolo her father had given him. And did he still play Lorelei? It was such a favourite of his! She remembered him wearing his Hitler Youth uniform on his fourteenth birthday. He'd told her he admired Hitler and hoped to join the S.S. The S.S.! Its very name had made her shudder with fear! Since then she'd always hoped he hadn't and prayed he was fighting for Germany as a soldier anything, even in the U-boats, anything other than the S.S.! She shook her head in despair; in this terrible war her family were on opposite sides. They were fighting each other! How will it end?

As she tried to rid herself of these awful thoughts, she saw the bus was entering Bootle and could see the masts and funnels of the ships in the docks. It made her think of Alan. He was somewhere in the Atlantic in the *Foxglove* trying to protect some convoy. She always worried about him, he and the *Foxglove* could be sunk too, like that destroyer the U-boat Captain claimed to have torpedoed. She remembered the first time she'd met him, when he'd come home on leave for a few days. Then almost eight months later the *Foxglove* had been in Bootle and he'd been able to come home on a couple of nights. That was when he'd given her his violin. That was when he'd kissed her! That kiss had made her feel wanted and yes, loved! She'd wanted to stay in his arms and be kissed again, but his mother had appeared and they'd hastily drawn apart. Then he'd had to go and the next day the *Foxglove* had sailed!

In her reflections she almost missed her stop, but the clippie* had shouted "St Luke's" twice, and hurriedly she'd got off.

"Hello, my dear," Mrs Bamber welcomed her. "How's your day been?"

"Fine, thank you, and the people are very nice."

"Good. But have you heard the news?"

"No."

"Coventry was bombed last night. According to the B.B.C. there's hardly a building left standing in the centre, and the ancient Cathedral is in ruins. Nearly six hundred people have been killed and just under a thousand seriously wounded."

Chapter 29

Two years ago, when he'd helped build that new Kibbutz at Alonim, Moshe had never thought he'd one day be wearing Army uniform and fighting for the British! He and many of the Jews had disliked the British, and for good reason, for they'd reneged on their promise to establish a home for the Jews in Palestine. Yet Chaim Weizmann, the Zionist President, wanted to support Britain in its fight against the Nazis and had sought to establish a Jewish force to fight with the British Army. The British had gratefully accepted his offer, though they wouldn't allow the force to fly a Jewish flag. And so when the French capitulated in 1940, making Hitler master of Europe, he and many other young Jews had put away their scruples and had enlisted. How else could he avenge the murder of his grandfather and the persecution of his mother and sister? He'd not had any news of them since boarding that train in Berlin over four years ago. With the family moving to Dessau and his mother and sister converting to Christianity, he'd agreed not to write, but he worried constantly. For all he knew like so many Jews they could be starving in some concentration camp or could have been murdered. All he could do was hope and pray they were still safe, but now he could do something positive, he could join the fight against that evil fiend Hitler.

He'd enlisted in Jerusalem and with the others had been sent to an encampment outside Beersheba, where given his own Lee Enfield rifle, he'd completed his training as an infantryman. Then with the other recruits he'd gone to Alexandria to join a Jewish Battalion attached to an English one, before they were both sent to form part of the Eighth Army in Libya. But their preparations and training for desert warfare in Libya were quickly halted. Though the Greeks were managing to repulse their Italian invaders, Britain had offered some military support and so at the end of October, Moshe had found himself and his battalion in a troopship, bound for Crete, where they were to relieve Greek soldiers guarding Souda Bay, so they could join the battle on the mainland.

For the next few months the war passed them by as they familiarised themselves with their defensive positions and enjoyed the local cooking and drank Retsina in the Heraklion taverns. But as the Italian invasion continued to falter, everyone began to predict that Hitler would come to the aid of his ally, Mussolini. Later when RAF planes arrived at Maleme, one of the three Cretan airfields, it seemed their prediction might be true, and not long after, troopships had arrived at Piraeus with British, Australian and New Zealand troops, destined to guard the Greco Bulgarian frontier against invasion by the Nazis.

On 6th April the Germans struck, attacking Greece through her borders with Bulgaria and Yugoslavia. Within days the heavily outnumbered Greek, British and Commonwealth forces had abandoned the Metaxis Line, the chain of twenty-four forts built on the Bulgarian border in the inter-war years and the vital port of Thessaloniki soon fell to the Germans.

Moshe and his comrades were devastated by the news. The British had been routed and within a few days! The Army in which they had enlisted seemed to be no match for the Wehrmacht. When their time came and he and his comrades faced the Germans he wondered how they'd fare. He hoped they'd not keep withdrawing. He hoped they'd stand and fight. He wanted vengeance for the Jews murdered by Hitler. He wanted to kill some Nazis.

Thankfully some encouraging news followed. The Allied army had stopped the German advance along the Haliacmon River, while a separate British force was defending a line based on Thebes, not far from Athens. But further news was sporadic and often contradictory!

In their defensive positions around Souda Bay, Moshe and his comrades had a grandstand view of Heraklion and the Bay. They would see plenty of caiques, the small sailing vessels the Greeks used for fishing or for supplying distant islands, but then they saw warships being attacked by Stukas. The cruiser HMS York had become a permanent resident in the bay. She'd been attacked by Italian motorboats loaded with explosives and, badly damaged, had settled on the bottom in shallow water. Moshe had met some of her sailors in Heraklion. They told him they were trying to make the hull watertight and re-float her.

On the mainland despite their hopes, the Commonwealth force outnumbered, ill-equipped and with little or no air support, had been unable to stop the Germans who entered Athens on April 27th. But though Greece had capitulated and the Nazi flag was flying on the Acropolis, the residue of the Commonwealth force fought on as it withdrew to the port of Piraeus. There despite almost constant attack by the Luftwaffe it was evacuated to Crete, where Moshe and his comrades saw the troopships arriving in Souda Bay.

Demoralised by the rapid German advance and having lost much of its armour and artillery, the Commonwealth force braced itself to defend Crete. Here the Allies would have the advantage of Crete being an island. To capture it, the Germans would have to launch a seaborne invasion and despite the threat of the Stukas, such an invasion would surely be countered by the Royal Navy. And with three Cretan airfields available for Allied aircraft, the defenders hoped to have the luxury of some air support. The defence of the airfields thus became vital, and Moshe and his company was sent to defend the airport at Maleme.

The Luftwaffe now changed targets. The troopships in the Bay were ignored, the airfields became the prime target. For two days they were attacked without respite and most of the aircraft and anti-aircraft guns were destroyed. Only a few of the precious RAF fighters survived and they were hastily withdrawn to Egypt. After the last wave of bombers, Me.109 fighters came to rake the airfields and their defences with their gunfire. Then there was a lull, to be broken by an ominous new sound, the roar of hundreds of three engined Ju52 transports, escorted by yet more fighters. Then all were amazed at what they saw! An enormous cloud of parachutes began to fill the sky, with men dangling beneath them. Now was the time for the defenders to fire and fire they did at these easy targets that drifted slowly down to earth. Many of the paratroopers were killed before they landed, but the majority survived and when they landed, they began firing as they ran towards them. Then gliders came, crashing and slithering along the badly damaged airfield before coming to a halt. They too made an easy target as they disgorged their troops. For the defenders, the airfield had become an easy killing ground, but it wasn't to last. Another battalion of paratroops had landed unopposed to the west and, able to form up without disturbance, came quickly to support their comrades on the airfield.

The fighting soon became disorganised with defenders shooting whenever they saw a paratrooper. When his first bullet had struck and Moshe saw his enemy fall, for a moment he'd felt a pang of remorse, but then he saw another trooper running and firing at him. He shot him too; and then another. It was a battle fought fiercely until the sun set and brought with it a welcome lull, doubly welcome for Moshe and his comrades were running low on ammunition. How many he'd killed he didn't know, but he'd survived, though two of his platoon hadn't! Later under cover of darkness they began to withdraw to the south to re-group and re-arm and by dawn they'd moved to the west of the airfield, where they launched a counter-attack. They had some success at first, recovering a defensive trench the Germans had taken the day before. But then Me109's came to strafe them with their murderous 20mm canons. Several of Moshe's company were killed or wounded, but again he was lucky! Following the Me109s came Ju.52s with yet more paratroops. The fighting escalated and gradually the Allies were forced back as the Germans gained ever more ground. When after a long and brutal day darkness came and it was clear the airfield and its buildings were now in German hands, the order came to abandon the fight and withdraw to the beaches at Sfakia on the south coast. No one had heard of Sfakia, but in the darkness they stole away to join the six thousand other British and Commonwealth troops tramping along a narrow mountain road. As the dawn came they prayed for fog or mist to give them some cover, but their prayers went unanswered and the sun rose in a cloudless sky. Then came the dreaded Me109s to strafe and harry them without mercy. But at last they saw the sea and warships lying offshore to rescue them. Footsore and weary, they followed the others down the winding narrow track that led to the crowded beach and the welcome fleet of boats collecting soldiers from the water. Then it was their turn to join the orderly queues of men making their way down to the water's edge to wade with rifle held above their heads to the waiting boats.

As he'd waited to join the queue, Moshe had thought of those who'd been killed and wounded. They'd managed to bring the more lightly wounded with them, but some had been left behind. He worried about them and prayed especially for any of the Jewish Battalion, that the Germans would treat them as prisoners of war like the others.

When he reached the boat it seemed full, nevertheless he was told to "come on" but as he struggled to climb onboard, the boat tilted so badly he thought it was about to turn over; but thankfully it didn't. Then it was heading for a destroyer and they were clambering onboard, to be taken below and given tea and sandwiches. It was the first food he'd eaten for days! More and more troops came to join them until there was hardly any room to turn. Then they felt the ship begin to move. He and his comrades had been rescued!

Chapter 30

Klaus walked past the Stuka assembly line to the hangar. Despite its vulnerability, the Stuka had done great work against the English in the Mediterranean, sinking countless ships, and in Greece also, where its role in close support had been applauded by the Wehrmacht. Indeed in tactical roles where little opposition from enemy fighters was expected, the Stuka had proved its worth. It was only in a strategic bombing role against well defended targets that it was so vulnerable. This seemed to have been recognised by the Luftwaffe, who kept the assembly line busy meeting orders for yet more Stukas.

With a heavy heart he entered the hangar. There it was, this problem child of his. It had first flown almost four months ago, but was now jacked up on a cradle waiting for the new engine to be fitted. In the first test flight, the pilot had been able to maintain level flight when rotating the tail fin by the small and judicial use of the ailerons, his modified rudder controls had given easy steering whether the tail fin was in the up or down position and the interlock to prevent the undercarriage being lowered unless the tail fin was in the up position had worked. All had gone well, except for the plane's disappointing top speed. There was little chance the plane would be ordered by the Luftwaffe unless this could be improved. So a more powerful engine was needed and after some considerable evaluation he'd decided on the Daimler Benz 601. That was the biggest engine he could fit without a radical redesign of the front end. The DB 601 produced 10% more power than the Jumo 211A it was replacing. With that engine he was sure the plane would do at least 550 kilometres per hour, as fast as the Hurricane.

The new engine had at last been delivered and today they'd been busy preparing to install it. So far all had gone well. It was time for lunch.

When he returned to his office to tidy up, his Secretary told him that the Managing Director had phoned. "Oh!" he'd replied. He'd returned his call and had been invited to his office. A downcast Otto Tauber met him.

"Ah! Klaus, we've had a letter from the Reich Chancellor for Aviation. He's withdrawing funding from the Ju187!"

"Oh! My God. Does he say why?"

"Yes, he says the plane's too slow, slower than the Spitfire and even the Hurricane!"

"But he hasn't given us time to work on that."

"Yes I know, but unfortunately for Junkers, Focke-Wulf have modified their fighter the Fw190 for a dive-bombing role and it's much faster than our Ju187."

Klaus was devastated! His plane had been rejected because of its slow speed! Yet with the new engine he was sure its speed would match that of the Hurricane, even exceed it. His innovative design was to be abandoned, without giving it a fair trial! It was a cruel, cruel blow! He felt dismayed, he wouldn't be given time to perfect his design, his unique design. What would he do now?

"It's a sad blow for Junkers and for you too Klaus."

Kluas remembered that day as if it was yesterday. It had been a disastrous day! After that bombshell they'd moved his problem child, the Ju187 to a little shed-like hangar and boxed up all its plans and documents, in case it should be revived. Then his team had been dispersed and he'd been assigned to the Ju88 team to assist with its modification for a night-fighter role.

Working as an assistant rather than the head of a team had given him little job satisfaction, but that was the least of his worries. Now he feared the status he seemed to have acquired with Hermann Goering as the Chief Designer of an aircraft which had caught his eye, would become devalued. That could have worrying consequences for Golda and him!

For three months he'd worked diligently on the Ju 88. The modifications were relatively simple, requiring little creative thinking and he'd tried hard to hide his dissatisfaction. Then once again he'd been summoned to Otto Tauber's office.

"Klaus," Otto gave him an encouraging smile. "I've been very conscious that we've not been making the best use of your skills since the demise of the Ju187, and it seems the Ministry of Aviation has similar views." He stopped as he reached for a letter on his desk.

"We've received this letter from the Ministry instructing us to release you for other work." He shrugged his shoulders. "The work they have in mind is not specified, but they require you to report to the Director of Weapon Development at Peenemunde in a week's time, where you will be given accommodation for you and your family." He paused and handed him an envelope.

"They don't say what your job will be, but they've enclosed this letter for you. It may give more details."

Klaus thanked him and had retired to his own office to read the letter. It gave little more information than that which Otto had given him, except that he would be working on the production of a Vergeltungswaffe, a Vengeance Weapon. A Vergeltungswaffe? A weapon to seek vengeance for what? For the bombing of our towns and cities? The enemy air force had been mounting an ever-growing bombing campaign, and their bombing accuracy was slowly improving. U-boat bases, Luftwaffe airfields, Railway stations and marshalling yards had been the main targets, but Junkers had been bombed too, though only the runway had been hit and that had been easily repaired. But in the bombing many civilians had been killed and their houses destroyed. Was this new weapon to seek vengeance for this? Was the Führer planning a campaign of revenge attacks on London and other English cities? What was this weapon? He could think of nothing else. When the day's work ended he hurried home to tell Gerda.

"Peenemunde?" she asked. "Where's that?"

He hadn't known himself until he'd studied a map. "It's a tiny village at the western end of an island called Usedon on the Baltic Sea. The nearest town is Karlshagen, not far away. The Wehrmacht has a weapons development establishment there, with a small airstrip and some workshops and accommodation."

"Oh! It doesn't sound very nice. Where will you find a home for us? In Karlshagen?"

"Dearest I'm told accommodation will be provided for us, but where it will be I don't know. We'll have to wait and see. I have to report there in a week's time with you dearest."

He could see Golda was pleased she'd be going with him, but nevertheless it was clear she was unhappy to be moving, to be leaving behind her new friend Christel and her precious garden, but it had to be!

"Dearest, for safety, we mustn't divulge where we're going, nor give our new address to anyone."

Golda nodded. "Yes, and when we get there we must go to church too. I suppose the nearest one will be in that town, whatever it's called."

"In Karlshagen, dear. But there could be one in Peenemunde."

Chapter *31*

It was her 19th birthday, but she hadn't told anyone, not even Mrs Bamber! But that morning all thoughts of her birthday were put aside as the bus wandered through the bombed buildings. Could Britain survive such devastation? It worried her, the papers were always full of the bombing. While cities like Coventry, Liverpool, Manchester, Plymouth and Portsmouth had all been badly damaged, London for the past eight months had been the main target of a sustained bombing campaign, which the papers called the blitz. She'd heard that almost a third of London's streets were now blocked with debris from bombed buildings and every main railway terminus had been put out of action at some time or another. Fifty thousand houses had been destroyed, thousands of people killed and many more injured and as the year closed, fires were still smouldering all over the city, which had been the target of a great incendiary raid on December 29th. Surely the Londoners couldn't take much more! And Lord Haw-Haw* in his programme *"Jairmany calling"*, was gloating over the success of the U-boats in the Atlantic and was pouring contempt on the feeble British Army that had been so quickly driven out of Greece. The British, he claimed, were losing their will to fight and would soon be suing for peace! Victory for the Nazis, he said in his German accent, was inevitable. Everyone claimed to laugh at Lord Haw-Haw, but should they? After all, the events he reported were true! It was only his assumptions about the morale of the British people and their determination to fight on that could be challenged, that were wrong. All Britain's former allies had given up the fight against Hitler. Might Britain do the same? Such a possibility terrified her. In countries overrun by Hitler, his anti-Semitic policy was being enforced and as rigorously as it had been in Germany itself. If Britain surrendered she and all Jews in Britain would be at his mercy! She thought of her parents in Germany. Were they still free? The possibility that they might be incarcerated in a concentration camp haunted her. She didn't even know if they were still alive! They could have been killed like her grandfather. Would she ever see them again? Only her father's expertise with the Stuka bomber might save them. His Stukas that were proving their worth in the London blitz, the blitz that Lord Haw-Haw prophesied would lead to a British surrender!

Yet everyone kept saying Britain would win. But did they really believe it? She hoped and prayed that they were right. But she wasn't so sure. Passing through the Ops room on her way to the office, she'd snatched a quick look at the board that showed the convoy losses. Two hundred and ninety-nine merchant ships had been sunk by the U-boats in the first five months of the year yet only ten U-boats had been sunk! She'd done some mental arithmetic. That meant sixty ships had been sunk each month! And how many poor sailors had been sent to their death, drowning in the unforgiving ocean? She daren't even think! And how could those sunken ships be replaced? Could Britain build 60 merchant ships each month? Surely that was impossible! And only ten U-boats had been sunk! Just two a month, they could easily be replaced, she was sure! She'd shaken her head in despair, to her there could be no question about it, Hitler and his U-boats were definitely winning the battle.

She fingered the crucifix her father had given her. Those statistics had shaken her. With such losses how could Britain survive? Perhaps there was no need for Hitler to invade. With such losses Britain might be starved into submission! Food had been rationed since the outbreak of hostilities and the ration had been reduced time and again as the war progressed. Recently it had been announced that even clothing was to be rationed!

"We've got a new tape for you," Sue said as she loaded it into the machine.

Hedwig switched it on and began to translate, but as usual it was a just a lot of chatter and an occasional burst of laughter. Someone was telling jokes about the English! It made her laugh too! But then she heard that familiar voice *"Good morning sir, we have five new arrivals today. This is Oberleutnant zur See Heinrich Boddenburg,"* Hastily she stopped the tape, Heinrich Boddenburg? Heinrich! Heinrich her cousin?

Sue gave her a questioning look. "Are you alright Hettie? You look as if you've seen a ghost!"

"Yes, yes, I'm alright, it's just that he's called Boddenburg, the same name as me."

"Is he a relative?"

"No, no, it's just a coincidence!"

Shaken, she switched the machine on.

"And what was your U-boat?"

"U-71 a Type VII boat, sir."

"One of the latest. So how many patrols did U-71 make?"

"Two, sir and in total we sank 5 freighters and 2 oil tankers."

"That's a good score. But how were you sunk?"

"An escort made several attacks, but as escorts have to pass overhead before releasing their depth charges, it's possible for a good Captain to dodge them, and that's what our Captain did. But then without any escort near us, we were hit! We could hear an escort's Asdic but it was still some way away! It certainly hadn't passed overhead, so how that depth charge was delivered we've no idea! It couldn't have been dropped by a plane, we were in mid Atlantic where not even our Condors can operate, and the convoy had no aircraft carrier. So it's a complete mystery."

"Could it be some new weapon of theirs? Or maybe some new tactic?"

"Possibly sir, but none of us can think what it could be!"

Hedwig switched off the machine. "Have you got all that, Sue?"

Sue nodded. "Yes, but we've never heard of a U-boat being attacked like that before. I wonder how that depth charge was delivered! I'm sure this will give the Intelligence people something to think about!"

"Well," Hedwig smiled, "Let's hope we've found something useful." She switched the machine on again.

"So how many survived?"

"Only eight of us. With four others I tried to release the life raft, but the boat must have been badly holed for she went down very quickly. There must have been 10 or maybe 12 of us left swimming. The escort was nearby, but it circled us before it stopped to pick us up. It was probably checking there wasn't another U-boat nearby and by the time the escort stopped to pick us up only eight of us were still swimming. I was one of the lucky ones!"

Hedwig switched off the machine, she could hear no more. "What a terrible story Sue!"

Sue nodded. "Yes, those poor men in the convoy and in the U-boats face a terrible death. I wouldn't have the courage to be one of them."

"Nor would I, Sue. Just hearing about how that U-boat sank frightened me! I think we need a break and anyway it's almost time for lunch."

Hearing Heinrich's voice had been a shock for Hedwig and she desperately wanted to be on her own. There was only one place, the lavatory.

Thankfully she closed the door and sat down. That definitely was his voice! Hearing him talk after all these years had rattled her. Thinking about the family, the family she was unlikely ever to see again, had become too upsetting and she always tried hard not to forget them. But then she'd heard his voice! It was as if he'd come back from the dead! Heinrich her cousin always overshadowed by Horst, had always been a kind friendly boy. One who laughed a lot and always put others first. Well thankfully he was safe now and never again would he face death in one of those awful U-boats.

Hearing him had brought back so many memories. How wonderful it would be to talk to him, he might have news of her mother and father. If she told her boss that Heinrich was her cousin, would he allow her to meet him? Perhaps on the pretext of getting more intelligence? No it was a crazy idea and anyway when the family had moved to Dessau they'd kept their address secret, so how could Heinrich know any more than she? No, she had to be content with the knowledge that at least one of her family Heinrich was safe!

That afternoon she found it difficult to concentrate, but fortunately the tape had nothing but chatter and banter on it and finally it was time to go home. On the bus she heard his voice again, heard him retelling that awful tale of his U-boat sinking and how he was rescued. She felt so pleased to know he was safe and wondered what his brother Horst was doing. Heinrich would know. Horst, she felt herself smiling. Horst, he was so good looking, but then she remembered Alan. He was somewhere out in the Atlantic escorting those convoys. He was different from Horst, so different. Not so good looking, but he had a pleasing face and he was honest, considerate and kind and without fanatical views like Horst. She admired him and enjoyed being in his company! Yes, she had to admit she'd grown to like him, even to love him!

The sound of the clippie shouting "St Luke's" ended her musing and she got off and approaching the Vicarage, saw the front door opening. A smiling Mrs Bamber held out her arms. "Happy birthday, dear Hettie." She gave her a welcoming hug and bade her, "Come into the sitting room, Ronald's there," and leaving her to find her own way, Mrs Bamber disappeared to return a moment or two later with tea. The Vicar wished her a happy birthday too! Hedwig was mystified. "How did you know it's my birthday?"

"Ah! The Vicar smiled. "Ve have our vays!" Hettie laughed. "Well you are clever and your German is excellent!" Mrs Bamber who was lighting the one candle on the cake apologised, "I'm sorry Hettie it's only one, but candles are so hard to find nowadays!"

Overwhelmed by her kindness Hedwig felt she really must call her Aunt Dorothy as she'd been asked to do so many times. "But Aunt Dorothy you've made a cake, though everything's rationed!"

"Well my dear it's only a little sponge cake. I used one of Lord Woolton's* recipes!" As she began to pour out the tea, the Vicar pointed to the clock.

"Dorothy dear, it's almost 6 o'clock, we mustn't miss the news." They were just in time to hear:

"This is the BBC Home Service. Here is the news at 6 o'clock on Monday 22nd June, read by Alvar Liddel.

At 3.15 this morning Germany attacked her former ally the Soviet Union on a broad front from the Baltic to the Black Sea, unleashing a massive war machine of some three million troops supported by more than three thousand tanks, seven thousand guns and nearly three thousand aircraft. Reports indicate that Soviet forces are offering little resistance as the Germans race eastwards.

The Prime Minister Mr Winston Churchill has sent a message to the Soviet President Joseph Stalin offering Britain's support as the Soviet people fight to repel the Nazi invasion."

There was a stunned silence as they digested the news. The Vicar was the first to speak. "What incredible news. We have an ally once more, we're no longer fighting Hitler alone."

"Yes, but," Dorothy broke in "will the Russians be able to stop Hitler?"

"Well, Russia's been taken by surprise, that's why the Germans are advancing so quickly, but they'll stop them soon enough."

It was indeed incredible news. Britain no longer stood alone in the war against Hitler. Now she had the Russians as allies. But would they be able to stop Hitler?

Chapter *32*

The officers of Einsatzkommando 3 had been bidden to attend a briefing by Brigadeführer Franz Blobel, the Commander of Einstazgruppe A, of which their Kommando formed a part. Like the others Untersturmführer Horst Boddenburg expected that something big was being planned. Could it be an advance to claim the other half of Poland that the Russians had occupied so quickly in September?

There was an expectant hush as the Brigadeführer arrived. He began by warning everyone that what he had to say was Top Secret, then spoke about Operation Barbarossa, the planned invasion of the Soviet Union. The Wehrmacht and Luftwaffe, he told them, were now positioned and ready to attack and it was expected that the Soviet Army, now in disarray after Stalin's recent purge of his Generals, would offer little effective resistance. The Führer he told them, was confident of a rapid advance and expected Moscow, Leningrad and Stalingrad to be captured before winter. Then victory would be in their grasp.

"While Einstazgruppen A, B and C will not take part in the fighting, they have an essential role," he told them. "At a recent gathering Obergruppenführer Reinhard Heydrich gave us our mission. It's a simple one, but a vital one. It is to liquidate all the higher cadres, officials and leaders of the Soviet Communist Party and state, and to instigate and encourage pogroms against the Jewish population." His audience nodded in approval and Horst could hear murmurs of agreement and a lone voice saying "Das ist gut."

The Brigadeführer continued, "The Führer made his purposes clear when planning Operation Barbarossa. He sees Communism as a growing danger, which could overwhelm the Reich in years to come. Therefore this must be a fight to the finish, for while we may defeat the Soviets now, if we don't eradicate all traces of Soviet Communism, in thirty years or so once again we shall be confronted by the Communist foe. So the Führer is determined that the Bolshevik Commissars, the Communist intelligentsia and the Jews must be exterminated." Again he paused and again his audience muttered their approval.

He went on, "Einstazgruppe A will be attached to Army Group North and will be tasked with making the area and towns it captures free of Communists cadres and of course, Judenfrei. Your Kommando has won itself a good reputation here in Lodz, with many Jews exterminated, but I shall expect even better results in the war against the Soviets."

With that he departed with instructions for the Kommando to be ready at noon the following day.

The supervision of the Ghetto having been delegated to the Orpo*, Horst and his colleagues were left busy packing away their smart black uniforms, digging out their field grey ones and getting ready to move. They didn't have to wait long, for in the early hours of Sunday 22nd June the Wehrmacht struck on a 1,800 mile front from the Baltic to the Black Sea. Three days later Horst and his Kommando, following in the wake of the army, entered the town of Kaunas in Lithuania.

As Intelligence had foretold, the Lithuanians freed from Russian domination welcomed them. Local nationalist and anti-semitic groups were quickly recruited and reinforced by prisoners released from the local jail, quickly began hunting and killing local communists and the hated Jews. Horst and his men were hardly needed for within three days the local nationalists had run amok and some 4,000 communists and Jews had been killed. After that first unruly spasm the killings became more organised as the local officials and police began a systematic search for their quarry. Now Horst and his men became involved. They had found a glade in the woods outside the town where his men marked out a long pit which they partially dug. It was to serve as the place of execution and a routine was quickly established. The local Police would force Jews and the few communists remaining out of their homes telling them they were to be re-housed in a ghetto and that they could take only one suitcase apiece. Then formed into groups of fifty or so, they would be marched off under armed guard to the glade, where Horst and his men would be waiting. On arrival the first batch of Jews was made to dig the pit to a depth of two metres. When this had been done they were then made to hand over their bags and valuables, undress and stand in line along the edge of the pit. Any who refused were shot out of hand. This seemed to leave the others numbed with shock, and they stood obediently awaiting the bullets. As they were shot their bodies fell into the pit behind them and when the shooting was finished, earth was shovelled over the bodies and their clothes and baggage examined for any gold, silver or other valuables, such items being fed into the Nazi coffers.

For Horst and his men this became a daily routine as group after group came to be executed; it seemed the steady flow of Jews would never end. Aware that some of his men were becoming distressed by this constant killing, Horst reminded them that the Jews were Untertmenschen, sub-humans, and though it might be a distasteful task, there was no place for them in the Greater Reich and they had to be exterminated. Most of his men had nodded in agreement, but he'd heard one or two whispering "if we lose the war, we'll have to pay for this." He'd rounded on them saying "The Wehrmacht is almost at the gates of Moscow. We cannot lose the war!"

And he would remember his Reichswehreid*, his Oath of Allegiance to Adolf Hitler, in which he'd sworn loyalty, bravery and obedience to him. Then he would tell himself, he was a mere tool carrying out the Führer's decree! But nevertheless the constant killing was troubling him too. Were the Jews really Untertmenschen? His aunt Golda was a Jew, but she wasn't sub human. He remembered how loving she was and how when he was a little boy, he loved her too. And then there was his cousin Hedwig who would play her violin when he played his flute. How could she be sub human? Often after a day's killing when such thoughts worried him he would be unable to sleep. Then in an effort to forget he'd play his piccolo, his beloved piccolo which transported him into another world.

After a while the flow of Jews to be executed began to slow and though it was difficult to keep accurate records Horst estimated that he and his men had killed some eight hundred and fifty Jews. There were occasional days without any killing to be done and after one such happy day yet another group arrived and were lined up along the trench. All were Jews, filthy Jews he kept telling himself, for whom he had the greatest contempt. Most were elderly and all were bedraggled, save for one young girl. As they were ordered to undress he couldn't take his eyes off her. She reminded him of that shapely Jewess in Lodz he'd bought for five zlotych. She'd had beautiful breasts too, just like this girl. Remembering that Jewess in Lodz excited him, and as the young girl took off her clothes before him, his eyes devoured her. She was tall, with braided hair and had striking eyes, the colour of sapphires. But when their eyes met, hers were full of fear and accusation. He looked away, his eyes drawn to her young enticing breasts. Suddenly he needed a woman. Could he? He smiled at her and heard himself saying,

"Tell me your name."

She made no reply. She seemed paralysed with fear.

"Tell me your name", he repeated.

At last she spoke "Kotrina."

"Take a step forward, Kotrina".

But she didn't. She seemed too terrified to move. He looked into those sapphire eyes of hers.

"Kotrina don't you want to live? You are too beautiful to die. Take a step forward."

She moved and stood before him, her eyes wide with fear.

"Go, it would be a pity to bury such beauty as yours in the earth. Go and wait for me at the entrance."

She looked at him in disbelief.

"Go," he said.

She hesitated for a moment and then she started walking. He watched her, admiring her supple movement with eager thoughts of lying with her. But then reality struck. He a Gestapo officer sworn to serve and obey Adolf Hitler, was sparing a Jew for his own use! How could he? Hastily he drew his Mauser and fired. She seemed to freeze as the bullets struck, then she fell.

For a second he wondered what his men would be thinking. He looked at them and laughed. "Thought we needed a bit of sport eh?"

But they didn't laugh! Hurriedly he shouted, "Take aim, fire."

The shots rang out and he saw the Jews collapse, all but a few falling backwards into the trench. Now as usual it was time to finish them off, to despatch the wounded. He beckoned his men forward to do the deed. When they'd finished, the naked bleeding bodies lay heaped up on one side of the trench and as usual he led his men down to spread the bodies more evenly, ready to be covered with earth.

Pulling those bodies around and being contaminated by them had become his worst nightmare, yet as a loyal member of the S.S. who'd sworn a personal oath of loyalty, bravery and obedience unto death to Adolf Hitler, it was part a job he had to do. All he could do was to tell himself and indeed his men that Kaunas was now almost Judenfrei. But no doubt they'd be sent to make another town Judenfrei and the carnage would start all over again! Sometimes when he couldn't get the sight of those naked corpses out of his mind he'd wish he'd joined the Kriegsmarine like his brother Heinrich, or the Wehrmacht, anything but the S.S.! But like so many of his friends in the Hitler Youth he'd been mesmerised by the Führer and the S.S. and having sworn that oath of loyalty and obedience he had no choice but to do Hitler's will. And his will? The Brigadeführer had made it clear, the Bolshevik Commissars, the Communist intelligentsia and the Jews must be exterminated! So he had to put brave face on it and not show his men know how he felt. But it was become more evident day by day that it wasn't just him who'd become disturbed by this constant killing. Many of his men were equally disturbed and like him getting solace from drink, some being drunk and unfit for duty the following morning! He'd dealt firmly with them! But it was clear that many were becoming mentally disturbed by the killing and more than one were deliberately aiming wide. He'd spoken to them more than once to remind them of their oath of obedience to the Führer, that they had to obey his will, but it only had a limited effect and the executions were taking longer and longer.

The Sturmbannführer* who was aware of these problems had told the officers of his Einsatzkommando, that Obergruppenführer Reinhard Heydrich had been tasked by Heinrich Himmler the Reichsführer of the S.S. to propose a final solution to the problem of exterminating the Jews. What his proposals might be no one knew as yet, but a new method to replace the execution of Jews by rifle fire was apparently being developed. The Sturmbannführer told them this would entail the use of special vans capable of carrying up to seventy people. They looked like furniture removal vans and were airtight when the doors were closed. The van's exhaust pipe would be connected to a tube giving access to the interior.

The Jews would be made to enter, supposedly to be taken to a place of work, the doors closed, the engine started and the van would move off. As it did so the exhaust would fill the van with carbon monoxide killing the Jews trapped inside. Their death would come within fifteen minutes or so, then the bodies would be buried.

Horst and his fellow officers were full of admiration for this simple solution which would help to alleviate the distress experienced by the execution squads. They waited with growing impatience for the delivery of such a van to them.

Chapter *33*

Hopes that the Russians would stop the Germans soon faded as Hitler's army raced eastwards sweeping aside all resistance, seemingly unaffected by the Russian scorched earth policy. But despite the German early success and fears that the Russians might capitulate, the United States and Britain began supplying the Russians with aircraft, artillery, tanks and munitions by means of Artic convoys, which were very vulnerable to attack. Ju88 torpedo bombers and Stukas were a constant threat requiring the convoys to be escorted not only by anti-submarine escorts, but also by cruisers and destroyers fitted with anti-aircraft guns to provide air cover. The convoys were also threatened by the battleships *Tirpitz* and *Scharnhorst,* the pocket battleship *Lutzow* and the heavy cruiser *Admiral Hipper* based in the Norwegian fiords.

For Britain, however, the German assault on Russia relieved her from the threat of invasion and the constant bombing of its cities virtually ceased. But in December the Japanese attacked the US Naval base of Pearl Harbour in the Pacific without warning, and invaded Malaya. Now the conflict became a truly world-wide war. And for the British, more bad news was to follow with the sinking of the battleships *HMS Prince of Wales* and *HMS Repulse,* and the loss of Malaya, Burma and Singapore. The war in the Far East now stretched Britain's resources and that of the Empire to the limit, but thankfully it gave her a new and powerful ally, the United States of America.

In the European theatre with the growing need to supply Britain with American troops and ever greater quantities of arms and munitions, winning the Battle of the Atlantic became ever more imperative. Former passenger liners sailing independently at speed now zig-zagged* across the Atlantic bringing American troops to Britain without loss, but the convoys continued to suffer. Hedwig saw the statistics. In December 1941, 11 merchant ships, 1 Escort Carrier* and 2 escorts had been sunk for only 5 U-boats destroyed. In January 48 merchant ships and 3 escorts were sunk for only 1 U-boat. February was even worse; 73 merchant ships and 4 escorts lost for 2 U-boats.

Continued sinkings on such a scale threatened to bring Britain to her knees. It was the Liberty ship that saved her. The simple and easily built Liberty ships based on a 1940 British design, were constructed in 18 shipyards in the United States. On average they took just 42 days to build and with 18 yards building them, it meant that one Liberty Ship was entering service almost every other day! Now there was hope that the number of merchant ships being built might begin to compensate for the number being sunk! By war's end 2,710 Liberty ships had been built, the first named the Ocean Vanguard, being completed in August 1941.

In the spring of 1942, with so few U-boats being sunk, the number of U-boat prisoners remained a trickle, yet Hedwig continued translating the eavesdroppings from the Prisoner of War camp. Most was chatter, but then one day some prisoners began talking about a new torpedo being developed for the U-boats. It was an acoustic torpedo, which they called the Gnat. She heard one of them explaining it to the others. *"It listens for the noise made by ships' propellers and then steers toward the sound, until it hits its target." "But does it work?"* she heard another ask. *"Yes of course, it will have been well tested before it's issued to the boats."*

When her boss Lieutenant Matthews read her translation he was very excited. "What a weapon! This'll keep the scientists busy, they'll have to think up some defence!"

His excitement had made her feel she could at last be making some contribution to the war effort. That the intelligence she'd uncovered might give those brave men in the convoys more protection against the U-boats. On her bus to and from work she often saw the merchant ships that had survived the Atlantic crossing, as they sailed upriver for Bootle or Liverpool. She'd begun to recognise their national flags. Most flew the British flag, the Red Ensign, but she'd seen Canadian, South African, Swedish and other flags she'd not recognised. And recently she'd seen the Stars and Stripes. Sometimes she would see an escort too. After the merchant ships it looked so small! How could it withstand the gales? Every time she saw them, she always read the numbers painted on their sides, hoping to see K125, the number of Alan's ship the *Foxglove*. But she never did! She did worry about him. Escorts were being sunk by those terrible U-boats as well! Oh why must Alan be at sea? Why couldn't he be in Intelligence like Fred Matthews? He'd be safe then. It was a cruel irony, her cousin Heinrich who had manned one of those awful U-boats was safe, yet Alan the man she'd grown to like, she hesitated, grown to like? Even love? He was facing continual danger at sea, unlike Heinrich in his Prisoner of War camp!

On her way to the office as she passed through the Ops Room, she always looked at the board showing the monthly losses and secretly kept a record. In the seven months December to June, 97 merchant ships had been lost and 8 U-boats sunk. But as the months progressed, she'd seen that the number of U-boats sunk was slowly increasing, with 12 sunk in July and 15 in October. It was certainly beginning to look hopeful!

November 1942 came and for the first time the British began to feel Hitler really could be defeated. Though his armies were at the gates of Leningrad in the north, Moscow in the centre and Stalingrad in the south, the age old ally of the Russians the winter snow had come to their aid and at last the Germans were held at bay with their tanks and motor vehicles bogged down in snow and mud. And in North Africa British Forces had achieved a great victory against Rommel and his Afrika Corps at El Alamein. Winston Churchill the British Prime Minister, speaking about El Alamein and the country's long struggle against the Nazis, said at the Lord Mayor's luncheon "this is not the end, not even the beginning of the end, but it is perhaps the end of the beginning."

Hedwig had always been surprised by the reluctance of the British to admit defeat and their conviction that somehow victory would be theirs, yet when a few weeks later on the bus home, she saw a mighty battleship steaming slowly up river, she herself began to feel it might be true. It was the *Duke of York* coming in for minor repairs after defending an Artic Convoy and sinking the German battleship *Scharnhorst*. What a sight she made!

And four weeks after Christmas she'd seen two of those little escorts coming up river and with hope in her heart had read the numbers painted on their sides. For a moment her heart stopped. She saw it. She couldn't believe her eyes. There it was K125, clearly painted on the ship's side! It was his ship, the *Foxglove*! How wonderful! She might see him today! She wanted to rush home and tell Mrs Bamber, but she couldn't, she had her work to do.

Oh! How difficult it was to concentrate. She had to tell Sue, how she hoped to see him when she got home. Sue had given her a hug! "Oh! Hettie how wonderful. You must worry about him so." She didn't reply. How could she tell her how worried she was? She changed the subject. "Well we must get down to work. What have we got today?"

"There's yesterday's transcript for you to check and we have another tape."

"Shall we do the tape first? Let's hope it's not as boring as they've been lately."

Sue started the tape. *"Before we sailed,"* Hedwig heard a German voice say, *"We saw the U 459 coming in. She was enormous. We couldn't keep our eyes off her. Later we learnt she was the first of the Milch Cow boats. She'd just finished her work up and was ready for her first patrol."* Another voice interrupted. *"Milch Cow? What's that?"*

The first voice continued, *"It's a Type XIV boat much, much bigger than the Type VIIC and it's designed to act as a supply ship for other U boats and replenish them with fuel, torpedoes and food, so they can stay longer on patrol."*

She heard an angry groan, then a voice. *"Isn't a normal patrol long enough in those Iron coffins of ours, without extending it? Doesn't our precious Admiral Dönitz know what hell it is in a U-boat?"*

There was a general rumble of agreement, then the first voice continued, *"Well there are easy pickings off the coast of America, and that's no doubt where Admiral Dönitz wants our U-boats to be and the Milch Cows will be waiting for them."*

The conversation had continued, dwelling on the rigours of life in a U-boat on patrol and what a boat would do if the Milch Cow they were seeking had been sunk. When the tape came to an end Sue looked at her. "That's the first we've heard of these Milch Cow boats. Lieutenant Matthews will be very interested in this."

And he was. "The Milch Cow! He exclaimed, "That'll make a prime target for the Yanks. Sink a Milch Cow and you'll save a lot more U-boat sinkings. The Admiral will be very interested in this. Well done Hettie!"

Thankfully the time came to go home and she hastened to catch her bus, her hourly bus, but there was no sign of it. Had she missed it? No, the others assured her, though no one knew why it was late. But then after nearly half an hour it arrived, already full. Resolutely they clambered aboard to stand crowded in the gangway. With a jerk the bus started, but it seemed to go at a snail's pace. Would she ever get home? He could be there! After what seemed an age the bus stopped and a few passengers left and there was room enough for her peer out of the window and see they were nearing Bootle. Would it ever get to Crosby? Would he be there? But he wasn't, however Mrs Bamber was overjoyed when she heard her news.

"If his ship's only just arrived he'll not be with us today, Hettie dear, perhaps tomorrow."

Tomorrow came and with it the long ride into Liverpool. As the bus drove through Bootle all she could see were the walls of the warehouses with a mast or two rising above them, but whether one of them was the *Foxglove's* she couldn't say. But she had seen the Foxglove yesterday and surely he'll be home tonight. She must be patient!

Sue gave her a friendly smile. "Did you see him?"

Hedwig shook her head, "No, but I'm sure I will tonight! So what have we got today?"

"Dear Hettie, I do hope you will." Then she gave her the transcript of yesterday's translations and Hettie settled down to read. Oh! There was the usual boring chatter and then came all she'd heard about the Milch Cow. She read it carefully and signing it gave it back to Sue. "The boss will enjoy reading this," Sue said as she hurried off.

She came back smiling. "I left him reading it. He kept saying 'This is excellent.' So let's see if this tape has anything to tell us."

She loaded the tape and Hettie began. It seemed another boring tape but then she heard a voice talking about a Schnorkel. Schnorkel? Had she heard it correctly? She stopped the tape, rewound it a little and started it again. Yes, Schnorkel it was! The voice continued *"Just before we left Kiel we saw a boat that was being fitted with the new Schnorkel."* Another voice interrupted, *"New Schnorkel? What's that?"* The first voice continued, *"It's a modification which allows a submarine at periscope depth to suck air into the hull so that the diesel engines can be run to propel the boat and charge the batteries."* Another voice chipped in, *"That's great, but how does it work?*

The first voice continued. "*Well the boat is fitted with a long pipe which has access to the interior of the boat by means of a hinged joint and at its other end it has a float operated ball valve. In use the pipe is raised to the vertical and with the submarine at periscope depth, its top is just above sea level, allowing fresh air to be sucked in and the diesel engines to be run. The float will stop water entering the pipe if there's a big swell or if the boat goes below periscope depth.*" Doubts about its practicality were expressed and many questions followed, but the speaker who had told them about the Schnorkel seemed unable to answer them. Then the talk had reverted to the usual banter and idle chatter.

With the tape finished, both agreed the tape had yielded valuable information. Sue said she would type it straight away and asked Hettie to find Lieutenant Matthews and ask him to come to the office in an hour's time, when the transcript would be ready. When at last Hettie found him, he told her the last transcript had been well received by the Admiral, and asked whether the latest transcript was equally exciting.

"I hope so sir, but come and read it!"

He came and did so

"Well done Hettie," he said, "this is fantastic. It'll be great news for the anti-submarine boys! They'll want this, and so will the Admiral. Sue, do you have a duplicate?"

"Yes, sir, I have two carbon copies."

"Right, stamp them SECRET and give me a copy for the Admiral." And as he disappeared with the transcript and Hedwig for her bus, Sue wished her "Good luck."

Chapter 34

They'd arrived at Peenemunde station and met by an Army driver, had been driven to the Research Centre, where the Vergeltungswaffe weapons the V-1 and V-2 were being developed. The car had stopped at a bar across the road, but after a brief conversation between driver and sentry, it was allowed to proceed into the Research Centre, that occupied the northern peninsular of the Baltic island of Usedon. The village of Wolgast with its little port, standing on the western end of a long sand-spit where the river Peene empties into the sea, had become home for the accommodation blocks and administrative offices and across the river a collection of buildings marked the area where the weapons were being developed and test launched. The site also housed the Aerodynamic Institute, with its wind tunnel, hangar, workshops and airstrip.

The driver had stopped outside one of the accommodation blocks, where they'd been met by the warden and taken to their apartment on the third floor. Adequately furnished, with two bedrooms it looked out over the port and the sea beyond. Golda remembered Klaus pointing to the sea and saying,

"Over there's Sweden, neutral Sweden not too distant, perhaps 130 miles away, no more." He'd given a deep sigh. "How wonderful it must be to live in a land where Jews are safe and can live in peace!"

Then he'd shrugged his shoulders, "Will we ever feel safe in Germany?"

She'd reached for his hand, "Dearest as long as we're together, we must be thankful."

Klaus knew she was right, they had to be thankful; they were still together. But would it last? To him it was incredible that his aeronautical skills had served to protect them from Hitler's hatred of the Jews, but would it continue? Having a non-Jewish name, her conversion to Christianity and her regular attendance at Mass surely helped. Helped them to avoid the terrible persecution.

Though never mentioned in the newspapers, most Germans were aware of the barbaric treatment of the Jews not only in the Greater Reich, but in Poland, Russia and the Baltic States too. The elderly, children and those unfit for work were being systematically slaughtered, while those deemed fit for work were used as slave labour to build fortifications and excavate huge underground shelters for munition factories, to be manned by yet more slave labour. Most people knew something about it, but no one mentioned it. To talk about it would be to recognise its veracity! But it was true! His brief imprisonment in Buchenwald had revealed all too clearly the irrevocable hatred the Nazis had for the Jews, and the brutality and inhumanity displayed when implementing Hitler's doctrine.

The following morning he'd reported to the Director of Weapon Development, who after swearing him to secrecy, had told him the V-1 flying bomb had completed its series of test flights successfully and was ready for production. Now all their efforts were concentrated on the V-2, the rocket propelled ballistic missile. He mentioned the three key technologies needed to build such a weapon; the design and production of the large liquid-fuel rocket engines, the supersonic aerodynamics of the rocket's body, and the design of the gyroscopic guidance system. The aerodynamics and the development of the body had been led by Marcel Gunsch, but he had recently died, struck down by a heart attack. Now he Klaus was to replace him.

"Work on the V-2," he continued, "began here at Peenemunde in September 1939 and three years later in October 1942, we had our first successful launch, when the missile reached an altitude of 52.5 miles. And now here we are in May 1944 with its development almost complete. But we still have a major problem. Of twenty-six successful test launches last month only four reached the target area. The other twenty-two failed due to in-flight breakup on re-entry into the atmosphere. We don't know why this happened, maybe the build-up of pressure in the fuel tank when the missile enters the increasing atmospheric pressure at lower altitudes causes fuel to escape, maybe the warhead explodes, or perhaps the body of the rocket is not strong enough. We just don't know. Herr Gunsch and his team were reviewing the design of the body when he died. So now mein

Herr," he'd given him a searching look, "We look to you to lead this review, report your findings and propose any remedial action."

"How long have I got?"

"I want your report as soon as possible."

"Is the in-flight break-up the only problem?"

"No, no. We have others. The guidance system is unreliable and erratic." Klaus had left with the break-up problem already perplexing him, and had been introduced to his team; all well qualified and intelligent men, who had worked on the V-2 since the early days. He'd asked what they thought caused the explosions. Almost to a man they told him they didn't believe as some did that the war head had exploded. In earlier flights when some had exploded just after launch it had always been blamed on an explosion of fuel. Could the change in pressure on re-entry allow un-used fuel to leak and explode?

One lonely voice suggested that static electricity generated on re-entry could be the cause, a possibility that Klaus thought valid. Yet another asserted his belief that the rocket's body wasn't strong enough to withstand the forces of re-entry.

Over the next months he and his team had evaluated the possible causes and had concluded that the front end of the missile did indeed need strengthening. So they'd designed a tube to fit around it to give added strength and also extra insulation against static electricity. The tubes had come to be known as sleeves and when the "sleeved" rockets were test-launched in August all re-entered the Earth's atmosphere without breaking up. But still the guidance system gave trouble.

Klaus and Golda had now been in Peenemunde for several months had attended mass in the local church of St Peter's in Wolgast every Sunday, and had begun to make a few acquaintances. They especially enjoyed their Sunday afternoon walks in the cooling on-shore breeze. Watching the sea birds and the occasional ship or fisherman's boat passing by, helped them forget the war. One of their more regular walks took them along the sands to the little airstrip whose marker beacon stood on the beach. Golda was puzzled! "Is this ever used?" she'd asked. "We never see a plane landing or taking off!"

"It's used now and then," he'd told her, "but only by light aircraft bringing important visitors to the island. There's a small hangar too with a couple of mechanics to service and fuel the planes that do land here."

Despite the pressure of his work, their isolation and restriction to the Research Centre, Klaus and Golda were happy. She and Klaus had become used to her new name of Gerda and were pleased that everyone seemed to accept her as an Aryan. And like all those living in Peenemunde she and Klaus were thankful that the enemy bombers, now raiding Germany night and day, seemed to show little interest in the place. There'd only been the one air raid in the previous August, when the RAF had caused considerable damage to the V-2 production line being built on the island. But though it had been the first and only raid of the war, such was Peenemunde's obvious vulnerability that a decision had been made to move the production line to the Mittelwerk site in Thuringia. A huge series of underground tunnels were being excavated in the mountains there by forced labour from the concentration camps at Ebensee and Mittelbau-Dora, from where the labour to man the production lines would also come.

After that one raid in August, the bombers had strangely left Peenemunde in peace. Yet despite this peace many were becoming increasingly worried about the war in the east. The happy days of victory in Europe and North Africa and the headlong advance into Russia were but distant memories. Some even worried Germany might lose the war. The possibility of an American and British invasion of France gave Golda hope that their armies would be successful and drive into Germany to liberate it from the Nazis ideology and oppression. Many others without admitting it, began to share her hope too, though not for the same reason. Theirs was motivated by the fear of being occupied by the Soviet army whose troops were renowned for brutality and rape.

And on 6th June Golda's hopes were answered when the wireless announced that American and British armies had launched an amphibious assault over the beaches in Normandy. The announcement ended with the confident assertion that the enemy forces would be driven back into the sea as they had been before, at Dieppe*.

But they hadn't been, and by mid-July when the nation heard of the failed assassination attempt on Hitler at his "Wolf's Lair" headquarters in Rastenburg, the Allied armies in the west had captured Bayeux and the port of Cherbourg. The only encouraging news was that the V-1 flying bombs were now regularly falling on London and south east England. One report said as many as one hundred a day were being launched.

Meanwhile test firing of the "sleeved" V-2 rockets had proved successful, but the troubles with the guidance system still persisted. A meeting to discuss the problems and find a solution had been arranged for August 5th to be attended by General der Flieger from the Reich Ministry of Aviation. Like other important visitors he had arrived by air the day before and was scheduled to leave again in the afternoon of the sixth. His visit however was badly timed for on the night of 5th August the RAF launched their second attack on Peenemunde. One of the test flight stands was destroyed and buildings nearby were badly damaged and a number of people killed or injured.

Klaus and Golda had taken shelter along with their neighbours and had emerged safely and unhurt and early the next day Klaus had hurried to his office to see if any of his buildings had been hit. Shortly after he'd arrived Herr Griem the Director of Weapon Development had telephoned.

"Klaus, I take it you were not injured in the raid last night."

"Herr Griem, thank you for asking. I'm pleased to say neither I nor my wife Gerda was harmed. We took shelter with our neighbours and all are safe. And I'm pleased to report none of my buildings seem to have been damaged either, except for a few broken windows."

"That is good, but unfortunately the General's pilot has been killed."

"Oh! I am sorry to hear that. There must have been other casualties?"

"Yes, I'm told ten have been killed and about fifteen have been injured, but now I need someone to fly the General back to Berlin after the meeting tomorrow." He paused. "He came in a Goldfinch, not the usual Stork*."

"Did he?"

"Yes Klaus, a Goldfinch. I'm told that was one of your designs."

"Yes, it was. It proved to be a good trainer."

"I'm also told that you flew in the last war and have flown since."

"Yes, that is so Herr Griem."

"Well Klaus I'm sorry to have to land you with this responsibility at such short notice, but it's vitally important. I'd like you to fly the General back to Berlin tomorrow."

A plane! He's giving me a plane to fly! They could escape in a plane! He was so excited he feared his voice would tremble. He paused as if considering the matter. It gave him time to compose himself.

"I will do that willingly Herr Griem, but I must have a practice flight or two. It's a while since I've flown an aircraft."

"Certainly Klaus have your practice flight. I will tell the General you'll be flying him tomorrow."

"Herr Griem, the airstrip people need to be told that I'll be flying the General home tomorrow and most importantly that I will be having a practice flight this morning and to have the plane fuelled and ready. Will you do that?"

"Yes, I'll do that Klaus. Fly safely," he said.

Am I dreaming, Klaus asked himself? I've got a plane to fly. I could fly Golda to Sweden. Sweden, where we can be free! Excitedly he left the office and headed home. Sweden was only one hundred and thirty miles away and he had a plane!

He let himself in and found Golda in the kitchen. He hugged her, "Dearest I've got a plane!"

Bewildered, she looked at her beloved husband, his face lit up like a child's on finding a new toy!

"Klaus, whatever do you mean? You've got a plane?"

He let her go. "Yes dearest, I've got a plane. I've been asked to fly the General to Berlin tomorrow."

"To fly an aeroplane? Why you? You haven't flown for years. Why are they asking you, why you of all people?"

He told her of his conversation with Herr Griem. Then he smiled, "But I'm not flying the General to Berlin tomorrow dearest, I'm flying us to Sweden today!"

She looked at him, her eyes wide open in shock. "To Sweden? Is this true? It's not some wild dream?"

"No, no Golda dear. It's true, and the plane is one of my Goldfinches, I can fly that. Surely it must be an act of Providence."

He saw her face light up. "Do you really mean we'll be in Sweden tonight?"

"Yes, yes, dearest, so let me tell you of my plan."

He told her about his practice flights and how he'd fly them to Sweden, that she could take nothing except her handbag, which she should fill with her money and jewellery. Then she should go to the beacon on the beach at the end of the strip, and wait there. She must be there by half past ten.

She would see him take off and after five or ten minutes he would land as near the beacon as possible. Then she should run to the plane and scramble into the front cockpit.

Realising that this was a lot to ask of someone unfamiliar with flying, he explained with care, how she would climb into the cockpit while he kept the engine running. He made sure she understood how to fasten her safety straps securely and that she must keep her head down so no one would see her in the cockpit as he taxied back for a supposed second practice flight. Only this time they'd be on their way to Sweden!

He looked at his watch. It was nine-thirty, time to go. He kissed her, wished her luck and left. As he walked to the airstrip, he tried to visualise the controls of the aircraft he'd designed and flown so long ago. Suddenly he felt nervous, would they end up in the sea? Once they'd taken off, they could never return. If they did they'd be at the mercy of the Gestapo, and the Gestapo knew nothing of mercy!

The Goldfinch was standing ready when he arrived, but it was only ten minutes past ten. It was too early to take off! Having checked that she was in fact fully fuelled, he had to waste time so painstakingly, he started his pre-flight checks, running his hands carefully over the fuselage, moving the ailerons, the rudder and elevators by hand. Then he checked the wheels and stood back as if he was admiring the beauty of the plane. A glance at his watch told him it was twenty minutes past ten; at last it was time to go. He climbed into the rear cockpit and helped by a mechanic, strapped himself in. The engine started effortlessly and he began his in-cockpit flight checks. It was half past ten, she should be there by now. He waved away the chocks, opened the throttle and the Goldfinch began to move as he taxied towards the end of the strip. Feeling the joystick in his hand thrilled him and as he lined up for take-off, memories of flying his Fokker D VII during the war returned. But he chased them from his mind, he had to concentrate! It was now or never! He opened the throttle and the Goldfinch began to accelerate and as she bumped over the uneven ground, he watched the air speed indicator needle moving on its dial. At forty he pushed the stick forward, the tail came up and the speed increased. The needle passed eighty the stall speed, and at ninety he gently pulled the stick back and she was airborne. The beach and sea was not far ahead and there near the beacon, he saw a figure. It must be her! He gave a great shout of joy. All was going well and it was great to be flying a plane again after all these years. He headed a mile or so out to sea, then turned inland, rehearsing in his mind, the drill for landing. He'd always made good landings before and he would do so now! He passed the airstrip to starboard then a mile or so later he turned onto his approach run and began losing height. As he passed the fence marking the inward end of the strip, his altimeter read forty feet. He eased the throttle back to reduce speed and lose height and gently lifting the nose he felt that reassuring bump as the wheels touched the ground. "Well done Klaus," he shouted as he taxied towards the beacon. Then he saw her, running head down towards him. He braked and there she was climbing onto the lower wing and heaving herself into the forward cockpit.

"Well done love! Keep your head down, you mustn't be seen!" he shouted. She waved a hand, "Of course."

He revved the engine and got her moving again, turned and headed back.

He could hardly believe it, it had gone so well, but it wasn't the time for congratulations, they still had to take off and make that long flight to Sweden and safety.

At the other end he'd turned and after a quick prayer had taken off, "No, Herr Griem" he muttered, "Not for a practice flight, it's Sweden this time."

Now he was flying her with increasing confidence and as the beach passed beneath them, he saw Golda's head appear. She gave him a wave and he shouted "Sweden, here we come!"

Chapter 35

She couldn't wait to get home. Alan could be there, but she'd been delayed leaving the office and had arrived breathless at the bus stop just as the bus appeared. Thankfully she got on and sat on the one remaining seat. It wasn't her favourite, it looked out over the boarding platform, but it was the only one free. What an afternoon it had been! Hearing about the Schnorkel had made her feel she was doing something worthwhile. Lieutenant Matthews had been excited by it. What would the Admiral think? She hoped it would be useful intelligence and that it might help in the war against the U-boats. She wanted to tell Alan about her work and what she'd discovered, but she knew she couldn't tell him. It was secret.

She watched the familiar scenery passing by, another merchant ship coming up river with a tug leading it, a fishing boat going out, the outline of Birkenhead on the other bank, and then the approaches to Bootle. The bus slowed and drew to a halt. Some people got off and others got on. Then she saw a navy man. She couldn't believe her eyes. It was him! It was her Alan! He moved from the boarding platform into the body of the bus. Then his face lit up. He'd seen her!

"Hettie, Hettie dearest, it's you." As he leant forward to kiss her the bus bounced over a pothole and he almost fell into her lap. Her arms reached out for him and held him as his head brushed against hers. She felt him kiss her forehead. Then as he regained his footing, they were laughing and she heard herself calling him dearest.

"You've grown a beard!"

He stroked it, a ginger bushy one. "Yes. No-one shaves at sea, at least not in our lively corvettes. They roll even in dry-dock!"

She laughed at the impossibility of it.

"Do you like it?"

She giggled, "Well Alan it's part of you and I like all of you."

"Do you? You do? That's good 'cos I'm fond, very fond of you."

Hettie could feel herself blushing. No one else was talking. Everyone was looking at them. It was embarrassing! Especially when the lady sitting next to her got up and offered Alan her seat.

"I can see you two haven't seen each other for a long time and we love our sailors, so my dear, sit down by your love."

Alan thanked her, telling her how kind she was. As he sat down it seemed everyone was smiling at them and she was blushing all the more! He reached for her hand and gave it a squeeze. "It's lovely to see you," he whispered.

"Dearest, I knew you were home. I saw your ship coming up river yesterday. I could see it was the *Foxglove,* I saw her number K125."

"Well done," he laughed. "Those pendant numbers have their uses!"

Hettie smiled, "I told your mother I'd seen your ship. She was as excited as me. She'll be expecting you." She'd seen he had a case with him. "Can you stay the night?"

"Yes. The ship's in port for a boiler clean and I've got leave till Monday morning, so we have three whole days together."

Three days together! How wonderful, but how could she tell him she had to go to work tomorrow; that they'd only have just Saturday and Sunday! She saw the church and the bus slowed to a stop. They got out and as they reached the gate, the front door opened and his mother ran to greet her son, hugging and kissing him.

"Oh! Alan dear it's wonderful to see you. And you've grown a beard, just like your father did, when he was in the Navy."

Hettie studied Alan as his mother fussed over him. He had such a manly figure and that beard made him look a real seaman, like that bearded sailor she saw so often on the packet of Players cigarettes her boss always smoked. Alan was tall too, over six feet, almost a foot taller than her, just as a man should be!

She heard mother and son talking.

"Mum, I've got a ration card for my leave," he was saying. "I don't know what it'll give you, but I hope it'll help." She heard her thank him, "How kind of the Navy, but Alan dear when I told one of our parishioners you might be coming home, he gave me a rabbit he'd shot, so," Hedwig heard her give a little chuckle, "we have roast rabbit for supper."

And later that night as they enjoyed the rabbit, Alan and his father swapped stories of their time at sea. She heard Alan speaking of the convoys, of the gales and the U-boats. It made those cold statistics displayed on that Ops Room board come alive. She wanted to tell him what she did, though not what she translated, but she could only say she worked at Convoy Headquarters. The two men talking of their time at sea and her work with the Navy created a strange bond between the three of them, making her feel sorry for his mother who seemed excluded from the conversation. But soon his mother broke through!

"So Alan dear, what do you want to do tomorrow. You certainly won't want an early call will you?"

"No, no mother dear. I shall enjoy my bed. But," he laughed, "perhaps after a late breakfast I could show Hettie the beauties of Crosby."

"Oh! My dear. Hettie has to work, don't you Hettie dear?"

"Yes, Alan. I have to work tomorrow, but I'll be free on Saturday and Sunday."

He looked disappointed. "Oh! I'm sorry I won't see much of you till tomorrow evening then."

It was clear to all that he was fond of Hettie and for a moment no one spoke. Then he broke the silence. "How's the violin?"

"Oh! Alan I think of you every time I play it. I can never thank you enough for giving it to me."

"Oh! Hettie I was glad to give it you. I wasn't using it and I was horrified when you told me how yours was snatched from you. Perhaps you'll play something for us?"

"Yes please do," his father nodded, "We'd love to hear you play."

And so later that evening she'd played the piece she'd grown to love, Elgar's 'Salut d'Amour'. She'd begun nervously for she'd never played to anyone since coming to England, but as the piece progressed her confidence grew and she'd been delighted when at the end they'd all clapped so vigorously.

It had made for a lovely evening, the four of them delighted to be reunited; the four of them? But there was another four, her four, her mother and father, she and Moshe. They were a family too and seeing Alan being hugged and kissed by his parents had brought back that persistent longing to be reunited with hers, to be hugged and kissed by them. Would her longing ever be fulfilled? As ever its unlikelihood tormented her. Involuntarily she shook her head, she didn't even know if they were still alive. And even if they were, for all she knew, they might be locked up in some concentration camp. Thinking about them was too painful; desperately she drove such thoughts out of her mind. Thoughts of Alan replaced them, of him seeing her to her bedroom door. Neither of them had wanted to be parted, he holding her in his arms and telling her how well she'd played the violin, how he loved being with her and how he'd miss her tomorrow. Then pulling her gently towards him he'd kissed her. It was a long kiss, a tender kiss, a loving kiss. She'd never been kissed like that before! It had made her feel loved! Loved? That all-consuming feeling of being special, of being wrapped in the devotion and care of another. It was a blessing she'd never known before. She'd wallowed in parental love of course, but that was different! Never had she had love like this. Affection yes, the Bambers had given her plenty of that, and Sue in the office too, but love, love was intoxicating! But that loving embrace had to come to an end. "Dearest," he'd said sadly, "I shall miss you tomorrow, but we've the evening together and all day Saturday and Sunday. We must make every minute count!" Then kissing her lightly on the cheek, he'd left.

After he'd gone she'd found it difficult to sleep and had woken in the early hours thinking not of him, but of her family. She hadn't seen them for almost five and a half years! It was such a long time and now to her shame she was finding it difficult to recall their features! When she thought of her mother and father all she saw was their contorted grief stricken faces when they'd bad farewell at Dessau. Would she ever hug and kiss them again? And Moshe too? She thought about her beloved Aunt Liesel also and of her Uncle Wolfgang and cousins Horst and Heinrich. The two families of her father and her uncle had been irrevocably divided by Hitler, merely because her family were Jewish and her uncle's Aryan! And now here she was helping the war against Hitler, while her cousins were fighting for him. How terrible it was that cousins should be fighting each other!

"How lucky Alan is," she heard herself mutter. "How lucky to be born English." He had what she wanted above everything else, a mother and father to love.

She'd drifted off into a fitful sleep and weary and drained she awoke and left for work. The day had dragged. She'd found it difficult to concentrate on her work, though luckily the day's tapes had contained nothing of any importance. At last the time came to leave for home, where she hoped Alan would be waiting for her.

He was, and opening the door gave her a hug. He told her how much he'd missed her and asked after her day. Then stroking his beard he gave her an enquiring look.

"Mum tells me there's dancing at the parish hall tonight. Shall we go?"

"Dancing?"

"Yes," he laughed, "you know Hettie. Waltzes and quicksteps and slow foxtrots."

"Well, I think I can dance a waltz, but the only other dances I know are German folk dances," she laughed, "and in one of them you have to yodel!"

He laughed too. "Well Hettie, I'm not good at yodelling, but we can dance the waltz and perhaps I can teach you the others. They're not too difficult!"

"Hello Hettie dear." His mother appeared "Alan tells me he's taking you dancing tonight, but you must have some tea before you go."

Hettie nodded "Yes, and I must change, I can't go like this!"

But what should she wear? How she wished she'd bought that pretty turquoise dress that had tempted her so. All she had was that dress she'd worn for her confirmation. It was white and very modest! Could she wear that? Mrs Bamber had seen her looking concerned and when Hettie told her what was troubling her, she'd produced some colourful chiffon and suggested she wore it as a sash or perhaps tied around her waist. It had certainly brightened up the dress and Alan had liked it!

The hall had been crowded and there were lots of American G Is* there. The Yanks had been in England for almost two years now and were popular with the girls for they were well paid and could be more generous than their British counterparts. They had also brought a strange new and exciting dance with them. Hettie had heard the girls in the office talking about it. It was called the jitterbug, and the Yanks whirled and threw their partners around in a way they'd found exciting. It was certainly different! It was so care-free, full of joy and movement, though she and Alan had been content to sit and watch. Hettie had told him she couldn't see the Germans doing the jitterbug! "And in any case," she'd said, "it would probably be forbidden!"

Most of the men dancing wore uniforms of one sort or another and some of the girls did too, but Alan was wearing his civilian clothes. He did stand out and one drunken soldier had accosted him, asking why he wasn't fighting for his country. Luckily another quickly pulled him away muttering, "Leave him alone. He's probably one of them conchies*!" It had made Hettie angry, she'd wanted to shout "He's in the Navy, fighting the U-boats," but before she could do so, Alan had moved her away, "Forget him", he'd said "He's drunk."

Though the incident had annoyed her, the evening had been fun and when the time came for the traditional last waltz, Alan had told her how well she'd danced! And as they walked home in the blackout, she felt his arm slide quietly around her waist. Then in the darkness he stopped and kissed her. She'd been hoping he would and responded willingly as he kissed her again. But it was cold, there was frost about, and they hurried home.

His mother met them. She and his father had been listening to the late night news. "The Russians have at last broken the siege of Leningrad!" she said. "How those poor Russians have suffered!"

"Yes," his father added, "Leningrad's been besieged for almost two and a half years and it's estimated one and a half million civilians and soldiers have died due to starvation or bombardment."

"And," his mother continued excitedly, "the RAF have bombed Berlin again. I must admit I do feel sorry for the people there, but perhaps it helps to bring victory!"

"Let's drink to that," his father added, producing a bottle of whisky. He grinned. "This is precious stuff nowadays, but with Alan home, we must drink to victory!"

They'd clinked their glasses one against the other and toasted "Victory". Hedwig sipped hers carefully. She'd never drunk whisky before, it had a strange taste and warmed her throat. Suddenly she was aware they were all studying her!

The vicar smiled, "I hope you're enjoying it?" Hettie looked uncertain. "I've never drunk whisky before, it's quite strong isn't it?"

They all laughed, savouring the golden spirit and discussing the progress of the war. Then Alan's mother declared it was time for bed, and having kissed his mother and bidding his father sleep well, Alan followed Hettie up the stairs.

They stopped by her door and he kissed her, telling her how wonderful the evening had been; that he loved her; that he wanted to be with her always; that when this war was over he'd never leave her. She'd nestled in his arms saying she loved him too, that she too longed for the war to be over and that she worried about him when he was at sea, praying for him to come home safely. They held each other closely as if they would never part, but then he'd kissed her again, and opening her door had bid her sleep tight, before leaving for his own room.

Monday came. What had happened to Saturday and Sunday? The days had gone in a flash and here they were sitting in the bus bound for Crosby holding hands and hoping the time to part would never come.

Saturday had been fun. He'd suggested they'd go for a bike ride offering her his mother's bicycle. She hadn't ridden a bicycle since she was a girl in Bremen, but she'd managed somehow, laughing as she wobbled. They'd cycled to Hightown where they'd strolled on the beach followed by tea in a little café. He'd asked about her family. It was a subject she'd always avoided before, but he'd been sympathetic, listening with so much concern that she'd told him everything! About her father marrying a Jew and being involved with the design and production of the Stuka dive-bomber, how he'd been incarcerated in Buchenwald Concentration camp because he'd married a Jew, and how Herr Goering, the Reich Marshal of Aviation, had ordered his release declaring his ability to design aircraft for his Luftwaffe could not be wasted! She remembered telling him she prayed for her father's continued success in designing aeroplanes even though this would help Hitler, since it seemed to keep her parents safe. And she'd spoken of her Jewish grandfather being killed by the S.A. and of her Jewish uncle and aunt's escape to Switzerland.

As she related all this to him, she'd watched expressions of horror, anger, disbelief and compassion cross his face. When she'd finished he told her "we English, to our shame, never thought the Nazis could be so merciless, so evil." He seemed relieved to hear her brother Moshe was safe in Palestine! Then she'd told him of her non-Jewish cousins. He seemed untroubled to hear Heinrich was in the Kriegsmarine, but was horrified when she said she feared Horst might be in the S.S. and possibly the Gestapo. Alan had seemed lost for words, he'd just sat there shaking his head as if he couldn't believe it. Then she'd asked about him.

He'd taken a deep breath as if to clear the image of her S.S. cousin Horst from his mind and had said rather proudly, that he'd been lucky to have been brought up in a country where people were free to express their opinions, criticize authority and belong to different religions or racial groups without fear.

"In England," he said "we take that freedom for granted, but I suppose that's what we're really fighting for!" He told her he'd always wished for a sister or a brother and he didn't even have any cousins! Like him his mother was an only child and his father's brother had been killed in the last war.

In the evening they'd gone to the pictures to see 'Casablanca', the film everyone was talking about, with Humphrey Bogart playing the owner of a gambling den frequented by German and Vichy French officials, who falls in love with the wife of a Czech Resistance leader desperate to reach the still neutral USA. The intrigue and mystery had transported them into another world and on the way home Alan had softly sung to her that unforgettable song from the film, 'It had to be you'! Then he'd kissed her and said, "Dearest, for me it has to be you!" What could she say? All she could do was surrender to his kisses!

When she awoke on the Sunday it had seemed strangely quiet and pulling back her window curtains she could see why. It was snowing, and it must have been for some time since everything lay under a deep blanket of white, contrasting with the blue-grey sky above. But despite the snow, they'd all gone to church, Alan's mother insisting that he should wear his naval uniform. His father had preached and led prayers for victory and to celebrate his son's homecoming, had told the congregation he would say the Naval Prayer. It was new to Hedwig, but she had found it very moving and had sought to remember it. But she could only repeat a little, which she recalled went:

'O Eternal God, who alone rulest the raging of the sea, who has compassed the waters with bounds until day and night come to an end;

be pleased to receive into Thy almighty and most gracious protection, the persons of those Thy servants and the Fleet in which they serve' She could remember no more, but she would learn it and say it each night with her prayers.

After the service, many of the parishioners had spoken to Alan, praising the Royal and Merchant navies for their bravery in the battle at sea. One elderly widow had said "Without the Navy we'd starve." While Alan had clearly been embarrassed by it all, it made her feel proud of him.

In the afternoon they'd played in the snow, building a snowman and throwing snowballs at each other. Oh! What fun they'd had!

But that was yesterday and now they were in the bus again. The dock gates of Bootle were approaching. He pulled her to him, told her he'd always love her, kissed her, grabbed his bag and jumped off the bus. He turned and waved as the bus began to move. It seemed her world had come to an end.

Chapter 36

Untersturmführer Horst Boddenburg consoled himself with a glass of schnapps. Usually in the evening he would play his piccolo to forget the war and the killing, but this evening he couldn't, the war was going so badly. Yet no one would admit it. To admit it would show disloyalty to the Führer. Somehow, but no one knew how, most people believed he'd yet bring victory. He remembered how shocked the nation had been to hear of the attempted assassination of the Führer a few months ago. Colonel Claus von Stauffenburg had attended the daily conference in the Wolf's Lair, Hitler's Headquarters deep in the Masurian woods near Rastenburg. He was carrying a timed bomb in his brief case and had been sitting near the Führer, but on some excuse had left early. After he'd gone the bomb exploded, but miraculously the Führer had not been killed. He'd survived with only minor injuries!

Stauffenburg and his many accomplices were later arrested and executed. But rumour had it that General Erwin Rommel had been involved too, for strangely a week or so after the failed assassination attempt, it was reported that he'd died, dying of a brain seizure! Had Hitler discovered he'd been involved too? That it was intended that he Rommel should replace him as Führer? If that was so, Rommel had to be executed. Yet to try him and execute him would reveal the disloyalty and treachery of a well-loved General, the respected Commander of the famous Afrika Korps! Surely Hitler wouldn't want that! If Rommel had indeed been involved it would be far better to say he'd died of a brain seizure, and bury him with full military honours! The subject was discussed with trusted friends in the safety of their rooms.   But in public everyone like him had voiced thanks for Hitler's survival. What else could they do? If one regretted the plot's failure, hoping that a successor might have sued for peace, one daren't say so. Such disloyalty could be met with death!

He'd admired Hitler, right from his time in the Hitler Youth, but now he'd begun to wonder whether a new leader might be able extract the nation from its terrible predicament. After the loss of the 6th Army at Stalingrad and that tank battle at Kursk the Wehrmacht was now being driven relentlessly back towards Germany. And in the west the British and Americans had launched a successful amphibious assault over the beaches in Normandy, and with the Allies advancing in Italy, Germany was now fighting and losing a war on three fronts! The future, if there was one, looked grim!

As the Red Army continued its advance, fears that the work of the Einstazgruppen would be revealed in detail, together with the identity of those responsible, had begun to worry the S.S. Commanders. For should they be taken prisoner, they could be held to account for what they'd done! Orders had therefore been issued that in future the bodies of those executed were to be burnt, to hide evidence of their killing. Then not long after, it had been decided that the bodies already interred in mass graves were to be burnt too! So his Kommando had had to deal with the bodies buried in that mass grave in the glade they'd used as an execution site.

It had been a terrible job. With forced labour the tangled bodies he and his men had shot had been uncovered. It had been a gruesome sight and there'd been so many! It was then that the savagery and the inhumanity of the killing of those people overwhelmed him. Did all these people have to die? But they were Jews, they had to be exterminated, it was Hitler's orders, wasn't it? But then an inner voice had kept telling him they were people, people like Hedwig and Auntie Golda, like him! He'd tried to ignore it, but it had kept on. "What would you do if you found the girl standing in line before you, ready to be shot was Hedwig your cousin?" That question had worried him before, but he'd always ignored it. It would never happen! But now he couldn't ignore it. Hedwig was undeniably a Jew and it would be his duty to kill her. Yet how could he? The S.S. called Jews the untermensch, sub humans, held them in contempt and taught all who sought to join its ranks that they must hate all Jews. But how could he hate Hedwig? They were cousins, her mother his aunt, her father his uncle. Was it right that all Jews without question should be exterminated?

Yet Hitler said they must and as an S.S. officer, he had to be obedient to his will. He had no option! He had to be obedient! He had to kill Jews!

Finally when all the bodies had been burnt, he and his men had been given a few days to clean themselves and prepare for their next task. This became clear a few days later, when Sturmbannführer Oscar Naumann called a meeting of his officers to discuss the worsening situation. He told them that the concentration camp at Klooga in Estonia had been captured by the Red Army. The attack had come so quickly that the camp had been captured intact and the Totenkopfverbande* (the guards) had been killed or taken prisoner. Only the Commandant and a few had escaped and did so, before all camp records could be burnt. This serious breach in security, he told them, was causing great alarm, for now the Russians may well have the names of the Totenkopfverbande who served there and other sensitive material too, even the *Dienstaltersliste der Schutzstaffel der NSDAP* (the confidential Seniority list of all S.S. personnel). This he said could be used as evidence against any member of the S.S. taken prisoner. Such a breach must not be allowed to happen again and it had therefore been decreed that if the capture of a concentration camp, labour camp or extermination camp becomes inevitable, every action must be taken to prevent such evidence falling into the hands of the Russians. All records and documentation must therefore be burnt and prisoners sorted into two categories, those fit for work and those unfit. Those unfit for work and all children must be shot. Those who are fit form a necessary resource for the defence of the Reich. So they are to be assembled ready to march westwards to the next camp. The movement of prisoners from the two camps in Lithuania will be supervised by this Kommando, and any prisoner who tries to escape or who falls behind during the march must be shot. But before the camp is evacuated, the bodies of those killed must be doused with petrol and set alight and the camp buildings torched. The Totenkopfverbande in the camps, he told them, know what to do, but our role is to supervise and assist where necessary, especially with the killing of the unfit.

When he'd finished, he asked if everyone understood what was required. A few quiet cries of "Jawohl Mein Herr" could be heard, then satisfied that everyone knew what had to be done, he continued, "Now we have to have a plan for our camps in Vilnius and here in Kaunas. Vilnius is nearer the front line and is likely to be attacked first. So Kaunas must be ready not only to evacuate, but also to receive prisoners from Vilnius."

A voice from the back asked "Mein Herr, if it becomes necessary to evacuate Kaunas, where would we head for?"

"Stutthof, that is the nearest."

The nearest? Horst thought. Stutthof must be at least two hundred miles away. How long would a column of prisoners take to march two hundred miles? Eight days, maybe ten?

After the plan had been outlined, the meeting dispersed, everyone looking thoughtful and no-one wanting to talk. The Russians would soon be upon them. Stopping them seemed impossible, they had an inexhaustible supply of men and tanks! All they could hope for was that the Providence which had saved the Führer only a few months ago would now inspire him with a master plan to save Germany from the Russians.

For a month or so the Wehrmacht had been fighting the Polish underground army in Warsaw as it mounted its uprising against Nazi rule. For some reason the Russians had stood back, letting the Poles and the Germans fight each other, and had directed its armies northwards towards the Baltic States. Army Group North, unable to stop them, was now retreating towards Riga and the Courland Peninsular and now with the Russians no more than a hundred miles or so from Vilnius, the order was given to evacuate its camp. A section of the Kommando was sent to supervise and assist, while Horst and his men remained in Kaunas preparing to receive the prisoners from Vilnius. But the Red Army's advance had become so swift that Kaunas was ordered to evacuate too! As they entered the camp they could here distant gunfire and saw fires in the camp as records and documentation were being burnt. Meanwhile the prisoners were being sorted into fit and unfit categories. Including children with the unfit was proving difficult, for mothers were hiding them under their skirts, making it hard to separate them. In the end he Horst had let the mothers join their children in the unfit section, and then having moved them away from the others, he and his men had had to shoot them. After that terrible time only a week or so ago, when they'd dug up those bodies to be burnt, it was a task he found difficult to face. But his men with their rifles at the ready were looking at him. As he braced himself to give the order to shoot, a mother broke away with her children and ran off. Hastily he shouted "Take aim, fire," then there was a rattle of gunfire and bodies were dropping. After he and his Sergeant had made sure all were dead, his Sergeant volunteered to find the mother who'd escaped.

"No, Sergeant. I'll do that. Take the men and help load the vehicles. Make sure the Gas Wagon is kept for us."

He found her hiding behind a hut, a young mother with her two children clinging to her. She looked at him, her eyes wide with terror, "Nein, Nein," she kept pleading. As he looked at her, that inner voice of his kept insisting, "It could be Hedwig, it could be Hedwig. You can't shoot her!" He looked at the girl again, but all he saw was Hedwig! Hedwig trembling with pleading eyes! He couldn't kill her! He pointed his pistol at the ground and fired three shots. The girl stood there, her mouth open in a state of shock! A feeling of relief spread over him and finding a few coins in his pocket, he said, "Take this and go."

Then hoping the three shots had satisfied his Sergeant, he'd joined the others. The two lorries had now been loaded with the camp's food, the Sturmbannführer had left in his Kubelwagen* and the long column of prisoners, some nine hundred and fifty of them, surrounded by the armed Totenkopfverbande and their dogs, had begun to shuffle off.

Now as he and his men were left to burn the bodies and buildings, he found himself praying for that young mother and her children. "Please God, let them not be found". Later while his men were dousing the bodies and huts with petrol and setting them alight, he began to realise that he, someone who'd never accepted God, had actually prayed to him; had asked God to let that mother and her children not be found! Was there a God? Was it God who'd made him fire his pistol into the ground? Whoever or whatever it was, he was thankful. Now he felt happy and relieved he'd let her go.

The October sun was low in the sky when they finished and the column couldn't be more than a three or four miles ahead. In the Gas Wagon they'd catch them up within ten minutes or so. But he'd found his men reluctant to climb aboard the van, and it was only after the Sergeant had checked and assured them that the vehicle's exhaust pipe was not connected to the interior of the van and one of the men had insisted he should check it as well, that the men agreed to climb aboard! By the time they'd joined the column it was already cold and frosty and they'd begun looking for a place to spend the night.

That was the start of an eleven day trek with little or no shelter at night and an ever decreasing column, as prisoners fell by the wayside and were shot. And all the time the aircraft they'd seen and the noise of artillery fire told them the Russians were not far behind. Twice they'd had to clear the road to let German troops heading for the front pass. They'd found that broken down lorry awaiting recovery. It was loaded with ammunition and some Wehrmacht food packs too. That was manna from heaven! The driver couldn't stop them. They'd taken the food, it wasn't enough to feed the column, but it would feed the guards, they needed feeding, they had a job to do! Then they found the Jerry cans. There were only two, reserved no doubt for the lorry itself, but the Gas Wagon needed fuel, so despite the driver's objections they took them as well.

They'd been on the march for nine days making no more than fifteen or twenty miles a day. It had been impossible to do more and now the food they'd brought from Kaunas had begun to run out! It had given the prisoners a daily meal of gruel and a little oats, barely enough to keep them alive. Even his men and the guards had had little more, the extra they'd had, had been gathered from the fields or the villages they'd passed through. But after finding that lorry they had those Wehrmacht rations, though they'd still have to do more foraging in the fields. But there weren't so many to feed now! The meagre rations and nights spent sleeping in the frost without cover had taken an increasing toll of their numbers. A rough count that morning had revealed the column held only five hundred and sixty-one!

Two days later on 13th October, they entered the little town of Stutthof and saw the camp buildings. The column stopped and sank gratefully to the ground, while he and his sergeant approached the camp. After being allowed entry he was taken to the Commandant, who told him that Sturmbannführer Naumann had informed him that prisoners from Kaunas were on their way. He asked how many there were and when told there were about five hundred and twenty, he said they could be accommodated as many of his prisoners had been sent as labour to help with the defences at Elblag. So ended the long trek.

Now Horst and his men could catch up with news of the war. The Red Army was indeed not far away, but had been held at Isterburg some twenty five miles south east of Konigsberg. Fearful of being trapped in

Courland, Army Group North was now fighting a rear-guard action to escape through the Konigsberg/Isterburg gap. They also learnt that the Führer had abandoned the Eagles Lair at Rastenburg and had moved to his Berlin Bunker under the Chancery building.

It was all bad news, though news of the successful V1 and V2 campaign against London gave them some comfort. The V2, it was claimed, was indeed a wonder weapon that couldn't be intercepted and struck its target without warning. It was claimed it had struck terror in the hearts of Londoners! But to Horst it wasn't the British or the Americans who would destroy Germany. It was the Russian hordes they would be the ones! Surely the Führer could see that! Surely he should be transferring the army from France and Italy to bolster the defence against the Russians! But he kept his criticism to himself. He couldn't be seen finding fault with the Führer!

Chapter *37*

On the Eastern front Memel had fallen to the Russians, Königsberg in Lithuania had been surrounded and the evacuation of Stutthof had been ordered with the withdrawal to Danzig. Now camp prisoners had to be killed and once more Horst and his men were to form the execution squad.

Time did not allow for the prisoners to be lined up for shooting, all they could do was herd them into their huts, douse the huts with petrol and set them on fire. After that wonderful feeling of relief he'd experienced when he'd spared that mother and her two children, Horst tried hard not to hear the screams of those trapped inside the burning buildings. But it was almost impossible even as he concentrated on directing his men to shoot those managing to escape. Now it seemed his only role in life was to kill. To kill defenceless people, people born of a Jewish mother, who were Jews, people the Führer said must be exterminated. How, how could this terrible killing be ended? Perhaps he should kill himself! Surely he deserved death more than these Jews.

The killing and the burning took barely two hours. Then it was time to set off for Danzig in the Gas Wagon. When they arrived, Danzig was in a state of chaos as preparations were being made to fortify the city against the impending Russian attack. Trying to find the rest of his Kommando he was directed to the Town Hall, now the Headquarters for the defence of the city. There he found his Sturmbannführer, and was told he and his men were to stiffen the city's defences and the Kommando was to join a Waffen S.S. unit and fight as soldiers! To fight as soldiers? To fight as soldiers? No more killing of Jews? He couldn't believe it. He laughed. For him it was like a stay of execution!

For some however to fight as soldiers was an unwelcome role. Their role had always been making towns and cities Judenfrei and in so doing had become well versed in using their rifles, but they themselves had never been the targets! They were unhappy, indeed worried. And when they joined their Waffen S.S. unit they were received with some degree of scorn!

But there was to be no fighting, for a few days later the order came to abandon Danzig and a fleet of naval ships and craft came to rescue them. He and his men had had to wait almost to the end before they were allowed to embark. It seemed to show the low esteem the Waffen S.S. had for them. But at last they climbed aboard a patrol boat bound for Stettin. Luckily there was little wind, but as he found the motion caused by the swell disturbing, Horst was thankful to remain on deck. The sea had never appealed to him, unlike his brother Heinrich. He wondered how he was, the last he'd heard was that he'd completed his U-boat training and was about to join an operational boat. Was he still alive, he wondered? In the early days the U-boats had been masters of the Atlantic, sinking more ships than the enemy could build. If it hadn't been for the Americans and their mass produced Liberty* ships, the English would have been starved into submission! But now it was rumoured that the tide had turned and the Allies were sinking more U-boats than Germany could build. He hoped Heinrich had survived, that perhaps now he was safe in some training job ashore or even in some Prisoner of War Camp in England. He sighed. The first year or so of the war had been a time of great victories, with only England left to conquer. How the nation had worshipped Hitler then! But now? Involuntarily he shook his head. If only the Führer had brought England to her knees before attacking the Russians! But he hadn't! At first it had seemed the Soviets would surrender as quickly as the French, for within a few months German troops were at the gates of Moscow, Leningrad and Stalingrad and everyone thought it could only be a matter of weeks before the Russians capitulated. But then after that dreadful defeat at Stalingrad it had been one long retreat for the Wehrmacht. And now the Red Army had crossed the Oder, taken Frankfurt and was approaching the outskirts of Berlin, Danzig had been abandoned and he and his men were being evacuated to Stettin.

In the West the Americans and the British had been held on the banks of the Elbe, but their expertise in river crossing would soon enable them to overcome that obstacle and advance on Berlin. Now the war was clearly lost and all that could be done was to hold back the Russians and let the Americans or British reach Berlin first. So even though defeat was inevitable, it was essential to save Berlin from the Russians and he was certain he and his men would be involved in this final battle. Holding back the Red Army with its huge arsenal of tanks, artillery and men, with a retreating Wehrmacht reinforced by the Volkssturm*, Hitler Youth contingents and S.S. units unfamiliar with land warfare, would be a formidable task. Many would be killed and for him death would be better than capture for if captured, he an S.S. officer who'd served in an Einsatzkommando making towns Judenfrei, would undoubtedly be tried as a war criminal and executed!

It had all gone terribly wrong! The Führer had promised to make Germany great again, but the war had been a disaster with the country now in ruins and defeat inevitable! His faith in the Führer had been ebbing for some time, but now it had gone altogether and with it that oath of loyalty. Now it would be a battle for his own survival!

"Survival," Horst muttered as he stood on deck watching the land slip by. He remembered once in Sturmbannführer Naumann's office, catching a glimpse of a secret paper. The Sturmbannführer had left it open while he answered his telephone. Driven by curiosity he'd read as much as he could. At the time he couldn't believe what he was reading. It was about helping senior officers of the S.S. escape Germany in the event of defeat and find refuge in friendly states. Argentina was one of them. He'd thought it was treachery, but he'd been sure it would never be needed. But now? For some it could be a life line! After defeat, it would be every man for himself! How he wondered, would he get to Argentina?

The boat was turning now as it entered the estuary, and in the distance he could see Stettin, crowded with the ships and boats that had brought them from Danzig. Having disembarked, his unit like the others was directed to a school where they were to be quartered. An officer from the Garrison was there to meet them. "The Garrison Commander welcomes you to Stettin," he announced, "and reminds you that today is the Führer's fifty-sixth birthday. Herr Goebbels will be speaking to the nation on the wireless and you should listen to him."

Horst had expected some inspiring words, but he could hardly believe what he was hearing. He remembered him saying "we stand behind our Führer: soldier and civilian, man and woman and child." They were words he'd expected to hear, but then Goebbels had descended into a world of fantasy! He'd gone on to declare that after this war Germany would blossom as never before! Her ravaged countryside and provinces would be re-built and the people would be happy, living in new, more beautiful cities and villages. Had he gone out of his mind? And he'd promised that we Germans would be friends again with all people! Did he really think the relatives of those we've killed will forgive us so easily? It had been rumoured for some time that the Führer, Goebbels, Bormann and the Generals in the Berlin Bunker were living in a fantasy world. It seemed so. Surely Herr Goebbels' message confirmed it! When the broadcast ended, he could hear muttering among the men, but one had to be careful. Disloyalty in the S.S. was a crime.

Chapter 38

On the 5th of June 1944 the long awaited Allied invasion of Northern Europe code-named Overlord, began when a vast armada of over six thousand ships, warships, merchant men and a myriad of landing ships of different classes braved the high winds to launch an invasion army of one hundred and eighty five thousand American, British and Canadian troops and its twenty thousand tanks and vehicles onto the beaches of Normandy.

Having heard the news with high hopes and great delight, the nation held its breath as it anxiously awaited further news. By D plus one, beach heads had been established on all the five landing zones, Utah, Omaha, Gold, June and Sword and within four days the whole fifty miles of beachhead from Sword to Utah was connected and cleared of mines and obstacles. Then the tugs arrived towing ancient merchant ships and huge concrete pontoons known as "Bombardons", all to be sunk to provide a breakwater to shelter the temporary harbour of floating pontoons forming jetties to unload supply ships, and floating roadways to lead vehicles ashore. Within a week this man-made harbour was operational and delivering an average of six thousand seven hundred and fifty tons of munitions daily and withstood the gale that sprang up on 19th June with minimal damage. Mulberry Harbour, as it was named was the result of lessons learnt in the failed Dieppe raid of August 1942.

As Allied confidence grew in an eventual allied breakout from the Normandy beaches Hitler launched his "Vengeance" weapon and by mid-June the V-1 flying- bombs were falling thick and fast on London and the south-eastern counties. Hettie's newspaper reported that Herbert Morrison, the Home Secretary had stated that the first flying-bomb had caused relatively little damage, but her paper was not so complacent, for it read:

According to figures issued at 6am today eighteen people have died and one hundred and sixty-six have been injured in flying-bomb explosions since the first six casualties in Bethnal Green, London on 13th June. Yesterday seventy-three flying-bombs fell on Greater London with twenty-four people dying in a single blast on a London pub. The flying-bombs carry a warhead of nearly a ton of explosive and its engine is programmed to cut out over its target, when it nosedives silently to earth and explodes. Damage can cover a quarter of a mile in radius, mainly by blast causing debris to strike down anyone standing nearby. The flying-bombs have been nick-named "doodlebugs" for the drone of its engine and when you hear its engine stop you must take cover immediately.

The next day's paper reported that:

A flying-bomb had fallen on the Guards Chapel at Wellington Barracks during the Sunday morning service. The building was almost completely destroyed and one hundred and nineteen worshippers, half civilian, half servicemen were killed and another one hundred and two seriously injured.

But mercifully for Hettie and her hosts, Liverpool was beyond the flying-bomb's range and the frequent air raids were now a thing of the past. And now that U-boats were rarely encountered in the North Atlantic, the convoys were regularly making safe passages. That was good news for her. The *Foxglove* and her beloved Alan would now be a little safer. But though she was still translating those eavesdropped conversations from the Prisoner of War camp, with the lack of new U-boat survivors, there was rarely any useful intelligence.

Recently when she had begun to wonder whether she was serving any useful purpose in the Headquarters Lieutenant Matthews had told her the Army might be poaching her for translation purposes.

On the bus home that night she had an odd feeling that some strange event awaited her. Would it be the sighting of K145? She always looked out for the *Foxglove* whenever she was in the bus, but there was no sign of her today. Perhaps the Army would be wanting her. Well if it did she would think about it then. She sat back in her seat and watched the river go by.

Yet still she had that strange uncertain feeling. The clippie's voice calling "St Peter's Church" broke into her uncertainty. Hurriedly she got off. Mrs Bamber met her as she opened the door.

Hello, Hettie dear. Here's a letter for you."

She took it, a manila envelope addressed to Miss Hedwig Boddenburg. Who could be writing to her? The only letters she received were from Alan and those earlier ones concerning her job in Liverpool. Mystified she took it to her room. Then sitting by the window she opened it. It was from Kindertransport.

Dear Miss Boddenburg, she read, *We have received the enclosed envelope addressed to you, with a letter asking that should we know your address, it be forwarded to you. Please acknowledge its receipt.*

She studied the writing on the envelope. It was her name spelt out in capitals. Puzzled she slit the envelope open.

Dearest Hedwig, It was her mother's handwriting! *Your father and I are praying that you are safe and well and that you will get this letter. We are both safe. Your clever father managed to get hold of an aeroplane and flew us to Sweden, where we have been made welcome and safe from the Nazis.*

Her eyes filled with tears of relief. They're safe! Wiping her eyes she read on:

We had to leave everything behind and could only bring money and my jewellery, so we arrived almost penniless, but the Swedes have been very kind and when AB Flygindustri, who built the prototype Stuka dive-bomber, heard that it was your father who modified its design after its early crash, they offered him a job. So dearest Hettie all is well with us and we pray that all is well with you too.

We've not heard a word from dear Moshe, but then we did agree not to write for our safety, so all we can do is pray for him and hope that when Hitler is defeated as now he surely must be, the four of us will be re-united.

She put the letter down. It was such wonderful news she could hardly believe it.

Chapter 39

"Copenhagen!" Horst congratulated himself as he sat with his piccolo and begging bowl under a tree. Somehow he'd made it and he'd heard of a ship unloading meat in the docks. Meat from Argentina, one of the countries in the Odessa plan, where S.S. members hoped to find sanctuary. He hoped to stow away on her before she sailed in the morning, then he might be safe!

The past months had been hell, unremitting, unforgiving hell. He and his S.S. unit had set out from Stettin hoping that Berlin might be saved from the Russians, that the remorseless sacrifice of the German people might be ended, that Hitler would accept defeat. For defeat had been inevitable for some time, all sane men had known that, everyone it seemed except Hitler!

They'd met up with the Third Panzer Division at Schwedt after a difficult drive through roads crowded with columns of people trudging doggedly westwards and carrying whatever possessions they could on their backs or in prams and handcarts. Every now and then there'd been an overloaded horse drawn cart or two and sometimes even a cow. It had been a terrible, distressing sight. Germany was being torn apart.

But then they'd seen the Tiger tanks of the Third panzers, the renowned Tiger tank with its 9cm gun and heavy armour. It had felt good to have the panzers on their side, it had given them confidence. But that confidence had quickly been tested a day later, when Soviet T34 tanks appeared. In the ensuing battle five of the T34s and 2 Tigers had been left in flames, but that didn't stop the Russians, for yet more T34s appeared and broke through the line, with infantry following in an attempt to encircle them. That was when he and his men had had their first terrible taste of war as infantrymen. In the unremitting battle that followed, artillery bombardment followed by a rush of tanks and infantry had been repeated time and time again. But though brave men had destroyed five more T34s with their Panzerfausts*, it had been a one-sided fight, the Russians seeming to have unlimited reinforcements of tanks, artillery and men, and despite their tenacious resistance, they'd been driven back to the Wasserturm. Only when darkness came did they have some respite. In the lull they counted their losses, eight of his men were missing and four had been lightly wounded. How the rest of the force had fared he didn't know, but they'd probably had equally large casualties. The savagery of the fighting had made it impossible to rescue the badly wounded who, despite their desperate cries for help, had had to be left where they fell, sometimes to be crushed under the tracks of a tank! Some had muttered "They're the lucky ones" for many were terrified of being captured by the Red Army. Death was preferable to that!

At dawn the next day it had been strangely quiet and the result of the Soviet bombardment could be seen. Hardly a building had been left undamaged, most were now just a skeleton of broken walls, while of others there was little trace, just a heap of rubble. Yet he'd seen life among the ruins, women emerging from cellars in search of food, and in the distance in the Tiergarten he'd seen blossom on the trees! It was spring, the first day of May. Mayday! Were the trees in bloom he wondered, to celebrate May Day for the Russians; for their inevitable victory? It was a disturbing thought! But then they'd been ordered to fall back yet again as the enemy had bypassed them to the north and they were in danger of being cut off. Their next defensive position was to be the Brewery in Schonhauser Allee. They'd loaded the few wounded they'd managed to rescue into the last remaining truck and set off. Now they were a mere hundred or so plus a few Volkssturm and the remnants of the Hitler Youth contingent. But they must have been spotted by enemy aircraft, for soon they were being shelled. Whilst all sought cover among the wrecked buildings, the truck was hit and burst into flames. Shell after shell landed among them, one close to him, killing two of his men and injuring others, but luck had been with him, he'd been unhurt. When the shelling had stopped a search was made for survivors and from the dead ammunition, water bottles and anything edible were recovered. Later that day about eighty survivors, including the Volkssturm and Hitler Youth, reached the brewery. It had suffered some damage, but there was beer to drink and a little welcome food. As the beer lifted their spirits, they'd reported their position and the number of men remaining and made a plea for food and ammunition.

But then a T34 appeared and yet more Soviet infantry. The brewery gave better cover and nursing their limited stock of ammunition until re-supplied, they'd managed to hold out for three days, after which they'd been ordered to withdraw to cover the central bus station. So under cover of darkness the force, now reduced to a mere fifty or so, had made its way through the ruins to the bus station. By then he was one of the two surviving officers. The other was a Waffen S.S. man senior to him, who was in charge.

In the morning the extent of the damage in this part of Berlin could be seen. Once again, he looked out on a scene of utter destruction, only the remnants of buildings remained. The mood of the men reflected the desolation surrounding them. Everyone was despondent. Wasn't it time for Hitler to sue for peace? It was clear the besieged residents thought so too, for many white flags, sheets or anything white could be seen hanging from broken windows or draped over the remains of buildings. Was there any point in further resistance? Most of Berlin was now in the hands of the Russians anyway. Were they fighting only to avoid capture? Capture by the Russians?

The Americans and the British could not be far away, maybe no more than twenty or thirty miles and the temptation to desert and flee westwards to surrender to them was growing ever stronger. Some indeed had already deserted, but a few had been caught and executed. So still they fought on, repelling the enemy as best they could, though thankfully the attacks were becoming less frequent and the sound of artillery fire less audible.

Then the rumours had begun circulating. "The Führer is dead. He's shot himself!" Whether it was true or not, everyone hoped it was. "Surely," some said, "What else can he do? The war is lost and he daren't be taken alive!"

Their hopes for an end of the bloodshed were answered the next day when Admiral Dönitz Hitler's successor, sued for peace. The fighting was ended and then it was every man for himself! Yes, it was time to go, time for his own Odessa plan! As soon as it was dark he'd slipped away and had begun his desperate escape and now here he was in Copenhagen! What a stroke of luck that had been, to stumble over that body in the darkness. He'd expected it to be that of a German or Russian soldier, but it wasn't. It was that of an old man. He'd dragged him behind the rubble, pulled off the man's coat and trousers and removing his S.S. uniform had put them on. They didn't fit too well, but so what, his S.S. uniform was too dangerous to wear. After buttoning up the coat he'd searched its pockets and had found a wallet with money and an identity card. He retrieved his own, the little money he had and his precious piccolo, then throwing his S.S. uniform further away he'd walked hurriedly on. From then on he'd become Karl Weber, a widower and lathe operator of Breittestrasse 331, Berlin, who'd brought him safely to Copenhagen!

"Good morning Corporal. Are you one of us?" The tall, burly Captain smiled at Hedwig.

"One of us, sir?"

"Yes, are you Jewish too?"

"Yes sir, I am. My mother is Jewish and so therefore I'm a Jew too."

"So Corporal Heather Bowden, tell me how you come to be working with us."

"Well sir, I was born in Bremen, but when I was sixteen my parents were worried about my future in Hitler's Germany and applied for me to come to England under the Kindertransport Scheme. And when I was eighteen I began working at the Naval Convoy Headquarters in Liverpool as a translator. The huts which housed the German Prisoners of War were bugged to record what they said and I was employed to translate their conversations. Nearly all were U-boat men and we got some good intelligence from them. But then in 1944 with few if any U-boats still on patrol in the Atlantic, we rarely had any new POW's so there was little worthwhile work for me to do. Then after D-Day* with the end of the war near, I was asked to translate for the Army in Germany. I was pleased to help and so I became a member of the ATS* and was given the rank of Corporal, and", she smiled "here I am ready for duty."

"Well we're pleased to have you. I am Captain John Eberle and I will be your boss. Like you I am also German and a Jew and my Jewish name is Gunter Ebestadt, but as I'm sure you know we don't use our Jewish names in this business," he smiled. Then he continued, "Until six months ago I was with the Jewish Brigade as we fought our way through North Africa and Italy, but now I've been attached to the Intelligence Corps to hunt down Nazi War Criminals. And you're here to help with the translation."

"Yes, sir," Hettie nodded

"So Corporal Bowden, what's your Jewish name?"

"Hedwig Boddenburg, sir. Though my mother is Jewish my father is not. That is why my surname isn't Jewish. But the Army told me as I may be working in Germany, I should change my name, and I settled for Heather Bowden."

"But your real name is Boddenburg?" He looked thoughtful, "I had a Boddenburg in my Company, but sadly he was killed by a land mine in Italy. Could he be a relation of yours?"

"Oh! I have a brother who went to Palestine before the war. He's called Moshe Chaim Boddenburg, please tell me it wasn't him!"

"Oh! My dear. I'm afraid it could be your brother, he was called Moshe, though I can't remember his initials. I am sorry I can't be more certain, but I will check with the Company."

"Thank you sir. I'm afraid it does sound like Moshe. He was always a fighter and I'm sure he would have wanted to fight in the war against Hitler."

Seeing her upset by the news, Captain Eberle offered her his sympathy and suggested she might like to have the morning free, but gratefully Hettie declined.

"Well then Corporal, you'd better report to the Sergeant."

The ATS Sergeant welcomed her, took down her details and said,

"Meet Corporal Alison Kerfoot, like you she's a translator too."

Alison smiled "Hello Heather, good to meet you. Tell me how you came to be a translator." Hedwig repeated her story, and then asked about hers and heard that her Jewish name was Aliza Krupnick, though now she was called Alison Kerfoot and that she and her family had come to England in 1937. That she had a degree in Modern Languages and became an interpreter in the ATS four months ago.

Though Alison was almost ten years older than Hettie, they became good friends and with her she had heard about the British Army entering Bergen-Belsen, one of the many Nazi concentration camps. The battle-hardy soldiers had been horrified by what they saw. A huge pile of naked corpses had greeted them as they entered the camp. The Camp Commandant Josef Kramer was quickly arrested and his male and female guards were quickly put to work burying the dead in a mass grave. It was later estimated that the number buried in that mass grave was ten thousand, but about thirty thousand prisoners, mainly Jews and gypsies were found to be still alive, though raging epidemics of typhus and dysentery were threatening to kill them. Army medical staff had moved into the camp to treat the survivors now being moved into the guards' accommodation huts, while the infected prisoners' huts were burnt.

The capture of Bergen-Belsen had given Hedwig's team a magnitude of work as all the guards and those prisoners fit enough to testify had had to be interrogated, as the guards could be tried for war-crimes. The sight of these once arrogant concentration camp guards testifying that they were merely cooks or office staff sickened her. She found she could only translate what they said, with disbelief in her voice.

What she heard and saw intensified her hatred for all things Nazi. Had her cousins Horst and Heinrich been involved in such terrible crimes? She was sure Heinrich had not. He had fought for Hitler in the U-boats and that to her was an honest and honourable way to fight for one's country. But she often wondered what Horst had done. The awful possibility that he'd joined the S.S. worried her. Had he? She'd heard that the office held a copy of the captured *Dienstaltersliste der Schutzstaffel der NSDAP* (the confidential Seniority list of all S.S. personnel). If Horst had indeed joined the S.S. his name would surely be listed there! So plucking up courage she'd approached the ATS Sergeant who managed the office and told her about her fears that her cousin might be serving in the S.S. and had asked if she could see it. It was given to her and hastily she found the page listing names beginning with the letter B. She turned over page after page. Then she saw him!

> Boddenburg, Horst Erich
> Rank Obersturmführer, Gestapo
> Seniority 1 March 1943
> Serving in Einsatzkommando 3
> Date of appointment 27 July 1938

NSDAP membership no: 125,307
S.S. membership no: 34,683
Date of birth: 7 April 1919
Marital status - single

Horst her cousin, the handsome cousin with those sparkling blue eyes and unruly blonde hair, whom she'd idolised, and with whom she'd played her violin to his flute, was a member of the Gestapo! And he was listed as serving in Einsatzkommando 3! She closed her eyes in horror! The Einsatzkommandos she knew were mobile killing squads tasked with the extermination of the Jews in the captured territories. Suddenly she felt she could see him now. Those blue eyes were now cold and arrogant and his mouth hard and merciless! If that really was her cousin, then like the rest he must be hunted down and brought to trial. She closed her eyes. How many Jews had he killed for his beloved Führer? She took one last look at his details, then closed the book and returned it to the Sergeant.

"Did you find him?" she asked. She nodded, but she couldn't speak about him. How could she ever have idolized such a fiend, a murderer, one who had served in an Einsatzkommando? She thought of her dear Alan. How gentle and considerate he was. He would make a loving honourable husband. There was no hatred in him!

"Dear God," she prayed, "Keep him safe."

They'd been in Copenhagen for the past ten days interviewing three high ranking S.S. officers who had been trying to get a passage on a ship bound for Buenos Aires as part of the S.S. Escape plan "Odessa". But today was a Saturday and Hettie, Alison and another had ventured into the city.

Copenhagen was such a happy place where unlike Britain and Germany one could escape from the damage and deprivation of the war, for Copenhagen appeared to be untouched by the war, only Shell House used by the Gestapo as their headquarters had been bombed and there was no shortage of food or Schnapps. And they enjoyed walking through the famous Tivoli Gardens with its carousels, cafés, gardens and lakes, where they found themselves in another world with musicians on the band stand playing popular music. They strolled around the lake feeding the ducks and as the music faded, they revelled in the wonderful peace. They could hear the ducks calling to one another and the chirping of the moorhens and then she thought she heard the distant sound of a piccolo. Cousin Horst used to play a piccolo. Daddy had given him one. She walked towards it. She could hear it better now, it was playing Lorelei! Was it a dream? Cousin Horst used to play that, it was his tune! Could it be him? Of course not! It was just a strange coincidence! But she couldn't rest, she had to find out! She left the others, "I'll be back in a minute," she said and wandered off. She could hear it more plainly now. Then she saw a figure squatting on the ground. It had a piccolo pressed to his lips. It was a ragged figure, it had a begging bowl.

"Please help," it said.

She reached for some money as she studied him. In the shadows she couldn't see the colour of his eyes or his hair, but she recognised his face, now showing the signs of age and war. It was him! Cousin Horst of the Gestapo!

"Hello Horst" she put a little money in his bowl.

By the look on his face she knew he'd recognised her, but he made no acknowledgment.

"I'm not Horst. My name is Karl Weber, I'm a German trying to find my way back to Munster, where I hope to find my family."

It was all lies, she knew. It was Horst, she had no doubt about it. It was Horst with whom she'd played her violin, the blonde blue-eyed Adonis she'd worshipped as a girl. But now it was a frightened Horst of Einsatzkommando 3, sitting there, aware that he would now be held accountable for those he'd executed for his "God", Adolph Hitler!

At last he acknowledged her. "You're my loving cousin Hedwig, aren't you?"

"Yes, your Jewish cousin."

"Hedwig, please help me. I need money to escape to Argentina!"

She looked at him. No longer the arrogant, merciless Gestapo officer, now a pathetic frightened man.

"Horst, how many Jews have you killed for your God, Adolf Hitler?"

He made no answer.

"Tell me Horst, how many?"

Still he didn't answer.

"Were there so many that you can't remember?"

He sighed. "Hedwig you're right, I can't remember. But I was bound by my oath of loyalty. It was the Hitler in me that did the killing!"

"Would your dear mother believe that?"

He made no reply.

She studied this pathetic ragged figure squatting on the ground.

"Were you proud to wear your Gestapo uniform?"

He said nothing.

"Well," there was contempt in her voice, "You look better in Karl Weber's rags." Then turning she said "I'll leave you with your conscience. May it and the faces of those you murdered haunt and trouble you for the rest of your life."

She should report him she knew, but how could she? He was the son of her beloved Aunt Liesel! She walked away.

The end

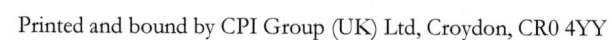
Printed and bound by CPI Group (UK) Ltd, Croydon, CR0 4YY